Dark Haven

By

Mandy Monroe

Paranormal Romance

New Concepts   Georgia

Be sure to check out our website for the very best in fiction at fantastic prices!

When you visit our webpage, you can:
* Read excerpts of currently available books
* View cover art of upcoming books and current releases
* Find out more about the talented artists who capture the magic of the writer's imagination on the covers
* Order books from our backlist
* Find out the latest NCP and author news--including any upcoming book signings by your favorite NCP author
* Read author bios and reviews of our books
* Get NCP submission guidelines
* And so much more!

We offer a 20% discount on all new Trade Paperback releases ordered from our website!

Be sure to visit our webpage to find the best deals in e-books and paperbacks! To find out about our new releases as soon as they are available, please be sure to sign up for our   newsletter (http://www.newconceptspublishing.com/newsletter.htm) or   join   our   reader   group (http://groups.yahoo.com/group/new_concepts_pub/join)!

The newsletter is available by double opt in only and our customer information is *never* shared!

Visit our webpage at:
www.newconceptspublishing.com

Dark Haven is an original publication of NCP. This work has never before appeared in book form. This work is a novel. Any similarity to actual persons or events is purely coincidental.

New Concepts Publishing, LLC.
5202 Humphreys Rd.
Lake Park, GA 31636

© copyright February 2011 Mandy Monroe
Cover art (c) copyright 2011 Alex DeShanks

NCP books are available at special quantity discounts for bulk purchases for sales promotions, premiums, fund raising, or educational use. For details, write, email, or phone New Concepts Publishing, LLC., 5202 Humphreys Rd., Lake Park, GA 31636; Ph. 229-257-0367, Fax 229-219-1097; orders@newconceptspublishing.com.

Second NCP Trade Paperback Printing: February 2013

Dictionary of foreign words used:

Russian

Mal-y-shka - Baby
Doro-gay-a – Darling (f)
Dorogoy – Darling (m)
Alyi - Scarlet
Da – Yes
Mi-lay-a -Sweet
Radast moya – My joy
Mater --Mother
Mne tak kharasho stoboy – I feel so good next to you
Ma-mu-lya- Mummy
Ya tebya lyublyu – I love you
Angel moy – My angel
Dobroye utro – Good Morning

Latín

Mel-lita – Sweetness
Del-icia – Sweetheart
Mel – Honey
Amore me-us – My love
Cunnus- Cunt
Ocellus – Darling (m)
Modus operandi – M.O. – Method of Operating
Magna Cum Laude – Graduate with Honors
In flagrante delicto – Caught in the act of sex

French

Merde – Shit
Elle dor(t) – She sleeps
Chérie – love
Ma bien aimée – My darling
Hein – Eh?
Ma petite - Little one
Ma petite Écarlate – My little Scarlet
Âme sœur du sang – Bloodmate
Zut- blast/damn
Mon dieu – My God
Au revoir – Bye

Abruti -- moron
Tu me comprends? – You understand me?
Non- No
Oui- Yes
La Terreur- the Terror (French Revolution)
Le petit mort- Small death- Orgasm
a la mode – in fashion
mon amour – my love
naturellement – of course

Chapter One

"Goddammit! Watch where the hell you're going, jerk off!" As the fancy sports car swerved out of her lane with seconds to spare before crashing into her, Scarlet Reves inhaled sharply and automatically braked to lengthen the distance between the two cars. Her breath was wheezing and her chest was jerking uncomfortably as she contemplated how damned close that had been, too damned close for her liking.

She'd been driving steadily along, minding her own business as she chatted to her friend on her cell's speaker phone, when all of a sudden the car had appeared out of nowhere in her rear-view mirror. Driving like a bat out of hell, the sports car had jerked out from behind her then dipped within a hair's breadth of her bumper in front of her, almost clipping the side at the same time, before speeding off ahead of her.

Glaring at the fool driver, who by now was hidden from her sight by the rays of the sharp, blinding sunlight, she hissed out a curse that incorporated all car owners who liked to scare the hell out of their fellow motorists!

"What's wrong?" Mary-Jane, Scarlet's best friend, asked sharply.

"Some jerk on the road nearly crashed into me!" Scarlet seethed.

"Damn. That would have been bad luck. What are you, ten miles from the dock? That would have made a killer headline. 'Woman dies five minutes away from dream vacation!'"

"Thanks Mary-Jane," Scarlet said wryly. "It's good to know that I'm worthy of a decent headline, if nothing else."

"Well, it's not something you read about every day, now is it? It would've been a true human interest story. A poor young woman, just moments away from her prize, three weeks stay aboard the brand new ocean liner that the whole world is talking about . . . . I mean, you can't get better than that, can you?"

"You almost sound like you want to read that in the paper, MJ," Scarlet accused teasingly.

"Of course, I wouldn't!" MJ said in a shocked voice. "But the journalist in me is always looking for a story, that's all. I can't help it now. It's become second nature to me."

"I know, I was only kidding," Scarlet said, her voice soothing now.

"Good!

You should know me by now, Scarlet. Hell, you would have thought twenty years of friendship would have taught you something!

With that being said, I still can't believe that you won this dream holiday. In fact, I still can't believe you actually applied! What happened to my practical, strait-laced Scarlet Reves, the woman who does nothing without planning it, months if not years in advance?"

"So I like to be prepared, okay! That's not a crime, is it?"

"W-e-l-l," MJ said, dragging out the syllables considerably. "You can be a pain in the ass, love. I mean, look at last week. I invited you over for pizza with Ryan and me, but what did you do? Rather than thinking, hey, I'm alone and have nothing more planned than a night in the laundry room so I should go and enjoy my best friend's company, you said no because of that very fact. I still can't believe you pencil laundry duties into your diary. You seriously need to get laid!"

"Charming!"

"It's true. I think a couple of good fucks and some guy, somewhere, would screw your brains on the right way this time. Hell, something has to give. Otherwise you're going to end up like one of those old cat ladies. No friends and no sex, just felines for companionship and kitty urine for perfume!"

"God, you know how to paint a pretty picture!"

"That's my job," MJ replied cheerfully.

"Look, my sex life is none of your concern. I'm very content with my vibrator, thank you very much. After the last few times of attempting to have anything that resembled an active sex life, look at what happened!

It's enough to turn a woman gay. Hey, if you weren't married, I'd probably be after you," she teased. "Anything but fool men, who think they're the be all and end all."

"Oh yeah, what happened to you was so bad, wasn't it?

I mean how dare your ex's behave so inappropriately? I mean Jack proposing just shows what a prick he is and Blair wanting to move in with you . . . ? God, what a jerk! Dammit, Scarlet, I think you must be the only woman on God's green Earth that could turn those two guys down.

You know Elizabeth? The girl in my office that looks like she stuck her fingers in the sockets?"

"Frizzy, Lizzy?"

"Yeah, well, she knew Jack before either of us did. You know what she told me, when the rumor bank started spinning about you dumping him after he proposed down at Luciano's?"

"No," Scarlet said with a sigh, not really wanting to know but giving in to her friend anyway. "What did she say?"

"She said that Jack was a complete jerk before he met you. He fucked women then walked before they even stopped climaxing. I think there was a bitter hint of experience in her voice. But the one and only Jack-the-lad Baines falls head over heels in love with you, wants to marry you, and have your babies, and you, you, have the audacity to say no! No wonder she glares at you when you come and meet me at my office. Hell, if it weren't for Ryan, I'd hate you. How you turned him down is beyond me."

"Oh, for God's sake, he wasn't that big a catch!" Scarlet muttered impatiently, checking the rear view mirror to ensure there were no more boy racers on the road.

"Only you, my dear, could say that Jack Baines wasn't a catch. Adonis reincarnate with brains and a position in one of the city's most acclaimed law firms and nice to boot!

Not a catch, my ass!" MJ said with a snort.

"It gets pretty wearing sharing your boyfriend with the vanity mirror, MJ," Scarlet pointed out testily.

"I think that the entire female population of North America wouldn't give a shit if they could just spend a few moments in Jack's bed. Hell, if Ryan wasn't the one, and fuck our friendship, I would have tried to get into his pants!"

"I sure am glad to know that twenty years of sisterhood stands for something!" Scarlet said with a chuckle.

"Oh, it does," MJ said earnestly. "But with a man that fine?

Hell, you'd have to be a nun to not feel something for the guy!"

"Well, I'm no nun. Jack was a nice guy, for a couple of dates and a couple of fun nights in the sack. In fact, yes, he was great in bed, but for anything more? No way. Not only am I not interested in anything serious at the moment, but Jack was a player. He liked the chase. Because I didn't really consider him God's gift to womanhood, it intrigued him, and he liked the idea that I wouldn't let him get away with murder just because of his pretty face," Scarlet said nonchalantly. "He's definitely not husband material."

"Ha! So you admit he was pretty?" MJ said gleefully, pouncing on this new admission like a lion pounced on a gazelle.

Fortunately for Scarlet, she was used to her friend's feline ways. "I'm not blind, MJ. Of course he's pretty ... pretty dull!" she teased mercilessly.

"Philistine!"

"Pushover!"

"Loser!"

"Bitch!"

"You wait until I tell Elizabeth. She already hates you for being the one to tame Jack, now when she finds out you think he's dull as well, she'll probably come and stalk your ass and you totally deserve it for shaming the rest of womankind!"

"Stop being so damned melodramatic. Look, enough was enough with both Jack and Blair. I didn't want what they wanted, so it was best to end it. The only demand my vibrator has is a request for new batteries. That's the only kind of commitment I want." In her mind's eye, Scarlet knew that MJ would be shaking her head sadly.

"But you're missing out on so much, babe," she said a little sorrowfully.

"I'm really not, MJ," she replied softly, not wanting to hurt the woman who was as important to her as her mother. "Not everyone has what you and Ryan have. I know that and so do you. Your marriage is a hard act to follow and if I'm honest, nothing less than what you have would make me even consider living with someone, never mind marrying the man!"

"I know what Ryan and I have is special, but you have to work at a relationship to get what we have. And I know you. You're not willing to even try." MJ sighed resolutely, resigned to the fact that Scarlet would never change. "What made you sign up for this cruise ship prize competition anyway?" she asked, changing the subject.

"I heard it on the radio at work. They were advertising the contest constantly, and, all of a sudden, I just thought, why not?"

"I can't believe you even gave it a shot. It's so not like you. I'm surprised you didn't start adding up the statistics of losing and whether or not it was worth the postage to even enter!"

"Oh, I did. But I decided it was worth my while to give it a go."

MJ snorted. "That's weird. It's just like you, but at the same time, so not."

"Maybe I'm tired of being boring, MJ," Scarlet said, her voice filled with exasperation.

"Never! You?" MJ said sarcastically before laughing mercilessly.

"Okay, maybe not entirely."

"Well, where is the first stop?"

"Key West."

"That should be fun. Remember Spring Break four years ago?"

"I didn't go." Despite herself, Scarlet's voice had tightened in discomfort.

"Oh, damn, of course you didn't. Silly me, I forgot about you and your damned pride. Talk about cutting off your nose to spite your face."

"Don't lecture me, MJ."

"I'm doing no such thing. I'm just saying that if you had had a little less pride and had let me ask my mom for a loan to pay for that trip, then we could have enjoyed Key West together!"

"That sounds a lot like lecturing to me!"

"Well it would to you, wouldn't it? I only speak the truth," MJ stated bluntly.

Scarlet sighed. "Maybe I do have too much pride, but there was no way I was going to ask your mom to lend me money to take a damned vacation!"

It was MJ's turn to sigh. "I know. I just had a great time and wish you'd been there, too."

"I'm glad you did, MJ, and I'll enjoy seeing it now. It should be nice. I'm looking forward to relaxing," Scarlet said, effectively changing the subject.

"Yeah, I think this will be good for you. You need some time to chill. You never know, there might be a guy on there that will break that practical streak and turn you into a lovey-dovey normal woman!"

"I doubt it," Scarlet said, the words coming out a little more dryly than she'd intended.

"Well, never say never. Would you ever have believed that I could fall in love either? But I did. The ultimate man hater turned one-man-woman and in a single shot! Saying that though, Ry is pretty pungent. Damn, I still can't believe it. You entered a competition that you had almost no chance of winning. You're turning into a new woman," MJ exclaimed with a teasing chuckle.

"Maybe I am and maybe I'm not," she replied hesitantly as she thought about what her friend said. "I just thought it would be a good idea."

Looking down at the road map she was using to find the damned docks, Scarlet determined that she was nearing the place where her first ever vacation was about to start. Despite the fact that she'd told herself from the moment she found out that she won that she wasn't going to let herself get carried away with emotion, a thrill of excitement rushed through her, and she felt a hum of adrenaline crawl along her flesh, leaving all the fine hairs on her body standing on end.

"You've just whetted my curiosity even more now!" MJ complained. "Since when do you have good ideas that involve anything fun? That's just not you. You plan and organize everything down to every boring detail. Creativity isn't allowed! In fact, why am I even your friend?"

"Because you love me. Really, that's why!" And anyway, you know I don't have time to be creative, MJ. You know how hectic my life is. Not only that, but you know how tight my budget is, as well."

"Yeah, I do," MJ admitted grudgingly.

"You also know damn well that I just can't spare the time. I wish that I could! I wish that I could just let my hair down, but you try working three jobs and studying part time for your law degree and you'll see you can't afford to not plan everything, to not be careful. If I wasn't so damned organized, I wouldn't be able to make it all happen, and I refuse to be in this position when I'm older."

"I know, Scarlet. I shouldn't have said anything. I know how hard things have been and still are for you. I'm sorry, honey."

"I know you are, MJ," Scarlet said softly, forgivingly. "I'm looking forward to not having to be organized for a while, though. If the opportunity hadn't been there and the timing hadn't been right, then I'd have certainly passed on this. I'm just lucky that I don't have another course at the college until after Christmas and that all three of my bosses actually let me have the time off!"

"Well, they all like you and know how good you are at your job. Plus, isn't this like the first time in forever when you've actually had time off?

How could they possibly have told you no?"

Scarlet laughed when she thought about what her friend said. "Yeah, I suppose you're right. And I'm going to make the most of this damned trip. Not only will I probably never be able to afford to do it again, but it's the chance of a lifetime to see more than just the states. I would never be able to afford a trip to Europe on my own. I feel so damned lucky."

"I wish I could go with you," MJ said wistfully.

"Me, too, it would be a lot more fun if we were both going."

"Yeah, it's a shame that I'm flat broke and that my

husband would kill me for vacationing with my single and very hot best friend for three weeks!"

"Not that I'm hot, but what does what I look like have to do with anything?"

"Ryan says that when we're together, I get more male attention because they all come flocking around you." MJ paused and thought about that for a second. "I just realized that I should be offended at that statement."

"As if! You know Ryan thinks the sun shines out of your ass. He'd just be jealous that you could be getting some other guy's attention," Scarlet said with a chuckle.

"Yeah, you're right. But I'll just bet you didn't know that jealous sex is even better than make up sex," MJ purred, sounding very much like a cream-sated cat.

"It is?" Scarlet asked, choking a little at that unexpected comment.

"Uh huh."

"Well, I will definitely have to try it sometime then. MJ, sweetie, I'm going to have to go. Judging by the huge ship in front of me, I think I've arrived."

"Duh. You think?" MJ muttered.

Once more Scarlet could picture her friend, sitting on her sofa, her legs curled up underneath her knees, twirling a long strand of curly brown hair around her index finger and her blacker than black eyes rolling at Scarlet's joke. "Bitch," Scarlet joked lightly.

"Take care, won't you, sweetheart?" MJ asked, her voice had become deeper, her tone more serious now.

"Yes, mommy. I won't talk to strange men, and I won't accept candy from people I don't know either," Scarlet said placatingly.

"Well, I don't know about that. I expect you to get laid, get some strange!

Have fun, but be safe!"

"Of course, I will . . . have fun that is. Don't worry about me. I'll have a great time. Bye, honey."

"Bye, Scarlet."

Smiling softly as she hung up the phone, Scarlet drove around for a little while and eventually found a parking space. It was a little further away from the ship than she would have liked, but at the same time, it was free and she dreaded to think how much three weeks of space rental would have cost her. It was worth the hike to park for nothing, especially since nothing was all that she could afford!

Jumping out of her battered little old car, Scarlet straightened the green skirt she wore before pulling her white T-shirt down so that it covered the waistband and settled correctly atop her hips. Reaching for her shoes, which she'd lain on the back seat, always preferring to drive barefoot, she popped them on. She grabbed her cell phone and charger and dumped them into her handbag before locking the car doors. Walking around to the trunk of the car, she popped it open with her key before reaching in and grabbing her one bag. Lowering her suitcase to the ground, she shut her trunk before making sure everything was locked one more time.

When she was done reassuring herself, she pulled out the handle of her suitcase with a flourish and began the short trek to the ship. Even as far away from the ship's docking bay as she was, the Moon Shadow was clearly visible. When she neared it and the crowds became heavier, her suitcase's wheels started to jam. As she looked down at them to see what the problem was, she accidentally walked into someone in front of her.

Jumping back, an apology was just about to cross her lips when she saw the sports car that had almost run into her earlier. The thought of apologizing disappeared instantly. A natural redhead, her mother had always told her, 'Scarlet in name and scarlet in nature.' She'd been very young the first time her mother had said that to her, but it hadn't been hard for her to figure out that she'd meant her temper was red-hot and quick to flare.

"Aren't you going to apologize?" the woman asked, her shrew's voice hard and coming out practically like a shriek.

"Only if you're going to apologize for almost running into me this morning," Scarlet murmured smoothly, managing to rein in her annoyance to just an aggressively raised eyebrow. Something about the woman really made her hackles rise!

"What . . . ?"

"You heard me!"

"You rude, insolent bitch. You should watch your manners around people like me," the woman hissed. Her features, while chic and à la mode, were ice cold, the blond beauty in complete contrast to Scarlet's fiery looks and nature.

The woman's sanctimonious tone made Scarlet's hackles rise immediately. "What the hell do you mean people like you?

I don't see a crown on your head, lady. You're just the same as me."

"Watch your tongue or I'll rip it out," the blond snarled and backed off and away.

Scarlet frowned at the retreating woman. She had a feeling that something else and not her had caused the other woman to hurry away. She looked around the crowded docks but saw nothing. Looking down at the gleaming metal of the luxurious sports car, Scarlet was hard pressed not to scratch a line along the body work with her key. It was tempting and damned difficult to stop herself from doing so.

It was the first time in her life where she had ever felt like doing something like that and the thought of acting upon that sudden impulse shocked her. For a moment, the desire to let her hair down and stop giving a damn had powered through her, leaving her feeling a little dazed and wistful. She secretly wished she did have the balls to scratch the bitch's car. She deserved it. Hell, she'd been lucky earlier that there had been no cops around because she sure as hell would've been charged with dangerous and reckless driving! Well, that is if she wasn't able to bribe her way out of a ticket.

Grimacing, Scarlet turned her back on the tempting idea that had been ricocheting through her head. She had to tell herself firmly that she was a grown woman who did not do mean things to other people simply because she didn't like them. Repeating the line like a mantra, she followed the crowd and felt herself slowly become charged with the holiday spirit despite the fact that her feet were already blistered from the long walk from the car to the ship. The drag of the suitcase's weight and broken wheels didn't make the short walk any easier as she felt the backs of her shoes rub against already raw skin and winced.

When she caught herself longing for her sturdy and comfortable boring work pumps, she admonished herself firmly. The heels she was wearing were sexy and made her legs look like a million dollars. Despite what she'd said to MJ, she wasn't averse to male companionship, especially in the bedroom department. If this torturous pair of hooker heels ensnared a few gorgeous men then wear them she would, blisters be damned!

Although she tried to deny it, MJ was right. She was turning into a bore. The problem with her life was that practicality had become the focus of her day. It was the ugly truth, and she was fully aware of that fact. But, unless she was practical, her life as she knew it would shudder to a complete halt, and that was something she just couldn't afford which was why this vacation she'd won was going to be all about throwing caution to the wind and enjoying three reckless weeks of adventure and freedom.

While the time away from work was something else that she could ill afford, she'd spotted the opportunity to do something magnificent and hadn't been able to say no, the possibility of taking her first ever vacation.

It was sad when she thought about it. She was twenty-seven years old and she'd never had a vacation, but when your mother was a single parent and worked all day, every day to keep the wolves from the door, you were grateful for the food on the table and the clothes on your back. She had never complained. She didn't regret anything about her life. Both her life and her mother's had been hard and had forged them into the people they were today, which was strange since, despite everything, it had made her mother a hopeless romantic and her a hardened cynic with a desperate need to better her life so that she could simultaneously enhance the quality of her mother's life as well.

She decided that her thoughts were too deep for the start of a vacation, so she mentally shrugged them away and glanced around at the crowd. As she began to board the ship, she noticed that almost everyone was wearing black. She was the only one wearing actual color. They were just wearing black, but it was like being surrounded by a gang or something. One big blotchy mass of black was a nasty sight to the eye.

The wheels of her case were still sticking and were hard to drag up the inclined ramp that led onto the ship. Blowing out a grateful breath when she reached the top and handed over her ticket and ID, she took an interested look around the deck and her gaze skimmed over the décor and, ultimately, the employee that was checking her in.

It was difficult not to stare in awe at the amount of black the guy was wearing. It was strange to think that this man worked for the cruise liner. His jet black hair was spiked into truly gigantic proportions. So much so that he appeared to have four little volcanoes running along the central line of his skull, the tips of which glowed with red dye. In fact, when she thought about it she realized that that was the only color in the man's entire ensemble. His black jeans were skin tight and ripped at the knee, fagged denim rips covered almost the whole length of his thigh and calf. His black T-shirt was tucked here and there with safety pins.

Unconsciously she frowned in thought as she looked at the man.

"Enjoy your stay with us, ma'am. Here's a map of the ship and an activity guide. If you have any queries, please don't hesitate to ask a member of the staff for more information. Have a good day," he said, a warm smile gracing his lips.

His voice was surprisingly polished and quite cultured, which was in complete contrast to his looks!

She nodded in response and went on her way. Looking about the luxurious deck, she was truly pleased with her prize. How could she not be?

The ship was beautiful. Just the thought of three week's vacation in itself was an awesome thing, but three weeks on this ship? Wow. It seemed incredible that frugal and poor Scarlet Reves was actually on board one of the latest and most talked about cruise liners in the world.

After consulting the map the employee had given her and walking around for about five minutes, she discovered an elevator that took her to her level. The ship wasn't as busy as she'd expected, but then everyone was probably in their cabin unpacking their bags and preparing themselves for the first night aboard. The few people that she'd seen so far were employees that were dressed similarly to the guy who'd welcomed her. Briefly she wondered who on Earth the cruise company had hired to design their employee's uniforms because, whoever the hell it was, they needed firing!

Eventually, after reaching her allocated floor, she found her cabin and walked into her suite of rooms. She'd expected a beautiful place to lay her head at night, but she'd never imagined such sheer luxury.

The first room was painted in a pearly white that reflected the sunlight that flooded in to the room from the wall of floor-to-ceiling windows. When she looked out the window she saw a huge expanse of sea. If that in itself hadn't been amazing, then the minimal but cozy style would have just blown it out of the hills for her. Low cream leather sofas were placed strategically so that they looked out on to the ocean. Kicking off her shoes, she found the caramel carpet was plush and soft beneath her feet. Walking further in she found there was a coffee table in the center of the room that truly was a work of art. Sticks of driftwood banded together with rough and oxidized strips of iron with a smooth piece of glass lying atop it. It was beautiful.

With a grin of sheer delight, she peered into the bedroom that had a bed that was practically the size of a tennis court with mounds of what looked like down-filled pillows on it. The same caramel carpet flowed from the lounge into this room and it was filled with similar furnishings as well. Earthy, natural paintings dotted the walls, and there was a beautiful ceiling light in the very center of the room. The glass of the fixture was obviously hand blown with small lights that filled equally small balls of glass until there was just a mass of glittery light. Somehow it reminded her of the way sunlight reflected off of the sea, and she thought that it was very appropriate for the suite.

Locating the bathroom, she discovered that it was a marvel in Italian marble and gloriously expansive to boot. In her whole life she'd never been anywhere so extraordinary, somewhere so special that it made her jaw drop in wonder. There was no doubt in her mind that she would enjoy every moment here. There was something very homey about the place. While the epitome of beauty, it wasn't so stuffy that she was afraid to touch anything, and she appreciated that quality about it.

Dropping her bag and suitcase on the floor beside the

bed, she immediately began to unpack. When she was only halfway through, though, she stopped and glared down at her luggage.

Why did she have to be so practical? Why was it so important that she unpack now?

Defiantly, she dropped the clothes into the suitcase and decided to plop herself on to the bed to test it out instead. Quickly stripping off her confining clothes, she jumped on to the feather-filled mountain. Sighing at the comfort after she'd landed,

She snuggled down and contemplated the freedom of twenty-one days' worth of vacation. Laughing gleefully, she stretched and laid herself comfortably out on the bed.

The combination of some recent heavy hours at each of her three jobs that she'd put in to make up for such a long vacation combined with the specter of pre-Christmas exams and a gloriously sun-warmed room made her eyes flicker shut and soon she napped peacefully.

* * * *

Sitting up with a squint, Scarlet smiled when she saw that her bedroom window was ablaze with the setting sun. Streaks of rosy heat and warm shots of orange splintered through the glass, and she yawned happily at the sight. Jumping off of the bed, she quickly hurried into the bathroom to wash up. There was no rush, but she wanted to explore some of the ship before the sun actually set and so she dressed speedily for the night ahead, selecting a formal black high-waisted pencil skirt. She combined it with a sweetheart neckline bustier that was a deeply hued bronze and really accentuated the gold highlights in her auburn hair. Not really feeling like worrying with her hair, she simply brushed her locks, feeling that her hair's natural wave was enough style for the time being. To complete her look, she put on a pair of black court shoes and hooked a pair of dulled bronzed hoops that MJ had lent her into her ears before she felt that she was finally ready to walk out of the door.

She headed back to the elevator she'd discovered earlier and began her perusal of the liner. As she explored, she noticed that it seemed like all of her fellow guests were dressed in black grunge clothing. What she'd earlier supposed to be a staff uniform was actually a style of dress that the entire ship seemed to be adhering to. Well, except her. Frowning, she studied the rips and tears and piercings then noticed that almost all of the guests seemed to be her age, which was indeed a surprise. In teenagers or people in their early twenties, sure, she'd seen this fashion. But in people nearing thirty? That was more than a little bizarre. If it wasn't so close to Christmas, she would have thought that everyone was dressed up for an All Hollow's Eve party!

Feeling unbearably uncomfortable in her smart and elegant wear, she tried hard not to fidget as she saw some stares being focused her way. It was almost a relief when a voice spoke over the loudspeaker as it took attention away from her. Hell, she'd splurged on a few decent outfits at a designer overstock outlet for this damned trip so that she wouldn't be feeling like a poor relation in comparison to the other guests! But as it was she would have out-styled these guys in her ancient, ratty pajamas!

"Welcome aboard the maiden voyage of the Moon Shadow. We hope you enjoy your stay aboard this fine vessel and are so glad that you could join us for the world's first ever vampire cruise ship! The captain and his staff are proud to welcome vampires and vampire admirers on board the Moon Shadow and hope that you enjoy all the extra amenities that we've laid on for you. Enjoy."

A themed cruise?

Why the hell had she only just learned that?

Feeling her redhead temper begin to spark, Scarlet had to fight to dampen the flames and breathed in deeply in an effort to relax.

A vampire cruise? Who the hell had even thought up that kind of crackpot scheme?

She seethed silently but then studied her fellow travelers and admitted that there was obviously a market for loons who thought themselves to be bloodsuckers. What the hell had she gotten herself into?

She'd expected three weeks of relaxation, visits to countries she'd never even hoped to visit, to see a continent that she'd always dreamed about seeing and now she had to share that dream with a couple of thousand crazy vampire lovers. Life just wasn't fair.

She'd finally convinced herself that it was alright trying

to stop being uber practical for a few weeks, but the idea of spending so much time on board a ship with mad people was not an enjoyable prospect. There was nothing more that she longed to do than leave the ship. The idea of having cabin fever amongst this madcap crowd was just too horrific to bear. There was no way in hell she was going to make friends with these people, not because she was prejudiced, but because they were. She could see that they thought she was weird for not being dressed like them. She knew that she would be spending all three weeks in solitude and while that wasn't altogether a bad thing, she had hoped for a little male company to while away a few days. No way did she want to fuck a vampire-obsessed loser!

Feeling the engines hum beneath her feet, she damned herself for breaking with her routine and taking a nap. Without even having registered the thought, she knew that the cruise liner was already sailing and knew that her only chance of escape wouldn't be available until the ship docked again. From memory, she realized that that was going to be in a three days time, which at this moment, seemed far too long a time to be spending with a bunch of crazy mother fuckers.

The cruise was lazily meandering around the Straits of Florida before heading along the East Coast and finally beginning its journey across the Atlantic Ocean. It would be stopping off at England, France, Spain, Italy, and Greece before heading back. Twenty minutes ago, the prospect of such a wonderful vacation had sent a shot of happiness fizzing through her blood. Now, it made her feel slightly depressed. The idea of being cooped up with people, who so obviously had nothing in common with her, made her feel down.

She didn't need people to feel content. If that were the case, then she would never have accepted the one ticket prize. But, seeing the very evident differences between herself and the rest of the ship's passengers was just too much to bear.

How could she, someone who as a child hadn't even believed in Santa Claus or the Tooth Fairy, now as a twenty-seven year old woman spend time with a bunch of people who probably actually believed in vampires or believed they themselves were vampires?

She just couldn't. It was a completely absurd notion and she knew that she would be leaving her dream trip eighteen days ahead of schedule. The thought made her sigh dejectedly, but it didn't stop her from tracking down a member of the staff and arranging the details of getting off the ship early. She quickly discovered, however, that there had been another undisclosed reschedule. Yes, they would be meandering around the Straits of Florida, but no, they wouldn't be docking off anywhere. So the earliest time she would be able to leave the ship was in seven days' time.

It had been difficult to rein in her temper when she'd heard that. Knowing that it wasn't the hapless steward's fault, she'd resigned herself to a week, and now, as she traipsed around the ship, she had to stop herself from cringing at the sight of all the vampire lovers. It was so terribly embarrassing to see grown adults who believed in Dracula.

Scarlet attempted to shift her focus from the guests to the ship, and she had to admit that even though she was upset at least that wasn't a disappointment. The whole prize had the makings of a sent-from-heaven vacation that the rest of the idiots on board could spoil. It made her itch in annoyance. The only consolation was that it was free, which was a great comfort. She didn't doubt that this vacation was setting these vampires back a hell of a lot of money. Thank God she wasn't paying exorbitant sums to be here!

Resolutely, she decided that the idea of spending seven days feeling gloomy was just ridiculous and so she was determined to enjoy the few days that she would have on board. It was something she would probably never experience again, and she decided that she should try and make the most of it come what may. The vampires and vampire lovers had stared at her funny, but they hadn't been overly rude or aggressive towards her. Sure, they looked odd, but they seemed a nice bunch of people and their seemingly normal behavior soon set her at ease. So long as there was nothing overly weird going on, she knew that she could handle it. At least she thought she could.

On a sigh, Scarlet realized that she was hungry, and so, with her map and activity guide in hand, she located the nearest restaurant and set off to have a bite to eat.

Thinking about the word bite made her cringe, and she damned all vampires for intruding into her once-in-a-lifetime vacation. She knew that if MJ could see her now, she'd be hooting with laughter. The idea that she, stuffy logical Scarlet Reves, was actually associating with people like this would just be too much for her to handle. She was too strait-laced for this sort of thing and would've never dreamed that she'd find herself eating in the same restaurant as a whole bunch of people who believed that paranormal monsters actually existed!

Grimacing at the thought, she sat down at a table and glanced around the Gothic castle she found herself in. Completely unlike every other public area she'd been in, this dining hall would have suited Count Dracula perfectly. All of the tables were lit by candelabra and covered in starched white linen and silver cutlery with shining drinking glasses. Decorative cornice moldings on the ceilings, the sepia colored plaster work contrasted smartly with the black walls and arched nooks that housed some pretty impressive stone friezes. Old world and truly beautiful in its own way, the fact that it was for vampires totally spoiled the affect for her.

The Gothic atmosphere combined with the chillingly dark violin adagios in the background totally unsettled her stomach. Before she could rush away to the sanctuary of her room, a waiter arrived. He wore tailored black pants and a white shirt with a frothy cravat at his throat. Handing her a menu, he bowed deeply and stood waiting patiently while she perused a list of foodstuffs that killed the small amount of appetite she had left. The menu read like a child's Halloween party: Eyeball and blood soup. Fang Steak with Witch's Tears. Quagmire of Gore.

"Is this for real?" she asked, unable to hide the horror in her voice.

"Ma'am?"

"These dishes? Are their names descriptive or just honorary? You know, because of the occasion 'first vampire themed cruise ever'?"

"Yes."

"Yes to which one?" Scarlet muttered exasperatedly.

"Both."

"You mean you're serving eyeball soup?"

"No."

"Please explain a little further."

"Our meals have been specially designed to tempt the palate while savoring the occasion. The names are strange but the meals are themed around them."

"So eyeball and blood soup is what exactly?"

"Spaghetti and meatballs," the waiter said with a flash of a grin.

Unable to help herself, she laughed aloud when she saw the man's teeth. "Are your teeth real?" she asked, a little curious.

The man raised a hand and fingered the pointed incisor teeth that graced his upper jaw. "Yes, ma'am."

"So you're a vampire, are you?" Scarlet asked, amused now.

"I wish."

The man spoke so wistfully that Scarlet almost snorted.

"My dentist furnished me with these beauties however."

"I'm glad to hear that!"

"I can recommend the spaghetti and meatballs, ma'am. Although a humble dish, our chef is truly excellent."

"Okay." Scarlet nodded and handed the waiter back the menu. "I'm placing myself entirely in your hands."

The waiter nodded. "Would you care for a beverage, ma'am?

We have a fine choice of bloods available for your discerning palate," he murmured softly, his face completely free from expression.

"I take it that's a fancy term for wine?"

The man said nothing. Instead he just waited silently for her to make a choice.

Pondering why the hell he hadn't admitted that the blood was just a weird name for wine, she shuddered a little at the prospect of drinking blood. "Water. I'd like still water with ice, please," she replied with a grimace.

Bowing, the waiter walked away silently, leaving her to her own company and to deliberate over the strange conversation she'd just had. Why on Earth would someone have their teeth shaved into points? It seemed completely bizarre to her and totally and completely unnecessary and dangerous. But, obviously, this was a way of life to these people. They actually believed in vampires and chose to emulate them.

Shaking her head at the thought, she glanced over the activity sheet she'd stuffed in her bag earlier along with the map of the ship and reviewed the night's entertainment. There was a welcome aboard party on deck four and a cabaret show on three. She didn't exactly fancy either choice but thought she would wait until having eaten before making her final decision. She dreaded to think what the entertainment staff considered cabaret for a bunch of vampires!

Hell, this whole thing was a complete and utter farce. She herself felt absolutely ridiculous and as though she was in a parallel universe. Things like this shouldn't happen to people like her. People like her planned everything so that surprises like these wouldn't occur, dammit. She couldn't believe that the first time in over fifteen years that she'd decided to let her hair down and relax, this was the result.

Nodding her thanks as the waiter returned with her water, she took a sip and looked around the room. Frowning a little, why she didn't know, she turned her head to the far left. It was an uncomfortable position, but she immediately understood why she'd been frowning. There was a man staring at her. Unblinkingly so. Even from the difficult position her head was in, she could see that his entire focus was on her.

Her skin tingled and her blood began to crawl sluggishly through her veins as an awe-inspiring desire worked its way languidly through her system. Not content with making her pussy wet, it wanted to wreak havoc with her organs, and she felt her heart slow to a dull thud in her chest before picking up the pace to beat rapidly like a trapped bird in the cage of her ribs. She gulped and turned her back a little to the left so that she could see him more easily.

Immediately he caught her gaze.

Cheeks flushing with an embarrassed heat, she tried to break away from his gaze, but she couldn't. It wasn't possible. Everything in him called out to everything in her. Her body, her entire being cried out in longing for a more physical manifestation of that all encompassing touch. His gaze had touched her everywhere and now she longed for his hands to do the same. In fact, she more than longed for it, she needed it urgently, craved it like a starving man craved food.

Her skin felt super-sensitive, her ears hyper-aware of the restaurant's hustle and bustle. Indeed, every single one of her five senses seemed wide awake and was responding to the sheer vitality in her admirer's gaze. Somehow, she could feel it like a caressing hand, and, unable to help herself, she shuddered as her pussy began to clench needily. She damned the emptiness and prayed for his cock to ease it, to push into her and complete her in a way she'd never before experienced.

The thought made her breath catch in her chest, and she ducked her head, more than a little ashamed of her response to this one man's gaze. Hell, she'd been looked at and checked over before, but something about this man called out to her and made her feel urgency for him like she'd never needed anything before. It was a rather frightening situation and one that she didn't appreciate finding herself in. She always liked being in control and nothing in this situation was within her grasp. Indeed she was more like the puppet than the puppet master, and she heartily disliked it while recognizing that she had no choice in the matter.

A little more blatantly now, she studied him and realized that, although he was dressed in black, he wasn't sporting the whole grunge and punk style that most of her fellow guests were wearing to the detriment of their looks!

He was dressed expensively if she wasn't mistaken. The suit he had on was exquisitely tailored and obviously designer. It fit him superbly and added to his already impressive aura.

He looked to be a few years older than her and a part of her wondered what had made him join this crazy cruise! He didn't seem the type, what with his New York suit and his playboy good looks. This man was not someone who joined in on things like this, just like she herself wasn't. Finding herself to be intensely curious about him, she almost jolted in shock. She was never curious about the opposite sex. She didn't care enough about them to want to know. But with this man, this stranger, she needed to know him and the thought frightened her.

Blowing out a pent-up breath, she took in the long brown hair that drifted along the line of his shoulders.

Normally she thought long hair on a man was effeminate,
but this most definitely wasn't. The long hair merely
enhanced his masculinity, something that was already
rather overpowering!

The long mink brown locks framed a square jaw that
housed a firm mouth. Neither fleshy nor thin, the lips were
perfect for biting and the thought made her pussy quiver.
His eyes were piercingly narrowed, but she couldn't
discern their color because of the distance between them.
His forehead was broad and led down to a thin blade of a
nose that should perhaps have detracted from his looks but
instead added character. His skin gleamed, and he truly was
the picture of good health.

In her mind's eye, she could imagine that expanse of
lustrous skin that tautly covered bunches of muscle and
tough sinew. She could see herself testing the curve of his
bicep with her teeth, feeling the strength and tightly leashed
control in between her jaw. She could imagine herself
licking the delineated line of his hip bone, that luxurious
line that started at just below his waist and curved inwards
to his leg. In the middle of that glorious area would be his
cock. Perhaps it was wishful thinking, but she imagined
nine inches of velvet covered steel. She imagined it filling
every single inch of her, and the thought made her sigh
hungrily.

This was the first man she'd ever seen who had inspired
lust at first sight in her.

* * * *

If he hadn't known his senses were beyond
extraordinary and completely incomparable to those of a
human, Vincent Duchette would have doubted them. For
the first time in his long existence as a vampire, he felt
unsure of his capabilities, as the last time he'd felt so
strongly, it had been upon meeting his one and only love
for the first time.

A young man of twenty-three, hunger and desire had
raged through his system upon meeting Véronique Du
Clair. Those heady feelings combined with tenderness had
made his world rock on its feet and he'd known
immediately that he had to make her his wife. In the two
hundred and forty years of his life and death, Vincent knew
that only she had raised him to the very highest peaks of

heaven and the very lowest caverns of hell.

Meeting her had made him feel reborn. Her death, at the hands of Robespierre's bastard minions, had effectively ended his own life. The day she'd been slaughtered at the guillotine had changed him forever, had filled him with a never ending despondency.

That was until now.

It was almost painful, this roar of awareness that was pounding through him. After such a long time of feeling nothing, the sensations bombarding him were like a punch in the solar plexus. Only his well constructed control developed over the many years of his existence stopped him from gasping as emotion after emotion powered through his veins until his ear drums burned from the rushing in them, his eyes felt blind from the flash of lights behind them, and his skin tingled from wave after wave of sensation attacking each nerve ending.

Gulping in a harsh breath, he took a deep sip from his glass and looked around the room. His eyes touched every person until he found the one who had brought him back to life.

Seeing the auburn haired angel perched on a chair chatting with a waiter made his heart stop in his chest. He took in every inch of her and processed the thoughts into some semblance of order. Gleaming porcelain skin that he longed to mark with his teeth was the first thing he noticed. Her emerald eyes were the next. They glinted in the light and sparkled with life. Her nose was small but suited the heart shape of her face. Her lips were full and a deep red, not stained from make-up but truly red. They were naturally formed into a pout, and his cock throbbed at the thought of that luscious pair of lips surrounding and swallowing him deeply.

Her breasts were large and were displayed supremely in the bustier she wore. He could see the bouncy curve and imagined the ripe berries at the end forming into taut peaks as he scored them with his teeth. He knew at that exact moment that he had to have her, that he had to bite her, and that he had to mark her as his.

In his mind's eyes, he saw her rose colored nipples framed by his bite marks, and once more his cock pounded against the tight confinement of his pants. He imagined the velvety smoothness of her blood sliding down his throat, and he was hard pressed not to cum right there.

Marking a woman was always a dangerous idea. Three times and she was your slave. Six times and she was your mate. He knew without even having to act that it would be difficult for him not to sup from her at least ten times during just one night of sex!

Her velvety skin would showcase his bites to perfection and each one would be like a work of art. He could see two framing her nipples and one at her mound. One on either side of her neck and two at her inner thighs. And that was just for starters. The main course would be her blood. He just knew that it would be like nothing he'd ever tasted, that the slip and slide of it in his mouth would bring him to his knees. For dessert would be the orgasm that would ripple through him as she accepted his cock and let him pleasure her until she climaxed.

The powerful need that was nearly overwhelming all of his senses almost frightened him, because he had to have her. To control the lust and desire for her blood would be more than difficult, it would be practically impossible. To satisfy his need, he would have to bite her, and he knew that once would not be enough. There was a fatalistic sense to the lust he felt for her and it worried him. Never having felt this deeply before, he knew that his life was about to change, and he wasn't sure that he wanted it to.

Watching her laugh and smile at the waiter made his possessive instincts rise. It was crazy to feel so intense, but he was helpless against the feelings mounting in him. The sentiments boiling inside him weren't within his control, and he was fully aware of that. He was also fully aware of how dangerous that was. Even after recognizing that fact, he felt himself rise from his chair and begin the walk towards her. It was almost an out of body experience. He didn't feel himself stand up, didn't register the walk or the passing of tables and people as he strode past. Suddenly he was in front of her and her scent blossomed inside of him, setting his blood alight and charging every particle of need that she had previously inspired in him.

Whatever happened during this voyage would change their lives forever.

Whether he was ready for that, he didn't know.

Chapter Two

Feeling a hand tighten on her left shoulder, Scarlet didn't have to guess to whom it belonged. She knew instinctively that it was the man who had been seated at the other side of the room, knew that it was the man who had been staring as intensely at her as she had at him.

Helplessly, her body reacted to that presence, and she gasped as a shudder chocked to the brim with arousal rolled throughout her body. It felt like an earthquake. The aftershocks just kept coming and coming.

"Do not be alarmed, ma petite."

His husky tone seemed to shiver throughout her system. The French accent merely enhanced the guttural timbre that seemed to quaver along every nerve ending that her body contained. She felt the pinch as the fingertips gripped her harder still before releasing her entirely and trailing them along the line of her shoulder.

He dipped them down and dragged them along the length of her collarbone.

She knew that this kind of touch was completely out of order, so intrusive that everything about it was just wrong, but she didn't care. This was different. Different how, she didn't know. She didn't understand why the hell she was letting a stranger touch her so intimately, but it felt so damn right that it would have been so wrong to refuse the caress. And that was what it was, a caress.

Her eyes fluttered shut as he trailed his fingers up her neck and along the lobe of her ear.

"My name is Vincent, Vincent Duchette."

"Scarlet Reves," she said in a hushed voice.

"Such a fitting name, ma petite."

Entwining a hand in the locks of her hair, he tugged gently, tipping her head backwards so that she was looking into his eyes.

Chocolate brown clashed with emerald and she felt her heart stop and her breath halt in her chest.

"Do you know how many times I've heard that?" she joked huskily.

"I can imagine," he said, smiling slowly. "But actually I meant your last name, Rêves . . . . In French that translates as dreams."

"Okay, I don't know how to take that . . . ," she murmured after swallowing nervously.

His eyes followed the movement of her throat.

"You can take it anyway you want while we dance," he said, although it was more of a statement than a question.

As soon as he said the words, she realized that a band had started up, replacing the recorded classical music that had been coursing through the crowded room.

He slipped a hand down her arm to grab the limb, and he tugged her up on to her feet.

"I-I'm not much of a dancer," she stammered uncomfortably.

"Do you think I give a damn?" he whispered with a faint smile.

Her eyes opened wide as she felt his callused hands brush along her sensitive palms. "You might when I step on your toes," she warned lamely.

A part of her really wanted to dance with him, just to feel his arms around her, but she didn't want to make a fool of herself either!

"If Vincent doesn't mind, then I'm willing to take the risk."

Spinning around at the intruding voice that was husky with a teasing lilt of Russian, Scarlet's eyes almost popped out of her head when she saw the two men standing before her. She gulped and stared a little blankly at the man who'd spoken. A shaft of despair rushed through her as she felt that same powerful torrent of attraction that she'd felt for Vincent thrust through her veins.

His hair was blond, short, and wavy, darker at the roots and tinged with the sunlight. She desperately wanted to run her fingers through it. Her fingertips tingled as though she could feel the warmth of the sun from his hair against her skin. His eyes were a strange pale blue, eerie and piercing. He had a Nordic look about him, but rather than pale skin, he was darkly tanned. Tall and lithe, his body was attired to perfection in a suit that was similar to Vincent's, perfectly and expensively tailored but black. It screamed designer brand.

"Nicholae, try not to alarm this lovely lady."

Her gaze shifted to the third man, and, as her gaze touched upon him, she swore that every single hair on her body quavered and stood on edge. Long hair that brushed his shoulders was blacker than a pitch dark night. His eyes were the scariest part about of him, though. Scary seemed like a strange word to use, but the color alternated so fiercely from one to another that it made her heart palpitate. Hazel was much too tame a word to use since it ranged from the deepest chocolate to the palest of greens and from dusky gold to sapphire blue. Something in his eyes touched her deeply, and, all of a sudden, her body felt bombarded with too many sensations. To feel so much for three men seemed so implausible that it was crazy.

She'd never even felt this way for one man, never mind three and at the same time. There was something so unbelievable about this situation that she felt as though she were dreaming. Hell, maybe this whole day was a dream and in a few hours she'd wake up and find herself on a normal, non-vampire cruise surrounded by retirees and married couples.

It seemed incredible that all these three different men were so intrinsically what she wanted in a man. It frightened her. This intensity of feeling for three men when she'd never even felt anything even remotely strong for her past boyfriends. She'd merely liked them. She'd never felt anything as earth-shattering as this.

"Who-are-you?" she asked stiltedly.

The sheer masculine beauty of their faces made her suck in a swift breath.

The long-haired man ducked his head in a formal bow that both stunned and pleased her. "My name is Lazarus."

"And you're Nicholae?" she asked the blond man.

He nodded, a slow grin forming on his unbearably sexy lips.

She blinked as she was blinded by each of the three men's stunningly gleaming smiles. Talk about blessed in every way!

"Why are you even talking to me?" she blurted out. The sudden unexpected verbalization of her thoughts made her cheeks flush uncomfortably.

These guys were beyond hot. If there was a measure of one to ten of 'hotness' then they were one hundred on that scale. A simple glance scorched her skin. A touch burned a brand on her flesh. She felt like whimpering at the thought of how intense one of their cocks sliding into her would feel. She imagined the heat would be enough to melt her insides and knew that any sexual experience with them would be beyond anything she'd ever felt, beyond anything she'd ever hoped to experience.

Why was it becoming so hard to breathe here? She wanted to raise her hand and flap it in front of her face, wanted to fan her blushes away and cool herself down. Maybe a dunk in the ocean would help that, seeing as she highly doubted a small draft would help at all. Knowing her luck, it would merely fan the flames. She felt like jumping into the sea and hoping to God that it cooled her down some because these three men were the epitome of masculine beauty!

"What do you mean?" Lazarus asked a little disconcertedly.

"Well, I-I, look at you!" She blew out a breath as she realized that her rather strange outburst was actually offending them. They were looking down at their suits as though they'd find soup stains on them. "Dammit. Look at you and look at me!" she mumbled uncomfortably.

"I think there is a compliment somewhere in that statement, gentlemen," the blond, Nicholae, said with a chuckle.

Unable to help it, her cheeks flushed once more. Every instinct went on alert as Lazarus stepped forward and cupped her cheek with a warm and distinctly rough palm. The brush of his skin against the smooth flesh of her face almost made her shudder as a need so potent almost choked her. "Why should we not talk to you, mellita?"

"What does mellita mean?" Scarlet asked in a hushed voice, the words coming out no more than a soft whisper.

He smiled faintly as his hand dropped down to trace his fingers along her neck and slid down along her collarbone to finally cup the ball of her shoulder. "It's Latin for 'sweetened with honey.'"

"Oh," she murmured dumbly.

He smiled again. "Your hair is the color of fire and your eyes are like gems. You've been touched by the Gods, and we, mere men, should bow down at your feet."

If he hadn't have been so deadly serious when he'd said the words, she would have laughed. Instead, she stood in awe as those words registered in her mind. "I don't think we know each other well enough to use terms of endearments."

Lazarus grinned at the other two men and chucked her under the chin. "Time means nothing, mellita. Yes, minutes blend into hours and hours into days, but in this magnificent plane, this means little. You know me as I know you, delicia."

"I do?" she asked, a quaver evident in her voice. Hell, these men turned her into a quivering mass of jelly. Where on Earth was the strong Scarlet from twenty minutes ago? The thought made her blink. Had only twenty minutes passed? She wasn't sure. God, maybe Lazarus was right. She felt as though she'd known him forever, felt as though her body recognized every centimeter of him and reacted accordingly by heating and blossoming with arousal.

He nodded sharply.

Before he could reply, Vincent interrupted. "Pardon me, Scarlet, for just a moment. I need to speak to my friends."

She blinked, a little dazed now, and sat down with a jolt. A feeling of something akin to being star struck made her slightly lightheaded. "Of course," she whispered.

Scarlet reached for her glass of water, seized it gratefully, and took a huge gulp to settle her nerves.

Her gaze helplessly followed the three, involuntarily glued to their asses. If she'd been able, she would have split her line of sight in three ways so that she could look at them simultaneously and not flicker hungrily between them.

Whatever they were discussing looked serious and as she finally took a deep cleansing breath, she wondered why on Earth these three men, men who looked like Gods and had to be rich businessmen of some kind to afford those damned suits, were on a vampire cruise. She truly felt as though her eyes were deceiving her, as though they'd magically superimposed these wonderful facades over the faces of three geeky vampire wannabes. She blinked twice to ensure that that wasn't the case and breathed a sigh of relief when Lazarus, Nicholae, and Vincent's appearances all remained the same.

Hell, she was a superficial bitch, wasn't she?

* * * *

"What the hell are you two doing?" Vincent spat angrily.

"What are we doing?" Nicholae asked dumbly. "What the hell are you doing?"

"I was blending in."

Lazarus laughed darkly. "I don't think that's what I'd call it, Vincent. Let's be honest, every woman's eyes were on your ass and every guy's eyes were on Scarlet's breasts. You couldn't have been more conspicuous if you'd tried!"

"I think you had more on your mind than blending in, Vincent!" Nicholae said pointedly as he lowered his gaze to Vincent's crotch. "I think your cock does, too."

"Bastard," Vincent spat and attempted to rearrange his crotch as unobtrusively as physically possible. He'd known that lust and arousal had fired through his system, but he hadn't realized his cock was hard. In his over two centuries of life, even with his beloved, his body had never taken over his mind to the extent that his arousal was on display. Perhaps it had happened when he'd been an untried boy but never since he'd become a man. That fact made him edgy. "Like you're not feeling the same way. Both of you. Since when do you call women mellita, Lazarus?"

"Since I met Scarlet," Lazarus replied easily.

The depth of feeling behind Lazarus' words really affected him. It perturbed him a little to find himself annoyed. How could he feel so possessive over a stranger? Or was it possessiveness? He'd never felt that way with Nico and Lazarus before. Women were easy meat to share between all three of them if the woman was consenting.

What made Scarlet so special?

It actually pissed him off that he was reacting so uncharacteristically towards her. In fact, scrap that, he hated that she affected them all so strangely.

It didn't help that she was just as powerless to resist this bizarre attraction that afflicted them all.

Because it was bizarre. There was absolutely no denying that.

"This is beyond belief. I've never had a mortal affect me like this before. Even as a human, no one has truly affected me to this extent. Not even . . . ." He sighed and shrugged uncomfortably, unable to finish what he'd been about to say.

Nicholae slapped him on the back, understanding without words what Vincent was referring to. "I know, Vincent, but times change, my brother."

"Perhaps. I just never really expected it to happen."

Lazarus placed a reassuring hand on Vincent's shoulder. "Scarlet is obviously your Achilles' Heel. Fear not, brother, it would seem that she is the chink in our armor, as well. Do you not agree, Nico?"

"Yes," Nicholae admitted a little sheepishly, slightly embarrassed to admit to himself how strongly the woman had affected him.

"You're the eldest, Lazarus, have you heard of a mortal affecting both vampire and werewolf alike?" Vincent asked with a troubled frown.

"I've heard of the werewolf bond, as have both of you. For a vampire there is a blood mate. To answer your question, no, I have never heard the likes of this before. It could just be an anomaly. It could be either about sex or about a deeper, truer bond. At this moment, I cannot be sure. Only time will tell." Seeing the despondent faces of his brethren, he chuckled. "Cheer up, stranger things have happened. We are all living proof of that," he finished on a nonchalant shrug.

"Aren't you bothered by this? Doesn't this worry you at all? The possible ramifications of what this could mean make me feel ill!" Vincent grumbled irritably.

"Not really, no. Two centuries may seem like a long time to you, Vincent, but when one lives for two thousand years it takes a lot more than 'possible ramifications' to bother me. I'm surprised you have to ask," he said with a dark laugh.

Vincent shot him an annoyed look. "Well, this is a little more than we're used to dealing with. Hell, slaying vampires means merde when we're talking about what Scarlet could mean to us."

"Why borrow trouble, Vincent? There's no point. Either she is our bonded mate or she isn't. If she is, then we'll probably feel a lot happier and more fulfilled than we are at this moment. If she isn't, then we'll pleasure her and she us. Simple."

"Dammit, Lazarus!"

"What do you want me to say, Vincent?

I don't have all of the answers."

"I don't need you to have all of the answers, Lazarus. I just need you to show some fucking sensitivity. Why do you have to be so goddamned blasé about all of this? I mean, my head is spinning as it is without you acting like this all means shit to you. You talk about our possible mate like this couldn't change our lives, as though Scarlet is just going to be some quick and easy fuck. I thought this was never going to happen to me, Laz. I thought Veronique . . . ." He stopped as his voice broke. "I thought she was my mate. Not a day passes where I don't think about her, and it turns out that she might not have been my mate after all. Do you realize how much of a betrayal that is to her memory? Or does that just mean jack shit to you?

"Don't be stupid, Vincent. Of course, it doesn't. Just because she wasn't your mate doesn't mean to say that you didn't love Veronique deeply. You're overreacting, because this has all come so unexpectedly. But we're all on thin ice here," Nico countered angrily.

"Oh, I'm sorry. Am I boring you?" Vincent asked sarcastically.

Lazarus sighed, refusing to let the emotions radiating from Vincent and Nicholae draw out any of his own, working hard to maintain his stoic demeanor. "Vincent, calm down. I was just saying that we should take the evening as it comes. Given our current situation and the options available to us, there's little else we can do, brother. You're foolish to think of Scarlet as some kind of replacement for Veronique, though. She's her own person, and, if we're fortunate enough to have her as our mate, then it's only fair that we go to her with a clean slate. You loved Veronique, we know that. But loving and needing Scarlet won't weaken that any. It's just different. The heart has an astounding capacity to love. It's not a betrayal to move on. If there is an afterlife and Veronique begrudges you any happiness you can get, then, quite frankly, you've wasted your love on her!"

Vincent's head shot up, and he glared fire at Lazarus, who merely raised a brow.

Finally bowing his head in dejected acceptance, Vincent nodded jerkily and tried to calm his anger. Perhaps he was overreacting, as Nico had said, but surely it was justified?

Neither man could understand. Losing someone who you had loved, almost since birth, first as a sister, then as a friend, and then as a man loves a woman, it wasn't as simple as grieving and mourning over her. It went further than that. Nicholae interrupted his perplexing thoughts.

"The lady is looking a little dazed. Perhaps we should return to her side?" Nicholae quietly suggested.

"Yes, let us not ignore her any longer. Have you had ample time to regain your composure, Vincent?" Lazarus asked politely.

"I have. But, to be honest, I don't know how long I'll be able to maintain it. Scarlet is receiving far too much attention. Combine that with our presence and there could be trouble."

"That is a possibility," Lazarus generously conceded, "but come," he said, changing the subject as he spread his arms to shepherd his brethren back to Scarlet's side. "Let us not worry about such things now. After all, time is on our side."

Even in his slightly riled state, Vincent couldn't hold back the smile at the picture Scarlet's face made which was a combination of bewilderment and shock with a somewhat glazed glassiness about her eyes. She somehow managed to portray to perfection exactly how he himself felt. To some extent, he could understand the kind of emotion that was bombarding her since similar feelings were hitting him with equal gale forces. Not one person in the history of his life had affected him the way Scarlet had. That more than perturbed him, it actually scared him. The love which he'd had for Véronique, his heart that she'd always possessed, even in death . . . for someone else to perhaps lay claim to that was a frightening thought.

The time after Véronique's death had been some of the worst years of his entire life. Everything about her death had made him mourn and grieve her passing deeply. The fact that he'd known her from being in short trousers, that they'd been childhood sweethearts, having been thrust together from Véronique's birth and the marriage alliance already agreed upon between their families, had pushed them together continuously. He'd loved her as a boy, as an adolescent, and as a man. To know someone and to love them wholeheartedly for such a huge length of time and then to lose them because of her noble blood was hideous beyond compare. To then be turned into a vampire against his will and to know that every single day for the rest of his immortal life he would have to wake up knowing that she was dead was just another nightmare that he'd had to live with. Every single shaft of pain thrust into his heart had strengthened his fortitude and control, only two hundred years later, for that to break upon seeing this beautiful woman.

Yes, he was aggravated by the sheer unexpectedness of this situation. He would be completely heartless if he weren't.

While it helped that Lazarus and Nicholae felt the same for Scarlet as he did, it equally perturbed him. He didn't want to share her if she was his mate. On the other hand, how could he deny her the two men he loved like brothers? If it was fated for all three of them to share her forevermore or just for the night, either way, he wanted her to know every one of them.

If she was their mate, then there were advantages to a shared bond. After countless years of slaying his evil brethren, the trio had managed to assemble a daunting number of enemies. For every single bastard vampire they killed, three more were created somewhere in the world. Two of these newly created vampires would become further prey for Vincent, Lazarus, and Nicholae . . . while only one had the chance of living decently. Scarlet needed protection from the evil of his kind.

Lazarus was one of the oldest of their brethren. If he had not heard of a woman attracting two completely separate and normally warring species of the paranormal genus, then what they were facing was indeed rare, rare enough to raise eyebrows. Perhaps it stemmed from the fact that they were blood brothers. Perhaps not genetically so, but spiritually and emotionally they were from the same stock.

Each man had stood by the other's side for the last one hundred and fifty years of their friendship. They knew the best and the worst about each other, knew what had brought them to the point where a restless despair rattled inside until killing those who caused that despair became all they lived for.

Vincent was proud of his role as a slayer, was proud of

this part of his life. How could he not be? Ridding the world of bastards, could there be a more worthy cause? And that role had brought him to this ship, to this special woman. His role as slayer had him seeking a vampire and inadvertently that same position could have led him to the one woman who would make their immortality more bearable.

* * * *

"Is everything alright?" Scarlet asked hesitantly.

Watching them during their private discussion had given her a few surprising glimpses into the men themselves. For a few moments, she'd seen an unbearable sorrow cast over Vincent's face like a dark and somber shadow that drowned out the sun. She'd seen the temper on Lazarus' face combine with a touching understanding. Scarlet had then seen on that ruggedly handsome face, that he felt Vincent's pain, that he too shared whatever was discomforting his friend. Nicholae had stood there quietly, as though offering silent support. But through it all, she'd seen the bond that claimed each of them, the bond that kept them altogether.

Nicholae smiled. In that instant, she saw past the role of charming rogue that he usually displayed and witnessed the real man. "Yes, Scarlet, in your presence, why shouldn't everything be alright?"

She laughed even though she saw through his facade, which, if she was honest, made him even more attractive to her, which seemed impossible when he made her panties go from bone dry to wet in less than ten seconds flat!

"I'll take that for the negative it is. Something's wrong, but we're all allowed our little white lies. It's just a misdirection of the truth," she said with a smile and a quick wink.

"You o-f-f-end me!" he declared very dramatically as he slapped a hand over his heart very comically.

"I'm quite sure!" she said, her voice dripping with sarcasm as she struggled to hold back a laugh. She was proud of the fact that she managed to grin drily at him.

"Would you dance with me, Scarlet?" Vincent asked in husky voice.

"Thanks for asking. I would really like to. I don't want you to think I'm making excuses so you'll leave me alone, but, to be honest with you, I don't know how," she

admitted on a deep exhalation that portrayed the extent of
her discomfort at her admission.

She wasn't sure what it was, but something about these
three men made her revert back to a nervous girl at her first
dance! If her friend MJ could see her now she just knew
she would be rolling about on the damned floor, thoroughly
enjoying this.

Having never felt this way about one man, never mind
three, she felt very disturbed by the entire situation. Those
emotions added to her nerves and made her feel trebly
unsure of herself. It was like being the geek at school and
then having three of the most popular, most handsome and
drool-worthy hunks actually speaking to her at the end of
the day. They only had to speak a few words to make her
start, a complete sentence made her tremble. God only
knew what a paragraph would do to her!

"You can take your first lesson on the dance floor with
me," Vincent answered her reassuringly. Ignoring her
complaints, he grabbed her by the arm and swept her up
and on to her feet.

She felt herself being part-danced and part-dragged to
the floor, and, despite her misgivings, she laughed happily
as he immediately tossed her out on one arm, just like the
ballroom dancers she'd seen on TV. Somehow, by
throwing herself into Vincent's arms, she also threw some
inhibitions away.

Having never had the time or money to pay for dancing
lessons, or the time to go out dancing in clubs, she knew for
certain that she couldn't dance. She hoped to God that she
at least had enough natural rhythm to soften the blow when
she tripped over Vincent's feet!

But she soon forgot all about her doubts because being
held close within his embrace felt so good it was almost
orgasmic. Feeling the hard sinew pressed firmly against
her, the solid bounce of muscle where she held him, she
knew he had to be the most ripped man she'd ever seen . . .
or felt rather. When she thought about that for a second, she
rectified, one of the three most ripped men she'd ever seen!
And the suit he wore, it was beyond delicious on him. She
was surprised at how she felt so supremely feminine in
contrast to his utter masculinity. It was like drowning in
something so completely different to you, something that

pleased and aroused you deliciously. Her upper torso was bare and brushed almost constantly against him. Her flesh tingled where it made contact with his and it felt seared by his heated breath. She felt so on edge that it was difficult to concentrate on moving at all, difficult to remember that she was dancing with one of the three most handsome men on God's green earth!

She tried not to think about why he or Lazarus or Nicholae were on this cruise ship. The suits told her that they had money. But that didn't surprise her since she already knew that the cruise cost a fortune. Their being here wasn't a mistake or a prize like with her trip. They were here on purpose and that little fact disturbed her as much as the confounded attraction she had for them.

Could they, like all the other crazies on the ship, seriously believe in vampires?

Was it even possible that these three guys could be so irrational as to believe in something so childish?

But, what the hell? Did it really matter if they believed in vampires?

She was going to be on this ship for the next seven days, not the next seven years of her life. Whatever happened here, whether they slept together or not, they would only know each other for a week, she didn't require a background check on any of them. She wasn't planning on starting a life with them, so why should she care whether they believed in vampires or not?

One thing she had to admit to herself was that she really appreciated their manners. If they were odd enough to believe in the undead, then it sure made them polite. They teased her, yes, but they did so much more than that, they charmed her. They were so smooth that it should have been wrong, but instead it was entirely intoxicating. As crazy as it might seem, they were like a drug she was very rapidly getting addicted to!

Feeling a hand clamp down on her shoulder, she was soon swept into Lazarus' arms and guided into another dance. It was official. Her worst fears were confirmed. She couldn't dance. But, somehow, when they pulled her close and held her in their arms, she could. Maybe it was only that they were just so damn good they made her feel like she danced like a dream, she couldn't really be sure. All she knew was that her feet felt like they barely touched the ground and she felt like some kind of southern belle who had been taught to dance from a young age until it was in her blood, the intrinsic knowledge of how to move and sway to the music as easy as blinking. That was how she felt. The notes of the music seemed to swirl around her until she forgot everything and anything. She weaved sensually to the movement and felt her sexuality surge through her, empowering her utterly.

As she was passed from man to man, their arms curled around her to pull her away from her current dance partner as they seamlessly pulled her into another dance, another song, almost another time.

It was dream-like, so perfect and enchanting that she knew the night would forever be in her head. She knew that she wouldn't forget it. How could she? It was in her blood now. This perfect evening was exactly that in every way . . . perfect.

It was only when her head dropped against Nicholae's shoulder that she felt some disturbance in the air. When a hand tapped her on the shoulder, she felt and heard the growl roll from Nicholae's -call me Nico's- throat. It vibrated up and out his chest and she could swear she actually felt the tremble of his chest wall. At that moment she almost pulled away from him, but quickly realized after one look at his face that to do so would have both offended and hurt him and neither of those were something she ever wanted to do, even if he could growl like a dog.

Before she got the chance to twist around to see who'd tapped her on the shoulder and to get a look at what had caused Nicholae to react like that, she noticed that his incisors were pointed and extremely long. As she blinked in astonishment, surprised at having not noticed that about him before, her breath halted in her lungs as she actually watched them retract before her eyes. Unable to help it, she froze in his arms just before she collapsed against his torso. She didn't understand what the hell she'd just seen, and while it had frightened her, strangely enough, she realized that Nico didn't, but only God knew why!

Her mind whirled as Nico spun her around and away from the man who'd tapped her on her shoulder. From her position against him, she watched over his shoulder as

Lazarus and Vincent dragged the man off to a quiet corner in the restaurant. As he swept her around the floor, she kept her eyes glued to their position and almost fainted at what she saw next. If her eyes weren't mistaken, if she could believe the information her retinas were transmitting to her brain, the eyes of the men she'd been dancing with all night glowed a disturbing shade of red.

She blinked in disbelief. When the image before her didn't change, she buried her head in Nico's shirt. He'd removed his jacket earlier that evening, she recalled that his scent had flooded her senses and it had been so powerful, had such a debilitating affect on her that it had almost floored her. Now she took comfort in that as she tried to hide from what she thought she'd just seen.

Maybe there was something in the water the cruise ship was serving that made ordinary people believe in the impossible?

Hell, for all she knew the cruise ship could've been piping weed through the vents and making everyone high. In comparison, cannabis floating through the air conditioning units was a lot more plausible than believing in the undead!

She tried to collect herself, to collect her thoughts. She was high on how Lazarus, Nicholae, and Vincent made her feel. She wasn't high on some manufactured drug.

She wasn't entirely sure if that realization made things better or worse!

Hell, if she could let herself believe what she'd seen, she would be admitting to . . . something. What that was, she didn't know exactly.

Blowing out a breath, she tucked herself further into his arms and tried to forget, tried to block out the disturbing images, tried to rationalize what had happened. She was determined not to have her perfect night spoiled by something that had probably been a glitch in her sight.

* * * *

Nicholae tightened his arms around the woman in them and knew, beyond any shadow of a doubt, that she was his mate.

Before his death, his father had told him of the effect a mate had on the wolf in every were, and she had hit every single thing on the checklist his father had given to him, made him feel everything he'd been told he would feel.

Thinking about his father was difficult. Even now, even after over a hundred years. They said that time healed all wounds, but he knew that Vincent, Lazarus, and himself were testaments to the contrary. For what seemed like almost the entirety of their lives, they'd been filled with a never ending grief and an unhealthy thirst for revenge that seemed to consume more and more of them with every passing year, consumed what little bit of humanity they still possessed.

Scarlet didn't know it, but she was a blessing in disguise.

For so long, their lives had been taken up with vengeance and now, with Scarlet here in his arms, he knew that that would change. Their lives would change and for the better.

Lazarus, more than either he or Vincent, needed Scarlet with a desperation that had only recently become apparent. He'd been getting a little harder and little colder as each month passed. Of course, it was only natural. After two thousand years of witnessing the evil human beings and immortals seemed to revel in and fighting against the inhumane evil of vampires and the like, how could he help but change? What he needed was Scarlet's softness. What Lazarus needed, now more than ever, was her love to change all of that.

Nicholae could only hope that she wanted them as much as they wanted, no, needed her.

It was a lot to ask. Of that he was fully aware. Their way of life was completely alien to her. In fact, it was more than alien and completely foreign. The breadth of the distance between their lives and the reality of hers, he didn't bear thinking about, but if they could ease her in to the truth of their real identities, of what they truly were, then there was hope.

When he felt her head fall against his shoulder as she nuzzled into him, he took a deep breath, inhaling her scent as the nape of her neck brushed against his ducked chin. "Are you tired, Malyshka?" he murmured as he pressed a soft kiss to the exposed flesh behind her ear.

"Hmm. What's that mean?" she asked with a sigh and buried her face into him a little more. It felt so good to be encompassed in his strong arms.

"Malyshka?" he asked.

She nodded in response.

"Baby, " he replied. As he let the words register, he almost shuddered in relief that she wasn't repelled at his calling her something so intimate after only one night of knowing each other.

"Nice," she said, rubbing her forehead against his shirt.

"Do you want to go sit down and have something to eat? You haven't had anything yet, dorogaya."

"I don't want to, but I am tired."

"Come," he murmured and relinquished her from his grasp, partially. He still hooked an arm around her shoulders and dragged her close. He liked the feel of her relying on him for support as she practically wobbled her way back to her table, so fatigued was she!

Feeling guilty, he nodded at one of the waiters who had held back Scarlet's dinner, in acknowledgment that she was now ready for her meal. Nico seated her and sat down close to her. She didn't seem to be too uncomfortable being the cynosure of both the other two and his own gaze. They watched as she was served and somewhat dreamily began to eat her meal.

He'd ordered a steak, which he consumed with a lusty greed and watched as Vincent and Lazarus drank some blood. He felt amusement crease his mouth as he realized that Scarlet hadn't a clue that her companions were actually drinking human blood. He had to duck his head to hide his grin. It shouldn't have been funny, but in the short time he'd known her, he could tell that her feet were so firmly on the ground, they were stapled. And that was where the difficulty lay in her accepting them for what they were!

Damn!

"I don't want the night to end," Scarlet murmured mournfully.

He instinctively realized that she was not used to feeling something like that. It was completely nonsensical to her practical approach to life. Wishing for something that was totally out of her control was a waste of time and energy to her. He could sense her shock at feeling this way.

Vincent laid a hand on the table's surface, palm up.

Scarlet quickly scrambled her own against his.

"It doesn't have to end, chérie."

"I know. It's just been such a lovely evening, that I'll remember it forever," she said with a sigh as she tightened her fingers around his."

Touched, Nico smiled faintly. "Do you not think that we feel the same, dorogaya?"

"I suppose," she muttered.

"We're on this ship for three weeks, mel, there is no reason why this evening cannot be recreated every night," Lazarus said with a soft chuckle.

"I just don't do things like this, that's all."

"Why not?" Lazarus asked.

"I just . . . . Well, I have three jobs, so I don't get that much time to relax. Plus I have college work as well, so I just don't have the time to do things like this."

"Well, it's time to change all that," Nico grinned.

"I don't know if it's as simple as that, Nico."

"Well, it should be."

"I mean the only reason I'm even here is because I won the damned ticket."

"There you go. Fate!" Vincent added positively.

"Even then, I had to make sure that I could get time off at all three of my jobs. Then I had to make sure my Mom would be okay . . . in the end, she was more excited than I was! She pushed me to come. I was going to turn the offer down . . . . I'm not saying this to be maudlin, I'm just saying why this night has been so wonderful . . . ," she said, sighing heavily before she took a sip of her water.

Hating to see her so melancholy on what for him, was a truly joyous occasion, he dragged her closer and tucked her under his arm. When she was settled in the crook of his arm, Nico bussed her temple and let her sit there quietly. The other two obviously agreed with that silence and a peaceful ambiance overtook their table. It was a huge contrast to the hustle and bustle that was going on around them.

Early evening had disintegrated into the early morning and people were dancing, obviously imbibing heavily from the bar and it was easy to see that these people had been enjoying their night of revelry. He could only hope that the majority of the human guests had been drunk enough to not fear the small glimpses of inhuman behavior, they'd all exposed them to.

He knew for a fact that his teeth had bared at the man attempting to hook up with Scarlet, his beast had taken control and acted aggressively. He knew that Laz and Vincent's eyes had glowed at the same guy he helped to chase off from wanting to dance with Scarlet. Not only that, but Lazarus for what must be the first time in his life, had lost control. As they'd danced, they'd floated. As one of the oldest vampires walking the Earth, he had talents and gifts that to a human were like superpowers and completely out of the ordinary. Thankfully the guests on board the ship were all sympathetic to vampires, as they were the friends and companions of the vampires holidaying on the ship. Although they weren't exposed to too much paranormal behavior for fear of rumors spreading, they were somewhat used to the extraordinary.

That's why it had been a surprise to hear about Scarlet's competition to win a ticket for this cruise, after all, the company had guaranteed a safe passage for the vampires on the ship. Nicholae could only assume that fate had played it's wicked hand and had somehow managed to ensure that all three of them met their bonded mate. Perhaps there had been a mistake in the cruise ship's admin department. A nice and bland cruise ticket had winged its way to a vampire and the human female had received a surprise to end all surprises!

Thank you, Fates! he thought gratefully as he began to stroke the soft wisps of hair on Scarlet's cheek.

They sat together silently and watched as the dining room slowly emptied.

Hearing a soft sigh escape Scarlet's mouth, Nicholae's eyes flared at that perfect O of her lips.

"Elle dort," he whispered in French, the language they all used to communicate in, and smiled softly at the pretty picture she made, lying relaxed in a deep sleep, slumbering against him. Relying on him to protect her and keep her safe. The thought almost made him howl.

"We should have put her to bed earlier," Lazarus admitted with a sigh.

"There are a lot of things we should have done earlier. You do realize that we've effectively wasted a night's hunting?" Vincent said somberly.

"Worth it though, wasn't it?" Nico joked.

"Oui," Vincent conceded wryly.

"It's not like the bitch can leave the ship, Vincent. Elizabeth is holed up with us for the next seven days. There's plenty of time for us to catch her. She has to know we're on board by now. Some of her minions will probably have sent out the word that we're after her. Kind of like vampire Chinese whispers," Nico smirked. "She'll probably be staying low for the first few days of the journey."

"I can honestly say that I don't care if we catch Elizabeth or not. Scarlet," Lazarus said, pausing to sigh in frustration. "I don't know what the hell she is to us, but whatever it is either one night stand or mate, Elizabeth can go to hell."

Silence reigned for a few moments as Lazarus' words registered in his and Vincent's heads. They'd both known how close to the edge Lazarus actually was and that statement, just reinforced how dangerous a ledge he was perched on. If Scarlet could ease that any, drag him away from that perilous edge, then Vincent and he could only ease that path.

They all tensed as Scarlet moaned a little and fidgeted within his embrace. When she practically hurled herself even further into his arms and snuggled even closer into him, they all smiled at each other.

"I should take her to her room," Nico said with a grin.

"Lucky devil," Lazarus chuckled. "If she didn't look so damned comfortable, I'd wrestle you for her."

Nico laughed and hugged her tighter as he stood up. "I might see you back at the suite, but if I'm lucky I won't," he teased and laughed at their curses. "Look in her purse, her key card will be in there. What number is she staying in?"

Lazarus did as requested and handed him the card and told him the number. Before they both left, in a gesture that before meeting Scarlet would have made his mouth drop wide open, they both pressed a kiss to her temple and wished her good night in their own mother tongues.

Carrying his mate to her room was a feeling beyond compare. Why it should affect him so much, he didn't really know. But it satisfied the beast in him to be caring for her and holding her and keeping her safe and protected.

Shaking his head at this folly, he led her back to her room and through the suite to her bed, where he laid her gently upon the mattress. Turning around, he headed to the windows and lowered the shutters. Almost ten hours had passed since they'd first met Scarlet and the dawn was approaching. The sun shot a blaze of red across the horizon and he knew that all the vampires would be scuttling back to their bedrooms. Only the ones over two hundred years old could day walk. Only for the last few decades had Vincent had that talent and it was damned easier now that he could! A lot more convenient at any rate. It meant they could investigate the hiding places of their targets more easily and save a lot of time. This in turn, saved lives. For as soon as an evil vampire was slain, countless humans were saved.

The bitch they were hunting could be a particularly evil young blood, or an aged vampiress with no conscience. If it was the former, then she would definitely be hiding away. The movies exaggerated the effects of the sun on a vampire's skin. They didn't incinerate as one ray of light touched their skin. They merely suffered a case of extremely painful sunburn. Five minutes in the sun could give them first degree burns and as their immune systems weren't all that great, it could take years for the burns to completely heal. For that reason and that reason alone, they stayed out of the sun. Vampires were vain creatures. Even Lazarus and Vincent were afflicted with that particular sin! If this Elizabeth was the latter and had lived for many, many years, then she could walk about easily and cause more havoc.

Although the humans on board were mostly protected by their vampire companions, there was always the danger that she could attack them. Laz had first heard of Elizabeth through an old friend. He'd told Laz about a vampiress who boasted of her number of human kills. It wasn't conjecture, there was factual evidence in police records about every single one of her three hundred kills.

In their eyes, any vampire who could be proud of such an abominable record needed slaying. The danger to human kind was just too immense for them to allow her to continue existing.

It said a lot for Scarlet's effect on Laz that he actually was willing to let the bitch go, if it meant discovering more about Scarlet's importance in their lives.

For Nico, it wasn't about discovering. He already knew that she was his mate. His blood pounded the message, he couldn't be more sure. He knew it like he knew he was blond and of Russian descent. Having never discussed it with either Lazarus or Vincent, he wasn't sure what it took for a vampire to admit he'd found his blood mate. Whether it was through a transfer of blood or by their scent or whatever, he didn't know. But something told him that she was meant to be shared between all three of them.

Surprisingly, that didn't disturb his wolf.

But how could it? He'd shared so much of himself with Laz and Vincent that this was just another aspect of his inner self. She was his mate and he knew, just knew, that she was made for all of them.

* * * *

"Bastards," Elizabeth spat as she ducked into a small nook and hid from the long haired slayers that were searching for her. There was something poetic in one's creation hungering for one's blood. She knew Vincent very well indeed. Lazarus was a different matter. She'd heard of him but thankfully had never had any dealings with him . . . until now.

She was used to being one of the oldest vampires in any company and knowing that he was almost a thousand years older than her, had made her shy away from him and avoid any associations with him. Especially considering how completely different they both were. He fought on the side of humans, while she treated them like the slaves and dogs they were.

Vincent was an unworthy opponent. She could destroy him in an instant. She had spawned him, had made him into what he was today. If she couldn't kill one of her own, then she deserved to be slaughtered!

Hell, he was eight hundred years younger than her! It would be shameful to even consider the prospect of him being able to kill her. The possibility made her snort scornfully.

She'd played with Vincent for long enough. It's not that torturing him further didn't interest her, but she was bored with toying with him. It was no fun going over old haunts, and she fully admitted that there was very little more she could actually do to him.

Vincent had first come to her attention when she'd first seen him at a ball in Paris, when he'd turned down her offer of a night of passion. She'd spied his masculine beauty, admired his strong form from across the ballroom. Being a celebrated beauty herself, she hadn't expected to be rejected, and there was truth in the old adage, 'Nor hell a fury like a woman scorned.' Hatred had festered angrily within her breast, and she'd planned the perfect revenge.

The beauty of being a vampire was that time didn't matter. Vampires had an endless source of it. So three years meant little more than three hours to a vampire and three years after being scorned, the French Revolution or la Terreur had been in full swing. Elizabeth had sought out his fiancée's hiding hole and had hand delivered the address to the National Guard. Soon his heart's desire had been under the guillotine, her head plopping indelicately into a woven basket.

That hadn't eased her disdain any. She'd struck the final blow by deciding to kill him. Unfortunately, she'd been disturbed while biting him. Unable to drain him entirely, she'd spawned another vampire who was now aiming to kill her.

The irony didn't amuse her.

She didn't doubt that he hadn't a clue the vampire he was seeking was his creator.

Now that amused her.

Vincent was merely a distraction from her real opponent however. Lazarus was a completely different kettle of fish. He was dangerous, and that pissed her off. Because of him, she would have to tread carefully, and she hated that fact, as it went entirely against the grain.

She'd only recently learned that this so-called brotherhood had been baying for her blood. It hadn't perturbed her at all until she'd seen Vincent boarding the cruise and she had realized that they were there for her, were there to annihilate her.

Bastards.

She refused to die at the hands of some rag tag bunch of miscreants.

It wasn't she who was going against nature, but they! What kind of vampire didn't hunger for a human's blood? What kind of vampire protected the humans and slaughtered their own brethren for damaging the puny race of mortals? They were the unnatural ones, and they were hunting her! What a damned nerve they had!

The evening had been a revelation. Elizabeth had to admit this relationship or whatever it was, developing between the mortal and the three immortals, was indeed intriguing.

Against the werewolf and Vincent, the vampire she herself had created, Elizabeth could easily fight and kill them both. Lazarus would not be so easy. Adding this woman to the already volatile mixture actually eased her path. This mortal woman was a potential weakness and she intended to use it against them.

Lazarus' intense reaction to this woman, combined with the other two's, made her extremely suspicious. For a two thousand year old vampire to behave so bizarrely with a human woman made her think that perhaps, she was his blood mate. It was rare for a vampire to meet a blood mate. The sheer amount of time that a vampire lived combined with the fact that they had to be at the right place at the right time at the right year at the right decade etc, etc . . . . Every vampire had one, but finding them was another matter entirely. His conduct indicated that this redhead was indeed his blood mate and if she was, then she was Elizabeth's perfect weapon of destruction.

Killing a vampire who had seen two millennia would indeed be a coup. Killing the other two members of his brotherhood, a team of ruthless slayers internationally renowned and feared by all, would merely enhance her reputation. She'd be infamous amongst her kind, known throughout the world, revered for her strength and cunning.

The more she thought about it, the more the thought pleased her.

She would wait and see how this situation panned out.

Either way, she would not be the one to die. Of that, she was sure.

* * * *

Peering through the slats of the blinds, Nico squinted his eyes against the strong sun. A part of him sighed as the warmth penetrated the glass and heated his skin.

There was something peaceful and tranquil about the situation he found himself in and only then did he realize how raucous and 'noisy' his life had been up to now.

It seemed that every single part of his life had been filled with strife and, until now, until he'd found his mate, did that feeling oscillate through him.

The knowledge that she was laying behind him combined with the sounds of her soft breathing added to the soothing ambiance that seemed to cleanse his very soul. He sighed deeply as a happiness he'd never felt before simmered gently in his blood.

In truth, he couldn't afford to feel anything for this woman. All three members of the brotherhood couldn't really afford to have a mate of their own in their lives. Every day was a fight for survival, another day to find an out of control immortal and slay it before it could harm any mortals. But fate obviously disagreed that they couldn't afford a mate, and it had been preordained that they feel more than just something for her.

A mate became the other's entire life. As time passed and the bond grew deeper and stronger, it became impossible to live without one another. If one of a pair died, then only the very strongest of Alphas could survive the grief. It just wasn't in a wolf's nature to be without one's mate. Until this moment, he'd never recognized the truth behind that fact, had never understood how damned hard it must have been for his father to live without his mother for so long.

Scarlet was already filling in the gaps in his soul. His parents had been mated for eighty years before his mother's death had separated them. The thought of spending eight decades with her and then losing her was a hideous and impossible thought.

To immortals, eight decades was a flash in the pan and felt more like eight years. It wasn't nearly enough time, and he mentally congratulated his father for the sheer will and brute strength it must have taken to continue living. He also thanked him for loving his son so deeply that he'd managed to go on without his mate.

To be without Scarlet after eight decades together would be like a hundred knives lodged in his heart. It would be like a surcease of pain that would be never ending, constantly torturous, continuously at the front of his mind.

"Nico?" Scarlet's voice was husky and sleepy.

The sound of her voice sent shivers down his spine. She affected him in ways that were most bizarre to him. Since his mother's death, he'd felt apart from the world and only bonded to his father. He'd become a melancholy child thereafter and that had only worsened when his father had been taken away from him. His world had become isolated and focused solely on revenge from that point. Unhealthy obsessions had ruled him until he'd finally succeeded in killing the bastards who had taken his father. The only high point in a prolonged time of unhappiness was meeting Lazarus and Vincent. Vampires and werewolves were natural enemies, but that had never been an issue with them. For some reason, they'd bonded and now he questioned whether Scarlet was ultimately the reason why.

It made sense.

"Yes, Scarlet, it is I."

Until the words escaped his mouth, he didn't realize how thick his accent was. His words were clouded with his guttural Russian, and he knew that she would find it difficult to understand him. Having spoken English fluently for over one hundred years, it was rather strange to hear his accent return. But, then, she did seem to move him in mysterious ways. It was just another piece of evidence that proved how she was chipping at his control without him even realizing it.

"Why are you standing by the window?" she asked through a deep yawn, her words a soft purr that slithered over him like the softest of silk.

There was something of a slumberous cat about her, he thought, as he watched her stretch lazily against the sheets. The move just simmered with sensuality. It was all the more powerful because of her lack of awareness of it. It was just another intrinsic part of her nature and something she herself didn't recognize.

She was the sexiest woman he'd ever seen, and she was his. He felt almost like howling his triumph at capturing this delicious woman for himself. But instead, he chose to retain his dignity and respond to her question. "Where would you prefer me to stand?" he asked, turning away when he realized his voice sounded more gruff than he would've liked. But he couldn't help it. Speaking to her in English was rapidly draining his control. He wanted to speak to her in his mother tongue, to shower her with affectionate terms that proved to her how important she was coming to be in his life.

"I'd prefer you to be here with me. I'm cold," she said.

Without looking at her, he knew that her lips would be formed into a pout. The thought made his cock hard. "Be careful for what you ask, alyĭ," he warned softly.

"Why?

Will you hurt me?" she replied, her voice equally as soft as his.

"Never."

"Then what have I to fear?"

"I'm not a kind man, Scarlet. You might not like the real me."

She chose to ignore that statement and pressed him further. "Come and hold me, Nico."

"I fear that you do not know the repercussions of what you ask," Nico answered stiffly.

"I'm not a little girl, Nico. I know exactly what I'm saying!" Impatience made her voice sharp, and she hated that she sounded like a shrew. Was it so long since she'd tried to entice a man into her bed that she'd lost the art form of it?

Saying that, though, she'd never really had to work all that hard to seduce a man. It just wasn't that difficult to get a man in bed, so she was never lacking a partner.

Recently, however, she'd been segregating herself from the opposite sex. Men were contrary creatures, and the fact that she didn't want them and just their cocks seemed to intrigue them. With her last four bed partners, they'd wanted something deeper from her, and she hadn't been willing to go any further than the bedroom with them. The relationships, if that was what they could have been called, had ended rather quickly.

It probably sounded quite heartless and cold, but she couldn't help but find it all rather insanely comical. If she'd been looking for a partner that she could spend the rest of her life with, then men would have avoided her like the plague. She supposed it was Murphy's law.

It was with some astonishment that she realized that she actually wanted Nico to hold her close. Sex had never been about emotion for her. In that regard, she'd always been quite masculine, she supposed. She hadn't needed hugs or kisses to put out, she'd done so willingly.

For her, sex had always been about arousal and need, not something that was filled with emotion. It had been more of an itch that needed scratching. She had quite a high sex drive so it wasn't something that could really be ignored. But she'd been celibate for the last eight months because she was sick of men believing they'd fallen "in love" with her because she was so different from other women. They thought she was playing hard to get, but she wasn't. She didn't care enough to play anything.

That's why this came as such a shock. She actually wanted Nico to hold her close. She wanted to snuggle with him. Until now, the word snuggle had never even been in her vocabulary! Before Nico, the thought would have made her feel antsy, queasy. It was such an anathema to her ordinary self. But now, there was nothing she wanted more than for him to take her and hold her in the protective embrace of his arms.

Men had always been a distraction for her, a distraction both from work and her ultimate goals in life. She'd wanted them transitorily, and a part of her realized that she didn't particularly want that impermanence with Nico, or Lazarus, or Vincent.

The thought made her frown, but she realized that she had no other choice. This time, the situation was out of her hands. She was leaving in seven days, although that could be rearranged as the duration of the trip was three weeks. Either way, there could be no permanence in this situation. For the time being, she could bask in his, hopefully their, attentions and affection and then when the trip was over and they went their separate ways, she could go back to work feeling rested and sexually satiated and ready for the upcoming term at college.

Why he made her feel things that were so contrary to the normal her, she didn't know. The emotions he and the other two inspired in her were really odd, but, she had to admit, at the same time rather intriguing.

Scarlet had never felt this way before about anyone! That three men could trigger such similar emotions in her was unheard of.

She was willing to play it out and see where it led, because ultimately, she was safe. As soon as the cruise ended, she could go her own way with no recriminations or arguments. It would end with a goodbye kiss and a promise to meet up in the future, something that would never come to fruition.

"Believe me, I know you're not a little girl," he stated baldly.

His gruff voice shivered delightfully along her nerve endings. "Then what's the problem!"

"There is no problem, as long as you understand what this could mean."

Scarlet frowned. "What do you mean? You're starting to worry me, Nico."

"There is no need to be frightened," he said with a heavy sigh.

She hesitated, unsure of herself, unsure now whether or not he really wanted her. "Don't you want to come to bed with me?"

In the gloom of the darkened bedroom, she could see his body moving towards her position on the bed. She watched as he began to strip off his clothes and felt frustrated at the lack of light. The sun was gleaming outside but not enough to light the bedroom itself. She just knew that his body was a work of art, and she almost cried out as the sight was denied from her. Wearing a suit, he was like a sexy archangel. Without it, she was sure he'd be mouthwatering. Blowing out a breath of disappointment, she soon felt the bed shift beneath her and could hear his breathing become louder in the quiet room as he approached her.

Reaching a hand out for hers, he grabbed it and led it to his cock.

At the first touch of his heated skin, her heart began to pound in her chest and her breathing halted in her throat. It was difficult to think, difficult to focus. All rational thinking and function was clouded by what she was holding in her hand.

"Does it feel as though I don't want you?"

She noticed that his Russian accent had returned. The

sound made her quiver all over because it was so guttural and deep, so thick with need and arousal. It turned her on more than she could ever have imagined.

Hesitantly at first, her hand began to stroke up and down his length. Her fingers inadvertently measured him, and she realized that she'd never been with anyone that was so large. He would fill her right up. The thought made her pussy quiver hungrily. "No, I know you want me," she whispered huskily as she continued to stroke his hard length.

"Good," he said, cupping her breasts in his hands.

She regretted the barrier that was between them. She sat up and bent over, offering him her back to remove the bustier from her body. She felt his fingers pull the two sides apart and when he ran a rough fingertip along the curve of her spine, a powerful shudder made her body tremble excitedly. The thought of that same fingertip touching her clit was like pressing tinder to a flame. Hot and cold shivers ran over her nerve-laden flesh and she knew that as soon as he penetrated her, she would climax. She was already on the cusp of cumming now, something that was out of character for her, and she knew that when he did thrust into her, the orgasm would be beyond belief.

She felt almost breathless at the prospect.

Sitting up again, she tugged the bodice away and fumbled with the zipper at her side. Unfastening it, she wiggled on the bed to remove it and soon lay there with just a pair of panties on.

For some reason, she felt unbearably vulnerable lying there with just her pussy covered. She'd been in more exposed situations, but something about this felt different. Not bad different, but just different. Somehow it felt as if he could see all of her in the dark, that his eyes were tracing every part of her body, that he was fully aware that she knew that he was absorbing every single inch of her, and that thought made her slightly nervous. But, she realized, it was a ridiculous notion. How he could see her when she couldn't see him? He couldn't, of course.

When he placed his hand on her belly, she felt the heat and weight of it, felt almost branded by his touch. It was a strangely intimate sensation, and she reveled in it. She felt his fingers inch lower and felt the tug as they moved underneath her panties. With a gulp, she closed her eyes as his fingers touched the small strip of hair there and then wiggled further down so that the tips of the digits were mere millimeters from her clit.

Rolling her hips upwards, she silently urged him on and cried out when he complied.

He started speaking gravelly in Russian.

The words, although meaningless to her, seemed to set her even further on fire.

He began to rub her clit roughly.

When arousal rushed through her veins, she stared almost blindly as a climax to end all climaxes set her body alight. Crying out, she rocked her hips faster and faster.

Sensing her urgency, he moved his thumb to her clit and plunged his fingers into her depths.

Yelling brokenly, she shuddered as his fingers penetrated her deeply and scissored inside of her. They were so big, and the sensation was unnerving. Her climax had already rocked her, but this kept her on the knife's edge.

It was almost like pleasure and pain. Feeling so full was uncomfortable but pleasing at the same time. She needed that fullness. It enhanced her arousal as every single nerve ending was being touched and caressed simultaneously. She thought of his cock and how big it had been in her hand. The realization that it was bigger than all of his fingers almost made her faint.

"More," she whimpered, her voice breathy and filled with desire.

He mumbled something in guttural Russian.

She cried out at the sound.

Removing his fingers from her pussy, he took hold of the panty barrier she was still wearing and ripped them clean off her body.

Perhaps his roughness should have scared her, but it didn't. It only served to fire up her own passions. With a warrior cry, she sat up and pushed him away and on to his back, more than a little surprised that he allowed her to take charge.

Climbing on top of him, she gripped his hips with her thighs and let his cock brush against her pussy. Leaning over him, she dipped her head to press her lips to his.

Flicking her tongue along the curve of his mouth, she felt almost weak with longing as his tongue came out to duel with her own.

The stroke of his tongue was gentle, soft, and she could almost feel all his power being restrained. The feeling both pleased and disturbed her. It pleased her because she knew he was holding back for her sake. It disturbed her because she wanted him as mindless with need as she was. A part of her knew that as soon as he thrust into her, that restraint would desist, so it didn't altogether perturb her, and she continued to enjoy the gentle love play.

Perhaps it wasn't meant to do so, but her need was already on slow boil once again. She felt it as it simmered beneath her skin and knew that she'd never felt so hot so fast after climaxing before. The effect Nico had on her was incredible.

Rocking her hips, she brushed the scorching hot flesh of her pussy lips against his cock and felt him stiffen as she did so. A small smile graced her mouth at his reaction, and she repeated it. Once, twice, until he grabbed her hips and stopped her.

"Don't play with me, dorogaya!" he warned gruffly.

"Why not?" she teased with a pout.

He groaned a little, but, rather than chide her, he forcibly rocked her hips against him.

"I'm a glutton for punishment," he grumbled.

Laughing, she pushed her hips away from him and reached down to grab his cock. Stroking it a little, she then lined the entrance of her pussy over the head of his cock and began to press herself down on it, to spear herself on his turgid flesh. She was relieved that she was in charge of putting him inside of her. She knew that, as over-excited as he was, if he'd been in control he probably would have hurt her because of his massive length and girth, inadvertent though it may have been.

She took her time and just knew that he thought she was teasing him, but she had to genuinely restrain herself as she accepted him inch by inch. It was with a relieved sigh that, after a few minutes of struggling, she finally accepted him to the hilt. The unusual sensation of over-fullness was both shocking and wonderful. It was like being impaled on something, and every inch he touched felt scorched by the branding of his cock.

Blowing out her breath, she slowly rocked her hips and felt the rumble of his random Russian murmurings course through her entire being.

Grabbing a hold of her hips, he began to help her move, at first lifting her upwards and then pushing her back down on his cock so that he filled her entirely once more.

His body was tense beneath her. Every muscle strained as she accustomed herself to him inside her. She only relaxed when his hands moved from her hips and one went to her clit and the other to the pucker of her ass. The treble assault was almost overpowering. Her hips moved faster and faster as desire shot through her and feeling his pinch and play, was like being sent to heaven and back again. So close, yet so far.

His fingers sped up and as they did so, she reached her climax. Head flung back, she cried out as sensation after sensation pummeled her. Emotions rocketed through her system and she felt almost burned by them. Her pussy gripped him tight and she felt and heard him cry out. The sound was gutturally primal and a part of her felt so primitive as he bathed her womb with his seed.

The feel of it, the feel of him was so magnificent that she continued to cum. It was almost like a light show in her head. Splashes of color and fire bounced around her mind and sounds seemed to batter her ears.

When the powerful lights and sounds stopped battering her, she slumped against Nico's chest and almost purred as he wrapped her up within his embrace.

If she'd been an outsider looking at the two of them, she knew that she would have laughed. They clung to each like a drowning man clung to a lifeboat. Both shuddering and quaking as the aftershocks rattled along their flesh. She felt relieved by his heavy presence beneath her. His sheer solidness was comforting, when her world was being rocked and was shifting on its axis by what had just occurred.

It was with great relief that Nico wrapped Scarlet tightly within his arms. Something about her presence atop him soothed something inside of him, something that until this moment, he'd never realized needed soothing!

The countless women he'd slept with had never touched

him so deeply, had never stirred the beast in him. It had been with great shock that he'd partially shifted as he came. He knew that she hadn't realized and could only be relieved at that. His eyes had shifted and his claws had sprouted from his fingers, while his muscles had bunched fiercely as they'd expanded and grown bulkier. Never had that happened before.

It seemed incredible that the heart he'd almost forgotten about was pounding after what had just happened. It was as though her heat had scalded the ice around it and now it was beating fiercely to her tune.

He didn't have to be told that she was an independent woman that was used to her way of life. But something about her, made him feel needed. It was a nice sensation.

Feeling her sleepy yawn rumble against his chest, he grinned and tightened his arms about her a little more fiercely.

"Why are you playing the vampire, Nico?"

He laughed. "I didn't know I was."

She batted her hand against his side. "You know what I mean. Why are you on a vampire cruise?" she mumbled wryly.

"If I'm anything, dorogaya, I'm a werewolf."

"A werewolf?" She frowned and mentally sighed in resignation. Why was life so unfair? Here she'd met the three most delectable men she'd ever laid eyes on and they were mentally disturbed. That was just typical.

"How did you become one of those?" she asked curiously, eager to see how he would embellish what had to be a fantasy. It was easier to humor him than to call him out on his obvious act. Damn, she knew how to pick them, she thought drily, inwardly groaning.

"Why, I was born one, born into a noble family, milaya. My father was king and my mother was the queen."

"Was?

Have they passed away?" she asked, a little more alert now.

"Da. They died a long time ago." His voice was a little harsh with the unwanted memories. Although it was a long time ago, it still wasn't easy to talk about. But how could he deny his mate the knowledge of his past?

"My mother was killed in the forests by hunters, seeking

wolf pelts. My Father died at the hands of a rival, who illegally wanted to rule my family's kingdom. I left soon after his death. It was either that or be killed myself. I was far too young to seek vengeance for my father's death at that time."

"I'm sorry, Nico. Did you ever return?" she asked softly.

"Da. I had my vengeance on those who killed my father ten years after his death. My people wanted me to return as their alpha king, but I couldn't. I appointed a childhood friend to take my place. He is a good man."

"Why couldn't you be their king?"

He was surprised at the question. He'd rather expected her to run screaming from the room when he admitted that not only was he a werewolf, but he'd killed for revenge too. Either she was a lot more open minded than he'd first thought or she was too tired for it all to register. Of course, it could be worse than that, she might not believe a damn thing he was saying and was just going along with it because she thought he was crazy and making up the story or she thought he was the kind of crazy person that believed his "story" was the truth!

It would be even more of a shock to the system if she believed that!

"I didn't feel fit to lead them, dorogaya. How could I?

I was tainted; they needed a pure man to be their king. I'd killed the bastards who had murdered my Father, but it wasn't enough. I was a young man and filled with hatred and a need to stop the injustices in this world. My soul was restless and I knew my people needed a leader who was there for them. Not someone who was constantly seeking out vengeance. I left and met Vincent and Lazarus years later. We've been together ever since. I credit them with keeping me on the side of good. For far too long, my heart was dark."

She lifted her head and looked at him, really looked at him. Her eyes stared into his and he felt as though she'd seen deep into his soul.

Without a word, she snuggled back into his embrace and nodded her head against his chest.

He wasn't sure whether this conversation would be relegated to her thinking it had all happened in a dream. A part of him hoped it wouldn't, hoped that she recognized it was the truth and that he wouldn't lie to her about his past.

She was the first woman he'd ever told about his parent's murder and the subsequent path of revenge he'd taken. After Laz and Vincent, she was the third person in the world to know of the circumstances that had turned him into the man he was today.

He doubted she realized how hard it had been for him to disclose any of that sordid tale to her.

Chapter Three

"Lucky bastard," Lazarus chuckled as he watched Nico stride off with Scarlet hugged to his chest. "She's definitely his mate, you know," he added softly.

Vincent's head spun around to focus on Lazarus' serious face. "Definitely?" he demanded hoarsely.

Nodding his head smoothly, Lazarus patted Vincent on the shoulder and squeezed down.

"How do you know?"

"Their scent changed," he replied simply.

"How is this going to work then? I-I've never reacted to another woman like that and neither have you . . . ."

"Until we bite her, we won't know for definite if she's our blood mate now," Lazarus said with a shrug.

"Bullshit. You don't need to bite her to know," Vincent muttered angrily.

"No, I don't, but you do."

"Well, is she your blood mate?"

"Yes," Lazarus admitted with a slow nod. "I believe she is also yours, but until you taste her blood you won't believe it."

"It's not that I don't want to believe it, Lazarus. It's that I'm in shock. I never expected to have a mate, I always thought Véronique was my blood mate even though I hadn't known her as a vampire and that I'd lost my chance forever."

"I know, Vincent. If I'm honest, I did as well. However, the fact that we have a blood bond with Nicholae has always made me suspect that something of this nature could occur. Vampires and werewolves are natural enemies; in fact our bond is an anomaly. No self-respecting vampire would dream of bonding with a were, but we did. There had to be a reason why. It appears that Scarlet is that reason."

Vincent sighed. "It's worrying, Lazarus. We don't have the kind of life that means we can support a mate. We're in constant danger, hated by all the evil ones of our kind. She would be in danger. Is it not kinder to let her alone, to let her lead her life without adding our complications?"

"I don't think it's as simple as that, Vincent."

"What do you mean?"

"We can't leave her."

"Why not?

Don't we have a choice?"

"Not particularly. We need her blood to sustain us. You are correct though, it would be a kindness to leave her alone. Our way of life is a danger to her and it would be better for her protection to not be with her. But we have no choice. A vampire is immortal until he meets his mate. Upon meeting his mate, he is partially immortal."

"Partially immortal?

There's no such thing, Laz."

"There is where a blood mate is concerned. If anything happens to her, we can't continue without her. Like I said, we need her blood. While we sup from her, she becomes immortal and one pint of her blood will sustain us for far longer than one quart of another's. It's mutually beneficial."

"This is so much more complicated than I ever thought it would be. We came here to find that bitch and now we have a mate to protect while we try and slay Elizabeth."

"The Fates work in mysterious ways, Vincent."

"That's no answer, Laz."

"I think you'll find it is. Don't regret meeting Scarlet, Vincent. She's our other half."

"I don't regret it. It's just difficult coming to terms with it. We're here for a reason and we can't slay Elizabeth if Scarlet distracts us. And she's already doing so, so don't tell me that it won't happen."

"I make no such claim. Rather than looking upon meeting her in a negative light, you should see it positively.

The beauty of having Scarlet is that we're stronger and
more efficient. In her own way, her blood protects us and
improves our skills. While she does need protecting from
the more evil ones of our kind, we are more able to secure
her. It's a symbiotic relationship."

"That doesn't take away from the fact that we need to
find Elizabeth," Vincent said consideringly.

"No, it doesn't. But there are seven days before she can
disembark from the ship. We have seven days and nights to
find her."

"True."

"I know you don't like this situation, Vincent. I
understand that. But it's only because you're still hurting
from losing Véronique that you can't see how precious
Scarlet is to us."

"I wouldn't say that, Laz. I can well recognize that
Scarlet is precious. It's not that I still grieve for Véronique,
I mourn that she had to die so young and so cruelly. I didn't
even react like this with her, so I can easily understand
what Scarlet may mean to us."

"What she means to us, Vincent. Not may mean to us."

"Stop being pedantic," Vincent said with a grin.

"It's too damned hard not to! What do you reckon we
don't see him until this afternoon?"

"You're right, lucky bastard."

"Yeah. That we're not jealous is very positive, you
know?"

"I suppose it is. Just means that we are meant to be
bonded together, doesn't it?"

"Yes, it does. I'm most relieved because I've never
heard of a similar bond to this one of ours."

"No, me neither but then I'm not as old as you," Vincent
remarked pointedly.

"Charming!

It will be interesting to see how this situation pans out,"
Lazarus said quietly.

"You sound like a little boy pulling the wings off a fly."

"What a wonderful image."

"You are getting colder, Laz. Less feeling."

"Hmm," Lazarus agreed easily. "I know. Scarlet's
presence should stop that. We'll have to bond her to us,
otherwise she might run."

"I don't even want to think about that. Let's deal with it as it comes, Laz. Look, enough talk about Scarlet. We need to talk about Elizabeth."

"There's nothing to discuss."

"Of course there is. The plan that we had, isn't going to work. We expected to find her on the first day and spend the rest on vacation!

Obviously we haven't found her so she's hiding and we never thought she would be powerful enough to do so. She's obviously a lot older than we calculated."

Flicking at a crumb on the table, Lazarus smiled coldly. "She is. I caught her scent today."

"You did? When?"

"She saw us with Scarlet. She was there when we were dealing with the man who wanted to dance with Scarlet."

"Damn. Then she knows that Scarlet is our mate?"

"It's more than likely, yes."

"Hell, then Scarlet's in danger."

"She very well could be."

"Dammit, Laz. You need to give me more than short responses! I need answers! What the hell do we do?"

"We roll with the punches, Vincent. There is very little else we can do!"

"Surely there's something more."

"Not particularly. I think we should let Nico stay with Scarlet, have him act as a bodyguard. His skills are more in that area than the slaying anyway. It must be the dog in him," Lazarus said with a chuckle.

Vincent's lips quirked before he controlled them and maneuvered them into a frown. "What aren't you telling me?"

Lazarus shrugged. "I don't tell you everything, Vincent."

"No and don't I know it!"

"She's at least a thousand years old."

"Fuck. You're joking. Zut! Then it's imperative that Nico stays with Scarlet. There's no way in fuck will he be able to protect himself from a Vampire that old!"

"Why do you think I suggested it?" Lazarus said pointedly. "She'll be spiteful and spoiled. So she'll try and toy with us, all the while thinking she'll get the better of us. Her ego won't let her realize that I'm stronger than her and that if I sup from you, I'm ten times stronger." He shrugged. "It's just a case of finding her. She's curious, which will ultimately be her downfall. She's recognized that we're acting strangely around Scarlet, so she'll think she can use Scarlet against us. There are a number of situations that could arise from this new piece of information, that's why we have to take it as it comes. Her age means that no plan can be concrete. The way to win is to be flexible, because win we shall."

Vincent blew out a breath. "Do you need to rest tonight?" he asked, changing the subject. He'd seen the cold flicker of piercing cerulean blue in Lazarus' eyes. They only flickered that color when he was filled with a controlled rage.

"Yes, I think I do," Lazarus answered calmly and finished the glass of blood he'd been drinking all night.

At that moment, Vincent was doubly glad they'd met Scarlet during this trip. No matter how confused it made him feel, he fully recognized that Lazarus needed her. That cerulean blue was seen far too often for his liking. If Scarlet could stop that, then it was all for the good. He'd do anything to ensure Lazarus' soul remain on the right path.

He was such an old vampire that it was amazing he'd stayed on this path of righteousness. Lazarus' strength and mental agility grew as each year passed. He was at the peak of his power and that meant it was all too easy to fall from the path of good as everything bored him now. He knew everything, had seen everything. There wasn't enough to excite him intellectually and spiritually. Vincent truly believed that only his and Nico's presence had protected Lazarus from that course.

With Scarlet's help, and if she was as vital to them as Lazarus insisted she was, then Laz would be protected and around for a lot longer.

As much as it killed him to think it, if Lazarus had continued in the same vein as he had recently, growing colder and less sensitive to human feeling, it would eventually have become necessary for the slayer to be slain.

* * * *

Rubbing the sleep from her eyes, Scarlet yawned hugely and stretched out on the huge bed. She snuggled under the blanket a little longer until she gradually awakened enough to realize that she was in an empty bed. The thought made her open bleary eyes and sit up to look around the bedroom.

"Nico, are you there?" she called out, her voice husky with emotion and the memory of the passion they'd just shared.

Silence was her only reply and she realized that Nico had left some time during the past few hours. The thought made her scowl at the beautifully appointed room. She'd always been the one to leave her partners alone in their beds. It was odd that the boot was now on the other foot and she had to admit, that she didn't like it one little bit. It just didn't sit right with her.

She was no stranger to one night stands. She recognized the sordidness behind them and didn't really appreciate them beyond the fact that they eased a need that sometimes, she couldn't scratch herself. And while it probably hadn't bothered her partners that she'd left them alone in their beds, it was a hard pill for her to swallow.

No matter what she'd told herself the night before, their time together had meant something to her. That he'd just left her meant that that feeling wasn't reciprocated by Nico. The connection she'd felt and had been so damned sure he'd felt too, obviously was just a figment of her imagination because otherwise, he wouldn't have left her.

A part of her felt bereft and while she told herself to not be silly and so soppy, it was out of her control. She genuinely couldn't help that she was feeling a kind of loss. It was difficult to chastise herself, when the emotion was so powerful, so difficult to ignore.

Ordinarily, she would have been damned glad that he'd left. Pleased that there hadn't been the usually uncomfortable morning after, but she wasn't. She should have been relieved that he'd left as it meant that he believed there was nothing more meaningful behind the sex, but it pissed her off that he'd just left her in the lurch.

The bastard.

Why should she be feeling this way when she was obviously just an easy lay for him?

It seriously pissed her off that she'd just had the best, most fulfilling sex of her life and he wasn't in agreement.

She'd expected to wake up this morning and have some more of those delicious climaxes he seemed so adept at handing out and to wake up to nothing, just sucked. Talk about disappointing!

This taught her that if she saw him again during the trip, that she had to treat him like she treat every other man in her life, with indifference.

Okay, so that could be easier said than done, but this proved to her that all men were jerks and would shit on her as easily as breathing.

The thought made her nod self-righteously and with a smirk, she recounted the conversation they'd had the night before.

She almost sneered at herself for believing him. But now, she recognized that it had just been bullshit. That he'd been spinning her a line. She didn't like that he'd had her believing him. He had had her feeling sorry for him, when he'd told her about his parents' deaths. She felt like such a sucker to have believed that kind of bull-crap.

Scarlet should have realized then and there that he was just toying with her. He obviously hadn't taken her seriously to spin her that kind of line. It was so difficult to not feel like a fool.

Why this time was different to every other, she didn't know, but it was. Everything about this was so damned different. She hadn't exactly been around the block, but she was used to this kind of thing and she could honestly say that never before had she felt so hurt about a one night stand.

She grimaced and jumped out of the bed, shaking her head as though to clear it, and headed towards the blinds. Opening them with a vicious tug, Scarlet blinked at the setting sun and realized that she must have slept the damned day away!

Rushing towards her bag on top of the dressing table in the corner of the cabin, she fumbled around for her mobile and checked the time.

She had twenty minutes before dinner started and as that thought was processed, she realized that she was damned starving.

Rushing about because she was hungry, Scarlet grabbed a pair of black linen, wide-legged trousers and reached for a slim-line red waistcoat. Poppy red, it had darts in the waist that made her look tiny. There were buttons running down the very center of it, huge black ones with crystal jewels that took the outfit from day to nighttime.

As she headed to the shower, she tried to stop thinking about Nico and the night before. Jumping into it, she quickly soaped up and scrubbed herself clean. For some reason, she felt dirty.

The truth was that during an ordinary one night stand, both she and her partner were there for sex. Nothing more and nothing less. But the night before hadn't been like that. He'd been as into her as she'd been into him. For him to leave her like this, made it seem sordid somehow and she didn't like feeling like that one little bit.

Toweling herself dry, she sped up as her stomach grumbled once more. Quickly dressing herself, she dabbed her hair dry and brushed it before French-plaiting it. Adding some high Court shoes, Scarlet grabbed her purse and headed out of the door.

She rifled through her bag again and looked for the map of the liner she'd been given yesterday. Scarlet was determined to eat in another restaurant and hoped to God that she didn't see any of the three guys she'd met yesterday.

Obviously she was vulnerable to them and she refused to be vulnerable to anyone!

She moved down a level and headed to the seafood restaurant that was on this deck. She wasn't that great a seafood lover, but there was sure to be something on the menu she liked. Even if it was something like prawn cocktail or clam chowder.

Despite herself, she felt a little out of place amongst the crowd at the restaurant. Everyone was in twos or foursomes and she was the only person who was by herself. She felt as though she was the cynosure of all eyes as she sat down at her table. It wasn't a particularly nice feeling, but it lessened the dull throb her empty stomach was making.

Ordinarily, she was used to eating alone. She hardly ever ate with someone and if she did, it was with MJ. As a child and teenager, Scarlet had always eaten with her mother. But now, the distance was so far between them, that it would have cost a fortune to commute back home every day for dinner. It was a sad fact of life and she had to admit that she missed her mother's chatter.

When the waiter came to take her order, she asked for clam chowder and a glass of white wine. As soon as the man left, her bag began to vibrate and she reached for it and sought out her cell phone. Flipping the lid, she smiled as talk of the devil, her mother was on the other line.

"Mom?" It was so like her mother to be checking up on her.

"Baby!"

I'm sorry to disturb your vacation." Patricia's voice was slightly breathless.

"Are you okay, momma?"

"Of course, baby. I- I just have some news for you."

"Well, it doesn't sound like happy news, mom . . . ."

"Oh but it is, sweetheart! You'll never guess, but I've met someone."

"You've met someone?" Scarlet repeated blankly.

"Yes!"

"Where? You don't date!"

"He's wonderful, baby. You'll love him!"

"I will? Are you serious?"

"Oh yes, deadly serious and we're both serious about each other," Patricia said softly.

"Where did you meet him?"

"You know Laura, that new girl that started at my office? Well she asked me to go with her to this new bar that had opened and there he was. His name is Charles and he's such a gentleman. He makes me feel so young, baby. He's the one, Scarlet," she whispered.

"The one?"

"The one I've been looking for since forever!"

It was hard to refrain from rolling her eyes at her mother's romantic nature. She was so naïve, it was quite frightening at times. She'd been like this for the entirety of Scarlet's life and at times, had been more of the daughter rather than the mother. Scarlet had been watching out for her mother since she was old enough to realize how ditzy Patricia could be!

"You're not saying anything, Scarlet," Patricia said anxiously.

"What can I say, mom?"

"That you're happy for me, of course!"

"I'm happy if you're happy," Scarlet said hesitantly.

"Oh, I am, baby. He's so wonderful. I can't believe I've found him. I was almost thinking I was out of time, but it's not and he's here," Patricia said excitedly.

"I'm glad that you've found him, mom. How long have you known each other?"

For the second time, her mother sounded unsure and she felt guilty for diminishing Patricia's sheer happiness at finding her dream man. But it was a question that had to be asked.

"Well," her mother's gulp was almost audible. "Two days." The words were hushed.

"Two days?" Scarlet screeched.

"When you know you know, Scarlet," Patricia said defensively.

"How can you know he's the one when you've only known him forty-eight hours?"

"I just know."

"Look, there's a difference between lust and love, mom."

"Don't lecture, Scarlet O'Hara Reves!"

Cringing as her mother rolled out the one weapon in her arsenal, her hated name, Scarlet grimaced. "I'll lecture all I want to keep you safe, mother. Honestly, you need a keeper!"

"Somehow I've managed for fifty-two years, Scarlet!"

"No, you haven't!" Scarlet retorted angrily. "I've been looking after you for as long as I can remember, so don't start acting as though I haven't. Now, be serious, you can't feel so strongly for someone after two days of knowing him. What's his name, for God's sake?"

"I refuse to be chastised like a child!

And his name is Charles."

"Stop behaving like a child then. Be real. God, he could be an Axe-murderer, or anything!" As she spoke, her voice grew a little more panicked.

"Charles is not an Axe-murderer!"

"How the hell do you know?"

"Because he isn't. I won't hear a bad word against him, Scarlet. You haven't even met the poor man! He's a wonderful human being and I'm lucky to have found him."

"Stop talking about finding him. You were in a bar and he picked you up! God, I can't believe this. I go away for a day and already you're hooked up with some damned stranger! He could be a gigolo for all we know! Is he there now? I just know he is. Put him on the phone right now!" she demanded fiercely.

"The last time I checked, Scarlet, I was the mother here!"

"Stop trying to change the subject and let me speak to him!"

"He's in the shower," Patricia muttered over a huff of exasperation.

"Oh . . . my . . . God!
He's in the shower. You mean you're sleeping together! Have you at least been using protection?"

"Scarlet!"

"What? Have you?"

"It's not like I can get pregnant," she said sullenly.

"You haven't, have you? Go to the pharmacy or the closest market right this minute and buy some condoms. There's much more that can happen than just finding yourself a middle aged mom! Haven't you heard about STDs?"

"Of course, I have."

"Well then, protect yourself from them! Just do it for me! P-l-e-a-s-e mom! I won't be able to sleep at night if you don't," Scarlet told her mother and spoke louder as Patricia began making blustering noises of embarrassment and denial. "I don't give a damn about your embarrassment, mom, I care about your health! Be safe!"

"Alright, as soon as he gets out of the shower, we'll go to the pharmacy."

"Thank you," Scarlet said over a sigh of relief.

"I can't believe I'm being lectured about protection by my own daughter!"

"I wouldn't be lecturing you if you'd used your common sense, mother! He's a stranger. There's no telling where he's been. He could have anything!"

"Stop talking about him like that! He's a good man. If you say one more bad word against him, I'll hang up. I swear it!"

"Dammit." Scarlet exhaled roughly and rubbed a hand over her eyes as she tried to gather her composure. "Okay. But please be careful and don't get hurt."

"I won't, darling," Patricia murmured softly, all anger removed from her voice.

"Good. I love you, mom."

"I love you, too, baby. He's just finishing up in the bathroom. I promise we'll go to the store now, okay?"

"Good! Take care."

"I will. Enjoy the rest of your vacation, honey."

Closing her eyes at the dial tone that suddenly met her ears, Scarlet had to refrain from calling her mother back and demanding more information about this stranger. Her mother wasn't the sort of person to engage in one night stands. She was a total romantic. She'd never dated because she insisted that she would know instantly when she met her soul mate.

Ever practical, Scarlet had always had to bite her tongue when her mother had come out with those kinds of sentences because she herself didn't believe in soul mates. She didn't even really believe that monogamy was something that any modern day couple could live with. Dealing with her obstinate mother, who was strangely the complete opposite of her in almost every way except for her stead-fast determination, was incredibly tough at times.

She was the ultimate idealist. And that was why Scarlet was terrified. Her mother had only had one brief relationship, which had resulted in only one brief sexual encounter, years before she'd decided to conceive a daughter through artificial insemination. All of that combined to make her the next thing to a virgin. That this stranger had basically initiated her mother into sex scared her deeply. Her mother had to seriously believe they were meant to be together to sleep with the man.

The good news was they were going to go out and buy some condoms. She was furious that they hadn't already been using them. What kind of man didn't carry condoms?

The thought made her freeze.

Nico hadn't used protection last night.

She'd been getting on to her mother and she could very well be pregnant with a baby herself. Or, like she'd told her mother, infected with some hideous disease. The disturbing thought made her panic.

She gulped down the glass of white wine that the waiter had delivered during her phone conversation and breathed down a sigh of relief as the alcohol hit her blood. She'd completely lost her appetite now.

She felt like such a hypocrite. How could she judge and lecture her mother for not having the foresight to use protection when she herself hadn't? She felt unbearably stupid. She knew the dangers of not practicing safe sex, yet she'd completely forgotten about them. Condoms had been the last thing on her mind! Her mother had told her it was unlikely that she would get pregnant but there was every chance in the world that Scarlet could!

The waiter set down her bowl of chowder. "Can I have another glass of wine, please?" Scarlet asked in a voice husky with worry.

She stared at it for a minute and grimaced before pushing it away. Her stomach felt tight at the thought of swallowing any of the soup. If she had just one spoonful she knew that she would be sick. The thought made her feel even more nauseous.

"Is it wise to not eat one's dinner?"

The voice was smooth and immediately recognizable. She didn't have to look up to know it was Lazarus.

"No, it's not wise. But I feel too sick to eat, that's all," she said haughtily.

"Why do you feel sick?" Lazarus asked with a quirk of the brow.

He seated himself without her invitation, something she thought most odd because he was extremely courteous. He must have realized she would have refused him, had he asked.

"I just do. How's doggy boy?" she asked coldly.

"I take it you mean Nicholae?" Lazarus questioned equally as coolly.

"Of course, I do. I've never felt so cheap in my damned life!"

For the first time, she saw surprise on his face.

"Cheap?" he asked hesitantly.

"Yes!

Cheap!" she spat. "I don't like being just abandoned after a night like we shared!"

She didn't care that she was being indiscreet; she was feeling furious and hurt and wanted to hit out at someone, anyone.

"Abandoned? I doubt he abandoned you, mellita. He just had duties, that's all."

"Duties? On board a cruise ship? Does he work here?"

"Of course not. We seek a vampire. We're slayers, you know." His voice was matter of fact.

She blinked.

"Slayers?"

"Yes."

"Are you crazy?"

"No, not at all," he replied with a faint smile.

"Well, that's most comforting!"

"I'm glad to hear it. He didn't abandon you, Nico would never dream of behaving so crassly."

"Is it crass to wear a condom?" she spat furiously. "I could be pregnant!"

Her eyes widened as she watched him sniff the air.

"What the hell are you doing?" she asked quickly.

"Determining whether Nico's seed has taken root in your womb."

"Oh my God, you are crazy."

"I'm not actually. I'm just very old."

"Oh yeah, I'm sure. What are you, thirty?"

"Two thousand and thirty actually. Close but no cigar," Lazarus told her with a wicked smile.

"You expect me to believe that?"

"Why not, it's the truth."

"So reassuring."

"You're not by the way."

"Not what?"

"Pregnant."

"How do you know?"

"Your scent hasn't changed that much. Nico's is there, but that of his child . . . no, it's not there yet."

"Yet?" she squeaked.

"Yes, yet."

She was treated to that slow infuriating smile again.

"Have you eaten anything?" she asked on a deep exhalation.

"No."

"Do you want some of my chowder? It seems a shame to waste it."

He shook his head but thanked her. "You're willing to

break bread with me though, that's a good sign."

"It is?" she said wryly. "I just hate waste. More like too many years of living on the poverty line, I think."

"Ah. I can understand that."

"I doubt it, if that suit's anything to go by. That would probably pay for my rent for two years."

"Yes, it is nice, isn't it?"

"Very," she said dryly.

"Not now, but when I was a boy, my father was killed and I had a family of brothers to care for. We owned a farm so there was some food yielded from our crops, but not enough to satisfy three growing boys."

"I'm sorry about your father. How old were you?"

"Fifteen."

"I never knew my father," she murmured wistfully.

"He died?"

"No. Well at least I don't think he did. My mom chose him from a list of donors and I was created in a laboratory. Not a very nice thought really."

"The joys of technology. I for one am grateful for it, if it means that it created you," he said suavely.

"Hell, I never thought my birth could be deemed as charming!"

"Everything about you is charming."

"I'm sure! Are you positive you're not hungry?"

"Vampires don't eat mellita."

"We're not still playing that game, are we?"

"What game?"

"The whole vampire and werewolf game!"

"I'm afraid that's no charade. For most of the riff raff here . . . ," he said, waving a hand to encompass the majority of the crowd in the restaurant, "it's a game. There are very few real vampires on board. Vincent and I are two of them. Nicholae is a werewolf and a very royal one at that. Did he tell you his story?" he asked with not insubstantial interest.

"If you mean about hunters killing his mother and his father being killed by rivals, then, yes, he did."

"It's no fabrication, Scarlet."

"I can't believe that you expect me to believe you're vampires and werewolves. This is madness."

"Perhaps it is. Can you play chess?"

"Not very well, I know the basics."

"Good. You can come and play a set with me in our quarters."

"How am I supposed to stand a chance against playing a two thousand year old man?"

"You're not," Lazarus said with that infuriating smile of his.

"Oh, so I'm supposed to lose, am I?"

"Yes."

"Charming. Why should I want to come to your quarters just to lose at a game of chess?"

"You'll like the outcome, I promise."

"Why?" she asked suspiciously.

"You'll have to wait and find out."

She rolled her eyes at his sally and considered his proposal. There was no harm in playing a game of chess with the man, but a part of her was tired of appearing so green in front of them. She'd spent the majority of last night in their company and had acted like a dazed and star struck teenager! Tonight, she would make a fool of herself playing chess against an expert- it wasn't exactly her idea of fun. She hoped that they realized she wasn't just a pretty face. She had brains and was intelligent; she just hadn't had a chance to prove it to them yet. It appeared that she wouldn't be doing so tonight either!

"Will you come?"

"What will you do if I don't?" she asked, tongue in cheek.

"Lie prostrate on the floor and beg you attend?"

"Well, I wouldn't want to shame you too much," she replied as she stood. "Come on then, lead me to your quarters, Lazarus."

"Anything for you, my lady," he said with a small bow that made her smile. He reached for her arm and led her out of the dining room. They said little as he walked her to their cabin and she had to admit that as she made each step, her breath grew heavy with anticipation.

"Do you share a suite with Nico and Vincent?"

"Yes, of course. We share most things."

She quirked a brow. "Women?"

"Sometimes, but I meant our . . .shall I say, career choice, pushes us together."

"What, the slaying?"

"Yes. We work as a team."

"The vamp squad, huh?"

"I suppose so, yes."

"I'm actually starting to believe in this crap, you know. Are you hypnotizing me into believing?"

"Actually I'm not."

"You mean I'm becoming delusional?"

"Well, I wouldn't say that exactly. Especially seeing as it's the truth. But then, you don't believe that either."

"You really know how to be reassuring, don't you?" she murmured exasperatedly.

Little more was said as they wandered down the hall and reached his suite. He reached in his suit pocket for his key card and the door was open in a flash. She chanced a peek into the suite and saw Vincent and Nico sitting on the sofas reading some books. They both looked as suave and elegant as ever.

As she stepped over the threshold, Nico's head shot up and he graced her with the warmest smile she'd ever seen.

She immediately felt guilty for doubting him. She could see in that smile that he hadn't meant anything by leaving her alone today. Scarlet didn't know how she knew that. But she did.

"Milaya!" he said with a grin and jumped to his feet to come and greet her. He pressed a kiss to each cheek then one to her mouth.

She smiled and just like that, all her earlier resolve to act indifferently towards him disappeared. She could almost feel it dissolving into nothing.

Vincent stood more slowly and walked towards her steadily. He came to her and reached for her hand, pressing a kiss to it, he then leaned forward and pressed a kiss to her cheek. "Chérie."

She nodded a little shyly and it was with relief that Lazarus grabbed her hand and led her over to a small table, where they'd set up a game of chess. He seated her first then settled himself opposite her. The other two returned to their earlier seats, but she knew that they had their eyes on her.

"You said that you know the basics of this game, yes?" At her nod, he smiled faintly. "Perfect. We shall be playing strip chess."

A gurgle of laughter escaped from her chest as she finally understood why he'd been so pleased that she wasn't a chess expert.

"Oh, so that's your game is it?" she murmured amusedly. "What if I don't want to play?"

She'd never expected them to want to play something so tawdry. They were so well-mannered and gentlemanly, but then her mother had always told her to never judge a book by its cover. She supposed that in this case she actually had!

It didn't overly perturb her

"I'm sure you wouldn't be so cruel!"

"I don't know," she said with a false hesitation. "What's in it for me?"

"How about for every move you win, I take an item of clothing off and you gain an orgasm."

"I gain an orgasm?"

"Yes. However many pieces you remove from my set, then you will have that number of climaxes."

Her lips twitched. "Sounds more interesting."

He clapped his hands together and moved his first piece. She wasn't so altogether bad at the game that she couldn't take him on. She managed two pieces before he took one of her pawns and he told her to remove her waistcoat.

She grinned as she unbuttoned it and exposed her bare chest to the room. As soon as 'they' were out, Scarlet knew that she had all of their undivided attention.

She managed to wangle another two pieces of Lazarus' off the board before he totally slated her. First trousers, then panties and then each shoe.

At least she hadn't totally humiliated herself. She may have been totally naked, but Lazarus was dressed in nothing but a pair of boxer briefs that highlighted every single solid inch of his cock and the firm muscles of his butt, which she'd seen when he'd bent over to take his suit trousers off. And his shoes.

"So how many climaxes do you owe me?"

"Four, mellita."

"That seems like a decent bargain," she said with another twitch of her lips.

"Yes, it does, doesn't it? We shall be sure to keep you

consulted throughout the duration of the night."

"The night? Hmm . . . you have a lot of stamina then?" she murmured huskily, a taunt in her eyes.

As she spoke to him her left hand came up to cup her left breast. She fondled the nipple and tweaked it. She smiled as his eyes locked on to her fingers and could practically feel the other two's eyes on her as well.

She felt unbearably aroused to be at the very center of their attention. There was something very sensual about it and she felt unbearably sexy and proud of her body. She liked her figure and thought she looked okay naked, but before them, she felt like a sex goddess.

A part of her realized that to them, she was a sex goddess. Their goddess, and she reveled in it. Felt that power resonate through her. It was a very empowering feeling and she felt damned good.

"Luckily for you, I do," he murmured, his eyes still focused on the hand caressing her nipple.

"What about you, Vincent? I already know about Nico," she said blithely.

Her right hand stroked over her stomach and down to the apex of her thighs. She began to finger herself and had to refrain from smiling at their quick intakes of breath.

She heard Nico murmur something in French and tut-tutted. "English, boys. Don't you know it's rude to speak another language in front of someone who doesn't understand? What did Nico say Lazarus?"

"That your pussy feels divine," he replied bluntly. His mind obviously focused on her hands.

"It does, does it?" she hummed and removed her fingers from her pussy. She leaned an elbow on the table and offered her hand to him. "What about taste? Does it taste good?"

His eyes changed from the piercing blackish brown that was habitually there to an icy green. It was almost like looking in to a cat's eyes. She realized then that his eyes changed color according to his mood. Green must be arousal, because she could see through the glass table that his cock was hard.

Leaning forward, he reached for her hand and held it as though he were about to kiss the top of her hand. Rather than kiss it, he flickered his tongue along the fingers that

were moist with her juices. She couldn't help the small
shudder that racked her frame as he supped and licked
along the digits. Once more he spoke in French and the
other two laughed.

"I'm going to start getting pissed off, if you keep talking
in French!" she warned with a pout.

Nico stood up and strode towards her. Standing behind
her chair, he bent over her and pressed a kiss to her
shoulder. "Laz says you taste like nectar of the Gods. And
he's right," he whispered.

He traced a line along her shoulder with his tongue and
it sent a roiling wave of need over every inch of her flesh.
His hands worked in between the line of her arm and chest
and came around to cup her breasts. She shivered as his
fingers plied her nipples. Then shrieked as his hands pulled
away from her all of a sudden and he sped around to her
side, grabbed her by the legs and somehow hefted her up
and over his shoulder like a bag of potatoes.

She smacked his back with her fist. "Hey, you could at
least give me some warning, Nico!" she yelled in
exasperation.

He ignored her but smacked her on her bare butt before
heading into one of the bedrooms that was an offshoot from
the main salon. He tossed her on the bed and when she'd
settled and had stopped bouncing, she looked up to see the
three men staring hungrily at her.

It should have felt predatory, but it didn't. It was the
sexiest experience of her life.

She stretched against the covers and grinned as almost
as one, they all jumped on to the bed. She'd never been in
anything but a twosome, so how the mechanics of it all
worked, she wasn't entirely sure. Something told her that
the men did know and rather than feeling peeved, she was a
little relieved. It sure helped to have someone know
something about what they doing!

Vincent was the first man to kiss her on the lips. As he
pressed his mouth against hers, she luxuriated in the feel of
his lips against her own, soft yet firm. Warm and smooth.
He was a fabulous kisser. He'd never fully kissed her or
touched her before, so she was somewhat nervous about
feeling him so intimately.

Scarlet didn't know why, but she felt as though she

knew Lazarus like she knew herself. Only God knew why, because she knew him as well as she did Vincent. But there was something timeless about Lazarus and when she looked into his eyes, she felt at peace. It was rather disturbing she had to admit.

As Vincent took over her mouth, she felt someone crawl in between her legs and her every muscle tensed as she waited for the touch that was about to come. When it finally did, she felt breathless with anticipation. Vincent was sucking the flesh at her throat and it was unbearably arousing to feel him suckle that flesh. When Nico's tongue, because at the touch of his mouth she knew it was Nico's, flickered against her clit, she cried out. It was so insane a feeling that she felt like she was dying. It was that intense.

Her hands came down to clutch at his head and she almost pitied him, because she was sure she was suffocating him, but she didn't care! The flicker of his tongue at her clit was just so amazing that she felt the flicker along every inch of her. His fingers were deep in her cunt and he kept scissoring and twisting them inside her. At every thrust, she cried out.

Vincent's mouth had just reached her nipple and she cried out gaspingly as he bit at the nubbin. Feeling unbearably naughty, she cupped Vincent's cheek in her palm and tugged upwards and away from her breast. She smiled at him to let him know she wasn't rejecting him, just moving further up the bed. Digging her elbows into the bed linens, she dragged herself upwards and back against the pillows. Settling herself higher, she then grabbed Vincent's head and moved him back into position.

She knew she'd confused them, but didn't care. They didn't ask any questions and just got right back to what they'd been doing, which was fine by her!

She began moaning and tugging at both Vincent and Nico's heads. "More," she whimpered. "Please."

It took a few times for her voice to be more than just a breathless whisper. But finally they heard her, and she groaned gratefully. Suddenly, she was alone on the bed with just Lazarus for company. She gulped as he pressed himself along the length of her body and settled his hips against her own. The slow slide of his cock into her pussy made her gasp. Flinging her head back, she gripped his hips with her thighs and tensed as he entered her to the hilt.

She began to breathe normally, as he allowed her time to accommodate herself to him and during that time, she watched the other two rearrange themselves on the bed. Somehow it was almost seamless, it wasn't awkward or uncomfortable. It rolled perfectly into one. Vincent came up to the level of her head and pressed the weeping tip of his cock to her lips.

Something about the entire situation set her blood on fire, and she knew that she'd never felt so god damned right as she did at this minute. Everything felt perfect. It felt wonderful and made excitement simmer beneath the surface of her skin.

She pulled her mouth tight around Vincent's cock and tried to swallow him as deeply as she could. She wanted to taste his seed, needed to make him lose his control. He was so cool and controlled that she had to stop it, had to free him from that self-imposed prison.

When Lazarus began to thrust into her, she cried out around Vincent's cock and swallowed him a tad more deeper than was comfortable. But she made herself relax and pressed her cheeks against his hardness.

Her eyes fluttered shut as Lazarus seemed determined to make her cry with lust. Every part of her felt branded by him and it was so insanely special that she actually felt the small beads of tears at the corner of her eyes.

The long slow slide was endless. It never sped up, never slowed down. It was constant and made her crazy. She needed him to go faster, needed him to fuck her. But she couldn't complain with Vincent's cock lodged in her throat, could she?

Instead, she tried to rock her hips to entice him, moved her body and stretched against the sheets, tried everything to make him move faster, but it didn't work.

Small whimpers escaped her mouth and were muffled by Vincent's cock, but Laz heard and she didn't have to look at him to know he was smiling faintly. There was something faintly sadistic about the never ending pace. He was trying to drive her insane. She just knew it and it was working damn him!

Finally, when she felt she couldn't take anymore, she began to sob.

"Enough Lazarus!" Vincent commanded in a gruff voice, ordering his blood brother to stop.

Her body was trembling and minute shivers and shudders quaked her small frame. She felt mindless with pleasure and entirely unsure of herself. She couldn't concentrate on Vincent's pleasure. She kept him tucked into her mouth, but Scarlet was so focused on the maddening slide of Lazarus' cock into her cunt that she could think of nothing else.

Eventually, he conceded but rather than pleasure her. He pulled out. Completely out.

She began to sob once more as a crazy, mindless need assailed her. It felt like she would never come and she was so damned close to the edge that she'd practically begun falling off of the cliff.

Feeling fingers circle the entrance to her body, she tensed as she recognized Nico's touch. Wondering what the hell was going on, her muscles stiffened and strained as she tried to remain as still as possible in the vein hope that someone would make her cum.

When simultaneously, she felt the fingers disappear and a tongue move in its place which was then combined with her swift impalement upon Lazarus' cock, she came.

As simple as that, it was over and just beginning.

It was almost frightening what was happening to her. Anything else she'd ever experienced, even the power of the night before, was nothing in comparison to what was going on at this moment.

She felt like her system was shutting down and starting up at the same time. She felt deaf but could hear everything. Blind but she saw more than she'd ever seen in her life.

The sensations were so powerful that feeling the splash of Vincent's cum at the back of her throat just finished her off. The taste, the scent, it just magnified in her head until a black calm washed over her like a wave rolling over a sandcastle, dissolving into nothing, making it as one with the beach again.

At the very peak of an orgasm that was unlike anything she'd ever felt before, her mind blacked out and took respite in the soothing nothingness before her.

Chapter Four

With a jaw-cracking yawn, Scarlet opened her eyes to the new day.

The first thought that registered was that yet again, there was no other person in the bed or in the room but her.

Dammit.

And wasn't that just a crappy way to start the day? Especially after the magic she'd experienced just twelve hours ago!

She should have awoken feeling great, satisfied with the world at large, as her itch had most definitely been scratched! Hell, she was probably one big scratch!

Never had she felt so sexually fulfilled in her entire life. So on that note, she should have a great big smile on her face, but she didn't and it was all because it was rather disconcerting to find herself alone in bed for the second time in as many days.

Was she being paranoid, or perhaps just a little insecure?

Having never ever experienced either emotion where men were concerned, she wasn't sure. She'd never cared if a man had left after sex, because more often than not, she'd been the one doing the leaving! She'd never felt insecure because she's always been in charge of her relationships. Men had always taken her as they found her, and if they didn't like it then they could just go to hell. They'd never had any influence on her, so it was hard for her to understand why in this case, they actually were influencing her emotions. She had to admit that she didn't really like it.

Prior to meeting Nico, Lazarus and Vincent, Scarlet had always been far too focused to get bogged down with what the opposite sex thought of her. Something that MJ had always rather envied her. Maybe having never had a father figure in her life like her best friend had, she didn't see why men were so all-fired important. Her mom had always wanted a man, believing in soul mates as she did, but Patricia had never needed one and there was a huge difference between the two. She'd managed to raise a well rounded, intelligent, practical daughter, who had the drive and the burning need to succeed. Patricia had done all this by herself, with a helping hand from her mother and on just one wage packet.

Sure, there could always have been more money in the pot, but that would have been for luxuries. Scarlet had always had food in her belly and good clothes on her back. She had seen how well her mother had coped and the difference was that Patricia had chosen to do it alone, had chosen to have a child by herself. That independent streak had been passed down to Scarlet and she had definitely seen that men weren't the be all and end all in a woman's life. Sure, her mom was of a different opinion to her, wanting the man of her dreams to discover her and live happily ever after as she did. But it didn't matter because either way, Scarlet had been exposed to an environment where women could cope easily on their own. Where men weren't necessary and they certainly weren't imperative to her happiness, just a nice welcome addition when they helped her to satisfy any urges she had at the time.

So to start feeling things that were a complete anathema to her ordinary way of life was both perplexing and disturbing. Yesterday, she'd jumped to conclusions and in the end, she'd been wrong. Nico hadn't abandoned her, hadn't used and then discarded her. Well, thanks to the welcoming, warm and dare she say, loving smile he'd graced her with last night, she knew that. So why was she still having doubts? Why was she questioning why they had left her alone again?

It shouldn't have bothered her, but it did. She should have thought, well at least there's more duvet for me, but she didn't. Maybe she was being paranoid, but the doubts were hard to still when she didn't understand why they were there in the first place.

The more she pondered on that thought, the more she wondered whether or not it was a problem of her own, her own issue, and had nothing to do with the men at all.

She and MJ had been friends since kindergarten. Their moms had been friends and knowing how inexperienced Patricia really was with men, MJ's mom had been the one to talk about the birds and the bees with her, when she'd just turned thirteen.

She could still remember that afternoon with a fond grin. Laura, MJ's mom, had sat them down with cookies and milk and a few bowls of candy. Having been summoned to MJ's living room, they'd both thought they were about to be told off for some act of mischief, of which there had been many, but instead they'd been greeted with junk food, which they'd immediately pounced on.

Laura had stammered her way through explanations of sex and the feelings it aroused in a girl and MJ and Scarlet had just sat there, jaws open, candy half-hanging out at the thought of wanting to actually touch a guy at all.

When Laura had assured them both that eventually they would lose that disinterest, she'd then graced MJ and Scarlet with three pieces of advice that Scarlet had personally never forgotten.

One, to treat them mean and keep them keen. Two, never let yourself be used and abused. Three, there was one rule for men and another for women.

Those rules had been her gospel through the emotional morass that was high school dating.

When other girls had been hurt by jerk jocks or fucked then discarded, Scarlet had remained strong and never let herself be touched emotionally by the guys in her school.

When other girls had run crying from the cafeteria because there were whispers of them taking it up the ass at Kissing Creek with their current boyfriends, Scarlet hadn't. If any talk of her had ever spread in the locker room then that was it. Over. She hadn't reacted with tears but with a cold anger that had stopped any gossip in its tracks.

She could remember one time, when she'd slept with a guy at home, during one of her mother's night shifts. She'd sucked him off and the next day all the guys had started to look at her differently. When they'd seen her in the hall, they'd stuck their tongues against their cheeks and moved them back and forth in a parody of oral sex.

Scarlet's fiery temper had a way of cooling quickly and when she'd realized that her boyfriend had spread rumors about her. She'd followed him to one of his classes and had MJ stall his teacher. She'd walked into his classroom, he'd been joking and talking with his friends when she'd entered. The class had hushed, not knowing what to expect, and he, the bastard that he was, had had the audacity to just stand up to greet her. Cool as a cucumber, Scarlet had walked in with a sweet smile and walked towards him. She'd kissed him on the cheek then grabbed his cock and balls in her hand and squeezed. Hard.

When she'd finally released him, she'd dumped him as he lay writhing on the ground and had walked out without a backward glance.

From that day on, her boyfriends had known not to spread any crap about her.

Her looks had helped, that she would admit. She'd had the choice of the guys in her class and in the years above her too and that had given her an edge. She'd been in control of picking who she dated and slept with and when.

She'd been hard. She'd been cool. But she'd also known how to have fun and still did. Even if MJ did call her a stickler for organization! The combination of all three qualities however, had meant that she'd been respected as well.

At this moment in time, she wasn't feeling respected.

Dammit!

She was annoyed because Scarlet knew that she'd inadvertently and at some point during the last two nights, handed over control to them. And that pissed her off more than words could express.

Having never been in this situation before, she was floundering and that was why she was feeling so mixed up.

She was insecure and paranoid, because she didn't know how to cope in this kind of environment where she wasn't taking the lead.

Last night in bed, that had pleased her more than words could say. She'd been at the very center of all their attentions and had felt both cosseted and like their own personal sex goddess.

But now, in the cold light of day, she was feeling a little wary.

Nothing could come from the sex they experienced together. At the end of the cruise, they would go their separate ways and never see each other again. The thought saddened her and she recognized it to be another part of handing over control. Another weakness that had crept in.

The thought made her start in shock. Frowning, she contemplated whether or not it was a weakness that she alone had or whether they shared it as well.

The sex was brilliant; deeper and more exciting than anything she'd ever known. There had to be a reason for that and it had to be on more than her own side. Because she could see in their eyes that they felt it too. She had felt it the night before when she'd danced with them.

That intense recognition upon meeting each other for the first time had affected not only her but Nico, Vincent and Lazarus as well.

The attraction they felt for each other was more than deep, it was at the center of her very core; at the center of their cores.

She knew them and Scarlet realized that they knew her. Intrinsically. They knew what she wanted, when she wanted. She knew where to touch and how. It was as though they'd already met years before and had learned everything about each other.

The shapes of their faces were imprinted on her retinas. She knew the bone structure of their faces, recognized it like she would looking at herself in the mirror.

The thought was stunning. Almost like a blow to the stomach because what she was thinking was more than just irregular for her. It was completely crazy.

Scarlet didn't believe in soul mates. She didn't believe in marriage or being with one person for the rest of her life. She flitted about from man to man at her own discretion and did what she wanted when she wanted.

Soul mates didn't come into it.

So why did she think they were the other half of her soul?

Why did being with them complete her when countless other kind, charming, handsome men hadn't?

What was it about them that just clicked with her, that resonated deeply within her?

Why was everything about them so damned right?

Sitting up with a gulp, she stared blindly ahead. The bed faced the windows and she looked directly out on to a sunrise. The rays of the sun were warming and lit the room up to her gaze. Not that she saw it. Her mind was turned inwards, contemplating things that shouldn't be contemplated. Things that she couldn't, wouldn't believe in.

Locking a hand to her throat, she jumped off the bed and ran out of the bedroom. Searching for her purse, she eventually found it on a console table that was placed by the entrance to the suite. Grabbing it, she located her cell and rang MJ, praying to God that she was awake.

She felt sick with relief when she heard her friend's grouchy greeting.

"Scarlet?

What the hell are you doing waking me up at this time of the morning?"

"MJ?" Scarlet told her breathlessly. "I-I, you're not going to believe this. I swear you won't."

"What's the matter?" MJ said a little more lucid now. The urgency in her voice was most reassuring to Scarlet's frazzled nerves.

"You remember when you said that I was to meet someone and get my head screwed back on but right this time . . . ?"

"Yeah," MJ said and Scarlet could just picture the puckered frown on her friend's forehead.

"I've met three men."

"Three?"

"Yeah, three," Scarlet repeated then winced at her friend's hoot of glee.

"Ryan," Scarlet heard the covers on MJ's bed rustle. "Ryan, Dammit, wake up. Scarlet's sleeping with three men!"

"MJ, I didn't ring you to gossip with Ry!"

"I know, but you know I tell him everything anyway. So I thought I might as well save time by telling him now. He says, are you using protection? You should see him, he looks like a mother hen whose feathers have been ruffled. You'd think he was your mom," she said on a chortle.

"Shit."

MJ's voice was more subdued now. "Scarlet O'Hara Reves, you better not be telling me that you've met three strange men on board a cruise and you've been fucking them without condoms?

Are you out of your god damned mind?" she screeched.

Scarlet winced as she heard Ryan's angry voice over the phone.

"What the hell is she doing?

Tell her to get to a pharmacy right this minute! There must be one on board, surely?"

While she was rightfully concerned about her continual stupidity as regards to lack of protection, she couldn't help but enjoy their concern for her. It was wonderful to have friends that cared, really cared. She appreciated them more than she probably ever told them. The thought made her feel guilty.

"You don't have to repeat that. I heard," Scarlet muttered as she bit her lip nervously.

"Ryan says, 'Good'!"

"I know I've been stupid, but that's not what's concerning me."

"Not concerning you?" MJ said with another screech.

"No."

"You are crazy. I knew I should have taken this trip with you. You're so blocked up creativity wise that I knew you'd go mental on board with three weeks of nothing to do but enjoy yourself. You're not used to it. I blame myself."

Her tone was so mournful that Scarlet couldn't hold back a laugh.

"Think it's funny. Do you?" MJ said with a huff and Scarlet knew that she was being treated to one of her friend's killer glares.

"No. But you make me sound like, I don't know, some kind of creative dunce! I can have fun, you know! In fact, I frequently have fun and with you!"

"I know you do, but usually it's scheduled and with me to watch over you," MJ fretted.

"MJ, stop! Stop panicking!" Scarlet ordered. "I love you, you know that don't you?"

"Don't change the subject and don't think you can soften me up by telling me that. I do know it by the way and I love you too. But still, Scarlet, what the hell were you thinking?"

"I wasn't thinking. I'm still not thinking clearly where they're concerned. I'm . . . I'm starting to feel things."

"Feel things?" MJ repeated confusedly. "What things?"

"You know . . . ," she said, gulping.

"I wouldn't ask Scarlet if I understood!" MJ said exasperatedly.

"Well," Scarlet cleared her throat. "I-I keep sleeping in and they're not there, you know?"

"You fall asleep with them?" MJ said, her voice astonished. "But you never do that!"

"Believe me, I know!

And to be precise, two nights ago I slept with Nico and woke up to find him gone. Then last night, I, well, I slept with all three of them and none of them are here!"

"Ryan," MJ directed at her husband, who was obviously still a part of this three way conversation. "Our baby has actually grown up!"

"Stop teasing, MJ. Tell me what the hell to do!"

"I'm not teasing, it's called emotional development. You actually give a damn about these guys. Although I admit it's unorthodox, you probably need three guys, you nymph."

"Charming!"

"Ryan says maybe he should have married you," MJ said with a snort.

That statement was followed shortly by a very audible yell from Ryan.

"Dammit, MJ, you know I hate it when you pinch me!" he bellowed.

"Then don't make me jealous, sweetheart!" MJ murmured.

"I thought you liked jealous sex," Scarlet replied, butting in to her friend's conversation without compunction. She was used to these kinds of conversation and Ryan listening to them both chat.

"Oh yeah, so I do. Well, that's one good thing that's come out of this early morning wakeup call!" MJ said, sounding much more chipper at the thought of a tumble in bed before she had to get up to work.

"This can't go anywhere, so there's no point in feeling anything. At the end of this stupid cruise, they'll go their way and I'll go mine. Help me, MJ! What do I do?"

"Do? There's nothing you can do. Just hope they're not jerks and pray to God that you won't get hurt!"

"That's it? You have to be kidding me?"

"Nope," MJ said cheerfully.

"There has to be something! I mean, I could get . . . ."

"Yes?"

"Well, I could, she gulped. "I could easily feel about them the way you and Ry feel about each other," Scarlet whispered.

"Seriously? Are you joking? You're falling in love with

these guys?"

"No! I'm not joking! That's why I'm freaking out. I don't even know what love feels like. It could have been love at first damned sight and I wouldn't have a fucking clue. All I know is that I've never felt like this about any guy before. Never mind three of them! I saw them and my heart started thundering in my chest and I couldn't breathe or think or do anything.

"I'm questioning why they keep leaving me alone in bed. Do they think I'm cheap for sleeping with them so soon? Do they think I'm a slut for taking part in a foursome with three guys that time-wise are strangers, but in my head, I feel like I've known them for decades . . . ?

"I have all these doubts and I don't know what the hell to do with them! I've never doubted myself and now, when I'm not with them, that's all I fucking do! I'm so confused and it's scaring me, MJ."

"Well, they sound perfect for you, and I know you're scared, I understand, but there's nothing you can do. Just be careful, honey. With both your heart and your body. You don't want to get hurt."

"Trust me, I know I don't want to get hurt. I don't even want to feel this way! I mean they're almost perfect, but they . . . ." She hesitated, unsure of whether or not she wanted to tell MJ that they thought they were vampires and werewolves.

"They, what?" MJ asked curiously.

"Oh nothing. It doesn't matter. You'll never guess this next part though," Scarlet cleared her throat and quickly changed the subject. "I didn't realize before we set sail, but this is a themed cruise. It's all about vampires and the undead."

"Oh my God! I would have loved to have seen your face when you realized that. Let me guess, it took you five minutes to decide you were going to leave early, am I right?"

"Dammit, how do you know me so damned well?"

"It's a gift," MJ chortled.

"Bitch."

"Vampire-lover."

Scarlet snorted. "Thanks."

"I can understand why you're freaked, babes, but there's

nothing that can be done here. You just have to go with the flow. Nothing more you can really do."

"Damn," Scarlet whispered.

"Yeah. But if they're as great as you say they are, then I'm sure you'll be okay in their care."

"I can only hope so," she said with a heavy sigh. "I'm sorry I woke you up but I had to talk to you. Go and enjoy your jealous sex."

"Don't worry I will, but dammit, Scarlet, buy some condoms and stay safe, alright?"

"Yeah, I will. Take care, MJ. See you soon. Give my love to Ry."

"Will do. Bye honey."

Scarlet dropped her cell phone back into her purse and grimaced. She felt better for having spoken to MJ but it hadn't exactly gotten her anywhere, had it? She just had to hope that they wouldn't fuck her over.

God, is that what women the world over did every day?

How the fuck could they cope with this mass of negative feeling swarming them?

Will he hurt me? Will he dump me? Will he treat me like crap?

Hell on earth, no wonder MJ had always envied her her cool.

To be besieged with these awful doubts was just too hideous to bear. And she had all of this multiplied by three, dammit!

Her only hope was that she was sure that they were affected by her as she was by them. So she could only pray that they felt the same about her and she was pretty sure they did.

She reacted to them in completely contrary ways, but last night, Lazarus had deeply affected her. There was something about him, about his eyes that really touched her and resonated deeply within her. There was something that told him he was on the edge and rather than frightening her, it calmed her.

Weird, she thought with a shake of her head. But then, what about the last two nights hadn't been weird? She'd never experienced anything of the like and it was beyond curious. It was life-changing and she'd been damned please with the way her life was. She hated change, dammit and now, everything about her was changing.

Her perception of herself and the world around her, the way she viewed male and female interaction. She was seeing a whole new side to everything, and she didn't like what she saw!

She was growing accustomed to being with all three of them and after only two nights. She was growing used to this fiery attraction hitting her like a punch to the gut. And dammit, after years of sleeping alone, she had to admit that she was growing rather accustomed to being tucked up against someone's side.

Two nights ago, Nico had sprawled his body against almost the entire width of the bed. It was either lie practically atop him or fall off the edge of the bed!

It hadn't been a hard decision to plaster herself up against him. In fact, there hadn't been a decision to make. It had been wonderful breathing in the same air as he, every inhalation had encompassed his sultry, musky scent and she'd been perpetually aware of him the entire night. His hard muscles had pressed into her, but it hadn't been uncomfortable. It had been nice. A constant reminder that he was a man; stronger than her, a protector.

In fact, that was something she'd noticed about all three of them, they made her feel super feminine. She was everything womanly to their supercharged masculinity. It was an intriguing feeling and a rather primitive one at that. One that she was learning to revel in, just as she had the night before.

After the rather exciting interlude she'd shared with Vincent, Nico and Lazarus, she'd awoken to find herself surrounded by men. They'd rearranged themselves around her so that she was in the center of the bed and she was protected by a wall of muscled, smooth bodies.

It was rather disappointing to be surrounded by three of them one minute and then to be alone the next. Having always slept primarily alone, it was definitely a change to be surrounded by such hunks. She was deeply perturbed to realize that she enjoyed sharing her bed with these three.

Another part of her, the part that wasn't freaked out by what was happening to her, was intrigued as to know which two men had slept next to each other, but she pushed that thought to the side.

In fact, it was too damned huge to push to the side. It was there, right in front of her face.

Not only had she just experienced a foursome and for the first time ever, she'd actually watched and been intrigued and aroused by their touching and pleasuring of each other.

In fact, she'd been more than aroused; it had made her so hot so fast that it was amazing she hadn't self-imploded. She could honestly say that she had never experienced anything like that. It had been an instant turn on, something that no amount of foreplay had ever managed to inspire in her in the past.

If being in a foursome hadn't have been exciting in itself, then that was like plopping a thousand cherries on top of the cake.

Just thinking about it made her all hot again, the thought of what she'd experienced and what she'd seen was like setting hundreds of thousands of fireworks alight. The thrill, the sheer rush of it was now flooding her bloodstream and she was entirely conscious of the fact that she was naked in their suite's living room.

Last night had been like a hundred fantasies come to life and something she'd never thought to experience. If she were truthful, something she'd never even really thought about. But now it had happened, she knew that it had changed her for the rest of her life.

Seeing what she'd seen, feeling what she'd felt, Scarlet knew that to go back to ordinary sex would be so difficult. You couldn't experience the bounty of heaven then fall back to Earth and not feel cheated.

Closing her eyes, she gulped and determined that she was going to get dressed and head off for some breakfast. She hadn't eaten hardly anything during the past two days and her stomach was really feeling it.

Her head might be muddled but if obviously didn't affect her appetite!

The thought made her wrinkle her nose as she bent down to pick up the clothes she'd strewn aside the night before. Leaning over she reached for her waistcoat and panties then her trousers. With one hand fisted around her trousers, she shrieked as a callused hand slid down the very center of her bare pussy.

"What the fuck?" she screeched then upon realizing that it wasn't an attacker but one of her men, her already shaky knees collapsed from under her. Rather than fall to the ground she was soon swept up into a pair of strong arms.

"Don't do that to me," she muttered in annoyance, then ruined the effect by nuzzling into Vincent's shirt. She didn't have to look into his face to know it was him. His scent surrounded her, her body recognized his. It was strange but then she was kind of getting used to that.

Now she was with him, any earlier doubts or concerns vanished into thin air. Scarlet just reveled in being held by him. It was the same with Nico and Lazarus as well. They totally took over her thoughts when they were all together.

If they never left her side for a moment, she'd never have any doubts. But it was hardly practical, was it? The thought made her smile and she pressed a kiss against his shirt-covered chest.

"I couldn't resist, chérie!" he murmured suavely and walked her into the bedroom.

"Well, next time, resist, buster!
I felt like my heart was going to explode!"

"Don't be melodramatic, you knew it was me." His voice was confident and she wondered how he knew that she had been able to recognize him.

"Not at first I didn't! I thought I was going to be raped!"

"No, merely ravished, ma bien aimée!"

She laughed as he tossed her on the bed, her arms and legs spread to gain her balance and also to tease him. She'd felt his cock pressed into her side when he'd held her in his arms and saw no reason to not encourage him further.

He immediately took advantage of her new position and his fingers slid right to her cunt, as though they were a heat seeking missile.

"I need to shower," she murmured as her back arched and her legs tightened around him to keep him exactly where he was.

"Perhaps. But only if you shower with me, non?" he retorted, his fingers moving as he spoke.

She smiled slowly and nodded her agreement. When he lugged her back into his arms and transported her from the bedroom to the bathroom, Scarlet thought that life couldn't get much better than this, being transported around by a man who would make Adonis weep with envy.

The bathroom was a miracle in itself. It was a cream and gold washroom that positively gleamed and glowed. There was nothing in it apart from the large shower head in the very center of the ceiling, a faucet, a towel rack then a shelf for toiletries. It was rather impractical but stunningly opulent at the same time. It was an odd adjective to bestow upon it, because there was nothing in the room that was really grand, but the sheer emptiness was appealing and she just knew that she was about to be fucked on the floor directly beneath the pounding shower spray. The thought made her tingle happily.

Depositing her to the left of the shower head, Vincent walked to the faucet and moved the dials around until luxuriously soft warm water began to cascade before her. She walked into it with a pleased sigh and watched as he began to strip another of his twenty grand suits as though it was an old pair of sweats. He dumped the beautiful thing on the floor as though it meant nothing and reached for some toiletries, which he placed beside her on the floor.

It was hard to really concentrate when he was walking around with no clothes on. Her eyes kept moving to his cock, that swayed with his movements. Either that, or they'd focus on a rippling muscle here, or a flex of a bicep there. The phrase poetry in motion could have been written for him. His body moved fluidly and just seeing the small everyday movements of him preparing for a shower set her blood alight much faster and more powerfully than another guy sucking at her clit would do.

When he eventually joined her, his hands were cupping some liquid soap. "You will smell like a boy, but for me you will smell delicious, hein?" he murmured.

So saying, he began to massage the soap into her hair and the scent of a very masculine, very well known aftershave brand soon perfumed the air. It felt very decadent to have him attend to her. She knew that her hair would tangle but didn't care. She let him cleanse her hair then her body and finally, when he had her squeaky clean, did she see the intent in his eyes change.

"On the floor, ma petite," he ordered, smoothly rolling to his knees and thus to the floor as he spoke.

He sat in the lotus position and when she sat knelt

before him, he grabbed her knees and spread her legs. Placing her hands on the floor to her side, she steadied herself as he dragged her forwards and her legs upwards so that she was resting almost entirely against him.

Her head and shoulders rested on the warm floor, but her back was tilted to a diagonal and her legs were thrown over his shoulders. She thought he was going to eat her pussy, but he didn't. Somehow he supported her and kept her comfortable while he spread her legs as wide as they would go and at the perfect angle for the cascading torrents of water to pummel at her clit.

At the first splash, the muscles in her belly rolled and she tightened them in shock. At the second and third and fourth, her hips began to rock because they were the only parts of her body of which she had control. Water flowed down and flooded her upper torso. Sometimes, she swallowed it as she gulped in much needed air but the entire position, the water, everything, just got to her.

The very width and length of the shower head meant that the entire stretch of her pussy was being bombarded with the weight of water. It slipped into her cunt, barraged her clit and rolled down her ass. The way he spread her legs meant that her pussy was wide open and it felt as though it were drowning under the barrage of water. It was such an exciting feeling that she found it difficult to concentrate on anything but the here and now.

With other men, her mind could have been diverted along to next day's schedule. Not with Vincent. And not with Nico or Lazarus either.

The deluge of water kept her on the brink for such a maddening length of time, it felt like torture. It was almost too much pressure but not enough, too much heat but not enough. Her legs were spread too far apart but not enough. The water that slipped into her cunt was delicious, but not thick or full enough to help ease her need.

Everything about this position kept her on the knife edge and she knew that all three of them enjoyed doing that to her.

It made the orgasms awe-inspiring, but waiting for them to happen was almost heart-breaking.

Vincent moved his hands from her legs so that he wasn't spreading them apart. He changed her body position by

slowly sliding her even closer towards him. Now her
shoulders were against his feet and her head tilted
backwards so that almost all the water sluiced over her
body and into her face. She had to turn her head to the side
to get any air to her lungs and her eyes had to be clamped
shut to prevent any water entering them.

Being sightless and a little panicked by the lack of air,
she didn't realize what he was doing until he moved. She
was too busy moving her head about to find a position that
allowed her to breathe comfortably. She eventually found
one and realized that he hadn't touched her since he'd seen
her efforts. Scarlet felt relieved that he'd waited for her to
get comfortable.

He had one hand at her lower belly and that pressed her
to him and so supported her back, while the other made her
scream. One, two, three, four fingers thrust into her cunt. It
was almost too hard a thrust, but it was what she needed.
The maddening constant drive of that relentlessly pressured
water was unbearable and so transient, so unsolid that the
feel of hard, callused fingers was like a soothing balm.

Her hips rocked sharply upward as she began to cum
around his hand. She felt her pussy cling and grab at his
fingers, felt it mold itself around them as though they were
a cock and needed to be held tightly until it spewed with
cum. It was with some disappointment that she realized no
cum would be splashing her cunt this time. The small hit as
it walloped her hot pussy was an extra final touch that just
prolonged her climax even longer.

Without it, she felt almost incomplete and even though
she was climaxing, it wasn't enough. She dropped her hips
away from Vincent and rolled off his body awkwardly to
get out of the position he'd placed her in. Panting with
need, she quickly pressed him backwards so that he now
lay on the floor and she quickly sat astride him. His cock
was just two inches away from her and she sank down on to
it with a needy whimper.

He was big. They were all big and her pussy had to fight
to accommodate them, but Vincent had a very wide base
and she cried out as her cunt came to it. She felt almost like
a woman possessed, she wanted all of his cock, needed all
of it in her. That last climax hadn't fulfilled her, had merely
heated her blood and made her even hungrier. She needed

every inch of him inside her. Her cunt demanded it. She rode him up and down, each time trying to push herself further on to him and each time sobbing as she couldn't.

Leaning forward, she spread her fingers wide and rested her hands on either side of his head to give her a good measure of support. The position meant that her tits were dangling right over his face but she wasn't thinking about that. This new position meant that she had a better angle and it was easier for her to thrust herself on to him. She bounced atop him, determined to swallow him entirely and cried out as Vincent's hand split up, one to her tits and one to her clit.

She was already so wet, that it was easy to slide up and down him. But the added incentive of his fingers against her pleasure zone, made her hips rock faster and harder and deeper. After what felt like hours, but what was really only a few minutes, she managed to work all of him inside her cunt.

That fuller than full feeling made her just rest against him. Anything else was too much. Breathing hard, she kept her pussy close to his groin and rather than thrusting now, she rocked back and forth.

Small whimpers escaped her throat as she felt herself reach the very precipice and as she fell, only Vincent kept her grounded. His hands clung to her hips and he helped her keep rocking against him. It was a wondrous feeling to feel the splash of his seed, to know that she had pleasured this amazing man and satisfied him made her feel almost high.

To know that they were both experiencing such heavenly pleasure and at the same time, just magnified everything. She'd never had an orgasm where both she and her partner had cum at the same time, until now.

His shout rang out and mingled with her cries. As she collapsed against his torso, both their chests rose and fell rapidly as sensation washed through and over them in a continual wave, which was only enhanced by the water falling from the shower.

It was such a sensual moment that she knew she would never forget it, because how could she? Such pleasure could never be forgotten. The feel of his skin against her, the sound of his breathing, the scent of their pleasure-sated bodies was just magic.

She rested against him easily, comfortable in her nakedness and protected by the arms he placed snugly around her.

"We should get up and turn the water off," she sighed practically.

He laughed. "Anything for you, chérie!"

She tried to roll from him but he wouldn't let her and somehow, with what seemed like inhumane strength, he lifted them both from the floor and walked to the faucet to switch it off. He then moved them to the towel rack and only then, did he let her stand on wobbly legs. She dabbed herself dry and then leaned against his strength. She felt entirely drained of energy and in need of a nap, but contrarily, felt as though she could climb a mountain as well.

They stimulated such contradictory emotions in her that it was incredibly inspiring.

He grabbed her towel and began to dry her hair and she let him. She let him do something for her that was so amazingly intimate, and Scarlet loved it, enjoyed his gentle but practical touch and sighed when he finished and once more lifted and carried her back to the bedroom and to the bed.

Snuggling into the covers, she smiled when he moved to her back and curled his body against her own. Being so close to each other was very intense and although they hadn't known each other long, even though it felt like forever, she was intensely curious about him.

Last night, she'd thought that he was so immensely controlled and his emotions deeply contained. She supposed she'd recognized a kindred spirit. But, at this moment, she knew his defenses were down and her curiosity was so powerful that even though she didn't really want to know the answer, she asked him anyway. "What made you decide to become a vampire, Vincent?"

She felt his jolt of shock and knew her question had surprised him, but she also knew that he would answer her even though it had been quite impertinent. It was, after all, a highly personal question, and she had no real right to ask for such private information.

"Do you believe in vampires, mon amour?" he asked,

his words coming out slightly stiff, stilted.

"I . . . I don't know what to believe. If you had asked me two nights ago, then I would have told you resolutely, no!

But, despite myself, I can't understand why Nico would lie to me. He says he's a werewolf. I have no reason to disbelieve but, at the same time, no real evidence to the contrary. I suppose, if I'm honest with myself and honest with you, I'm fence sitting, Vincent."

"Always be honest, Scarlet. It's the only pure commodity left to the world," he said somberly.

"I try, Vincent."

"I'm pleased to hear that," he said, pausing for a second as he thought about his next words before he sighed heavily. "Very few men and women choose to become vampires. Only those who are intrinsically evil want to defy nature and live forever. There is some truth behind the human myths of the undead. Most of them are unbearably evil and their cause is hopeless. They are inhumane. They have forgotten every ounce of their human natures. They attack randomly, wishing to decimate the human population. They can kill thousands without even a blink of the eye. Sometimes, though, they do not finish the job and the result is another vampire is born from their mistake."

"Was it very painful?" she asked, rolling over so that rather than be curled against him, she was facing him yet still embraced within his arms.

"I cannot lie to you, chérie. Yes. It was very painful. It is torturous to be born a vampire, especially when you're not guided into your new life. In fact, it is so difficult that many of these new unguided vampires do not have the strength to survive, but, on a rare occasion, some do, and I am one of those few," he finished softly, his voice filled with pain, emotion.

"I was first born in the year 1770. From the cradle, I was set to be betrothed to the Du Clair family's first daughter. Five years later, Véronique was born, and, even though I was young, I thought she was a beautiful child. We grew up as childhood friends. As we grew, so too did our friendship. Our burgeoning passion became an entity unto itself.

I was blind to everyone else, to everything else around me. I didn't see the political unrest. I only had eyes for Véronique. But none of that stopped the French Revolution from coming. I was ill prepared for what came next. Despite my best efforts to protect her, Robespierre's bastard minions took her from me, took her to the guillotine. To my shame, I drank myself into a stupor to forget and I awoke as a completely different species. I have vague memories of being bitten by a woman, of the pain and the suffering from both the bite and the process of changing. There is little else though," he said with a shrug that hinted at his annoyance at that fact.

Scarlet frowned and bit her lip. Raising her hand, she cupped his cheek and stroked it, trying to imbue all the tenderness she felt into that one small touch.

Even though it was impossible, even though it was crazy, she believed him. Just thinking that she possibly believed what had to be a lie, almost made her rear back in shock. Only concern that he would feel she was rejecting him made her keep still.

"It's okay, chérie. I understand that it is completely out of your realm of comprehension. You will become accustomed to it, though," he said reassuringly, a soft smile playing on his lips.

"I will?" she squeaked, her eyes opening wide in shock.

Again there was that soft smile in conjunction with a slow nod. What the hell did that mean?

She blew out a breath. "What happened after your . . . rebirth?" she whispered, a trace of the astonishment she was feeling evident in her voice.

"I tried for America, the land where dreams are made and I was fortunate. I started a cotton plantation and the rest as we say, is most definitely history."

"Do you still own the plantation?"

"I own the plantation house and the land, but I don't grow cotton anymore."

"What do you do?"

"Are you sure you want to know?" he asked with a raised brow. At her nod, he smiled ironically. "I slay vampires like the one that created me. Lazarus and Nicholae do the same."

"Vincent," she whispered hesitantly.

"Yes, chérie."

"This is most inappropriate, but I'm starving. Could we possibly have something to eat?"

He chuckled. "I have to admit I was not expecting that! But, of course we can, Scarlet. Maybe food will help you come to terms with my words, hein?

Reach for the phone, it's on your bedside table. Dial two for room service and order whatever your stomach requires," he told her.

She did as he said and ordered pancakes with bacon and eggs then returned the phone to its place and snuggled back into his arms. When she did, he sighed heavily with what she thought was a faint tinge of relief.

"Yes, I'm relieved," he concurred, cannily reading her thoughts. He then dropped his chin so it rested against the top of her head. "I feared you would run scared from the room."

"I'm made of tougher stuff than that, Vincent!"

"Maybe, I've never told any woman my story, you know?"

"You haven't?" she asked and couldn't help but feel special for that fact.

"No. Why should I?"

"I don't know. Why have you told me?"

She could hear the smile on his face. "You know, Scarlet. You just haven't admitted it to yourself."

Scarlet frowned, confused by his words but before she could speak the doorbell rang out and Vincent climbed out of the bed to obtain her food order for her.

Rolling over on to her belly, she propped her head up on her hands and stared blindly as she tried to contemplate what Vincent had just said. Despite all common sense, there had been such sincerity in his voice that she had been unable to do anything but believe in his story. As she thought more about it, she realized that depth of sincerity had been in Nico's story, too.

The thought made her gulp.

Did vampires and werewolves really exist?

Was she insane for believing in their stories? Perhaps deranged for starting to believe these unlikely and unusual tales were true? Or were they the ones who were mad?

Perhaps it was just one of those things that was so crazy and so improbable that it was true.

That somehow made sense and stopped that burning sensation of nerves in her stomach.

"Well, that didn't take long!" she remarked when she heard the door open.

"What didn't take long?"

Rolling over on to her back, Scarlet grinned at Lazarus. Strangely unsurprised to see him there. "My breakfast! Is Vincent bringing it?"

"Ah, is that what was in the cloche?"

"I hope so! I'm starving."

"You see, we're good for your appetite," Lazarus commented with a faint smile.

"And a lot more besides," she retorted with a cheeky grin then clapped her hands as Vincent walked in with her breakfast. "Vincent, you are a darling!"

She arranged herself in the bed so that she was covered and sat cross legged so that she could place the tray atop her thighs. Vincent removed the cloche with a flourish, bowing low and he leaned forward to kiss her cheek.

"It is time for my shift, chérie. I will see you later, ma petite Écarlate."

"What shift?"

"We're searching for a vampiress called Elizabeth. Her crimes against humanity are too numerous to count. Lazarus will remain with you until Nico returns later," he said with a smile then clapped Lazarus on the shoulder before he walked out. "Au revoir."

"He will get dressed before he leaves, won't he? I don't think a sheet can be classed as appropriate attire for a cruise, do you?" she asked with a cocked brow.

"He will get changed in his room."

"Whose room is this?"

"Mine," he said with a possessive growl. "It pleases me that your scent permeates this room, you know?"

"My scent?"

"Mmm," he hummed.

She watched as he sniffed the air.

"You smell like me actually," he said.

"Vincent must have used your soap on me," she admitted and popped a sliver of pancake into her mouth.

"That sounds intriguing."

"Oh, it was. In fact, the entire morning has been. Vincent shared his past with me. As Nico did the night before, but then, you know that."

"Yes, I knew that. I also knew that Vincent would share his past with you as soon as he had the opportunity. It seems you're very easy to talk to, Scarlet."

There was something about Lazarus that made her feel as though he were testing her. Why she felt like that, she wasn't sure. Scarlet was fully aware that she affected him deeply and so could only think, that this was just his nature, to be suspicious and cautious.

"What are you thinking?" he asked curiously.

"I was thinking about you," she admitted honestly.

"Well, isn't that flattering," he said in a cool seemingly disinterested voice.

It was a statement, not a question.

"Perhaps."

She shrugged and ate some more of her breakfast. As she ate, she contemplated him further. There was no doubt that he was fascinating. He was so unique, even amongst Nico and Vincent, who had their own qualities that she highly appreciated. But Lazarus was a conundrum, a puzzle and that appealed to her perversely contrary nature.

"I was thinking if you were always so suspicious, actually."

He smiled faintly. "Were you?

Now that's very interesting. Most women find me unutterably charming, you know. Trust my âme sœur du sang to disagree with that fact," he told her with a chuckle.

"What does that mean?"

He laughed heartily. "I don't think you're ready to know, Scarlet," he replied, the humor in his voice still redolent.

"I'm not a child to humor, Lazarus!"

"I wondered if your temper was as fiery as your hair."

"Now you know and don't change the subject. I can speak a little French, you know," she huffed and shrugged her shoulders, inadvertently telling him how poorly her language skills were. She glared as his lips twitched. "Why do I always feel as though you're laughing at me?"

"Because you're adorable, I usually am. But it's not at you, ma petite. Normally, I have very little humor. Ask Vincent and Nico. They will tell you how rare it is to see me smile. I bring out your appetite and you bring out my smile," he told her with an earnest face that she just knew was staged and that was hiding a smile. Damn him.

"Blood sister," she said.

"I beg your pardon?"

"A translation of what you just said," she told him with a smirk of triumph.

"Ah, but that is a . . . literal translation shall we say, and quite wrong by the way, Scarlet. You shall have to wait to know more. But, you won't have to wait long, I fear."

"How old are you, Lazarus? Really?"

"I told you yesterday that I was two thousand and thirty years old."

"Why am I starting to believe all of you, Lazarus?"

"Perhaps, because it's the truth?"

"But your truth goes against everything I've ever believed in," she admitted with a sigh.

"Humans are told very little of the vast amounts of paranormal activity that takes place in their world. It's no wonder you're finding it difficult to believe."

"Vincent says that only a rare few choose to be vampires, is he right?"

"Yes. We were both accidentally turned. Have you finished your breakfast?" he asked interestedly. At her nod, he took the tray away and placed it outside his bedroom door. "There is a mere two pints of blood that make the difference between dying and being reborn a vampire."

"Can't you do something that proves you're a vampire? So that I don't have to think I'm crazy?"

"If you see proof, you'll still think that you're crazy, mellita."

"I know, but still, please?"

He walked towards her, where she lay on the bed and grabbed her hand. He separated her fingers and reached for the index finger which he raised to his incisors. Human length one minute, almost three inches longer two seconds later. They almost reached his chin.

The sharp point on the edge of the two teeth made her shudder and a drop of blood beaded at the tip where it nicked. She gulped as he lathed the small wound with his tongue and it immediately healed.

"Did I just see that?" she whispered hoarsely.

"Yes," he replied seriously.

"Vampires actually exist," she breathed and shook her

head. Her mouth opened and closed as her brain registered and processed what she'd just seen, but even that didn't make it any less amazing.

"You believe?" he asked with a quirked brow.

"How can I not?" Her voice was gutturally deep. "You really are two thousand years old?"

"Well, that's not entirely accurate."

"You really had me going. For a minute there I thought . . . ."

He interrupted her before she could finish. "You'd have to add thirty years to that to be correct."

"My God, you're really Roman, aren't you? This is incredible," she breathed. Her hand came up to touch his face, her fingers hesitantly caressed his features. "How old were you when you were reborn?" she asked.

His eyes had closed at the pressure of her fingers against his face. He didn't open then when he responded. "I was fifteen, almost sixteen."

"That doesn't make any sense to me. You look like you're almost thirty?"

"We age infinitesimally. In two thousand years, I've aged fifteen years."

"Wow. Who needs plastic surgery," she joked. "My logical nature is telling me I can't believe this, but, strangely enough, I do."

"I'm glad you do," he said with a smile, and he meant it. He didn't know what he would've done if she didn't believe him. Thankfully, he wouldn't have to deal with that hurdle. He tried not to think of the many others he would have to face.

"Hey, wait just a minute. Is this one of those secrets that means you'll have to kill me now that I know?" she asked with a skeptical scowl.

"No." He laughed and shook his head in wonder at her being able to find amusement in this situation. "I wouldn't have told you if that were the case. But, again, when it all has time to register, you'll understand."

"Just because you're over two thousand years older than me doesn't mean you can treat me like a child, you know?" Scarlet said with a pout.

"That's true. Fortunately for us, I'm not treating you like a child. I'm just not overfeeding your brain. I don't want it to explode with shock, mellita. You've had to process a lot today," he joked.

"Damn. You make me sound like a dumb ass. I don't like thinking that you see me as intellectually inferior."

"Believe me, I haven't underestimated you, Scarlet."

"Good. Why is it that Nicholae and Vincent have told me about their pasts and you haven't?"

"Perhaps it is because I'm naturally reticent?"

"Perhaps, but I doubt it."

"Hmm, maybe you're right. It's more likely that I haven't had the opportunity to bare all . . . that is if you really want to know?"

"I wouldn't have said anything if I didn't want to know, would I?"

He shrugged. "People say many things they don't actually mean. You'd be surprised."

"No, actually, I wouldn't. I want to know, Lazarus."

"Like Vincent and Nico's, my story isn't a happy one. But then, no vampire's tale actually is, I suppose. My family was slaughtered and I, for the most peculiar of reasons, was saved to lead this life."

Blinking in shock at the unemotional answer. "Slaughtered? You mean slaughtered like animals?" Scarlet whispered, blinking in shock at his unemotional reply.

"Yes," he murmured, his head tilted to one side at her shock.

She frowned and blew out a breath. "You can't be serious? Do you realize that you just said that with an entirely straight face?"

"At the time, I had never seen anything like it. In the two thousand years since, my mind has replayed what I witnessed that day over and over again, and I've seen the same thing happen to many others that were just like me."

Gripping the sheet in her fist and keeping it close to her body, she climbed off the bed and walked towards him. She stopped an inch before him and raised a hand to his face. Her fingers gently traced the line of his jaw. "You actually witnessed their deaths?" she whispered, horror coating her words like an oily film.

Her eyes were trained on the ever changing colors of his eyes, and, as he nodded his answer, she saw them turn a peculiar violet shade before flashing a dazzling cerulean blue. It was the only change in his expression. Had she not been looking for the slightest of nuances, she was certain that she would have thought him to be totally unaffected.

"Your control is astounding," she said in a voice husky with unshed tears, tears that this man could not shed himself.

"Time heals many wounds."

"Not this one, I think."

"Perhaps you are correct," he answered, a wry smile quirking his lips upwards.

"I know I'm correct. Your eyes tell the truth that your mouth is unwilling to admit," she said as she feathered a gentle finger along the line of his eyebrow.

Surprise flickered across his features. "Let's just say that vengeance still rides me," he admitted with a soft grunt.

"What happened?"

"My mother died when I was nine, just after giving birth to my youngest brother. My father managed to marshal himself together after she died, but it was for naught. He died a few years later. The flu was more than just an inconvenience back then. It was a killer. I was left alone to raise my brothers. The location of our farm was imperative to our survival. We were completely out of the way and had no neighbors. My father had always been a loner and had settled on the land for that reason. Surrounded on three sides by mountains, there was only one way in and one way out."

He breathed in deep as though he could still smell the air he'd once breathed as a boy, could still feel the sunlight that had warmed his skin, as if he could still hear the gentle rustling of the crops on the warm breeze.

Scarlet's eyes were trained on his face, and she studied his features minutely, as it was the only way to gauge his true reaction. His eyes had turned hazel, and she knew that thinking of the land made him happy.

He continued his voice heavy with the burden of the sordid tale. "Death was a part of living back then. Very rarely did parents survive to see their children reach maturity. It was hard but because we were isolated, we were left alone and lived off the fat of the land. We could have been taken for slaves or . . . God only knows. I don't like to think of how close we played it for so long.

Eventually, it had to end; I should have known that and made some kind of defense, done something to protect them, dammit."

His jaw tensed and she could see that his fury, his anger over what had happened, was just as strong as it had been two thousand years ago. Her heart sank in her chest when she realized why he was so angry. He wasn't just angry at what had happened, he was angry with himself. It had been his duty to take care of his family and he felt as if he'd failed them. He felt guilty. "How were you to know, Lazarus?" she interjected softly. "You were a boy yourself, not a man. Being the eldest doesn't mean that you weren't still a child! You were a farmer, not a soldier. How could you be expected to think about defense?"

"You can't understand, Scarlet. Life was different back then. Average life expectancy rates were only about thirty-five to forty years. I'd lived almost two quarters of my expected life. I was a man, mellita," he admitted gruffly. "I should have protected them, but I was unable to. One day, out of the blue, we were raided, and, seeing as there were no defenses, it was almost as though I'd welcomed them on to our lands. It was night when they came for us, and they were soldiers trained in stealth. Had it been day time, maybe we would have been able to hide, but not at night when we were in our beds and we were up against something that we'd never even known about. Not only were they soldiers, they were vampire soldiers," he said with a cold laugh. "We were dragged from our beds, beaten, tortured then slaughtered. I watched as they killed my brothers and welcomed the release of death but it did not welcome me. I was . . . less fortunate than my brothers. I remember nothing of the transition, don't remember being reborn. I just knew that I was a monster."

"You're not a monster!" Scarlet exclaimed on a hushed but insistent whisper.

"I felt like one. Do you know what I did when I awoke?"

She shook her head and bit her lip. His voice very rarely broke as he spoke about his ordeal, but every time it did, it broke her heart. She felt it crack deep inside at the torment he and Nico and Vincent had all suffered.

A part of her was disgusted at herself for actually doubting Nico's story originally. Their three tales touched a part of her that had never been touched by a man. MJ and her mother were there, but a man had never gained entry into her heart and with these sad recountings of their histories, they'd stormed down her own defenses and walked in.

How she was to cope with that, she wasn't sure. But deal with it she would.

"I didn't know what I was until I woke up and looked around and saw my brothers on the floor. I'd been tortured with them, the soldiers had toyed with us all . . . done unspeakable things to us, yet I was totally unharmed when I awoke. Every wound completely healed. Fingers that they'd cut off had magically been reattached. I realize now that I was fortunate. They'd left us in the stables and I was sheltered from the sun. I woke at night and weak and I admit, deranged with grief, I buried my brothers' bodies and just walked away from our land. I couldn't stand to be there a moment longer. When the sun's rays began to burn my flesh the next morning, I ran for cover and found a simple stone shelter. I slept and awoke again at night and came across a goat that must have strayed from its herd.

"As a human, I would have killed it and eaten its meat. Yet I could literally sense the throb of its heart; feel the pulse of its blood run through its veins. I didn't want the meat, I wanted the blood and I drained it of life in my desperate hunger for sustenance.

"In all my years of slaying, I feel the most guilt for murdering that hapless beast. There was no need to kill it. In all my years since, I've never killed any creature from which I've supped. I slay the evil of my kind, but not the helpless."

He shook his head. "Ridiculous, isn't it? To feel shame for killing a goat that would have ended up in a stock pot regardless."

"Oh Lazarus," Scarlet whispered. "You can't help the way you feel, baby."

He shrugged and placed a hand on her hip to tug her closer to him. "No, I can't. I won't lie, Scarlet, I killed the vampires that murdered my brothers. It took hundreds of years. But their faces were imprinted on my minds. I enjoyed it too. I may have killed them, but I afforded them a decent respect- something that they didn't bestow upon my brothers or me. From that moment on, I continued on in the same path. Killing the scum of my new race and keeping the humans safe from their evil. I fell upon Vincent in his first year of being a vampire-fortunately for him. Emaciated because he refused to sup, I had to feed him animal blood until he would feed himself. A stubborn man is Vincent. Nico, we came across last century. The need for vengeance that burned within our hearts, burned in his."

"Revenge is a cold bedfellow, Lazarus."

He smiled faintly, the first genuine one he'd bestowed on her in the last half an hour of their conversation.

"As I'm sure you witnessed the night before, Scarlet, our beds are never cold."

Her lips quirked. "So the three bedrooms are just for show, then?"

"Well, we all sleep separately on occasion. Three . . . and now, four, in a bed can be rather confining. Although I think with you in it, none of us would ever retire to our own chambers."

"You're showing your age," she joked. "No one has chambers anymore."

He rolled his eyes. "Have I frightened you?" he asked her, his voice a little more serious now.

"I don't think you have," she answered hesitantly. "I don't want to run away from you, if that's what you mean. I don't like that vengeance still holds a large chunk of you, but why should my opinion matter to you?"

His eyebrow twitched upwards. "You'll see."

She narrowed her eyes and scowled. "I see I'm not allowed the full picture again."

"No, but surely I am," he murmured suavely and tugged at the sheet that covered her. It dropped to the floor and left her standing bare before him. His eyes flickered between delicious colors that told her more than words could express the riot of emotions she inspired within him.

His hands came up to cup her breasts and she shivered as his slightly cool flesh touched her own. Scarlet felt tiny goose pimples flicker up and cover her breasts and stomach. The little bumps were sensitive and she closed her eyes as his fingers tweaked the nubbin of her nipple.

"You like that, mellita?" he asked huskily.

She hummed her agreement. "Very much," he

whispered.

"I'm glad because I like touching you."

"Only like?" she said with a pout and almost purred when one of his hands slid down over the curve of her waist and hip and slid down in between her thighs.

He smiled a little more hungrily now as his fingers touched her wet pussy. Arousal was written over every inch of his face and the fierceness of it made her feel weak at the knees. There was something in that expression that told her it was just for her. That she was the focus of his need and that no one else would do. It shouldn't have pleased her so damned much, but it did.

Separating her legs a little, she stood on tiptoe and pressed herself against him. Her body touched every inch of his length and the crisp feeling of his suit touching every inch of her flesh was like a shock of cold water. Rather than being a turn off, it was a turn on. All of a sudden, hunger fired through her. So powerfully that she felt faint and was relieved for his support.

Her mouth reached for his and she clamped her teeth down on his bottom lip. She pulled it and bit down hard. Releasing him, she smiled at the mark of her teeth on the fleshiest part of his lip. She lathed it with her tongue and soothed the small ache. Lapping at his mouth, she rested her upper arms against his shoulders and used her forearms to hold his head in position. Scarlet flickered her tongue in and out and used pressure to penetrate his mouth.

His came out to play and she undulated her curves against him as her mouth and his worked together to push them into a frenzy of need. His hands clamped around her ass and he pulled her tightly against him. His fingers bit into her inner thighs and with sheer brute strength, he spread them apart and lifted her high against him. Pinning her against the wall with his torso, he freed his arms and began to unzip his fly and release himself from the tight confines of his trousers. His mouth bit at hers as he moved and when his cock was free, he pulled away and began suckling at her throat. His lips and tongue and teeth raked at the skin and she felt pressure as he bit down.

The sheer unexpectedness of the bite made her back arch, with pleasure and not pain. Her reaction was surprising. It completely set her blood afire and she had to cling to him, clamp her knees to his hips to remain upright. The bite seemed to last forever and the emotions that powered through her were so intense that she felt her pussy flood with moisture and small whimpers began to escape her throat. Her hips began to rock against him and she cried out as his cock brushed her intimately.

When he pulled away from her throat, she dug her feet into his butt. The loss of sensation was disconcerting. Her body throbbed with hunger and it was relentless. Her hands fumbled between them and she reached for his cock, whimpering once more with relief as she finally touched it and fondled the shaft with her fingers. The tip was coated with pre-cum and she enjoyed the realization that he was as excited as her.

She pushed herself against him and felt his body buck as her wetness dragged along almost his entire length. With a satisfying grunt, he quickly rearranged his body and slammed his cock into her. She clung to him and buried her face into his neck as he rocked his hips again and again, powering his cock deep into her and dragging against every single nerve ending that her pussy housed. Pleasure like she'd never known, even amongst these three men, made her moan weakly. There was a timelessness to it, like there had been last night. He seemed in no rush, leisurely stoking her need until she was mindless, thrusting into her deeply and slowly- touching everywhere and nowhere.

Her teeth found the curve of his shoulder and she bit down hard as he pressed his torso against hers and kept her upright by the strength in his upper body. His hands then came up to dig into her inner thighs and they inched their way upwards to the very apex where his thumbs slid along the length of her.

Delicately tracing her moist pussy, they stopped at her entrance and dug into her already overfilled cunt. Her teeth released the skin of his shoulder as her head tipped backwards as a climax ripped through her. It was almost painful. Her limbs trembled and her skin was filled with goose flesh. Everywhere was tender and sensitive, too tender and too sensitive. She felt on fire then she felt ice cold. Her eyes were blinded with light that soon went pitch black. A cacophony of noise assailed her ears to be replaced by silence.

She felt everything and nothing as bliss rocked her world on its axis. Thrills of sheer tumultuous excitement pounded through her veins making her breathless with euphoria.

Wrapping her arms about him, she clung to him as her body seemed to shuttle its way along a roller coaster ride. Her heart beat uncomfortably in her chest and her lungs ached as insufficient air reached them. But she'd never felt so damned good in her life.

She registered his orgasm and felt a silly feminine pleasure at being able to satisfy her man. Ridiculous, she thought. But could it be ridiculous when it made her so damned happy? She thought not. Maybe she was turning into a 1950's housewife, one who doted on her hubby and lived and breathed through him.

God, she hoped not. What a bore, she thought on a snort.

"What are you laughing at?" Lazarus asked lazily.

She smiled against his chest. "Nothing."

"That's a lie, but, after what we just did, I think I can forgive you," he conceded generously.

"My thanks, I'm sure," she said as she choked on another laugh.

He nodded benevolently and merely smiled as her laughter now pealed out into the quiet room. He lifted her away from the wall and walked over to the bed. Sitting down at the edge, he plopped backwards and took her with him.

Scarlet sat up and leaned over him. Putting her weight on her hands, which she placed on either side of his head, she smiled down at him.

"I like to see you smile," Lazarus admitted quietly.

"I'd like to see you smile more," Scarlet said with a twitch of a brow.

"In time, mellita, I'm sure you will be bestowed with many of my cheesy grins."

She snorted once again and shook her head. "I wait with bated breath!"

Lazarus' hands came up to cup her buttocks and smoothed a path along the curve of her hip and back. It wasn't a sexual touch, more for comfort and it soothed them both.

"Thank you for sharing your past with me, Lazarus,"

Scarlet said gently.

He nodded slowly. "How could I not tell you, hmm?" he murmured.

"Laz told you about his brothers, then?"

The intruding voice was overly loud in the silent bedroom and both their heads spun around to stare, startled, at the doorway. Nico stood there with a faint smile on his face.

"Indeed he did," Scarlet said after she'd recovered from the shock of his abrupt entry.

"You are blessed," Nico answered with a warmer smile. He walked towards them and placed a kiss on Scarlet's cheek.

"I thought you were supposed to be out finding Elizabeth, Nico," Lazarus said with a frown.

"I was. And then I thought of what I'd find here and I admit, was distracted."

Lazarus rolled his eyes. "More like you wanted to join in!"

"Maybe, I cannot tell a lie, Scarlet," he joked and clasped a hand to his heart.

"I'm sure," she said dryly.

"I must go, Scarlet," Lazarus said softly. "I'll leave you in Nico's capable hands."

She turned to face him and looked into his eyes. The turmoil of emotions in the enchanting orbs was astounding and she cupped his cheek and stroked the line of his jaw, as she'd done earlier to soothe him.

She looked deeply at him and nodded. "Take care," she murmured.

To which he smiled faintly and with that, she was quickly left alone with Nico.

Not exactly a bad exchange!

Chapter Five

The last few hours of the dying afternoon had been relaxing, Scarlet had to admit. Totally unexpected, but relaxing. For some reason, Nico had been happy just to hold and talk to her. While she'd been glad as some muscles were screaming their recent use, the greedy part of her nature was pouting. After all, you couldn't exactly overdose from orgasms, could you?

She had to admit that although it was something she'd never done before, preferring to escape to her own place after sex as soon as physically possible, she'd enjoyed just being with Nico. Enjoyed the feeling of closeness and taken serious pleasure from being held by him. While he had to be one of the sexiest men she'd ever set her eyes on, it was nice to appreciate other parts of his nature and not just his cock and six pack. Scarlet had truly enjoyed his sense of humor, enjoyed his anecdotes and he was extremely relaxing and easy to be with.

But then, she'd noticed that about all three of them. There was no edginess to being with them and she wasn't longing to run away and be by herself. Because with them, it was as comfortable as being by herself. No uneasy silences or edgy tensions. Just a pleasant and relatively peaceful way of whiling away a few hours.

Scarlet had always found the majority of men to have the biggest of egos and more often than not, they were totally and ridiculously inflated. But with Nico, Vincent and Lazarus, they should have enormous egos and yet they didn't. It was refreshing to have her opinion rearranged to include these three guys and learn that not all men were jerk offs that thought entirely with their cocks.

Perhaps it was the men she hung around with that were at fault. Having never sought anything serious from the opposite sex, maybe she'd attracted the wrong kind of guy. Guys like Jack and Blair, who were serial and serious womanizers. Guys who entirely believed that they were God's gift to women. She'd only ever used them for sex because any man who felt like that was just not for her. It had always aggravated her that some men felt like that and she had to admit, that a teeny tiny part of her enjoyed damaging their ego. She didn't do it intentionally, but the end result was always the same.

Take Jack Baines. He had proposed to her after over six months of dating and that had to be her lifetime record of sticking with a guy. Half a year had been hard enough, especially with Jack- one of the most annoying men on

God's green earth. In fact, she deserved a medal for putting up with him for so long! The only reason she had stuck with him, was because his cock had been a good nine inches and he was good in bed. Make that very good in bed.

The vain prick had known it though, which had reduced her pleasure somewhat, but he'd always been ready for a quick fuck and that was what she'd needed in him. Until he'd proposed, she had been happy to skirt along with him, drift along as fuck buddies who occasionally went on dates. He'd been relatively amusing and she'd usually enjoyed her dinner dates with him, but the idea of marrying him? No way! That thought had never popped into her head, only in a nightmare, anyway.

The entire female population of her town seemed to think she was mad, crazy for turning down his proposal. But really, she was the only one with any sense. Jack Baines was in love with one person and that was himself. It would always be like that and probably, if she'd been dense enough to actually marry the jerk, as soon as the ink was dry on their marriage certificate, he would be of chasing some skirt somewhere.

All the women that had flocked around him since high school had given him a superiority complex and rather than treating him appropriately, i.e. like the jerk he was, they fawned over him and let him get away with murder. Not Scarlet. Not in a million years. She would probably go down in history as the only woman to ever turn him down, but then, it seemed as though she was the only woman to have any sense at all. She'd enjoyed totally rearranging his opinion of himself and denting that humongous ego.

Her recent confusion over her feelings for Nico, Lazarus and Vincent had dropped her back down to Earth and with a bang. Scarlet wasn't a one-woman squad dedicated to bashing the ego of any and every arrogant male. Meeting these three extraordinary men had taught her that she was a woman, above and beyond everything else. And if the average woman felt the same way as Scarlet did for these guys but for Jack Baines, then she needed pitying. Because at least Nico, Laz and Vincent were decent human beings, capable of good conversation and better for more than just a good fuck.

It seemed that there was a first time for everything and

in Scarlet's case this was the first time her feelings had ever been engaged in her dealings with the opposite sex. Maybe because Nico was lying right beside her, she wasn't worried about handling those feelings. Sure, they were scary and completely out of the blue, but Scarlet was strong and could handle the depth of emotion they inspired in her. It was something to be cherished not denigrated.

"What are you thinking about?

I can almost hear the cogs whirring in your brain," Nico asked. He sounded a little sleepy and relaxed, which made his Russian accent more pronounced. The husky gravelly timbres sent shivers rattling down her spine. It was as though her very female body couldn't help but react to his intensely masculine voice.

"Nothing really," Scarlet fibbed. As she spoke, she stretched and nuzzled her butt into the down-covered mattress beneath her. Sighing at how comfortable she felt, she smiled up at him reassuringly.

"Nothing, huh? You women, why do you have to be so evasive?" he asked with a snort. Rolling on to his side, he traced a fingertip along the side of her temple and then tapped gently. "I think you're lying," he murmured softly. "In fact, I know you are," he said with a grin. Lowering his head, he pressed a kiss to her cheek and then dotted another one on her jaw and proceeded to nuzzle his nose into her neck.

"Well, not lying exactly, just thinking about nothing in general. It's not often that I can just relax and chill out in bed and just be, you know?

I'm way too busy, I have three jobs and with my studying at night, all my time is taken up with just day to day stuff. So it's nice just to lay here and think about nothing in general."

"Why all the jobs?" he said and cocked a brow in query.

"Money, of course. Well, lack of it, if I'm honest. My mother had no savings to be able to help me pay for my law degree, so it's all been on my shoulders. I have a breakfast and lunch shift of waitressing at a diner, then a secretarial position with a small firm of cleaners, who need me to keep their office in order. Then at the weekends I have another waitressing position in a bar late at night. It's taken me almost seven years, but this year, it's my last," she finished with not insubstantial satisfaction.

"You must be working, what . . . twelve hour days without your studying, right?"

"It's probably a little more than that. Two are part time and the other one is full time. With my studies, it's about eighteen hours a day. So it's definitely weird having nothing to do. But I'm enjoying it!"

"Is our company preventing the tedium from setting in?" he teased.

"Yeah," she said with a laugh. "I'd probably be pulling my hair out by now. My friend was actually a little worried about how I'd react to having nothing to do, especially without her there to entertain me!"

"You have your own personal trio of entertainment now though, huh dorogaya?" he murmured huskily.

"I do indeed. I need to speak to one of the stewards today. I rearranged my booking so that I'd leave after a week; I think I need to rectify that."

Nico looked sheepish. "Lazarus already dealt with that. He reverted your ticket to the original dates."

Scarlet frowned. "How did he do that? Hell, when did he do that?

How did he even know about it?"

"You don't want to know. I don't think even I do! But I do know he did it yesterday."

"I think I should be pissed off that you all went behind my back and changed my ticket," Scarlet scowled as she spoke.

"Should be? Does that mean that you're not?" His voice was hopeful.

"I'm partially annoyed but the lazy part of me is grateful that I don't have to deal with it myself. Don't do it again though, Nico, and tell Vincent and Lazarus as well. I'm used to dealing with things myself, I'm not a frail woman, I don't need men to deal with my business for me," she warned.

"I know you're not. I think Vincent does too, but Lazarus? He works in his own way, milaya. Don't forget, while we're not exactly from your generation, Lazarus' age means that he might as well have been born on another planet! Even though he's become more cosmopolitan as the years pass, where you're concerned, he won't be able to control himself. You will probably grate against his dictates in relation to you, but know that it always to ensure your protection and happiness," Nico told her earnestly.

"Dictates? Hell no, I won't be dictated to, Nico! And that answer just raises more questions and if you're anything like Lazarus, then you won't bother answering them either. All I got from him was: 'You'll find out eventually.' Or, 'You'll understand with time.' Do you know how frustrating that is?"

"I can imagine. But it's best if you handle what Laz is referring to, in your own time and in your own pace. You may find that you like not being in control all of the time, milaya. We're not the weak men you're probably used to dealing with from your own generation."

"Maybe I like having pansies for boyfriends! Plus I know what my time and pace is. You don't have to set it for me!" she grumbled.

"We're not doing anything of the kind," he argued. "But I can understand why you would feel like that. Please, just don't be annoyed at Lazarus. He's behaving in the only way he knows how, so keep that in mind, angel."

She rolled her eyes. "I don't see why I should, but I will. You bear in mind that I'm not used to this Nico. I'm in charge usually, so please recognize how hard this is for me, okay?"

"Yes, I understand. But it's really for your own protection, Scarlet," he told her sincerely and with a sigh she relented.

What choice did she have with that puppy dog look on his face?

There was some truth to his words. Although they weren't always rigidly controlled, it had been nice not to be in the driving seat these last few days. She was so used to taking charge of any and every situation with men that it was unheard of for someone else to be in control. These three men, although considerate and kind, were each Alphas. They wouldn't be led around on a string. Even though they all had their quirks, they weren't pushovers and that she had come to realize that so soon in the vacation could only be a good thing.

"I don't know what I need to be protected from, but no matter. I'm hungry," she said mournfully.

"Order something then, dorogaya."

"Aren't you hungry? Lazarus and Vincent didn't eat anything when they were with me, but then I suppose they drink blood. Yuck. Will you eat with me?"

"Of course, Scarlet. Do you want to eat in one of the restaurants?"

"Could we?" she said a little excitedly.

The idea of eating with him seemed so ordinary in relation to thoughts of bloodsucking vampires that at this minute, when she was feeling out of every comfort zone she possessed, it was nice to feel as though she were going on a date.

"Naturally, I will come to your suite and wait while you dress and then we can eat at a restaurant of your choice, milaya."

"That would be fabulous," she told him on a smile and hopped out of bed in search of her clothes. Which had once again gone walkabout?

* * * *

"Any sight of her?" Lazarus asked Vincent gruffly.

Leaning against the deck rail, Lazarus looked into the setting sun and waited for Vincent's reply. Two thousand years ago, the weak rays from a sunset would have scorched his skin hideously. Now, in the new millennium, he could stand here and behave like a human. Despite having spent the majority of his life as a vampire, where nothing was ordinary and everything was unexpected, he enjoyed the feeling of normalcy. Relished the feel of the heat of the dying sun against his face. It was something he never took for granted. Even after experiencing it more times than a human could even dream of.

Heat and warmth was something that every young vampire missed. Even though it wasn't necessary for survival, as it was with humans, by the time the young ones were old enough to not react to the sun's damaging rays, they all relished the feel of heat and the lack of dampness and cold that they thrived on during their early years of being undead.

Vincent sighed and Lazarus redirected his gaze to him. It should have been a happy time for them all, finding Scarlet-their blood mate, was a relief and should have been for Vincent as well. Lazarus knew that their slowness at discovering Elizabeth's whereabouts was troubling him, but looking at him now, Lazarus realized that there was more to the almost frightened look on his brother-by-bond's face.

"No, not really. I know I'm being watched- that's about all I do know!

But I haven't seen her. She must be damned good to keep herself hidden so thoroughly," Vincent admitted with a grunt. He sighed as he looked out to sea and shook his head in annoyance.

Lazarus tilted his head to the side with a frown. "It's not that she's good, Vincent. It's her age," he said comfortingly. "She can use that against you, that's all. I've seen her a few times actually. She's not unstoppable. They never are."

"You've seen her? Then why are we still looking for her? And why haven't you terminated the threat?!" Vincent asked with a frown.

"Time and a place, Vincent, I can't just kill her in the middle of a deck filled with people and human members of staff, can I? Hardly practical and extremely messy!" he replied wryly.

Vincent snorted. "Alright. Understood. At least you're more than a match for her. I know I said that Nico would be better off guarding Scarlet, I think I will be of no use either. I can't see her, I can sense her watching me, but that's all. Will you be alright dealing with her yourself?"

"Vincent, the day I can't handle a thousand year old vampire is the day that I need to be slain myself! Especially this one. She's arrogant and thinks she's unstoppable. Even worse than that, she believes she can righteously kill humans, as they're an unimportant species. She leaves herself open to attack and I'll be there when the time is right."

"I'm not saying you can't deal with her, I'm just questioning whether it's wise, that's all," Vincent said smoothly.

"You don't need to worry about that. Scarlet's presence has stopped the coldness that was invading my soul."

"Are you sure? We haven't even claimed her yet! Surely it's too soon to feel that way?"

"It isn't too soon, as time doesn't matter. You should

realize that by now, Vincent. Just having her here helps."

"Maybe," Vincent said, sounding totally unconvinced.

"Don't worry. I'll be fine."

"Even though I'm probably of no use to you, I'll definitely be around, Laz. No way I'm leaving you to handle her on your own. There's just no point in me seeking her out. I'm useless. Might as well be human. My senses don't pick anything up about her at all."

"Not to worry. She should be easy to handle but until I can get her, she could be dangerous. It's imperative that you care for Scarlet and keep both her and Nico safe. Elizabeth is a liability and with the amount of time we're spending with Scarlet, Elizabeth is going to scent her as a weakness and target her to get to us. If we lose Scarlet, Vincent, that's it. You know that, right?" Lazarus warned somberly.

"Don't be ridiculous. We're not going to lose Scarlet."

"Life has a funny way of playing tricks on a person, Vincent. We know that more than most. Be vigilant in your care of her, that's all I'm saying."

Vincent nodded.

"Is there anything wrong?" Lazarus asked softly, directing the conversation from himself to Vincent.

"Wrong? No. Not really," Vincent replied with a frown.

"Are you sure? You seem very concerned about something?"

He looked as though he were about to argue, but instead Vincent laughed wryly and shook his head. "Strange how you know me so well."

Lazarus nodded his head slowly in acceptance of that statement. He knew both Vincent and Nico far better than they realized. He said nothing, not wanting to discourage Vincent from talking about whatever was bothering him.

"She's more than I ever imagined and I guess I'm feeling guilty."

"About Véronique?" Lazarus guessed. "Why?"

Vincent nodded and blew out a heavy breath. "Because my feelings for Scarlet are so much more powerful than my feelings for Véronique were."

"There's no shame in that, Vincent. It's been over three hundred years since you lost her and you were a young man. It doesn't help, but a blood mate . . . well, they're the other half of your soul. How can that not feel perfect and astoundingly powerful?" Lazarus said with a shrug.

"It doesn't matter. I promised to always love her. She was to be my wife, Lazarus. I feel guilty that I'm not being true to her."

"Vincent, you can only be true to someone when they're alive. When they're dead, they're gone. Véronique died a long time ago, she doesn't know whether or not you have been true to her and if I'm wrong and the dead do look over the living, then I'm sure she'd be very pleased that you've found someone to make you happy! Two hundred years is a hellishly long time to mourn someone. In fact, it's more than that, it's unhealthy!

"Not only that, but when you were alive and were to be married to her, she was very likely the woman for you. Had your life panned out as planned by both your families, you would have married, had a few dozen children and then died of gout, for God's sake. Being a vampire is nothing like being a human male. You should know that by now. But I don't think you do. You're so hooked on what might have been that you don't recognize how vital Scarlet is to the vampire in you. You're still thinking with human sensibilities and that will lead to nothing but misery, my friend."

"I do recognize how important she is to me, Lazarus," Vincent admonished. "Mon Dieu! I'm not dim! The realization that she means more to me than anything I've ever experienced, is why I feel so damned guilty!"

"But there's no need to feel guilty!"

"Perhaps there isn't, but I can't help it. I'm sure as time passes, this will change. It's just growing accustomed to it. That's all. I don't think it will be hard!"

"Good, because it shouldn't be hard. You can't imagine how difficult it's been for me, over two thousand years as a bloodsucker and I've only just found her. It should bother me that I have to share her, but because we're all close and bonded by more than blood, it doesn't. Be thankful that you've only had to wait three centuries, my friend. After twenty of them, you start to believe that the time will never come, that you will never be completed."

"I am grateful, Lazarus. Please don't believe that I'm not," Vincent told him earnestly.

He nodded slowly and released a measured breath. "I'm glad to hear it."

"Of course, it's only been a little while since we met her, that's all. Although it seems like months, it's only been days. Add to this complicated brew a damned evil vampiress, is it any wonder I'm a little out of sorts? I don't like that Elizabeth hasn't been easy to find, Lazarus. Yes, you've seen her, but she's managed to hide from us. It doesn't bode well. We should have been able to find her today, but now, the sun is dying and the moon is about to rise and still, she lives. Scarlet is distracting us from our purpose and while it doesn't bother me, I don't like that the longer Elizabeth is on board, the more she learns about us . . .Which gives her control of this situation and leaves us in the dirt, perhaps in possible danger and our mate's life in peril! What do you want to do? Keep on searching for her, or return to Scarlet's side?"

"Scarlet is a distraction, Vincent. I make no bones about that. But on the other hand, as I've told you, she strengthens us imperceptibly. You won't have realized, but you'll be a far stronger slayer from now on. The only reason you probably haven't realized, is that Elizabeth is a good deal older than you. You're right that the longer she lives, the more time she has to regroup and shore her defenses, but I wouldn't worry about that. Like I said, she's far too arrogant for that. I think at this moment, when really, she should be doing exactly that-shoring up her defenses, Elizabeth is more than likely engaged in her evening entertainments. We won't hear a peep from her this evening," Lazarus bet with a knowing smile.

"Why? What's going on?"

"An orgy."

"Crap, you're kidding?"

"No. On the top level, one of the best staterooms on the ship has been hired for the occasion," Lazarus admitted with a smirk.

"How incredible . . . ." Vincent shook his head with a wry smile.

"What?"

"A few days ago, we would have joined in and enjoyed ourselves. . . Now, I haven't the slightest interest."

"Ah, that's the joy of having a blood mate," Lazarus

said with a grin and smacked Vincent on the shoulder. "She can make you cum in less than thirty seconds, make you feel like an untried boy of fourteen. Well, she could if she put her mind to it," he admitted dryly.

"It's far too fun prolonging her agony than it is to cum so quickly," Vincent told him. His eyes were flaring with lust at the thought of Scarlet and how she turned him on.

"That's very true, my friend. I never thought I'd see the day that I wouldn't be bothered about climaxing quickly!"

"I know! I thought she was going to explode the other night! When she started sobbing, remember?"

Lazarus smiled slowly and nodded with a pleased smirk gracing his lips. "Oh yes, I remember explicitly. I think we should find our blood mate. Knowing Nico and his stomach, they're more than likely in a restaurant somewhere. We'll meet them and enjoy the rest of our evening . . . . Especially seeing as our prey is determined to do exactly the same thing!"

* * * *

"I can't believe how lazy I've been this trip," Scarlet complained. Slipping the half-full dessert spoon into her mouth, she finished the last bite of her deliciously decadent coffee liqueur cheesecake with a sigh and slumped back in her seat glumly.

Almost immediately though, she perked up. It was impossible to be seated across from one of the most gorgeous men in the universe and not feel slightly good about oneself! Hell, especially when he would make Adonis think he looked ugly and in that suit. Dammit. They were killing her. She'd never thought that she was into the corporate look but all three of them, somehow managed to make a jacket and a pair of trousers seem like sex personified.

Tailored to within an inch of his muscular frame, the suit added to his aura of intense masculinity. He looked powerful and sexy and hell, did he turn her on! Her pussy was continuously wet around these three. They were turning her into a nymphomaniac and while, she'd always had an extremely high sex drive, it had never been like this before. Her nipples burnt and itched with the need for their mouths to sup from them. Her body was flushed and rosy from arousal and her pussy was already prepared for their cocks.

While it was odd beyond belief to sit here and eat a dinner when every inch of her was ready to fuck, she was slowly becoming accustomed to it. Her need was always simmering at the back of her mind and she knew that she had but to say the word and Nico would swirl her off back to one of their suites and fuck her until her eyes were crossed.

"I wouldn't say you've been lazy, exactly," Nico broke into her revelry with a wry snort. "Answer carefully, my ego is on the line here."

She chuckled. "Well, okay I've burnt some calories and spent more time passed out than awake. Sex is good for weight loss and insomnia and is damned good for my self-esteem," she added with a grin. "But no, I'm on one of the newest cruise liners in the world and I've eaten a few meals and done nothing else apart from study a few ceilings! Sex can be done anytime, I want to do something fun."

Scarlet thought it wise to do the sightseeing now, because she had a feeling that as the days passed, her need for them would treble at the thought of losing them at the end of the vacation.

Nico chuckled and nodded. "They were nice ceilings though. Six star ones at that. And if you don't say you relished why you were studying the ceilings then I think my heart will break."

His lips twitched in amusement as she cocked a disbelieving brow.

Heartbroken?

She wished!

Hell, she would jump through hoops if he felt even a smidgen for her!

The balance of power had definitely shifted from her to them and although she wasn't entirely okay with it, she was slowly growing accustomed to it. She would challenge any woman to not be overwhelmed with these three guys after her. It would be so easy to fall in love with them, dammit. Too easy, maybe she was already there.

The thought was like walking into a wall. She blinked quickly and blew out a deep breath before ignoring it and focusing all of her attention on Nico.

Instead of stamping her foot and screaming out her rage

at fate, she rolled her eyes. "Oh the melodrama! Ceilings aren't exactly the focal point of a room and you've seen one and you've seen them all! I want to do something special. Apart from ceiling-spotting! There has to be something on this damned boat that is innovative and fun, do you know of anything?"she replied saucily.

He shrugged. "There's a cinema."

"Is that it? I mean, I didn't, but you did- you must have paid a fortune to stay on this boat and that's all there is to do at night? Watch movies?"

"Well, I assume there's more than that, but I came across it today."

"I don't really want to watch a movie," she said on a sigh.

"I think most of the innovative activities are daytime ones. Like the wave machine in the pool, things like that. For night, there are a few clubs and the restaurants. We're adults, we're supposed to make our own night time entertainment," he joked and moved his eyebrows up and down naughtily.

She laughed. "Well, that's for later."

"You promise?"

Scarlet sat up from her slouched position and laid her hand atop the one he had resting on the table's surface. "Promise.", Smiling slowly, she gently stroked her fingers along his knuckles and along the length of his hand.

"Anyway, you've never watched a movie with me," he said with a wink and captured her roaming fingers in his palm.

She hummed in pleasure. "Okay, you're making a movie sound more appealing!"

"I should hope so!"

"Do you want to go now?"

Laughing, he nodded at her glass of wine. "Have you finished that?" he sighed.

She nodded. "Come on, I'm dying to know what's unusual about watching a movie with you."

He grinned. "Well, I'm glad you find me intriguing, milaya. This evening hasn't been a complete waste of time."

"Charming!" Scarlet huffed.

Nico stood and tugged her from her seat. "Thank you

kindly!"

Walking out of the restaurant, Scarlet's hand was tucked into the crook of Nico's arm. As they moved out of the dining hall, Scarlet's eyes couldn't help but fall upon a group of vampire wannabes.

"I saw this group when I first boarded and thought they were nuts. Are they really vampires?" she asked with a frown.

Nico laughed. "No. They're not vampires. The humans on board the ship are actually slaves. Apart from the staff. They're just in costume."

"Slaves?" Scarlet squeaked. Her very modern sensibilities shocked to the core.

"Blood slaves," he clarified. "They're attached to a vampire somewhere else on the ship."

"Why the hell was there a competition to win tickets for this particular cruise? Surely it was dangerous?"

"In a way, yes, because, like you, there was a chance that the winners would learn about vampires. But, at the same time, the company is only holding a themed cruise. They don't actually believe in vampires."

"So it's just a huge joke that's backfired? Because now the ship is filled with vampires!"

"I suppose so. The company doesn't actually know that though. I guess it's like hiding in plain sight. The vampires can be themselves on board this ship and none of the staff will think any the wiser."

"Why the hell would they decide to have a vampire themed cruise?

Surely it would have been more profitable to just open to the public in a more ordinary way?"

"God knows," Nico shrugged. "Either way, I don't think the company will mind. All vampires are rich. It comes with the territory. They amass huge fortunes as they grow, so the cruise liner won't exactly have lost any money. In fact, they'll probably have made more than if they'd just opened up to ordinary Joes. I imagine if it hadn't been a vampire-themed cruise, all the normal cabins would have sold out and maybe fifty percent of the suites. I know for a fact that all the suites were sold first and that every single double and single cabin has been taken. It's absolutely bursting to the seams."

"I still can't believe that I'm believing in what you three are. I'm actually discussing vampires with you-it just seems incredible to me! A few days ago I would have thought of calling out the doctors! I just don't believe in stuff like this."

Nico shrugged again. "You have to believe the truth. You couldn't exactly think otherwise, could you? How did Lazarus prove to you he existed?"

"Well, he stood there and I believed he existed."

"You know what I mean!"

"Yeah," she said with a laughed. "Just being obnoxious." Scarlet pointed to her canines. "He showed them to me. They were much longer versions than mine though. He bit me twice, too."

Nico halted.

Rather than dragging him along, she stopped too.

"He bit you? Twice? How did you react?"

"Well . . . actually . . . it turned me on." She felt her skin flush uncomfortably at the admission.

"It did?"

She shifted awkwardly and ducked her head to hide her red cheeks. "Yeah. Well, I don't know why, but I'm really comfortable with you three. I don't think you'd hurt me, and I certainly don't think Lazarus would either," she answered and shrugged her confusion at that admission.

"I'm glad to hear that," Nico answered huskily. That aphrodisiac for an accent was strong as he spoke. "Because we wouldn't dream of hurting you."

"There you go then. Why were you so shocked?"

"Because I expected you to freak out and run."

She snorted. "I may be a woman, but I've got as big a pair of balls as you three!"

Scarlet grinned as Nico laughed heartily at her quip. She smacked him on the arm. "Well- are you taking me to the theater or what?" she grumbled.

"Come, my lady, to the theater we go," he said and bowed low.

As they walked down the stairs to the next floor, Scarlet allowed herself to be directed to wherever the cinema actually was on the ship. She enjoyed people watching, and rarely got a chance to do any of it, what with her hectic life. Moving through the crowds of people, she spotted more of the vampire's slaves and shuddered at the prospect and thought about what it actually entailed.

"Why are they slaves?" Scarlet asked.

"Most of them probably asked to be made into slaves. Some will have been forced."

"Forced?"

"Well, if their vampire was attracted to them and it wasn't reciprocated, it's a surefire way to get the attraction flowing on both sides."

"You have to be kidding. It's like a love potion for the undead?"

"Well," Nico conceded with a scratch to the tip of his nose. "Maybe a lust potion. Most slaves are cool with it once they realize what they are. It means they live longer and have a better quality of life. Vampires are wealthy and it's like a code that they take care of their slaves."

"So I'm basically looking at human prostitutes and vampire Johns?"

"Yeah," Nico laughed. "To be fair though, some humans will be blood mates"

"Blood mates?"

"Soul mates, but joined by blood as well as souls."

"Wow, that's telling me nothing!" she complained and tugged on his arm.

"Well, I'm not a vampire. You're better off asking Laz or Vincent. I can tell you about werewolf mates."

"Oh my God, you're blowing my mind here!"

"I hope to blow it in a completely different way soon," he promised on a sultry murmur.

"Okay, I shall look forward to that!"

"Glad to hear it. Anyway, you won't be seeing a lot of the humans around here for much longer. There's an orgy tonight in one of the staterooms. Most of the ship will be there."

"You're kidding!" Scarlet asked astonished. She blinked her eyes at the thought of what an orgy would entail. "I've never been to an orgy before."

"You surprise me!"

"Hey!" She whacked him on the arm and rolled her eyes as he chuckled at her.

"Well, it does. If you're not used to those kinds of sexual situations, I would have thought you would have been rather overwhelmed with our own particular situation. That's all."

"Oh," she murmured, mollified at his explanation. "It sounds intriguing," she said wistfully.

"Tonight is not the best time to experience your first orgy, dorogaya. It's dangerous and I would never allow you to be in any danger!" he told her stoutly.

"Why is it dangerous?"

"Sexual tension is high and the adrenaline is pumping in the atmosphere. It's heady and if you're not used to that and not claimed in any way, then you're likely to find yourself bitten."

"Shit. Really?"

"Yes."

"You sound like you've been to quite a few of them." Even though she'd attempted to remove any and all traces of jealousy from her tone, she knew immediately that she'd failed. His face seemed to light up, but not with laughter . . . . That was more confusing than anything. He seemed almost pleased.

"Before you, milaya." He bent down and bestowed a few kisses on her nose and forehead and then swept his hand forwards. "We're here. What movie would you like to watch?"

Blinking at the tenderness in his voice and the actual words he'd uttered, Scarlet gulped and took a few seconds to take in her surroundings. She stood in the center of the theater hall and realized that he'd actually led her into the foyer and she hadn't known. She'd been so under his spell that he could have invited her to jump over the deck rail and she would probably have complied!

She sought out the movie list and almost groaned at the list of movies that ship had to offer. "God, did they all have to be about vampires?"

Nico chuckled. "Well, I suppose they're true to their theme. We should applaud them for that, milaya."

"Well, you can applaud all you want, because I sure as hell won't! I don't like these kinds of movies."

"I've already told you, dorogaya, you've yet to watch a film with me," he said huskily.

Immediately, she didn't give a damn about the movies' content. She just wanted to be in the darkened hall with

Nico.

Her eyes flashed along the movie list once more and spotted one of the latest films that had hit the teenage and adult world by storm. Millions of people couldn't be wrong, could they? Sighing, she pointed her finger to her choice and Nico bought their tickets and led her into the theater hall itself.

The lights were on, and she smiled as she took in the décor of the place. It was unlike any cinema she'd ever been in. Normally they had uncomfortable seats and sticky floors. This one was most definitely luxurious. The seats were like armchairs, cushioned to within an inch of their lives and big enough for two. That fact more than any of the other luxuries stuck fast in her mind.

Nico led them straight to the back of the theater and sat himself on one of the seats. He then reached for her and tipped her backwards so that she landed on top of his lap.

"So that's your idea, is it?" she asked as she squirmed to find a comfortable position and inadvertently rubbed his cock. She felt it grow hard beneath her. Damn, she loved to tease!

"You knew very well that this was my intention!" he murmured on a growl.

She hid a smile. Whenever he was turned on or slightly uncomfortable, his English became very stilted. It was a quality that made him endearing to her. She supposed it also helped that he found her so attractive that just sitting on his lap made him erect. But then, she was a woman, wasn't she? Who wouldn't feel damned good at being able to arouse this man?

The theater wasn't exactly crowded and she supposed that it was because almost all of the ship would be heading to that damned intriguing orgy. She had to admit that a part of her really wanted to go and see what was happening. And while, she had her own personal love slaves here, so she didn't have to go looking for anymore, she was curious and inquisitive as to what would be happening there.

"I'm glad that it's empty. Your squeals would have made everyone in the crowd unhappy!"

"I don't squeal!" she told him indignantly and looked around the otherwise empty theater.

"You do squeal. But don't worry. I like it. And I like

making you squeal more. There's no shame in it!"

She harrumphed and dug an elbow into his belly.

He chuckled mercilessly at her feeble assault.

She hadn't been trying to hurt him, but his mocking laughter made her want to do some real damage, but she thought better of it. Who knew what his retaliation would be?

But, she thought defiantly, she did not squeal, dammit!

"I take it you're as crazy about this film as the rest of the western world seems to be?"

"Ha! No. Teen girls falling in love with vampire boys isn't exactly my thing. I grew out of that kind of film when I was about fifteen. I picked it because I wouldn't care about missing the movie," she admitted without an ounce of shame.

"You knew I planned to have my wicked way with you, hmm?"

"I had an inkling," she admitted, smiling slowly at him.

All of a sudden, the lights went dark and the screen flickered to life.

Almost immediately, he pounced on her, his lips seeking and finding hers.

She relaxed into his kiss.

He licked at her lips and then began to nip the fleshy fullness of them.

She pressed herself against him and began to maneuver herself so that she was sitting astride his lap. Sitting sideways meant that she couldn't get close enough to him and it ratcheted up her frustration, something she didn't need when Nico was aiming to drive her crazy in more ways than this!

She'd worn a mid-thigh length skirt for dinner, it was an evening skirt despite its shortness, and she had teamed it with an extremely revealing top. The sleeves hugged her upper arms, leaving her shoulders bare. It was almost like a gypsy-style blouse, but the cut was such that there was a deep V at her breasts, which meant that they were almost entirely on show. Only her nipples and the outer curve were hidden from view. It was a difficult top to wear and definitely one to entice, but the discomfort of wearing the damned thing had been completely washed away by three things. The look in Nico's eyes when he'd first seen her,

the erection that had tented his pants when that look had
been transmitted from his brain to his lower body, and the
ease in which his hand could cup her at this exact moment
in time.

His fingers rasped along the nipple, tweaking it and
torturing it into a nicely erect little peak. She exhaled
deeply as he flicked the nubbin with his nail. Closing her
eyes, she cinched her skirt higher to free her legs a little
and moved closer to him, until they were almost chest to
chest. She sighed as his mouth ate at hers, as his tongue
thrust into her like she wanted his fingers to thrust into her
cunt. His lips incited her lust and made her want to howl
with frustration as she felt as though she would
spontaneously combust from a need so powerful it would
make a bomb seem like a small firework. Her hips rocked
against him and she began to murmur her need against his
lips. Her hands sought out his and when Scarlet eventually
found one, she dragged it to her thighs and slipped it
underneath the skirt that still covered her modesty. Well,
partially anyway.

She hissed at the first touch.

"No panties?" he asked with a grunt.

Scarlet almost smiled at his low groan, but it was too
painful to do anything but focus on his fingers. Two of the
tips were massaging her clit, while the other three had
plunged into her. Her need was almost embarrassing. She
could feel her juices slip down her cunt and knew that his
trouser front would be wet from her arousal. Perhaps she
should have felt embarrassed, but how could she? It wasn't
her fault, was it? She couldn't help that he turned her on so
much that her cunt had prepared itself for him in less than
two minutes flat!

Squeezing her inner muscles around his fingers, she
hissed as he dragged them in and out slowly but rubbed her
clit quickly. The contrary sensations were powerful and her
body felt battered by the onslaught of feeling his touch
inspired. When he removed the three fingers from her cunt,
she cried out, but almost screamed, when his wet and
slippery fingers began to rub at her clit. The sensation was
too much to stand. They moved faster and faster, her juices
merely increased his speed and when her climax hit her,
she fully admitted, that she squealed.

She squealed and moaned and groaned and whimpered as release was hers. Her body sang triumphantly as it whooshed its way through her system, touching everywhere and making it feel rejuvenated and fresh with excitement.

Collapsing against his front, Scarlet rested her head in the crook of his throat and shoulder. Almost whimpering at the pure undiluted essence that was Nico at that pulse point, she moved restlessly against him as need began to worm its way through her once more. Hell, she was seriously getting greedy.

On unsteady legs, she managed to climb from his lap and dropped down to her knees, which he gladly separated for her. She smoothed her hands over the length of his thighs and inched the tips over his iron-hard stomach. She explored his torso before settling at his belt and beginning to undo it. When it was unfastened, she quickly undid the zipper and made him wait a full minute before she touched him and freed him from the cage of his pants.

She actually counted sixty seconds and was surprised at how long it seemed. Despite the sound of the movie going on behind her, she could easily hear his breathing quicken, could see his chest rise and fall faster than before. Felt the minute tremble that overset him as she made him wait.

A hiss was her reward when she released him and she felt almost like grinning as she felt the soaking wet tip of his cock. She lay his cock against his belly and rested it there for a moment. The flicker of light from the movie highlighted its impressive length and girth.

"Don't you like this suit?" he asked gruffly.

She frowned up at him in confusion.

"You've destroyed the trousers and now my shirt," he told her with a wry grin.

She smiled and grabbed his cock, ensuring that she dragged the wet tip against the material even more. She heard his quick laugh and bent forward and lapped her tongue against the wet navy silk. Supping at the seed there, she then returned to his cock and in view of his good behavior, sucked all of him into her mouth. He hissed and his hands came down to cup her head. Knowing that he wanted to take charge from here on in, she allowed him to take control and let him fuck her mouth. Her hands quickly wrapped themselves around the base of his shaft, tightly so that he wouldn't cum so quickly but covered enough of his large length so that she wouldn't choke to death!

He moved quickly and dragged her head up and down so fast that she almost felt like a yo-yo. There was something about it though, that turned her on hugely. She tightened her mouth around him as much as she could and let him have his way with her. Removing one hand, she placed it around his balls and fondled them. Squeezing them hard, she heard his groan and almost smiled at the thought of him being almost entirely on edge.

Her concentration was so intensely focused on Nico's pleasure that she almost bit down hard when she felt fingers slide along her slit. Only the quick realization that it was Lazarus protected Nico from being severely maimed!

She almost felt like smacking Lazarus for frightening her to death, but his fingers made her back arch as they slid right to the heart of her and thrust. Once. Twice. Before he removed them from her and slid them around the crack of her ass.

She'd tried anal sex once but hadn't liked it, and, almost as soon as the tip of her partner's cock had touched her there, she'd pulled away and had refused to go through with it. In theory, anal sex would be hard with Lazarus, his cock was big and wide and it was a tight fit in her pussy, never mind her virginal ass, but she didn't say anything. She let him prepare her, let him drag her juices to her ass to lubricate her and let his big fingers spread her open and scissor her so that she could accept him.

She wasn't overly frightened or nervous, because she knew they would never hurt her, but also, because she was turned on at the idea of Lazarus in her ass. It meant that one of the other two could be in her pussy and the thought sent shivers over her spine. It was only then that she noticed Nico had freed her mouth and that her head was resting against his upper thigh. That he could release her without her noticing should have freaked her out. But she was growing accustomed to being a little out of it where these guys were concerned!

A slight frazzle of tension filled the air for a second and Scarlet realized that Lazarus had deemed her ready for penetration. No words had been spoken, but she knew it like she knew she was a redhead. Her thoughts were merely confirmed when she was lifted away from Nico and rearranged on the floor. Her butt was high in the air, but Vincent-she knew it was he, because of his scent- pressed her head down to the floor. She rearranged her arms so that she could lean her head atop them and waited for what felt like centuries for something to happen.

When it did, it was almost anticlimactic. Scarlet had to admit to being a little nervous. But it seemed that he'd coated himself in a copious amount of her juices and lubricated her asshole sufficiently that he slid in painlessly. The only discomfort came from his size. He'd penetrated her so easily that only when all of him was inside her, did she moan out at the unusual sensation of complete and utter fullness. Thanking God that he was giving her time to accustom herself to being fucked here, she tried to even out her breathing and relax. Because she knew that relaxing was the only way she would be able to accept his penetration.

After what felt like hours but must have been a good five minutes, she breathed out deeply and managed to relax a little around him. He took this as a sign and began to rock his hips gently back and forth. Each slow thrust made her cry out. But not in pain, pleasure. The sensation was overwhelmingly complex. Somehow it shouldn't have been pleasurable, but it was. It was such a powerful feeling that she gladly welcomed deeper and faster thrusts. He brought her to the edge of what felt like an apocalyptic climax before he stopped. She almost screamed in frustration, then decided to whimper as they rearranged her body from its current position. The new position made her feel lightheaded. The way she was situated, made her feel as though she were impaled and it wasn't a pleasant sensation.

She felt almost as though she were floundering and felt beads of sweat coat her from top to bottom at his cock's branding. She was now seated upon his lap, he'd spread his legs so that she was cushioned between his thighs somewhat, but until he pressed her back against his chest, Scarlet couldn't settle. She began to tremble from this deeper, newer penetration and soft whimpers escaped her throat.

Hearing them, Lazarus spat out an order and suddenly, Vincent was in front of her and Nico was behind Lazarus.

Her mind was dazed, but not enough so that she couldn't question what the hell they were doing! She felt herself being pushed backwards and realized that Vincent was doing the pushing and Nico was controlling how far backwards they fell. When Lazarus was fully against the floor, Vincent unzipped his cock and pressed it to her wet pussy. Realizing what they were about to do, she cried out and shook her head, but Lazarus shushed her and tugged her head to the side so that he could engage her mouth with his own.

Slowly, slowly, Vincent slid into her. Each inch was excruciating, filled with so much pleasure/pain that her mind couldn't cope with it. She willingly threw herself into Lazarus' kiss because Scarlet knew that her mind couldn't handle this new sensation that was pushing through her like a rocket powering into space.

When every inch of Vincent's cock was inside her quivering pussy, a shaky Scarlet pulled away from Lazarus' mouth and tried to assimilate what the hell her body was feeling.

She heard Lazarus snort and almost jumped when he whispered in her ear.

"Don't pretend that doesn't turn you on, mellita." He hummed his pleasure and his hand moved in between Scarlet and Vincent's bodies to slide down to the apex of her thighs. Once there, his fingers caressed her clit for a second before sliding down to her entrance and massaging some of her juices along the surface of her cunt. "You're squeezing me and Vincent too tightly and you're far too wet not to be aroused."

Her eyes flickered shut at his words, but she didn't need him to tell her that she was turned on. Scarlet knew she was, could feel the high-pitched throb of arousal as it flickered through her bloodstream. She quickly opened her eyes and watched as the same pleasure/pain she was feeling, flashed clear as day on Vincent's face. She lifted a hand and cupped his cheek, he looked deeply at her and whatever he saw there, must have reassured him, for almost as one, they all began to move. Her back arched at the feeling of those two cocks, and she felt almost as though her brain was going to blow a fuse.

Sensation after sensation began to assail her, too

numerous to count and too powerful to understand. She felt every inch being touched and massaged and caressed, while she continued to feel that mind blowing sense of being impaled, but now on two cocks instead of just the one. A part of her enjoyed being in the middle of the excitement, as it were, but she would have liked to have taken a closer look. Something told her, however, that whenever she was in their bed, be it for three days or three hundred years, that would never happen. She would always be at the center of their attention. How she knew that, she had no idea. But Scarlet recognized it as the truth.

The constant rocking and jostling thrusts seemed to shock her system more powerfully than the smooth plunges she was used to. The air seemed to be filled with sparks of arousal and desire and it merely added to the feelings that were hurrying through her. The constant bombardment to her senses shorted every circuit in her brain until she came. There was nothing poetic about this climax. She didn't soar through a sea of pleasure. Nor did she reach heights she'd never before seen. This climax was so intense, her body took over. Bombarded by so much, it began to shut down, bit by bit. Pleasure singed the fuses to every part of her body until there was nothing working and she passed out.

* * * *

Elizabeth enjoyed being right. It was something that happened more and more often over the years. She'd seen and experienced far too much to be caught out often and so it was with no surprise that she watched the three slayers hover over their mate as they pulled their cocks out of her limp body. She could scent their concern for their mate and almost sneered at the weak emotion that was powering through the younger vampire and the were. Lazarus, as per usual, was impossible to read. But she knew that he too would be feeling some worry for the woman he'd just fucked in the ass.

The sight of his cock sliding slowly into the woman's ass had been a turn on. That she had to admit. She would have liked to have fucked Lazarus, all that visceral power and knowledge and wisdom that was contained in his head was a huge aphrodisiac for her. But she knew that there was no chance of him fucking her now he had this feeble human woman. A part of her envied him finding his mate. In fact, a lot of emotions were roiling in her mind and most of them were beyond her comprehension. Lust, jealousy, need, envy, anger, hate.

It was unusual for her to feel much emotion in regards to the opposite sex. After so many years of toying with them, she grew bored with them almost instantly. But Lazarus intrigued her more than she cared to admit. She watched as they arranged the woman's clothes and the werewolf lifted her into his arms and began to walk out of the theater. Elizabeth knew without being told that they were going to pretend the woman had fainted and would use that as an excuse when they walked her through countless hallways to reach their suite.

She followed them silently. Pleased that Lazarus was so focused on his mate's welfare that he couldn't scent her. He had to be the first vampire to have ever done that and she was both annoyed and impressed at his power. She moved quietly amongst those of her kind and their slaves and watched as they carried her gently to their suite. Her last sight was of them walking through the door and to what had to be a bedroom. Her enhanced hearing enabled her to listen to their conversation once they'd dumped the woman on a bed and she was rather flattered that it concerned her . . . .

"Scarlet needs to sleep," Vincent said quietly. "If we leave her now, we can see if Elizabeth is at the orgy. It might be wise to reconnoiter the situation. Nico, we'll need your help for that."

"Are you sure it's wise to leave Scarlet?" the wolf asked.

This time, Lazarus replied. "I don't see why not. Like Vincent said, she needs to sleep and I'm sure Elizabeth will be at the orgy. I know two of her blood slaves are there, so I assume she will be too."

So Lazarus wasn't infallible then. The thought was a relief!

"Assume isn't good enough where Scarlet is concerned, Lazarus," the wolf told him gruffly.

"He's right, Laz. But Nico, we have to find Elizabeth and annihilate the threat."

That made her scowl.

"I wasn't intending on leaving the suite tonight, but I

realized that if we discover Elizabeth then we can finish this here and now. Amongst our own kind, we can slay her and not cause any trouble. The staff are human and aren't blood slaves. This could be one of our only opportunities to discover Elizabeth in flagrante delicto, and where we can immediately act. If she's caught off guard then there more of a chance of success."

"If you're sure . . . ," the wolf said hesitatingly.

Elizabeth wanted to scream in frustration at his dithering.

"I'm not sure. Scarlet's clouded my senses somewhat . . . . I never realized her ass hadn't been touched before," Lazarus admitted with a dazed sigh.

They were all still focused on what had occurred in the movie theater and the thought made Elizabeth smile slowly. At this moment in time, she had the upper hand. It was the first time since the beginning of her so-called vacation and she enjoyed the feeling of power, especially over Lazarus.

"Look, let's get this over and done with. If Elizabeth is at the orgy, she will be as pleasure-dazed as us. I just wish Lazarus and I had realized that this could be a perfect opportunity to end this before we'd come and found you and Scarlet."

Hearing this determined statement, Elizabeth quickly rushed away from the door and ran down the hall in the opposite direction to the elevator. She flattened herself against a door and waited until she heard them leave their suite and heard their footsteps in the hall. When the elevator whooshed away, she moved away from the door and stalked back to their room.

She had a plan and it would strike at their very hearts. Of that, she was certain.

* * * *

With a groggy yawn, Scarlet climbed from the bed and almost fell back down again as a lightheaded feeling struck her. The woozy feeling continued to assail her for a good five minutes, until eventually it dissipated and she stood on trembling legs and stumbled to the bathroom.

Collapsing against the toilet, she sat down with a sigh of relief and looked a little blankly around the room. When she felt a little stronger, she walked to the sink and turned the faucet on. Cupping the water in the palms of her hands, she drank lustily and felt a little better at being re-hydrated. Looking into the mirror, she blinked at her reflection and almost smiled, she looked like a woman who had just been fucked! She supposed she had and the thought made her grin. Tilting her head to the side, she noticed two little marks and realized that Lazarus must have bitten her again. She didn't remember him biting her, as that last time the sensation had almost made her cum from that alone! But it didn't matter. She fingered them and winced, as they were a little sore but almost instantly forgot about them as her stomach grumbled loudly.

She clambered into the shower and quickly washed herself. Sluicing the water over her, she sighed at the soothing sensation and realized that she must have been so groggy because she'd never had so much sex in her entire life! The thought made her laugh and she quickly washed up and when finished, she dried herself off. She returned to the bedroom and looked around with brighter eyes and realized that she was in one of the guys' bedrooms again. With a disgruntled sigh, she raided one of their closets and reached for a shirt. Pulling it on, she grimaced as it swamped her in material and then walked out of the bedroom and into the adjoining salon.

Seating herself in the armchair nearest the phone, she reached for it and ordered French toast and coffee for breakfast from room service. As she placed her order, something sparked her memory and she was damned glad it had, while the phone was in her hand, she dialed her mother's number and grumbled as there was no answer. Rubbing a hand over her face, she contemplated why her mother hadn't answered and had to stop herself from panicking at what Patricia could be doing at that exact moment!

It didn't help that she knew her mother was a grown woman. It didn't help that she'd been taking care of herself for a long time. Scarlet knew that her mother was in a precarious position at the moment where this so-called love of her life was concerned and Scarlet wanted to talk to her to ensure that she wasn't being duped or conned by some low-life con merchant!

Maybe it was selfish, but as thoughts of her mother, work, and her studies assailed her, she wondered where the hell Nico, Lazarus, and Vincent all were. When they were around they took up every part of her concentration until she couldn't focus on anything else, and she had to admit that that had been nice these last couple of days. They were like happy pills. When they were around, or even when just one of them was there, everything felt right with the world. And she enjoyed that feeling. It was almost as though they wrapped her up in cotton wool and protected her from the outside world and all its trials and tribulations. It was something she'd never thought she would enjoy, but once again, she'd been proven wrong.

She tried her mother's number once more and, at the lack of response, sighed wearily and hoped for their quick return from wherever the hell they were. Otherwise the French toast might as well be thrown away!

Chapter Six

"I can't believe that I'm not even hard," Nico said with a somewhat self-satisfied smirk. A feeling of intense well-being and contentment shot through him as he realized what was happening to him. Wondering if Vincent felt the same, he pointed a finger at the three women who had caught his eye, women who were currently sucking and licking each other's pussies. Shaking his head at Vincent, he grinned. "Nope, not even a twitch. Incredible," he breathed then with a satisfied chuckle, smacked Vincent on the back.

Most paranormal creatures were highly sexed and Laz, Vincent and himself were no exception to that rule. Hardly two days passed when they weren't either fucking each other or someone that had caught their eye, and while the three women had popped into his line of vision and with a bang, he had no desire to fuck any of them and he wasn't being big-headed when he knew that his presence would have been welcomed by the women on the floor.

Which celebrity had said that he didn't have to go out for hamburgers, when he had steak back home? At that moment, Nico could well understand what that guy was talking about.

These three very hot blondes were lying in the very entrance of the large stateroom that had been booked for this particular orgy. Their tits swung freely with their agitated movements, their tongues frantic and their bodies screaming with the need for release. All in all, it was an extremely interesting sight, yet his cock didn't respond. Hell, it didn't even interest his brain. He watched as though he were watching some kind of avant garde art display. He admired the twisting and muscularly taut bodies, enjoyed the rather hurried and harried sexual act before him, but it didn't actually affect him.

As an experiment, he thought about the woman he'd left behind in the suite he shared with Vincent and Lazarus. He smiled slowly as he realized his cock was hard. Nico had to hold back a laugh lest Vincent and Laz think he was crazy. But it amused him. That he could witness this frenzied lesbian sex play – what most guy's wet dreams were made of- and not feel a thing . . . Yet just thinking of Scarlet, not even in a sexual way and his cock was hard enough to fuck her. How crazy was that?

Lifting his index finger, he rubbed his nose and thought wryly that if he could, he'd be right in bed with his mate at that minute. He also thought about how just five days ago, had he seen this, played witness to this lesbian ménage à trois, he would have jumped in immediately and joined in the fun!

"Me neither," Vincent replied and tilted his head to the side to watch the women further.

Nico casually leaned forward and cupped Vincent's cock. "No, you're not," he reiterated with a slight grin, pleased that he wasn't experiencing this bizarre phenomenon alone.

"Abruti," Vincent replied with a snort.

"Hey, I'm no moron," Nico joked. "Just testing the waters." He grinned as Vincent flipped him the bird. "Charming!"

"That's me, Nico, I'm all charm."

Nico chuckled and looked around the room a little more closely. His eyes caught glimpses of some rather interesting positions that he knew Scarlet would soon be in, but other than that, he saw no real threat. Opening his senses, he sought any highly wrought emotions like fear or anger, but he found none, just arousal, desire, and passion. What he'd expected for the most part. Either Elizabeth wasn't here or she was and she was fully enjoying a night of fucking.

He couldn't say that he blamed her.

The barrage of moans and whimpers and sounds of flesh slapping against flesh, wet pussies being slid into by hard cocks, asses slowly being invaded by dildos with a pop was definitely arousing. But for him, it wasn't all that difficult to deal with. What was difficult to deal with, was the fact that Scarlet was back in their quarters and lying supine on his bed . . . He could be fucking her rather than messing around here and watching other people get laid.

The thought made him flinch a little. It was amazing how quickly a person's perspective changed when someone as mind-boggling as Scarlet entered one's life. A week ago, the need to kill and extinguish any life in Elizabeth's body had run supreme in his veins. Now, apart from the fact that she could be a potential threat to his mate, he didn't give a shit. All his thoughts were consumed by Scarlet, by the need to claim her and make her know what she was to him. He didn't mind waiting for that time to come but he resented any time he couldn't spend with her.

Frowning, he wondered if Vincent and Lazarus felt the same. They'd all been seeking Elizabeth in a rather haphazard manner. Not in their more usual focused way. It was disconcerting, but he wondered if Scarlet had changed them for good. Before finding Scarlet, he wouldn't even have dreamed of contemplating giving up slaying. But now . . . . Now things were different. He wanted her, safe by his and Vincent and Lazarus' side. He wanted pups with her, wanted a regular, safe life-well, as ordinary and safe as their lives could possibly be.

The thought made him think that perhaps it was time to return to Russia, to return to his pack and rule it as his father had done and his grandfather before him. The longing nostalgic thoughts shocked him, but these past few days had been shocking and full of surprises. Why should this be any different?

"Where have you gone?" Lazarus asked quietly, noticing Nico's preoccupation.

"Russia," Nico admitted with a sigh.

Lazarus cocked a brow in question.

Nico shrugged a shoulder in reply. He wasn't sure he could answer. He hadn't set foot in his homeland for almost fifty years. It was a long time away, maybe too long.

"If your mind is elsewhere, it's a good thing Elizabeth isn't here! Fat lot of good you'd be with your top half in Russia!"

"Don't worry, I only let my guard down after I realized she wasn't here."

Nico moved deeper into the crowded room in the vain attempt to stop Lazarus from asking him any further questions. In doing so he had to step over the three lesbians and almost fell over another couple who were in the midst of fucking each other's brains out. From experience, he could easily say that an orgy was more than just a rather out-there sex act. The whole of it was geared towards sexual pleasure at its most addictive. The sounds, smells and sights were -pre-Scarlet anyway- heady and exciting. The whole focus on cumming and sexual gratification and knowing that a whole crowd of people were feeling the same way buzzed through the room and added to the sexual tension.

He wondered how Scarlet would react if they took her to an orgy and although he knew she would comply, even if it was just for curiosity's sake, Nico knew that it would rile his wolf something rotten if he so much as felt another guy just looking at his mate while they fucked her. Because no way in hell would he share her with any other man. Vincent and Lazarus were different, but any other mother fucker? Not a chance.

Tilting his head to one side, Nico peered down at the couple on the floor and grinned. The guy's hands and feet were cuffed together. While his balls were imprisoned in a testicle cuff, his cock was throbbing as he ate his partner's cunt. There was a slight vibrating sound and Nico saw the guy's cock jerk. Looking down, Nico saw the purple end of a vibrating dildo in the guy's ass. He grinned again as the man's cock began to leak and Nico knew that there was no relief in sight for the poor bastard on the floor.

There were other more interesting sights to be seen, but it made him wonder whether or not he would enjoy being tied up. The thought was definitely intriguing. He'd never trusted anyone enough to be tied down, even Vincent and Lazarus. While they were his bonded brothers, they were also jackasses. He wouldn't put it past them to tying him to the bed and leaving him there while they went out and fed! But Scarlet?

No, he trusted her.

The thought pleased him. The truth behind it pleased him even more.

As did the thought of that kind of slow, withheld release that that man would soon be experiencing.

He was jolted back to thoughts on Elizabeth when Vincent clapped a hand on his shoulder as he directed a question at Lazarus. "We'd best get back to Scarlet if she's not here then, no?"

At Laz's nod of assent, Vincent spun around and began the slow climb over otherwise engaged couples towards the door.

Nico swiveled slowly and followed Vincent unhurriedly, fully aware that Lazarus was by his side and waiting to ask him a question. The waiting seemed interminable. "Why Russia?" Lazarus asked curiously.

Nico registered the question with relief. He hated being at the other end of one of Lazarus' psycho-analysis sessions, he always dug way too deep and with far too much insight. "Because it's home and as safe as can be, and I want to take Scarlet there," Nico admitted bluntly, knowing from experience not to bullshit, to tell the truth. It was easier and less painful that way!

Lazarus nodded slowly. "You're ready to take up the mantle of leader then?"

Nico grunted his reply. "Yes . . . maybe." He nodded and then sighed in acceptance. "Yeah, I am."

"You want us all to give up slaying?" Lazarus asked quietly, a slight frown beginning to crease his forehead.

Nico sighed in frustration and rubbed his eyebrows pensively. "Yes, I do actually."

"What if Scarlet doesn't want to go to Russia?"

He shrugged. "Then we don't go. It's just a thought, that's all. Just something that came to me when I realized I wasn't all that interested in finding Elizabeth. When I realized that my life no longer revolves around slaying the vicious bastards of our kind."

"No, our interest in slaying is waning, I must admit. It's a rather peculiar outcome, unexpected at that!"

"I won't force her into anything, Lazarus. Nor would I force you or Vincent. It would be a joint decision. It was just at that moment, I wanted to be home."

"There is no harm in that. We often visit Gaul for both Vincent and myself . . . You should have told us that you were sickening for home."

"I'm not sickening for anything! You make me sound like a pussy. And it's France, Lazarus. Not Gaul!" Nico grumbled.

Lazarus rolled his eyes. "As if that has any importance! Gaul, France, they're the same place!"

"I'm not going to argue with you!" Nico stated and held up his hand. "I just thought it was time to see how my pack's doing, that's all."

"Well, after we find Elizabeth then I'm sure we can forge ahead with that."

Nico nodded faintly and continued the walk through the corridors and back to their suite.

"Vincent obviously wants to get back," Lazarus pointed out as Vincent was striding about six or seven paces in front of them.

"Must be all the moaning and groaning," Nico replied with a grin. "He didn't have a hard on, but thinking about Scarlet in any one of those positions takes me to the brink of implosion."

"It is good that she's highly sexed. We do not wear her out."

"No, we don't. That doesn't stop her pussy from getting sore though. I'll have to heal it if it's causing her any discomfort," he stated easily, referring to the 'magic' in his saliva that promoted rapid healing. Lazarus and Vincent shared similar properties, but Nico had the added advantage of a longer and more flexible tongue in his partially shifted form.

"I'm sure she will love that," Lazarus said wryly.

"She won't have a choice," Nico said with a grin. "She told me you'd bitten her."

"Yes, I bit her twice. The first time it was an accident, the second time it was on purpose," Lazarus admitted.

"You'll have to be careful, once more and we take her

choice out of this."

"I know. I will restrain myself."

"Good."

"Do you realize that in the ten minutes it's taken us to get back to our rooms that we haven't really even thought about capturing Elizabeth more than once?" Nico sighed. "Dammit. We're running out of time. There are four days left until the ship docks and we have to find her soon. She's bound to know that we've been seeking her out in hope of assassinating her. She won't take kindly to that. It's either killing her or putting up with her vengeance for the next thousand years!" he finished sarcastically as he reached the door to their suite and waited for Vincent to slide his key card through the lock before they all entered their rooms.

"Scarlet! You're awake!" Vincent exclaimed and came to a standstill in the center of the hall. Both Lazarus and Nico bumped into him before shooting him a glare and moving off into the salon.

Nico walked over to Scarlet and tugged her from the sofa she'd been sat on and on to his lap. "You've eaten dorogaya?"

"Yes," she murmured with a sigh and slumped lethargically against his chest. Her hand came up to bury beneath his tucked-in shirt and lay warmly against his lower belly.

Lazarus frowned at her lax positioning on his lap. "Scarlet, are you alright?"

She hummed yes.

Nico watched Lazarus scowl and stride towards them. He lifted her head and peered into her eyes. It was almost instantaneous, the shocking change of his mood. From lazy hazel flecked eyes to the piercing cerulean blue that spoke of his rage. Nico watched as the blue remained prominent and almost tucked Scarlet deeper into his embrace. It wasn't that he feared Lazarus would hurt her. Just that he didn't relish knowing what had caused that fierce fury to bubble through Laz's veins.

Lazarus leaned down and studied her neck. "Vincent, have you bitten Scarlet?" he asked with a rough exhalation of breath.

It was Vincent's turn to frown. "No, of course not."

"Well, she's been bitten," he stated gruffly, fury making

his voice thick. He leaned closer and sniffed the small wound before dabbing over it with his tongue. Almost instantaneously, the wound disappeared.

Nico clutched Scarlet to him a little more fiercely. "It was Elizabeth, wasn't it? " he demanded angrily.

Lazarus' entire body seemed to stiffen as he faced them both and nodded. His hand came up to lift Scarlet's chin as she slumped even further against Nico's chest. "Scarlet, are you alright?" he asked as gently as his voice would allow. Feeling her droop against him just made him all the more fearful. For the first time in his adult life, he felt helpless. His mate was in danger, could be dying, and he didn't have a fucking clue what to do.

"Hmm," she murmured again. "Phoned mom and ate a slice of French toast, but I felt a little drowsy when I went to the door to collect it. I think I fainted," she finished dazedly. "I've got to watch her . . . ," she mumbled. "She's falling for a gigolo."

For the first time, Lazarus seemed startled. The cerulean blue of his eyes, the color that signaled his rage retreated for a moment. Dusky gold flashed as he blinked. "Did I understand that correctly?" he asked Vincent and Nico.

"Your English is better than ours," Vincent scoffed.

"Then why is she talking about a gigolo?"

"Obviously our future mother-in-law is a little reckless where the opposite sex is concerned!"

Nico laughed but quickly quieted as Scarlet roused against him. The movement exposed another bite to their gaze.

"I'll kill her," Vincent growled. "No wonder she wasn't at the orgy. She was here, the fucking bitch."

Lazarus nodded stiffly and leaned down again to lick the small wound. This time she flinched, and Laz had to lathe the bite again before it was completely healed. "Yes, she was here," Lazarus answered grimly. "And tried to do as much damage as possible by the depths of these bites."

"Why the fuck did we all go? If I'd been here, this wouldn't have happened, Lazarus!"

"We all make mistakes, Nico. She'll be alright, that's all that counts." He breathed out slowly and clenched his jaw in an effort to maintain control. "Do you remember being bitten, mellita?" he managed to ask, his voice curiously soft.

He was obviously a better actor than Nico had realized because while Lazarus' questions were gently spoken and softly put, they were the only things that were. Watching the man, he could literally see the fury that was pulsing through his veins. Had he been human, he would have suffered an apoplexy at such a sight.

"I-I, no. Not like before. I came before," she said with a drowsy smile, which disappeared a few moments later. "Remember hurt."

Those words made Nico rear back, his eyes clashing angrily with Lazarus' and Vincent's.

Scarlet grumbled at the jolting movement.

Nico made a soothing sound and stroked the length of her spine with one hand.

"She hurt our mate," Vincent spat.

Nico watched as both vampires' teeth came out into the open and their eyes began to glow.

He was fully aware that if Scarlet hadn't have been in his arms, he'd have partially shifted himself! Only he didn't feel like frightening the life out of his mate when she accidentally brushed against him and discovered fur! For her, he would battle his self control and hide that side of him from her for the moment. Eventually she would see him in his true form, but that moment was not now. Her welfare was more important to him than his wolf's fury. Even though that felt monumentally difficult to withhold too, when all the beast wanted to do was rip the bitch into shreds. He felt as though he was practically vibrating with rage.

"Scarlet, I want you to do something for me . . ." Lazarus asked quietly.

"Wha . . . ?"

"Nico, give me your wrist," he asked briskly. "You won't like it, mellita, but I need you to sip from Nico's wrist," he softly directed.

Vincent sucked in a breath.

"No, don't wanna," she mumbled grouchily and turned her face away like a moody toddler refusing to eat her vegetables.

"You have to, baby. It's really important. If you don't, then we'll have to take you to the doctor."

"Why?" she grumbled and rubbed her face into Nico's shoulder.

"For a blood transfusion. You've lost a lot of blood to be reacting like this to a bite."

"Don't wanna drink blood," she mumbled, her voice was somewhat slurred. She curled her nose and pressed her forehead into Nico's peck. Inadvertently she touched his nipple and despite himself and the seriousness of the situation, he felt the nubbin curl up and harden at her touch. His cock began to throb hungrily.

"Nico, give me your wrist." Lazarus watched Scarlet before he curled his fingers around the proffered hand. Nico felt the sting as the incisors pierced his wrist. It was a small cut, a small drop of blood escaped and he quickly held it to Scarlet's mouth. "Sup, mellita. It won't harm you," Lazarus encouraged quietly.

His words seemed to have a calming effect on her, she licked at the cut and moaned a little as blood coated her lips. All three of them reacted with shock at the tenor that moan took. It was heavily laden with arousal and they watched in astonishment as she began to undulate against Nico and started to suck hungrily at the small bite. Lazarus reached for Nico's wrist and pulled it away from Scarlet, he licked the wound and sealed it instantly then watched as Scarlet began to shudder. Frowning, he watched as those shudders deepen. "Touch her pussy, Nico. She obviously needs to cum. It will finish the healing process."

Nico nodded and easily slid his hands in between Scarlet's legs, his fingers unerringly reaching for her cunt. When they reached that heavenly spot, he hissed.

She moaned.

"Fuck, she's wet," he said, more to himself than anyone else in particular as his fingers made moist, sucking sounds as they slid through her juices. The sounds seemed to incite Scarlet even more.

Her hips began to rock awkwardly until with a feverish groan, she sat up and away from him then returned by straddling him. Her fingers worked at his fly, aching to release his cock.

Lazarus stopped her. Using his hand like a manacle, he grabbed her by the wrist, hushing her as she moaned and turned wild eyes to him.

"We need to claim her," he stated gruffly.

"Claim her? We can't! Not without her say-so!" Vincent exclaimed in a startled voice. "What's brought this on?"

"We've got no choice now that she's taken Nico's blood. I thought it would be okay, but her reaction is a complete contrast to what I'd expected." Lazarus informed them bluntly.

"If you knew there was a risk, then why the hell did you let her drink from me?" Nico demanded.

"Firstly, I didn't expect there to be any complications, dammit! And secondly, because you're the only one of us with warm blood flowing through his veins," Lazarus replied impatiently. "What did you expect me to do? Take her to the damned human doctor on board for a blood transfusion? How the hell would we explain that? Either way, be it from you or a doctor, she needed blood. I've taken from her and so has Elizabeth. She needed replenishment! I just didn't factor the previous bites into all this. It's obviously altered her body's reactions to paranormal DNA. And, anyway, it was going to happen at some point in time. I don't like taking her choice away anymore than you two do, but we have no choice either. There was never any way we were going to let her leave us, so don't play the damned martyrs!"

Vincent glared at him angrily.

"Fuck off, Vincent. Don't look at me like that! Elizabeth had drained too much blood. Scarlet needed that replenished. A regular blood transfusion would have helped, but taking Nico's blood, that of a werewolf and her mate? Hell, she's as fit as a fiddle now! She's just not her normal self."

"I still don't like it," Vincent muttered. "We can't just claim her without her even being fully aware of being claimed, dammit. Look at her. She's hardly cognizant of what's happening!"

"I know that, Vincent," Lazarus said patiently. "She needs to be claimed. Our seed and bites will complete the claiming and soothe her. None of this is going to stop until we fuck her," he finished simply, leaving the choice to them and received painful glares for his troubles.

"If we don't have a choice, then we don't have choice," Nico said gruffly, his hands grasping Scarlet's other hand

which was attempting to unzip his fly while her mouth was
buried in his neck, sucking at his ear, biting at the tendons
there and generally driving him crazy, especially with the
biting. His wolf highly appreciated that sensation.

"You're just saying that because you've got a hard on
and she's crawling all over you like fire ants at a picnic,"
Vincent retorted.

"What a lovely picture," Lazarus said with a faint smile.

"Well, you try and sit here with her all over you and try
not to want to fuck her. Hell, I've only got so much control.
What the hell are we going to do?"

"We have no choice," Lazarus told them both.

"There's always a choice," Vincent answered.

"Not in this case."

"Maybe he's right, Vincent. It's too late. Look at her."
He let go of Scarlet's hand which immediately scrambled
to his cock and hissed as she cupped him. Determined to
ignore it, he grasped her chin and pulled her head up and
turned her so that she could look at Vincent. "Look at her
eyes, Vincent. Look at them."

Dazed wasn't the word. He'd seen heroin addicts with a
craving for a fix with not dissimilar expressions and that
fact frightened him. He understood why there was no
choice. Either they eased her need and ultimately claimed
her or she would go mad.

Her body was already moving in frenzy, swaying and
clinging to him, her torso plastered against his. It turned
him on, but there was a desperation to her movements that
verified how vital it was they acted and swiftly.

Ignoring Vincent's disapproving frown, Nico planted a
kiss against Scarlet's lips and felt his body tense as she
threw every ounce of her sensuality at him. Her mouth
devoured his, their tongues stroked against the others and
the sounds of their panting soon filled the quiet room. Her
moans vibrated against his lips and it just rocked his need
until he had to move, had to touch her.

Pulling his mouth away from her, he grabbed the shirt
that covered her body and pulled the two sides apart.
Buttons flew but he didn't give a shit, he groaned at the
sight of her tits and bare pussy which were undulating with
her need. He was only allowed a glimpse before she
pounced on him again. Instead his hands sighted her,

covering the heavy swell of her tits, tugging at the nipples, tweaking until she began to whimper against him.

Letting go of one of the beauties, his free hand swept along the line of her waist, over her hips and down over her thighs. She tensed, her body stilling in anticipation for that final touch and when he finally touched her cunt, she slumped against him. For a moment, she rested against him, obviously enjoying the touch and when his fingers parted her pussy lips, trailing her arousal along the smooth channel there and finally hovering over her clit-only then did she begin to move. Her hips rocked freely, pushing down against his finger as she played with herself.

High pitched groans and whimpers escaped her throat and the sounds were like music to his ears. Each and every one of them seemed connected to his cock and he could feel it leaking, could feel the pre-cum gathering around the head of his cock and every single strand of DNA in his body longed to shove his erection into her warm, wet and welcoming pussy and impregnate her. Spawn the next generation of his family.

Her hips stopped rocking and instead her fingers once more scrambled at his fly and within seconds released his cock. She almost sprang from his lap as she moved to kneel before him. Spreading his legs, she shuffled in between them and her head lowered to his groin. His eyes were focused intently on her but knowing what she was about to do, almost made them flicker shut. While his body longed to join more intimately with her, to lose his cum into the clinging walls of her cunt, his brain wanted the moist heat of her mouth, the mobile length of her tongue licking him clean, sucking him deep.

The muscles in his thighs tensed when she rested the palms of her hands at the top of his legs and delicately, like a kitten lapping milk, supped at the cum that was leaking from his cock. He hissed as she pointed her tongue and dug into the small hole then followed the line of the mushroom-shaped head of his glans. Small flickers of the tensile digit had his body screaming for release and when she finally opened her mouth fully and placed her lips around the glans and sucked down hard, his hips lifted from the seat.

Panting, he jolted as he heard a door bang shut and looked up, watched as Vincent with a toiletry bag he'd obviously retrieved from one of the bathrooms grabbed at a bottle of lubricant. That Vincent was about to fuck Scarlet in the ass and that he would get a first row seat made his cock twitch. His hands came down to cup the curve of Scarlet's head and he had to admit, he pressed down. As wrong as that was, pressuring her into going deeper, it felt so fucking good that his mind seemed to separate from his body for a moment or two.

Lazarus' voice was gruff. "Are you turned on, mellita?"

Her hiss was audible. "You know I am, Lazarus," she murmured throatily.

After a few moments, Nico felt the heat of her breath against his own cock once more, and he groaned at the feel of that silky slipperiness.

Turning his head away at the sudden volley of moans that were escaping Scarlet's mouth, he saw the slow slide of Vincent's cock into her ass and groaned himself.

"Sit her back against your lap, Vincent," Lazarus ordered with a grunt.

"What?" Vincent murmured dumbly, lifting dazed eyes to Lazarus' piercing ones. The word finished on a hiss as he slipped a little deeper into their mate's ass.

"Rest her back against your chest and spread your legs so that you're balanced," Lazarus directed impatiently.

With a disoriented nod, Vincent pulled Scarlet to his chest and complied with Lazarus' orders.

"Fuck her cunt, Nico."

Nico willingly jumped on to the floor and watched as Scarlet squirmed against Vincent's chest. Despite the roaring lust that was flooding his brain, he had to hold back a grin-Scarlet's movements were obviously torturous as Vincent's eyes were practically crossed. That was the last thought in his head before all recollections seemed to melt away as his cock slid into Scarlet's unbearably tight pussy. His cock slammed deep and Scarlet reared up, almost knocking into him as her back arched.

Grunting, he stayed where he was for the moment, deep inside her cunt and only rocked his hips back and forth. The sensation was beyond comprehension.

By now, Scarlet was as taut as a string bow, and Lazarus added to that tension by joining in the melee. His hand around his cock, Lazarus began to jack off, slowly and teasingly, ensuring that he covered every inch before sliding his hand down again. He watched as Scarlet licked her lips like a cat sighting a succulent piece of fish. The thought almost made him laugh. He took his cock and rolled it over the curves of Scarlet's lips.

This time she licked the cum away and swallowed.

Lazarus' eyes dilated.

Scarlet slowly accepted the length of Laz's cock into her mouth and there was something so amazingly earthy about their mate accepting each of them into her body at the same time, that it just blew his mouth away. Fused every single brain cell he possessed and he knew that the other two felt it too. Almost simultaneously, Laz, Vincent, and he began to thrust.

A charge seemed to rush through the air, and Nico realized that something beyond their comprehension, even that of Lazarus' was occurring. It whooshed through the air like a back draft, exploding into a conflagration that seemed to burn their souls and melt them into dust. Every single one of his senses took part in this love play and as he thrust, his back arching to get even deeper into her, sweat coating his body at the exertion; he felt his soul join with hers. They seemed to twine around each other and he knew that it was happening to Lazarus and Vincent, too. He felt his heart pound as a part that he'd never known was empty, suddenly seemed full. It warmed him as nothing else ever had and as that wonderfully heartening sensation pounded through him, his arousal burst around him. Three sets of groans exploded into the air as Vincent and Laz also came, filling Scarlet with their seed and each making them their own.

* * * *

"Let him carry her, Vincent," Lazarus quietly requested as Nico swept Scarlet tightly into his embrace, growls escaping his throat and rumbling through the air. "His wolf will be possessive but that's because he's just claimed her. He's protecting her," Lazarus nodded at Nico, whose arms held Scarlet tightly and close to him. Scarlet, herself, was nuzzling into his neck and returning that clinging embrace as fiercely as Nico.

"Wish our claiming was as easy as his," Vincent grumbled.

Lazarus scoffed. "You know as well as I do, she's claimed. But I think we should stick to the formalities. Over the next couple of days, we need to keep on biting her. You know the rules. Six bites for a blood mate. Just for her protection. Her blood should be repellent to other vampires now. If Elizabeth bites her regardless, then I imagine it will poison her," he murmured with evident satisfaction.

Vincent nodded with a slight frown. "We'll keep Nico and her together at all times though. I don't want that fucking bitch anywhere near her."

"Come, time to be with our blood mate. I must admit I'm relieved. I know we took her choice away, but this extra protection is all to the good. It was killing me, knowing that she was going around the boat with this pack of riff-raff probably sniffing after her," he said with a faint smile of understanding on his lips.

"At least she's safe."

"Exactly," Lazarus said, satisfied and began the short walk to the bedroom Nico had taken Scarlet into. Once there, in the semi-darkness, he stripped off his trousers and shirt, his jacket lay on the floor in the salon. When naked, he climbed into bed and lay beside Nico, upon who laid Scarlet. Her soft soughing breaths were a soothing tonic and calmed his nerves. When Vincent, also naked, climbed in on the other side, Lazarus felt truly at peace and soon fell asleep.

* * * *

Scrunching her nose, Scarlet wiggled against the tasty but hard body she was using as a mattress. God, there wasn't an inch of softness on the entirety of Nico's body, she thought with a grumble then snorted because those muscles were so fucking gorgeous that it was hard to not drool whenever she saw them!

Rubbing her forehead against Nico's peck, she couldn't help but bite the muscled mass. Feeling the give of skin in her teeth was a pleasant sensation, one she compounded by breathing deeply and absorbing as much of his scent as physically possible. Her senses replete, she tilted her head upwards and blushed at the grin gracing Nico's lips and knowing look in his eyes.

"What?" she asked defensively, dropping her head back

down to his chest.

Nico's fingers came to grasp her chin and force her head upwards so that he could look into her eyes. "Dobroye utro."

"Huh?" she asked.

"Good morning," he repeated with a faint smile. "You're going to have to learn Russian, dorogaya."

"I am?"

He nodded and smiled faintly at her.

Blinking, she stared at him a little perplexedly. "Oh."

Her eyes dropped down to that small twitch of his lips and suddenly, she had a flash of memory. Instinctively, her eyes fluttered shut as she remembered Lazarus, standing at the side of the sofa, the zip of his fly open, his cock pulled through the opening and being sucked deep into Nico's mouth.

These three men had introduced her to something she'd never before experienced, but that had to be the sexiest fucking thing ever. Never in her life had she seen something like that. Something that had made even her blood tingle as it coursed through her body, making everywhere else throb as it passed through.

Just thinking about it made her feel a little dazed.

Nico smiled. "Shell-shocked?"

"In a word," she answered wryly. "Just thinking about last night."

"Ah," was all he said.

"Yeah, ah. I don't think, hell, I know, I've never experienced anything like that before.

"We aim to please," he said with a soft chuckle.

Scarlet prodded him punishingly in the side; his very muscled belly hardly gave way. She sighed. Damn, she loved his body. God, they were all gorgeous and for the next two weeks they were hers. Although she had to admit, that despite herself, Scarlet had appreciated when he'd said that she would have to learn Russian. It sounded as though there was a permanency to that statement.

How that would work she had no idea. Why would he want her to learn Russian though? He wouldn't, unless he intended seeing her again.

Having never wanted permanency in her life with men, it felt so odd to be relieved by the possibility of their wanting to keep in touch with her.

Something about them resonated with her, especially today. She felt different. Didn't know how or why, but she did. Felt closer to them and she enjoyed the look of intimacy that was flashing between her and Nico. It was one which declared to the universe that they knew each other and understood each other-to a point, she added with an inward grin.

She dropped her head back down to his chest and inhaled appreciatively. "Damn, you smell good."

"As do you, angel."

"Stop that," she said with a slight shiver.

"Stop what?"

"Speaking in Russian. You know it drives me insane."

He smiled wickedly at her and before she knew it, Scarlet found herself lying underneath him, her legs spread to accommodate his obvious desire to get as close to her as physically possible.

His cock rested at the apex of her thighs and she shuddered at that heavy weight lying there.

"I shall have to speak to you more often in my mother tongue then," he murmured softly and ducked his head to press a kiss against the side of her neck.

At the rasp of his stubble against her skin, she felt gooseflesh sweep over her body. "Hmm, maybe you should." Her voice was faint as shivers of pleasure overcame her and her back arched. Would she ever get enough of these three men?

He began to rock his hips back and forth and pressed the very tip of his cock into her. With a hiss, she froze and almost laughed at her earlier thought! Sure, maybe she couldn't get enough of them, but it appeared her body could!

"I think I need a break," she murmured apologetically.

He just grinned at her and shook his head. "I can heal you," he whispered insidiously and pressed a kiss to her ear. His tongue played with the delicate whorls.

She shuddered as desire pierced through her.

"You can heal me?" she repeated doubtfully.

Nico nodded slowly and slipped his delicious body along the top of hers. Just the feel of their flesh melding was enough to have shudders of sensation spreading like wildfire through her system. When he eventually settled between her legs, his hands cupped her inner thighs and spread her further apart and his head drifted above her groin.

"You smell divine."

She grimaced uncomfortably and made to get up. "I need to shower."

"No." His voice was gruff. "You smell like us." If his voice had been deep before now they were gravelly and she saw his eyes switch from his usual blue color to an almost piercing white.

She almost jolted back but the realization that this was Nico helped her calm down. Exhaling deeply, she dropped her head back down to the mattress and waited for the first touch of his tongue to her pussy.

When it eventually came, it was so delicate that it made her shiver. It was like a feather being drifted along a rather ticklish spot, only this touch didn't make her want to laugh. It made her body scream . . . made every nerve ending stand on edge, at attention!

His tongue flickered along her clit and down in between the channel of her pussy lips and finally, after endless, pleasure-drenched moments, it slipped into her cunt. The feel of his tongue thrusting into her, like a short tensile cock that manipulated all the nerve endings around her very entrance, made her back arch and her butt rock down into the bed. Her head pressed back against the mattress and tilted back as pleasure rocketed through her.

When that small, thick tongue became magically longer and thinner, her eyes almost crossed. She felt it dragging in places that shouldn't have been touched by a tongue, but it did and the feeling was beyond compare.

Her hands came down to grasp at his head, to press his face even closer to her and when he complied, a shriek of pleasure escaped her throat as he slithered that tongue in and out, in and out like an ultra thin cock that somehow managed to touch everywhere and leave nowhere free from its possession.

As it moved faster and faster, Scarlet felt herself reach a peak that while extraordinary, was like a physical shock to the system. She felt as though she were floating on a cloud, and rather than the usual orgasmic pleasure, it was a feeling

of well-being that drifted through her body. She felt
encompassed by a warm healing glow, a protected and
cosseted lover that was being cared for by her partner.

When she finally drifted back down to earth, Lazarus
was resting beside her. He too was naked but he was lying
on his side, head propped on his hand, elbow against the
bed. His other hand was twirling through some strands of
her hair.

"Enjoy that, mellita?"

Her voice was too husky to speak so she nodded.

He smiled. "Nico has been looking forward to doing
that."

"Has he?" she croaked.

"Yes. I knew you would enjoy it."

"His tongue . . . ?" she said with a blink of dazed
pleasure and confusion.

"Good, isn't it?"

"Good?" she repeated disorientated. "It was . . . . I don't
know what it was but wow."

He laughed and placed his free arm over her stomach
and tugged her closer to him. "Did I wish you a good
morning?" he asked as he pressed an affectionate kiss to
her shoulder.

It was her turn to laugh. "No, you didn't and shame on
you!" she teased. Relishing in the affectionate love play,
she dropped her head against his and nuzzled into him.
Nico then decided to lie down beside her so she was
sandwiched between them. It seemed as though all her
Christmas presents had come at once!

A short silence ensued. "Where is Vincent?" she asked
throatily, her voice still redolent with the pleasure she'd just
experienced.

"In the shower," Lazarus replied.

"Why? What time is it?"

"Nearly dinnertime."

"How long did I sleep?"She shrieked.

Nico smirked. "Don't worry about it, dorogaya, we wore
you out!"

She smacked him on the arm. "What time is it?"

"Almost seven."

"Dammit. This is my first holiday, ever; I didn't want to
waste the days in bed! Why didn't you wake me?"

Lazarus' lips twitched. "Scarlet, we've yet to reach our first destination. There's nothing to miss. You do not seem the kind of woman to spend your days in the bars or eating up a storm in the restaurants . . . . Your day hasn't been wasted."

She narrowed her eyes at him. "If I say that my day has been wasted, Lazarus, then it has. Just because you deem it so, doesn't make it the case. I'm perfectly capable of making my own informed opinions!"

He nodded slowly, his eyes capturing her own and holding them for what felt like timeless moments. Whether it was an attempt to subjugate her to his will, she didn't know, but either way it didn't work and she had the feeling that he was both impressed and irked by her steely will. Either way, she wasn't a woman that was easily dominated. Inside or out of the bedroom!

"Forgive me, delicia."

"There's no need to apologize, Lazarus, just don't treat me like a moron, okay?"

Nico hooted and received a pained glare for his efforts. "That told you!"

Scarlet cocked a brow at him. "What are you laughing at? Do you think all women should be treated as though they don't have the cerebral capacity to make their own decisions?" she demanded with a lethal softness.

Lazarus grinned. "She's got you there, trapped in a bait of your own making, my friend!"

Nico rolled his eyes and then grabbed Scarlet, tucking her into his chest, as he swirled over and on to his back. Scarlet placed her hands either side of his head and pulled herself up slightly so that she could looked down at him. Her hair fell haphazardly over her shoulders and trailed against his skin. She could tell that he liked it and the thought made her lips quirk softly. It was rather enjoyable being with men who appreciated every aspect of her. While a treat, it was a very rare one!

She dipped her head and pressed a soft kiss against his lips and tasted her juices on the firm and bite-able lips. The only other time that had happened, she'd stopped kissing the guy in question and had instead trailed kisses over his jaw and throat. This time however, the taste seemed to ignite inside her mouth. Every emotion she'd felt while he'd been licking her pussy exploded in her head and with a groan, her tongue pressed inside his mouth and began to tangle hungrily with his own.

It was almost as though they were fighting with their lips, but as they touched, a conflagration of sensation worked its way between them until they separated and stared at each other blindly for a second. A need so strong wormed through her system and with panting breaths exploding from her mouth, she ducked her head and tested her teeth against the sinew of his shoulder. Biting down hard, she felt his back arch as she bit and felt growls and rumbles vibrating through his chest. The sounds he made turned her on so badly that Scarlet felt a tremor wash over her and gasping for breath she looked up at him and saw icy blue eyes staring back at her.

Perhaps she should have been fearful. Run for the hills, or at least tried to dive into the ocean and swim back to land-anything to get away from what she was seeing. But she didn't. The completely different colored eyes she was staring into, eyes that belonged to a beast and not to a man, seemed to sear her very soul. She felt their gaze touch over her flesh and the possessiveness behind that glance raked her to her core. When they flashed back to meet hers, a whimper escaped her throat. They were loaded with meaning and when he grabbed her to him and spun over so that this time, she was on the bottom and he on top, she made no complaint. When he tilted her head to the side and began to rub his lips against her throat, she said nothing. When she felt the rasp of his teeth against her ear, she waited with bated breath for what she knew was about to come. And when it finally did, she screamed. Not with horror, but a pleasure so intense she screamed.

The pressure of his teeth against her skin, the sensation of it breaking through the thin line of flesh- it was orgasmic. Maybe it should have hurt, but her system was overloaded with pleasure. If it did hurt, then it just worked against that until she was practically comatose with the lust that was riding her.

Feeling a finger work its way between the folds of her pussy, stretching her cunt a little and rasping it with his skin, she hissed as another jolt of pleasure hit her. The finger fucked her and she gratefully accepted the caress.

When another hand lifted her foot and tugged it into the air, she shuddered as unknown hands began to caress the flesh there. Dragging over her toes and the soft skin of her feet, over her firm calves and to the muscles of her thighs . . . never reaching where that other hand was touching her but reminding her of that touch all the same. A mouth came up against her calf, she could feel the moist skin clinging to the limb and the harsh rake of another set off teeth made her shudder. When once more the skin gave way to marauding incisors, her back arched as another wave of exhausting pleasure overcame her.

The position dislodged Nico slightly, but he still sat there, his teeth against her throat, hanging there almost like a dog with a bone. It was comforting having him there and the situation was made even more wonderful when she felt the soft suckle of a pursed mouth around her nipple. She knew what was coming, knew she was going to be bitten again and when it came, when the teeth broke through the thin sheath of erect flesh she cried out. Her cunt clenched hard against the finger she was sheltering and an orgasm burst through her veins like a shower of fireworks. It was with great regret that she passed out from those amazing, delirious sensations.

"She's covered in cum," Nico said to the room at large as he moved away from the lax body of his mate. Dropping down at her side, he absentmindedly rubbed some of their seed into her flesh as he nuzzled his head into the pillow of her breasts.

"That's not going to clean it off her, Nico," Lazarus commented wryly.

"It smells good," was all he said before inhaling deeply. He sat up a little and buried his nose between Scarlet's tits and murmured his pleasure. "Especially here, all of us and her and sex. Delicious. Smell, Lazarus."

Lazarus smiled faintly at Nico's words but complied and took to the task almost like a sommelier testing an expensive bottle of wine. His eyes closed as he breathed in the scent. "God, she does smell good, doesn't she?" he answered, his voice guttural with desire.

Nico grunted. "I don't think I've ever experienced anything like that before in my life! I've never spontaneously cum before-not without touching my cock anyway. The woman's a marvel."

"The woman's your mate, Nico. That's all. Her power over all of us is enormous," Lazarus replied in French and jerked his head at Vincent. "You're saying little. What's the matter?"

Jolted back to the conversation, Vincent just frowned. "Nothing's the matter," he answered.

"What is it with you two? Why do you have to lie when you fully know that I can tell if you're lying," Lazarus directed this and an eye roll towards Nico.

"There's nothing wrong with me, Lazarus. Just thinking about Elizabeth that's all. I don't like this situation-Scarlet's near as dammit fully claimed, there's little more we can do in that regard to protect her. I just don't like it. I wish this damned cruise was nearing land, because I'd make us all get the fuck off of here. Sure, that bitch would be left on the loose, but I don't give a shit. All I care about is ensuring Scarlet's safety. I've already lost one soul mate, I'm damned lucky to find another and I will not lose her!"

The passion and the spit-fire French prodded Scarlet into wakefulness. "Talk about mind-blowing! What you do to me," she said drowsily, and, sitting up, she drooped back down to the mattress again. Like a jack in the box, she sat up once more, and, this time, her joints stiffened at her command and let her stay in position. Rubbing her eyes, she yawned as she looked over at the obviously riled man who was pacing about the room. "What's the matter, Vincent?" she asked sleepily around another yawn. "

His voice was clogged with the tones of his native tongue and it was hard to concentrate on their meaning when he spoke so sexily.

"Nothing is the matter, Scarlet," he replied easily.

But she could tell he was lying. Something was stressing him out, and she didn't like it. In a weird way, she wanted to protect him from whatever it was that was making him unhappy and seeing as it was the first time she had ever felt that way, it came as a definite shock to the system!

"Why say that to me when I can tell you're lying?" she asked, uncannily echoing Lazarus' earlier statement. She frowned when she heard the men lying beside her snigger a little and shot them a glare.

"Get off the bed, Nico. Vincent, come here. Lay beside

me," she ordered and pushed at Nico's supine body until he budged and moved away, allowing Vincent to take his place.

With an amused smile gracing his lips, Nico easily obeyed her dictates and moved to the other side of the bed and lounged at the very bottom of it.

Patting the space beside her, Scarlet smiled winningly up at Vincent, who almost begrudgingly sat down. She prodded at him until he was lying flat on his back and she curled into his side. Hooking her leg over his thighs and an arm over his chest, she settled into the position and waited for him to relax. Scarlet knew that he wouldn't tell her what was wrong, but if she could comfort him and make him feel better then that would simultaneously make her feel easier.

It was bizarre feeling this way for a man and not only Vincent, but Lazarus and Nico too. They all fought for the largest area of her heart but never won because they each owned a special part of it and the size didn't matter. She couldn't believe that she loved one man, never mind three! But she did and that was that. A part of her was sure that they would be meeting up after the cruise finished, she was sure that they felt similarly towards her. In fact, she knew it. The way they cared for her, protected and cosseted her . . . if these weren't manifestations of their caring for her, then she wasn't worthy of her law degree.

When she'd spoken to MJ the other day, she'd experienced for the first time that hideous feeling of insecurity. It was something she'd never felt before with regards to the opposite sex and now, as time passed, time which included these three men, she realized that feeling insecure wasn't necessary. Although post-cruise, she wasn't sure what would occur, she knew what they all had together was too strong to just let go and she knew that they realized that too. It was in the hugs and touches, the little unnecessary kisses and in the fact that she was always at the very center of their attention. It was an unbelievably heady sensation. Take now, Lazarus and Nico were behind her, watching her console and comfort Vincent and he, although obviously unhappy with something, wasn't taking it out on her. He'd settled somewhat angrily on to the mattress but had soon relaxed and calmed down. His body was turned into hers and a restless but gentle hand was playing in her hair.

As she relaxed into his side, she heard them speak in French again, but rather than be annoyed she just sighed and rested peacefully, until their words actually started making sense to her.

"My safety is paramount? What the hell are you talking about?" she demanded, shocked, and directed the question and a frowning look at all three of them.

Lazarus slowly curled upwards, his magnificent six pack gleaming with a slight sheen as he moved. "Tu me comprends, Scarlet?" he asked and tilted his head to the side in question.

"Oui. Naturellement. Yes, of course I understand you! I wouldn't have asked what the hell you were talking about otherwise, would I?"

"I thought you couldn't speak French," he stated calmly.

"I can't!" she replied. Annoyed at his hedging until she remembered the actual words he'd used. "I c-o-u-l-d-n-t," she said, rolling out the syllables in the word.

Lazarus nodded faintly. "Well, this was unforeseen."

"Dammit Lazarus! How often over the next few weeks is something unforeseen going to happen? Surely you realized something like this could occur?" Vincent exploded, his eyes glittering dangerously, evidence that he'd gone feral.

"Vincent!" she snapped. "You're not helping!" Scarlet inhaled deeply in a quick attempt to calm herself. "Does this have something to do with all the bites?" she demanded, directing the question at Lazarus.

He nodded.

"Are there any other side effects to this little sex play?" was all she said as she blew out a wary breath.

Lazarus shrugged. "Not that I'm aware of, but I never suspected anything like this could happen. It seems the more often we bite you, the more knowledge you take away from us."

"Well, you should have suspected, dammit. You've bitten her four times, she's your blood slave until you bite her further!" Vincent said, his voice gravelly with anger.

"Blood slave?" Scarlet said slowly. "I'm your blood slave? Nico, is that what you were telling me about? About vampires who didn't find their attentions being reciprocated, so they forced them on to unsuspecting victims?" Jumping from the bed, she grabbed one of the sheets that had loosened from the bed and wrapped herself in it. "What the hell have you done to me, Lazarus?"

"Mellita," he started.

"Don't you dare mellita me! How could you do this?"

"It's a necessary part of the claiming," was all he said.

"Am I supposed to understand that?" she asked the room at large.

"No. You're not. But there is no need to fear."

"There's every need to fear. Other people may be glad to find themselves forcibly attached to a vampire, but I'm not one of them. What the hell were you thinking of!"

"If you'd listen to me and stop being melodramatic . . . ."

She interrupted him before he could continue. "How dare you accuse me of being melodramatic! How dare you!" she yelled just before stomping out of the room and running out into the hallway of the suite. Once there, she pulled the front door open and with one foot over the doorjamb, a piercing stab of pain split her head in two. The ache was so intense it made her crumble to the floor, her head cushioned in her hands as she sank to the ground.

She was only aware of the pain and was relieved when it gradually lessened but until it had almost entirely gone, the echoes of it seemed to tumble around inside her head. When she felt a little more alive again, back to reality, Scarlet realized she was back in the bedroom and curled into Lazarus' chest. Realizing who was comforting her, she immediately pulled away and once more that pain began to ricochet like a bullet in the tight confines of her skull. Shattering and damaging wherever that searing intense heat hit.

Lazarus quickly pulled her back into his arms and began to rock her. "Please, mel, stay calm and relax. You will come to no harm here. Please delicia be at peace."

His words soothed her and when the ache began to dissipate, rather than immediately run, she stayed within his tight embrace.

"What's happening to me?" she asked huskily, her throat heavy with pain-filled tears.

"It's a part of the link, mellita. Until I bite you twice more, when you try to pull away from me mentally you will

feel unbearable pain. I'm sorry, amor meus. I never
intended this to happen," he said softly, his voice a whisper
so as not to hurt her further. He shot a glare at Vincent. "I
never intended for you to know what was happening."

With a grimace, she sat up slowly and narrowed her eyes
at him once more. "How many times, I hate being out of
the picture! What the hell is going on here? Don't you think
I deserve to know?"

Chapter Seven

It was a rather subdued group that sat together in the
entertainment lounge, in fact, the atmosphere would have
been more suitable in a morgue. The thought should have
been amusing, considering there were in fact two members
of the undead at the table, but it wasn't. The last couple of
hours had been a fucking farce, hell, more than that, a
complete disaster and the next few looked to be just as bad,
maybe even worse. It wasn't a welcoming prospect.

Scarlet and Vincent sat in a cold, fuming anger; Nico
looked subdued and bored and he sat on the borderline of
feeling both chastened and slightly dejected while
simultaneously feeling furious.

Scarlet was sulking with him. Actually sulking with
him. Not for being a bastard or behaving inappropriately,
but for trying to save her life. Not exactly anything of
importance, just the most vital part of his existence.

That was all!

What the fuck would she have preferred him to do? Let
her die? Because if they'd left it much longer, then that
would have happened. This very clear proof that he'd failed
to protect the most important person in his life just
managed to rile him up even more! There had been two
bites, one obviously to mark and take a small sup, then
obviously the blood lust had overtaken the fucking evil
bitch and she'd bitten again and taken much, much more.
Probably more than she'd even planned...the greedy
whore.

Leaving Scarlet drained wouldn't have been her

intention. Elizabeth had wanted to show Lazarus that he wasn't infallible, that she knew that Scarlet was his mate and that she could get to Scarlet at any time she wanted. That she could get to him any time she wanted.

Once, he could have taken that in his stride. A few days ago, with the will and desire to live waning, a dispassionate apathy overtaking his very being, he wouldn't have cared a damn if she had been able to get to him. It would have been a test and one he would have enjoyed winning. But now, with Scarlet in his life, the world was filled with color once more. He was feeling again and she was slowly becoming the very center of his existence. He was learning to love life once more and no way would he allow a malevolent, evil, power-mad vampiress take everything away from him.

So, bearing all of that in mind, what the fuck would Scarlet have preferred him to do? Lose her and then rapidly lose the will to live again? Let her die? Watch the life slowly drain out of her as her heart beat grew weaker, the blood pressure lessening as the lack of blood in her system began to take effect?

Well, she could sulk at him all the fuck she wanted, because at least she was alive to do it!

He sat back into the lounge seats with a self-righteous snort, crossed his right ankle over his left leg and casually waved a hand at one of the wandering waiters.

"Armagnac, four fingers." Seeing the man quirk his brows at the size of the drink, Lazarus glared at him in reply. A couple of moments later, he cradled the balloon glass in his hand and swirled the beverage. Taking a sniff, he savored the scent and took a gulp of the strong alcohol. Feeling the burn in his throat, he relished the sensation and settled back into what looked to be a long and drawn out sulking session.

Hell, it seemed as though he were in the doghouse and despite himself, despite feeling angry and most annoyingly, slightly chastened, he had to admit that there was amusement there too. In the two thousand and thirty years of his existence, he'd never experienced anything like this and it made the fact that he'd finally found his blood mate more real. You had to take the rough with the smooth and he had now experienced both sides of that coin and felt somehow closer to her because of that.

Strange really, especially when he considered that he had never been on the receiving end of a woman's sulk before. For two simple reasons, one, he'd never been around long enough to get into anything more meaningful than a quick fuck, and two, if he had, he simply wouldn't have tolerated it.

That may have been harsh, but he'd had no time for a relationship. No time to develop any feelings for a woman. Seeing his parents die and literally watching his little brothers being tortured to death hadn't exactly made him a well-rounded, emotionally-keyed up person.

No, if anything had dominated his soul, it was vengeance. A desire to take revenge on the bastards that had slaughtered his brothers as though they were cattle and make them taste their own medicine. It had taken a long time to train and become stronger as a vampire before ultimately finding them and destroying them. For two hundred years, he'd lived and breathed revenge.

When tension had threatened to overcome him, he'd fucked women as a stress reliever. It was nothing more, nothing less. He'd fucked when necessary, when his body had threatened to explode if release wasn't imminent and his hand didn't provide the requisite relief. After his need for vengeance was sated, and then had come the desire to protect the unwitting humans from the evil creatures that were now his kind.

Vampires had a large variety of people to fuck; each other, humans and then there were the blood slaves. With such a diverse selection of the female and male population on offer, he'd had no need for anything deeper.

Time had passed and his basic lust had never developed into a need to build a relationship with any one woman. Looking back now, he supposed that he'd always been waiting for Scarlet. Waiting to find her and feel this sense of completion that had always been lacking in his life. It seemed rather ironic that a few days into experiencing the sheer bliss of having his mate by his side, she was sulking.

Not exactly the best start to any relationship, but then, no matter how much they were meant to be together, their path would always be a hard one. It was and always would be the way of it. All three of Scarlet's mates had tortured souls, had suffered deep losses. They'd fought the evil of their kind and had made enemies. This was just the first step on the rocky road of their future.

Taking another deep sip, his eyes glanced over the perfect features of his mate. It was enough to make him sigh with pleasure. He fully understood the phrase, 'A sight for sore eyes!' Because she was beautiful and her anger, rather than detracting from said beauty, merely enhanced it. She vibrated with life, it resonated from every pore.

She was definitely worth waiting for.

He'd met many beauties over the course of his long life. Women, who would have done anything for him, let him do anything to them, play as large or small a role in their lives as he wanted . . . Yet, this one woman was all he needed.

Where they had inflated his ego and he'd rather harshly, while unintentionally, discarded them because his need for vengeance had overshadowed all else. Yet with Scarlet, she deflated his ego, left it lying sunken on the ground like a limp balloon and he craved more. Perhaps it was the nature of the beast, but it seemed damned perverse to him! But then these last few days were perverse in their nature too. She had this whole attitude with him because he'd saved her life.

As though that was a crime! He was being blamed for everything, for Elizabeth biting Scarlet, for the impromptu claiming...like he'd done everything deliberately!

Nico and Vincent had become so accustomed to leaning on him for all the information in any given situation, and in this case, because of that, the blame lay entirely upon his shoulders. It didn't matter that he could make mistakes as well.

That he wasn't infallible.

No, that didn't matter, dammit!

It was forgotten at convenient moments that he didn't know the answer to every fucking thing. And, the reality was, that in situations such as these, where he usually understood what the hell was going on, it was tough to be left in the dark. If they were confused, then so was he! He was used to understanding situations that were well out of other people's capabilities. When he was as clueless as everyone else, he felt a distinct disadvantage!

His age and his experiences were an admitted bonus and gave them an edge, of which the brotherhood made full use.

In the dirty skirmish between good and evil, every skill was necessary. His intelligence and extra sensory perception gave them that added extra, something that was a silent weapon, one that the evil of his kind couldn't comprehend. It sped up the brotherhood, enable them to slay faster and with more efficiency. These skills combined with Nico's and Vincent's own unique capabilities took their brotherhood of slayers from mediocre to world-renowned. But in knowing this, his brethren seemed to think he was God as well!

Unfortunately for all of them, he wasn't. Because of that, his blood mate and brethren were giving him the cold shoulder and as he sipped at his Armagnac, his fury began to overtake all else.

He wanted to rage at Vincent and Nico. Ask them if they truly believed he would want to claim his mate in such a clandestine manner? Would they have preferred her to die? Did they think that he didn't want Scarlet to be fully involved in the decision making process?

He was fully aware that as the leader, he was always the one under most pressure.

It was something he was entirely capable of handling. Yet, when he made an important decision, yet wasn't backed to the hilt and was derided for it, it just pissed him off. He detested being put in this position, hated the fact that he couldn't protect her from scum like Elizabeth. Why couldn't Vincent see the untenable position he'd been put in?

Anger and fury from Scarlet, he could understand, but from Vincent too? He could tell that Nico understood to a point, but he felt as though he were entirely on his own here. Even the way they were seated at the table indicated their distaste at what he'd done. A squat table sat in the very middle of a cluster of four club chairs. Three sat to the left and he sat alone on the right.

It shouldn't have bothered him, but it did.

Everything about this bothered him. He hated that Scarlet was pissed off at him, but if it meant keeping her safe, then it was worth it. She could be pissed off at him as much as she wanted to be as long as he didn't lose her, as long as she was alive.

Even if to him it was and always had been a simple

matter-take Nico's blood or die!-he could understand Scarlet's hesitancy to accept what had occurred, but for Nico and Vincent to complain too? The two men he was closest to in the entire world, and they were brooding and not speaking to him? How unfair was that?

Damn it, did they want Elizabeth to get her claws into Scarlet? Did they like the fact that their mate, the mate that all paranormal creatures spent all of their lives seeking, was in danger? "Don't you think all of this is unnecessary, Vincent? To be sulking with me as though you're a child or something?" he spat in rapid French, making sure that the anger in his voice was as evident as it was in the glare he speared him with.

"I'm not sulking with you, Lazarus. If I'm 'sulking' at anything, it's the lengths we've had to take to keep Scarlet safe," Vincent replied coolly with a narrow-eyed sneer.

Lazarus nodded slowly in understanding. "As long as that is the case, Vincent. After all, Scarlet's safety is something we all want. No, it's much more than that, it's imperative to all of us."

"You're forgetting, Lazarus, I can now speak French too," Scarlet butted in sweetly, the gaze she swept over him tinged with fire.

He nodded again, this time considering what she'd said. Indeed you can, he thought. He had forgotten her new talent with languages. This entire claiming just grew more and more bizarre. He had never heard of a blood exchange that resulted in the claimed mate taking on some of the paranormal partner's traits. Instant knowledge of languages was definitely a new one on the list. But then, he'd never heard of a pairing such as this either.

Vincent and Lazarus had broken with the norms when they'd accepted Nico into their brotherhood, so they weren't new to raising eyebrows in the paranormal community. This, however, was completely ground-breaking. In all his years, in all his experience, he had never heard of anything like this.

Two vampires with a werewolf and a human mate?

Incredible!

"My apologies, Scarlet. I did indeed forget."

"I've told you time and again that I hate you speaking over me, as though I'm not here. Is it really necessary to speak in another language? At least now, I understand what the hell you're on about, but it's still rude! Especially as you simply assume that I can't understand! And frankly, I've come to expect more of you, Lazarus! I thought you were more of a gentleman!"

"Well, I can only be grateful that you're thinking of me at all, Scarlet. I feared I was completely out on my own in the cold woods!" he retorted sarcastically and took another sip of his brandy. "You would think that I was the one to bite you and almost drain the life from your very body." He paused. "Instead I saved it. I find it incredibly disloyal of you to treat me like I'm some kind of leper and all because I made a mistake. I may be old and have a greater depth of awareness than either of you, but just because I'm old doesn't mean I'm a god damn oracle. I can make miscalculations, just like anyone else. Especially in situations like this, where my emotions are involved and not only that, but when we're in totally unchartered territory. I have known of nothing that is similar to the kind of ménage a quatre in which we find ourselves! So forgive me for that!" he remarked pointedly, cuttingly, to Nico and Vincent.

"Lazarus, we're not blaming any of this on you," Nico said soothingly. "I fear you're misunderstanding our silence. If anything it's contemplative and perhaps yes, there is anger, but it's directed at Elizabeth. Both Vincent and I understand that. But we can't expect Scarlet to accept it as we do. Naturally she has to come to terms with everything. And that can only occur with time."

"Well said, Nico," Vincent told him.

Scarlet crossed her legs and pointedly began to dangle and swing the high heel from her foot. The movement made every muscle in her leg clearly defined and despite his anger and hurt at their unfair attitude towards him, his cock jumped to full mast at her shapely curves.

He watched as she then crossed her arms and pulled them tightly around her waist, which simultaneously pumped up her tits over the sweetheart neckline and almost exposed the sweet curve of her nipples, skin that he longed to suckle and moisten with his mouth.

Her body spoke of growing agitation, and finally, when Lazarus could see from her body language that she was growing more and more exasperated and was about to explode, she uncrossed everything and sat forward in her chair. There was an urgency about her that almost made him smile with pride. It was still difficult to be with her and realize that she was his. It was a truly remarkable sensation.

"Look, is there no way this blood slave thing can be altered," she asked earnestly.

While her denial of what they were to her hurt, he could easily understand how confused she must be feeling. Hell, hadn't he experienced something similar when he'd been turned? Although she hadn't become a vampire, her life had forever changed and like him and Vincent, that had been without her say-so.

In his agitation, he began speaking huskily in Latin. "I'm afraid not, mellita. I truly wish things had been different, Scarlet. You don't think I wanted to force something like this upon you? Your safety is imperative to me and to Nico and Vincent. We only have one mate. In the entire length of our lives, in my own case over two thousand, there is only one . . . you. Now I have you, I don't intend for Elizabeth or any other cunnus to let you take you away from me." Although her eyes softened a tad, he could tell that she was still heartily pissed off at him. He sighed, the sound soft and filled with regret.

"I understand that, Lazarus, and I'm really very grateful for you all trying to protect me, but did you have to take my choice away? Couldn't you have told me what was happening? I-I don't exactly like being told what to do or being dealt a fait accompli, this is the most life-altering, shattering thing that has ever happened to me and I wasn't even aware it was happening, dammit!"

"I know, Scarlet, but what choice did I have? Look, we arrived back at the suite and Elizabeth had obviously broken in and bitten you. She had to have drained a fair amount of blood for you to faint and the only option was for you to sup at Nico's blood . . . . It was either that or go into a state of shock, Scarlet! We had to act and act fast! She'd bitten you twice, once to mark and to declare her presence and then the second because she'd obviously enjoyed your taste. Your blood pressure was dropping because you were practically drained of blood. If we hadn't returned at that moment, you would have gone into shock and died," he explained earnestly, watching with concern as her face drained entirely of color.

"What choice did I have? I didn't even understand what was going on until a few moments after I realized you'd been bitten and that in itself could have been too late! It was either you live or you die, and I had to make the decision. Yes, I took it away from you, but you can live hating me. I can handle anything but you dying and the fault lying with me because I was too much of a pussy to make the choice for you! So I stepped up to the plate, grew a pair, and, because of that, you're here and breathing, and your mood, the fact that you're sulking, is fine by me. At least you're here to be in a sulk," he finished gruffly.

"What are you saying to her, Lazarus? Look at her, dammit, she's paler than milk! And, for God's sake, speak in French! You know Nico and I can't speak Latin!"

Scarlet's fingers crept up to cover her mouth. "I can speak Latin now? Oh my God, what the hell is happening to me? What have you done?" she whispered faintly.

"Calm down, mellita, you've just taken on some of our capabilities and now you can use them, too. There's nothing to worry about. Indeed, they're quite useful . . . . But, Scarlet, if our presence in your life bothers you so much, then we needn't live together. At first . . . ." The thought of being without her was so repugnant, the words almost stuck in his throat. He just hoped she realized how huge a concession it was. It physically pained him to even give her the option and, judging by the glares and furious flashes of anger being pointed his way, he could tell that neither Vincent nor Nico were any happier than he was about it.

"No, that's not necessary," Scarlet said diffidently, looking down at the floor.

She didn't see the relief that swept over the three men seated before her.

Her teeth tugged at her bottom lip, and, he watched, enchanted, as her lustrous eyes flashed upwards to glance over him. He was charmed once more at the faint flush that graced her cheeks for a moment. Even though she probably couldn't hear them, Vincent, Nico, and he all sighed faintly in gratitude that they wouldn't have to go without her at all!

It was a great comfort to know that she was as affected

by them as they were with her. Perhaps it should have been obvious, seeing as she was their mate, but that wasn't the case at all. Because she was so vital to them, they were supremely unsure of her, but perhaps that was the way it should be.

"Scarlet, I understand that these are things you'll have to come to terms with. But we all want one another. You wouldn't want to leave us and we would never want to let you go . . . ," he replied softly.

As his words faded into the air, his extra sensory perception suddenly kicked in. His fingers released the balloon glass and the shattering shards of the broken vessel seemed to explode into the air, the tinkling crash echoing in a surreal way for what felt like hours. Almost in slow motion, a hand came out of nowhere and dropped infinitesimally on to his shoulder. Before it even touched his jacket, his own fist shot up and clenched around the intruder's wrist. He gripped the unseen adversary's forearm and using that and his own torso as leverage, he tugged the stranger forwards and over him and directly on to the table before him.

A groan of pain escaped the stranger's mouth and hearing it, it awakened him to reality and the fact that lying supine before him was an obvious member of the cruise's entertainment staff. Startled and obviously slightly injured, the man was dressed in a glittery red shirt, black suit pants and polished patent leather shoes. He sat up slowly and stiffly with a groan and a glare of confusion at him, which Lazarus grimaced at.

A feeling of guilt swept over him at the man's uncoordinated movements and he scowled over at Nico, whose faint smile had caught his eye. Lazarus swiftly stood up and grabbed the man's hand and tugged him upwards. The entertainment worker got to his feet with a tight smile and hobbled back to the stage.

Silence and shock reigned in the huge salon before a spotlight shot out of nowhere and hovered over their table for a moment. "Best Costume Winner!" A loud speaker positioned somewhere in the auditorium announced. Hearing Nico hoot and laugh at that announcement, Lazarus spun around to glare at them, and he sat down silently, not taking a step towards the stage as the spotlight

kept directing as it was from him to the stage itself. He
turned his back on the entire entertainment staff and faced
Scarlet, who was also hiding a smile at the decree that his
very staid and very expensive suit was a damned costume.
His eyes glittered at hers, but he was pleased to see her face
graced with amusement and not the anger that had so
recently been there.

The spotlight eventually faded when the man yielding it
finally realized that Lazarus wasn't going to go on the
damned stage and make a fucking fool of himself.

"Can we go back to the suite now?" Nico asked with a
smirk. "You would have drawn less attention if you'd
actually walked on to the stage. Now everyone's gawking
because you made a damned fool of yourself!"

"You're damned lucky that that guy could walk after
that! You've broken people's backs using that move in the
past!"

"Yeah, well, I didn't, mater. Look, can we leave? As
Nico kindly pointed out, I'm being gawped at. Can we at
least go back to the room? Or another lounge - something
for fuck's sake?"

Scarlet ducked her head but he could still see a grin and
despite himself, he laughed a little too, even though his so-
called new title of Best Costume was a joke. Exhaling
deeply, because he knew she was trying to swallow a laugh.
" Come on, let's go. Give Lazarus a reprieve. I'm almost
starting to get jealous. A lot of those looks are come-ons!
And not just from the women!" Scarlet said with a chuckle.

Pushing her chair backwards, she stood then walked
over to him, waiting for him to stand before grabbing his
arm and hooking her own into it.

He knew that she'd been teasing, but he liked that she
was a tad jealous. Because the grip in which she held his
arm wasn't just about joking! Her body was curled into his,
and, if he thought about how a few minutes ago, a country
wouldn't have been too far away from him, Lazarus
grinned at the traits she was displaying. There was definite
possessiveness in her clasp and as they strode out of the
room, Lazarus didn't have to turn around to see the whole
room's eyes on them to know that that was the case!

When they left the darkened salon, he leaned down.
"Am I forgiven then?" he asked quietly.

She stiffened a little but then looked up at him.

He loved the way her gaze was fringed by her thick and silky lashes as her deliciously haunting green orbs stared back at him fiercely.

"What do you think? Should I forgive you?"

Unable to lie to her, he shrugged before he answered her. "What I did was unforgivable, delicia. I cannot be anything but honest with you. But what I did was for your sake. You're a part of my soul, Scarlet, and I know you hate that I took your choice away, but can you imagine how vital you are to me?" he hedged.

She shook her head. "I know how vital you're coming to be to me, though. Was it truly a life or death situation, Lazarus?" Scarlet whispered breathily.

"In a way, yes and no. I knew that your supping from Nico would always cure you, but you could have died if we hadn't have acted so swiftly, so, yes. I won't lie. Nico was always an option but so was taking you to a human doctor. But there were so many ways in which that could all go wrong. He'd have to match your blood type, he might not have had the facilities on board. Not only that but I'd have to explain how you were almost drained and by four puncture wounds!

"It was an untenable position to be placed in and I truly believed that if you took Nico's blood, that of your mate and that of a werewolf, I just thought it would fortify our defenses. But I didn't take into account that I had bitten you and that Elizabeth had also bitten you and taken a lot of blood in the process. I had no idea that your body would start the claiming process, I didn't know that until you reacted to tasting his blood and that's the truth."

She nodded slowly. "I forgive you then, but unless it's a life or death situation, I never ever want you to do something like that again. When you first told me that you were two thousand years old, I thought you were messing around. Either joking or trying to, I don't know, or maybe trying to impress me because I was amongst some crowd of weirdo vampire fanciers. Now I know that it's true, I have to take that into consideration in our dealings together and what form that relationship is going to take.

"Because I know you come from a different age. I know you've lived through countless eras, and most of them where the woman was the lesser sex and incapable of making her own decisions. Not only that, but she didn't want to make those decisions, they were for her husband, her man. Well, I'm not like that. I can make my own mind up. I don't need a man to do that for me. Yet it seems as though I've been given three men who are all alphas and want to take over . . . I understand that there will sometimes be issues, but just keep me in the know. That's all I ask, Lazarus and I know Nico and Vincent, even though they might not admit it, defer to you. So tell them that, too," she said firmly.

"Don't forget that women weren't always so incapable in my time. I'm used to strong women; it will be my protective instincts that clash with your independence. Forgive me that, Scarlet. But I do know how you feel, and, even though it will be difficult, hell it will be more than that, to have you in my life is well worth it."

She smiled softly at that and leaned on to her tiptoes to press a kiss on to his lips. "That has to be the nicest thing anyone has ever said to me. Do you know that?"

"It had better be," he growled against her mouth and then laughed. "You may be surprised to realize this, mellita, but I doubt it will be as hard as you think for Vincent and Nico to come to terms with your ability to make decisions either . . . . Didn't you see how furious Vincent was? And Nico was as unhappy as Vincent when I told him we had to claim you. We're all on your side, delicia."

"I'm glad to hear it. Although . . . I don't remember being claimed," she said with a pout and moved into his body space, her torso rubbing sensually against his. "That can be rearranged, amor meus," he murmured gutturally and clamped an arm at her back and tugged her even closer to him.

Her hands came up to cup his head.

He almost groaned when her fingers tangled in his hair. The tips began to massage his scalp and he felt as though every nerve ending in his body had just stood on edge. Hell, it felt more like he'd been electrocuted and the current was still cruising over the surface of his skin!

His own hands slid over the luxurious curves of her hips and waist, before sliding upwards to graze the sides of her breasts.

Her fingers began to entangle themselves in his hair.

His own came up to capture the luscious red locks that tumbled about her shoulders, sparking tinder as they glowed against the peachy creaminess of her bare décolletage before flickering like fire against the black as night dress she was wearing.

He grasped the ends of her hair and locked them in his fist, then curled her hair about his wrist and wound it tighter and tighter until he controlled the movements of her head. His actions tugged her mouth from his.

She responded with a hungry moan. At his continued absence from her mouth, her dazed and aroused eyes sought his and her lips parted as she gently sucked air into her lungs.

With their gaze caught, Lazarus slowly but surely lowered his head. Each passing centimeter brought them closer and closer until there was but a hair's breadth between them. He watched her eyes flutter shut as his lips gently tugged at her own. His tongue came out and swept along the sweet curve of her upper lip, before singling the other out for equal attention. He flicked it and out of her mouth quickly before she could seek it before biting down on her lower lip to make teeth indentations on the fleshy fullness.

Unable to control them, his entire being now in his cock's firm grasp, his fangs grew. The burst of blood in his mouth and the sting of pain hardened his cock even further. He scraped the sharp tip along the soft flesh of her mouth and felt arousal shudder through his system as she moaned breathlessly.

Feeling a hand grip his shoulder brought him back to earth, and he was glad for Nico's swift reminder that they were in the center of the cruise's very busy lobby. It simply wouldn't do for one of the vampires on board to be seen biting a harmless human female. The thought fluttered through his mind and manifested itself in a grimace as he slowly unwound Scarlet's locks from his hand. Each inch that he released made a need to recapture it flood into his veins. She was his and he hated having to modulate his behavior, behavior that would tell every mother fucker in this damned vestibule that Scarlet was his and to take their sorry eyes from her ass.

It was damned odd to feel so possessive about her. Having never experienced the emotion before, it was rather peculiar finding himself feeling nothing but possessive whenever he was with her and spotted some bastard ogling her tits. He both longed to cover her up and show her off. The black dress she was wearing tonight was a perfect example of how confused she made him feel.

The length of black satin stopped at just above her knee, exposing her shapely calves to the world at large. It then clung tightly to every single curve her body possessed. Cupping her tits like a lover's hands, it pushed them out and showed the heavy weight to perfection.

Seeing the entire picture she made, pushed his cock from merely aroused into ready to fuck mode. He enjoyed seeing her dressed to impress, knew that that sexiness was for him, Nico, and Vincent. But the rest of the male population was also granted a sight of her loveliness and that made him as jealous as hell!

It was a contrasting position to find himself in, but as he'd so often told himself that night, being with Scarlet simply tilted his world on its axis and he just had to become accustomed to that, and, if it meant having her by his side for the rest of their lives, then it was damned worth it!

Dropping his head so that his forehead almost touched her shoulder, he tilted it so that his lips grazed her ear. His voice was guttural. "Do you want to fuck me as much as I want to fuck you, Scarlet?" he murmured.

Her breathy gasp moistened the skin of his throat. The soft moan merely sent bursts of need throttling through him until he felt like pushing her to the floor and fucking her there and then.

He knew, that despite the very public nature of this kind of coupling, Scarlet would be as ready for him as he was for her. He flicked his tongue against the shell-like curve of her ear and stroked the earlobe with the flat of it. Feeling her shudder almost made him smile. "I'll take that as a yes, Scarlet." Slowly rolling his hips against her own, he watched her reactions closely.

"You want my cock in your pussy, no? Mellita? I don't even have to touch your cunt to know you're wet. You want my mouth there?" he asked and nudged her throat with his nose. "You want me to suck you and lick your clit?" he asked, knowing full well what her answer would be. Her breathy groans were turning him on, and he was finding it harder and harder to maintain any kind of control.

When she finally spoke, her voice broke. "Yes, Lazarus. I do. I . . . ," she paused and rubbed her chest against his. "I really need you to fuck me, ocellus."

Hearing her call him darling, and in his own tongue too, made his cock start to pound in earnest. He knew there and then that if he didn't fuck her, and soon, he was in grave danger of having zipper tracks along the ridge of his cock for the rest of his life! "I shall fuck you, Scarlet. You're mine, do you know that?" he asked gruffly and relaxed when she nodded, her face open and without any misgivings.

"Come then, we shall return to your suite, for it is closest." Releasing her from his embrace, he tucked her into his side and began the five minute walk to the elevator, which, thank God, arrived swiftly. Two minutes later, they were walking into the entry way of Scarlet's set of rooms. His eyes glanced about the different setting and noticing the outdoor balcony which her salon opened on to. Intrigued, Lazarus grabbed her hand and tugged her with him as he walked.

Opening the French doors, he stepped on to the balcony. "Lean against the railings, delicia," he ordered.

Her eyes flared at the naked suggestion in his.

He smiled slowly and promisingly.

She hesitated a second before turning around and leaning her elbows against the shining silver bar.

Stepping close behind her, he settled his hands on her hips and ground his own against hers as he moved even closer to her. He pivoted them for a second, relishing the smooth slide of his trouser front against the silky smoothness of her dress. The sensation was like dynamite and arching backwards, he inhaled as he slid the zipper to his fly down and released his aching cock.

Resting the heavy weight against the small of Scarlet's back, he began to rock his hips and relished the feel of the satin against his cock. His cock began to leak pre-cum and although it was ruining her dress, he didn't care. He was marking her and the thought almost made him laugh, as it sounded so much like something Nico would do! Something entirely animalistic and primitive, but, if the cap fit, then who was he to deny it. Scarlet brought out the beast in him and that was the truth of it.

Her husky voice merely made his cock harden impossibly more. "I liked this dress, Lazarus," she murmured with a pout.

He leaned over her, bending his back as he crouched above her. "Hmm, I love this dress, too," he said, grinning at her breathy laugh which was tinged with arousal.

"Then why ruin it?"

"Ruin it?" he declared with mock-outrage. "I'm merely embellishing it, making it even more beautiful!" Her soft snort made his lips twitch. Moving his hands so that they rested at the hem of the dress, he slowly slid the fabric over the curve of her thighs and hips until it rested at her waist. Exposing her bare ass and even barer pussy to the elements and to his extremely turned-on gaze!

"You were naked all the time under that dress?" he said with a groan. "How do you expect my brain to function when you go without panties, huh?"

"Not my problem, ocellus," she murmured huskily. "Anyway, out of your mind with lust for me is how I want all three of you. Don't want you getting bored."

It was his time to snort at her. Like that was ever going to happen! He said as much to her and even though he couldn't see her face, directed as it was to the open sea, he knew there was a soft smile of smug possessiveness gracing the gentle curve of her mouth. It reassured him. That she was learning to feel more secure in their affections satisfied that primal beast inside him and settled any unease in his heart. More than anything he wanted her to be happy and learning that she was becoming more content and felt safe with her mates really pleased him.

Sliding his hands from their resting place at her waist down to the apex of her thighs, he savored the feel of that molten heat scorching his fingers. She was wet, so wet his fingers were drenched and easily glided through the engorged folds of her pussy. Her cunt lips naturally formed into a channel that eagerly sucked his finger inside and he teased her by resting the fingertip at the entrance to her body yet never entering, rocking back and forth at the cusp, dragging the length of the digit up and down her clit, before retreating from the welcoming warmth of her pussy.

He felt the tension overcome her, her muscles stiffened and her body tautened as though in preparation for a climax, which he gladly and swiftly gave her. Clasping a supportive arm about her waist, he clutched her there with his elbow and angled his arm so that he could hold her but simultaneously touch her. With this hand, he separated the outer set of lips and bared her clit, freeing it from its small hood. Then he coated his index finger in her juices and began to frig the now-naked nubbin.

Her breathy gasps and moans were music to his ears and quickly rose into high-pitched screams as an orgasm washed through her, leaving her limp and relaxed in his arms. Only his strength kept them from toppling over the side, lax as she was in his hold and a dead weight that could have pushed them over, unbalancing him as it did, but what a way to go. His woman in his arms, her cries of pleasure still echoing in his ears, her juices coating his fingers and his cock resting between the cheeks of her ass waiting to enter that scalding heat of her cunt . . . . Heaven.

Gently patting her clit with his fingers, he smirked as she tensed and undulated in his arms. He knew she was sensitive now but that didn't stop him. He wanted her so out of her mind that she didn't know who the hell she was. That her conscious mind didn't know she was with him and Nico and Vincent. He wanted her body to recognize them, for it to respond to theirs. This primal need that was ricocheting through him clamored for an answering response in hers and he was damned sure that he was going to get it.

Pushing four fingers into her drenched pussy, he scissored them inside her. The action made her moan but he did it anyway, in his mind's eye, he knew what he wanted to do and he needed her wet and relaxed for it. He'd only ever done this the one time with Nico and a charming and statuesque blonde he'd met in Berlin about eighty years ago, but he wanted to recreate that because the thought of it still turned him on and he wanted Scarlet to replace the German woman in his memories. It felt wrong thinking of another woman now that he had her and he intended to rectify that tonight.

He felt rather than heard her gasp.

"No, Lazarus, I don't want to do that," she muttered tensely, shaking her head.

He frowned, unsure of what she meant. "Scarlet? What don't you want me to do?"

"What you did with that woman."

Scowling in confusion, he gripped her hips firmly with his hands. "What are you talking about?" he muttered with a frown.

"The blonde, dammit, don't act like you don't know what I'm talking about!"

"Scarlet, I don't have to act confused, I am confused! Which blonde?"

"You said something about a blonde."

"I did?"

"Yes," she paused and ducked her head, he found it adorable that after all they'd done together, she could still flush with embarrassment. "Yeah, well it's okay for you to think it's funny that I'm embarrassed, but it's not, alright!"

"Scarlet, I didn't say a word!"

Her head whipped around to incinerate him with a glare. "You did, dammit! Lazarus, why are you even lying?"

There was a cough from behind him, and it was his turn to whip his head around and glare at whoever had just forestalled him from defending himself.

Nico held his hands up as he walked on to the balcony. "Lazarus isn't lying, dorogaya. He didn't say a word."

"Stop defending him, Nico!"

"I'm not, milaya, but it's the truth. He didn't say anything."

"Well, I heard something about a blonde and . . . ." she scoffed, her words trailing off into a murmur.

Lazarus softly grasped her chin in his fingers and looked into her eyes. "What was that, delicia?" he asked curiously.

She scowled at his question. "You know what I'm talking about!"

"I genuinely don't," he replied honestly, his eyes reflecting the truth of that.

Scarlet frowned in confusion. "You were saying about this German woman, which, by the way, Lazarus, isn't very tactful, is it? I mean, do you normally talk about old conquests when you're with the latest version?"

"I said nothing about a German woman," he said firmly, but, hurt, he released her. "I thought . . . ," he continued then paused, tilting his head to the side in thought before he continued, "I thought about her. I didn't say anything about her. Are you picking up on my thoughts, Scarlet?"

She shrugged. "I don't know, am I?

I thought you said that you wanted to replace the woman with me, and maybe to you that's the height of romance, but it isn't to me, Lazarus!" Scarlet paused and looked at him for a moment. "I-I saw you two with her. But I didn't realize I did. I just thought you were talking to me." Her eyes grew wider with every word that left her mouth.

Blowing out a breath, he tried to comprehend what the hell was going on. Picking up on some of their language talents . . . that he could explain. But reading his thoughts? Fuck, he'd never heard of anything like this before. He was in completely new territory, and it killed him to not be able to answer all of the questions in his mate's eyes.

"Well, I never expected this! Are you picking up on everything I think?" he asked.

She frowned, this time in concentration, but shook her head.

"If you were turned on, then you could have been projecting the image, maybe? Who was it? Ava?" Nico asked interestedly.

Lazarus nodded.

Nico glared at him. "Smart, Lazarus!"

"How the hell was I supposed to know? Anyway, my intentions were good!"

"You've probably frightened her to death!"

"Stop talking about me like I'm not here! And I'm not frightened! I just don't want to do it!"

Nico's eyes flared with remembered lust.

Scarlet pulled free from his arms and shot a glare at him. "Stop thinking about it!"

"Why do you think I wanted to do it, Scarlet? It was a highly memorable occasion for Nico and me, I would have preferred for yours to be the face I think of whenever it pops into my mind," he said suavely. "But, if it frightens you, then there is need for concern, mellita, you know we would never do anything to cause you fear."

She crossed her arms and started tapping her foot.

Somehow she managed to look regal and commanding despite her diminutive form and the fact that she was bare from the waist down! Hell, they must be in love, he thought with a wry inward smile.

"I'm not frightened, Lazarus! I've just never done anything like that before. You wouldn't fit."

"You'd be surprised, Scarlet," Nico said, his voice hungry and awash with lust.

She bit her lip anxiously at that statement.

As he reached to comfort her, Nico swept her against him and brought his mouth down to hers. He suckled at her lips for a second before lathing the part she'd bitten down hard on. His hands rested at her hips a moment before his fingers slowly trailed down to her cunt. Unerringly, they delved at her center as he spoke. "Just think, milaya, Lazarus and I would be here . . . ."

Lazarus watched Nico's fingers sink into her cunt.

"And Vincent would be here." This time, Nico's tongue swirled around Scarlet's lips.

"You wouldn't fit," she repeated throatily.

"It would be tight, but that's where the pleasure is."

Lazarus bit back a smile at Scarlet's moan as Nico moved his hand and simultaneously began to nibble at her lips.

"Would it hurt?"

"We would never hurt you, radast moya."

She curled into Nico's chest.

"I know. I've only really had vanilla sex, Nico. I know this is hardly plumbing the depths of BDSM, but this is still out there for me, okay?" she murmured softly.

"I know that, mellita, and so does Nico. If you're not ready, then that's just fine," Lazarus interjected truthfully.

"I don't like you thinking of this other woman, Ava," she stated possessively.

He could tell that her jealousy shocked her. Even though he couldn't read her mind, he knew from the expression on her fact that she'd never felt that way about any man before.

"I'm not thinking of other women, Scarlet. I'm remembering what happened, and, I won't lie, it was a turn on. I'm hoping that eventually you won't be so afraid and might want to try it. When or if you do, we're at your service," he said teasingly before striding towards them to stand at Scarlet's other side. His hand joined Nico's and, flashing a glance at him, their fingers touched and slowly, they thrust them into her. Once inside her pussy, they both moved alternatively, Nico moving up as he moved down. As he pressed backwards, Nico pressed forwards.

"Imagine," he whispered sibilantly in her ear. "Our cocks both here, touching you in different places in our effort to please you . . . ." Pressing his mouth to the curve of her throat, he released his fangs and scraped the skin there. As she hissed, he flicked his gaze up to Nico and together they inserted another finger.

Nico's other hand came down to rub at her clit.

They watched as Scarlet's body began to flush slightly, a warning of her impending orgasm.

Seeing this, Lazarus swiftly pulled down the sweetheart neckline of her dress and released her breasts from their covering. Exposing them to the evening air, he scraped his fangs along the delicate skin. He flicked his tongue along the firm pout of her erect nipple, and, hearing her heavy, panting breathing, he quickly bit down and relished the taste of her blood as it coated his tongue. It was almost as delicious as her pussy juices.

As he suckled harder when he felt the tremors overtake her body, felt each and every inch of her shudder as a climax worked its way through her system and detonated in every part of her being.

Their fingers were coated in her juices, they slipped and slid inside her drenched cunt.

It was hard not to push her to the ground and work his cock inside her as she lay there gasping for breath from the orgasm that was still quaking her insensate. And, although he wasn't trying to manipulate her, he knew that she would comply with his desire for Nico and him to share her pussy simply because she couldn't stand the thought of them thinking about another woman.

He could easily understand that. The thought of her with another man almost made the veins in his throat explode. A vampire's blood pressure was extremely low, but despite that, he felt at risk of an apoplexy and she hadn't even mentioned another guy! So no wonder she was aggravated by his thoughts about Ava! Moving away from her slightly, he let her rest in Nico's arms. "Where's Vincent?" he asked softly.

"He found Elizabeth's suite today. It seems she's started to frequent it now after not setting foot there all this week. He just wanted to make sure that she was there, where she should be and couldn't cause havoc here with us."

"We're going to have to sort her out, Nico and soon." Nico nodded and grimaced. "Not as easy as that. She's more slippery than expected and our minds aren't exactly on the game." Lazarus laughed; it was an odd mixture of frustration and anger. When his eyes glanced over Scarlet, tenderness mingled in with the other emotions.

"Yes, she has blown our minds, hasn't she?" Bending down, he pressed a kiss to Scarlet's temple. " Come, amor meus, to your bedchamber," he whispered huskily.

"You're showing your age again, Lazarus," she replied, her voice throaty with emotion.

He laughed. "When you've seen as many years as I have, Scarlet, it's easier to show your age than not!"

Nico lifted her into his arms and carried her from the balcony to the bedroom and as he set her down on the bed, Lazarus moved to the shades that were covering the window and opened them. The fading sunlight shone delicately into the room, tinting the world with a deliciously, delightful rosy-red hue.

It glinted off Scarlet's peachy skin and mated with the fiery locks atop her head and down below. Her disheveled appearance merely turned him on even more and as he glanced down at himself, saw that he wasn't exactly the picture of respectability with his fly open and his cock bare to the world, he grinned slightly to himself.

Scarlet's voice was tinged with lust as she spoke and it resonated deep within himself as her words hit home. "Touch yourself, Lazarus."

His hand immediately went to his cock and he let his eyes remain there, because he knew that she wasn't looking at him in the regular way. Her eyes were focused inwards on what she could sense through his thoughts and while that should have made his defenses scream, it felt too damn good and too right to complain. And so, he stroked his cock. His left fist alternating between clutching tightly at the base of the shaft and grasping his balls, tugging them down to stop himself from cumming too quickly.

His right hand slid firmly up and down, dragging his foreskin along the shaft as he moved. Sometimes his fingers would rim the edge of the glans, drag over the shining head of his cock and gently skim over the pre-cum that was gathering there. All the time he moved, he could hear Scarlet's gasps of pleasure, her whimpers of excitement until finally, he could take no more.

Striding over to the side of the bed, he pulled Scarlet around to face him, so that she was lying horizontally on the mattress' soft surface. He pulled her legs up and apart as he dragged her closer to him and tilted her ass up. Placing his hands underneath her butt, he let her legs rest against his torso as he brought his cock to her pussy and slammed into her.

His cock unerringly finding the way home as he impaled himself on her, allowed his cock to feel every silken inch as it slipped into her wet cunt. His eyes clenched shut as a mask of concentrated lust overtook his face. His hips pistoned into her as arousal worked its insidious way through his veins, tainting everything with the need to cum, to catapult his seed into her womb and make her his.

The thought made him shudder and when she clenched around him, her pussy tightening until it was almost painfully exciting to thrust into her, only then did he stop. His hands came down to once more tug his balls away from his body, because he wanted this to last and it wouldn't if he continued in this path. His eyes fluttered open to look into those of his mate and what he saw their set fire to his soul.

"I'm ready, Lazarus," she whispered huskily.

"For what, Scarlet?"

"You know what I'm talking about." He jerked his head. "I do, but I want you to say it. We would never force you into doing something you didn't want to do, delicia."

"I know that and that's why I'll do it."

"Scarlet, no other woman matters to me but you. You know that don't you? I can't wipe out all the woman in my past, even to make you feel better. But, and I'm ashamed to say this, they meant nothing to me. They were there for my pleasure and little else. I have caused a lot of unhappiness in my past and I'm not proud of that. I've had needs and

I've fulfilled them, but little else. But with you, you do nothing but fulfill me. Just looking at you completes me.

I've known you five days and my world is already beginning to revolve around you. As it should, you're my blood mate, you're my everything. While I'm grateful that you're open to new things, I don't want to push you into something you're not ready for, mellita."

"But I am ready, Lazarus and I thank you for sharing that with me, but I'm not doing it for that."

"Are you sure?" Nico asked gutturally.

"Deadly. I-I, at first, I couldn't contemplate that. You're both, well, you're both large, you know? And together, both of you inside me? Well, I couldn't imagine it. But I know that you would never hurt me.

That you take pleasure from my pleasure, so why shouldn't I trust you? I was wrong to be scared. Like you said, you would never hurt me and it just took a while for that to sink in." Curling upwards, she sat at an awkward angle and let her arms support her as she tried to get closer to him. A circus performer couldn't have moved any nearer to him, what with her legs resting against his body! But he knew she was trying to bring him closer to her, make him resume his thrusts and continue in the vein she wanted.

Slowly, he rocked his hips. Not too hard or too fast, but rhythmically. He saw the effort it took for her to support herself and so using brute strength, lifted her from the bed and up and into his arms. He felt her clench around him suddenly at the new position, which in turn made her hiss at the depth of penetration. And it took all his might not to spew into her there and then. Instead he exhaled roughly and directed Nico to lie on the bed underneath her.

Unzipping his pants and releasing his cock, Lazarus watched as Nico completed those actions before moving into position underneath Scarlet. Before he could release her atop Nico's body, Nico's hands came up and began to unzip the long fastener of Scarlet's dress. It was crumpled at the waist so there were a few minutes of tugging, but eventually she was naked in his arms. Only then did he release her and rest her atop Nico. He didn't have to read her mind to know that she found being naked, sandwiched between them while they were fully dressed a complete turn on.

His cock thoroughly coated with her copious juices, he slid easily in and out of her pussy.

"Don't stop, Lazarus," she murmured.

When Nico also managed to maneuver his cock into her cunt, she shifted on his chest, moaning as her hips involuntarily jerked upwards.

"Do you like that, angel moy?" Nico grunted and placed his hands on her hips and jerked them back against him.

Her reply was a groan of pleasure.

Lazarus continued on his path and slowly began to thrust his hips, and, with the help of his fingers opening her up to his penetration, he finally managed to enter her fully. It was a tight fit, which he wouldn't deny and although he tried to keep his eyes open for her sake, he couldn't. They flickered shut, unable to stay open at such unspeakable pleasure the view gave him.

He continued to pump into her, slowly. The slurps of her juices as her pussy strove to contain them both were loud in the silent atmosphere. When she finally accepted them both, they were all finely misted with sheen of sweat.

"Oh my God," she croaked. Her legs shifted on the bed and her head pushed back into Nico's chest as her hips began to rock.

Nico could tell she wasn't exactly comfortable with the fullness. "Calm down, milaya," he muttered gruffly. His hand quickly went to her pussy, and he began to stroke and caress her clit.

She shrieked at the sensation, her hips jerking at his touch and this time her head began to shift from side to side.

Nico's other hand came up and grabbed her by the chin. His lips sought hers.

Quickly the kiss became a conflagration of everything that Scarlet's body was screaming to release. Her teeth nipped and bit aggressively at Nico's. Her mouth sought his tongue and the two tangled together as Nico's fingers worked her clit and both sets of hips rocked infinitesimally in and out of her cunt.

Her breathing began to become labored, her chest rising and falling deeply as sensation after sensation began to build up inside of her.

Lazarus watched as a light flush deepened her peachy

skin to a delicious rose and added his own aid to Scarlet's impending climax. Bending down, he placed his hands on either side of Nico's head and dropped his mouth to her bare breasts. Both the movement and the shift of his cock inside her and the sensation of her breasts being caressed made her cry out with pleasure.

He nipped at the budded nipples, he suckled a little before his eyes sought the heated kiss Nico and Scarlet were sharing. Unable to help himself, he stretched upwards and began to suckle at her earlobe, dropped biting caresses along the line of her jaw. Unable to help himself, his hips began to pump in earnest now.

Nico's joined in as their lust began to spill over, the tension of their cocks being so closely confined and jammed together, their veins bubbling with a need to cum, to release their seed into their pussy, to revel in their possession of her. Their desire was merely augmented by the sound track of their fucking. Her moans and whimpers, cries and screams of pleasure were like a light to dry timber.

Everything in them, their bodies, minds and souls ignited as Scarlet's pussy began to convulse around them. Her undulating curves, her tight cunt, her extreme pleasure in what they were doing, they all exploded in their heads and as their lust burst into flames and their cum shot into her welcoming cunt, a fierce fatigue over-set them as everything they were, everything they represented and everything she meant to them shot into her, completing and fulfilling them all in ways they'd never imagined possible.

Chapter Eight

As his heart raced and adrenaline shot through his system like wildfire, Vincent was hard pressed not to panic. Hell, who was he kidding? Fear of loss, of a life without Scarlet dogged at his heels as he ran through what seemed like endless passageways, as he headed from the very north of the ship to the far south of it. He'd already started to panic, each step he took was laden with it and it wasn't going to ease any until Elizabeth was dead and Scarlet was safe in his arms!

He raged with frustration at the time wasted by having to move from one end of the ship to the other, but then he supposed that Elizabeth, once on board the ship and knowing they were baying for her blood, had requested a cabin exchange, one that was as far away as physically possible from his own set of suites.

The only thing that stopped him from screaming in aggravation was his ability to transmogrify into mist and slip through the hefty crowds that seemed to congregate in the most ridiculous of places. He was moving in hallways that led to cabins and suites, not at the very center of the entertainment halls! He'd passed twenty-head strong groups arguing about what and where they were going to eat for supper. Laughable when dinner had only ended two hours ago! Smaller groups of people lost in the maze-like passageways, attempting to find their way to the Lido deck to watch the starlit night over the blackest of oceans.

Hell, it seemed an unlikely place to gather and he could only assume that the Fates were having a chuckle at his expense, forcing all of these obstacles into his path until he was pushed to the limits. Pushed so far that he had to hold back from admitting he was scared, because if he admitted that, then it all came tumbling down, and he couldn't afford for that to happen at this exact moment.

No, he needed to get to Lazarus, to warn him and help him. When Elizabeth lay drained on the floor, dead and lifeless, only then could he relax. Admit how fucking scared he'd been. Then, he could laugh about it and take solace in Scarlet's presence.

The thought eased him some, but agitation and concern wiped that out, until he was impossibly more on edge than before. Maneuvering as he was around clusters of people; attempting to pass from one end of the cruise ship to the other and all in the vain hope that he could reach Scarlet before Elizabeth had a chance of sticking her claws in again.

She had Lazarus and Nico there to protect her, of that he was fully aware, but they were completely unsuspecting of an upcoming attack. They were practically defenseless and knowing them as they did, hell knowing himself and his own reactions to their mate, they were probably plunging their way into Scarlet's ever-so luscious and ever-so wonderfully greedy body!

They were totally unprepared to protect her and Elizabeth was a vicious bitch. She'd see that they were completely unaware of her presence, sneak in and somehow manage to snatch Scarlet from them. She had surprise on her side. And it was something she would take complete advantage of.

That he might even at this moment be too late, that she might have captured Scarlet made his always low blood pressure begin to increase. He felt the whoosh of blood race through his system, felt the light-headed buzz in his head as his emotions pounded their way through him, slaying him as they did. He'd known how vital a blood mate was to a vampire, but Vincent hadn't realized that it, that she would overtake his soul to the extent that she had.

When he took into account that he'd known Scarlet for less than five days, it completely blew his mind. Vincent's life had made a complete volte face. His heart, before meeting Scarlet, still mourning the loss of Véronique, his mind still filled with vengeance. Now, Scarlet had taken complete control of his senses. So much so that the thought of a life without her was impossible. It was enough to make him shudder at the thought.

He could finally comprehend that life without a blood mate was impossible. And although it saddened him, he realized that when he'd believed Véronique to have been his mate, she obviously hadn't been, because he'd managed to continue, he'd managed to survive. That wasn't a prospect for Vincent where Scarlet's life was concerned. He needed her like humans needed air to breathe, like fishes needed water for life. He'd known loss, but Scarlet's death would be more than a loss. It would be like a huge chasm in his soul. She'd worked his way into the very depths of his being and contemplating the danger she was in, made his body quicken with fury and fear.

Never a smart combination.

The brotherhood had known since Elizabeth's biting spree, that Scarlet was in danger. Before that they'd never even contemplated what mischief, what havoc the bitch vampiress could create. Now, in full aware of all the facts, it didn't make it any easier. When they said that ignorance was bliss, it truly was. While they'd realized Scarlet's existence was endangered, they'd believed that Elizabeth's true prey had always been Lazarus.

She had rich pickings for a vampiress of her notorious history, especially one who longed for more infamy and longed for world renown amongst her peers. Managing to kill Lazarus, one of the eldest undead walking the planet, would be a real coup for Elizabeth. Therefore, they'd not incorrectly believed that she would have focused all her brain power at toppling him.

It had been a comforting thought for all three of them.

Scarlet couldn't defend herself from Elizabeth.

Hell, Vincent and Nico couldn't either.

But Lazarus could.

If anyone could kill the evil bitch, then Lazarus was definitely the man for the job. Having just spoken with her dazed and mistreated blood slaves, Vincent had just learned that Lazarus was indeed her target, but she was going to annihilate him through his only weakness . . . Scarlet. Losing Scarlet would cause more than Lazarus' demise. He and Nico would be goners as well. She'd become that vital that fast. It was a scary realization but true nonetheless.

Annoyance threatened to topple his guise of invisibility. It was difficult keeping a cool, clear and calm head when he felt like screaming his fury at the fates. He was annoyed at himself and the brotherhood in general. Had they taken on this case the way they tackled every other, then Elizabeth would have been dead by now. Scarlet would be safe and they'd all be enjoying the remainder of this wonderful cruise. Hell, on other slaying missions, they'd managed to set out and kill some of their targets within the first twenty-four hours!

This target was dragging on and it was nothing to do with Elizabeth's skills. No, it was their distraction that was at fault, the fact that they couldn't keep their hands off Scarlet. That had kept the vampiress alive and roaming the damned ship for the past five days. He was fuming at their incompetence. Fuming that Scarlet was in danger because they'd been too busy playing with her to take care of business.

Vincent couldn't believe that it had taken him so long to

Mandy Monroe

discover Elizabeth's suite. He'd only thought to look for it this morning, when Lazarus and Nico had been 'protecting' Scarlet in their suite which basically meant they'd been fucking her brains out!

They'd all known that Elizabeth had been hiding out at the start of the cruise, but as time had passed, she would have felt safer. Safe enough to retreat to her own cabin and rest herself for the coming days as she plotted her actions.

It had taken him until this morning to place one of the pursers on the front desk under a trance and ask after Elizabeth's cabin number. He couldn't believe that it had taken him and the other two so damned long to make even the most minor investigations into Elizabeth's whereabouts.

It seemed laughable that their brotherhood could have failed to do something so magnificently simple. How the hell they'd managed to become so famous in their world as top slayers was beyond him. It just proved how Scarlet blew their minds. They'd never in their lives been so shoddy in their duties and if they ever had been, then they would have been slain themselves! Hell, no way would they have made it this far into their old age!

It was sheer luck that he'd learned about Elizabeth's upcoming plans. Seeing that Lazarus and Scarlet were about to 'make up', he'd let Nico watch over them and make sure that they were safe and well-guarded when they were so wrapped up in each other before heading off with Elizabeth's suite number in his head on a reconnaissance mission.

Well, it had been a success. So damned successful that he'd learned his mate's life was in danger, that their ineptitude had brought Scarlet to Elizabeth's attention. It was enough to make him steam. His head felt almost as though it were about to blow. Because while he cursed himself and Nico and Lazarus for being so damned foolish at letting Elizabeth live so damned long, it had been completely out of their hands.

He himself had seen Scarlet first, and seeing her had set his senses alight. There was no way that he could have ignored her, or she him. He'd felt alive. For the first time in a few centuries, he'd felt like a living, breathing man and not like an empty shell of a vampire. When he'd set his eyes on her, his head had rung with hosannas! Knowing that Nico and Lazarus shared his feelings for Scarlet, he knew that they would have experienced the same sensations. How could you fight that?

The answer was, you couldn't.

And while he hated himself for putting her life in danger, how could he regret meeting Scarlet on this cruise? Lazarus' existence had been hanging on the very brink, his lack of caring for humans had grown more and more evident. Soon, he would have had to be slain. Scarlet had stopped all that. The thought of a life without his mate and Lazarus was too difficult to even contemplate.

So while she had completely fucked up their modus operandi, while they didn't know which way was up and which was down, and while he fully recognized the fact that they'd messed up and now had to deal with the consequences, he couldn't regret meeting Scarlet at this point in their lives.

He just hated that she was in danger. After what he'd just witnessed, he knew that she was, knew that the consequences of letting Elizabeth roam free would be mighty. Vampires were honor-bound to treat their blood slaves well. That he'd seen their mistreatment with his own eyes shocked him to the core. If she couldn't protect those she was supposed to protect, then how would she treat a woman considered her enemy. Even worse the woman of her enemies.

She obviously kept them drugged, at least to a point. Perhaps it pleased her to have them so befuddled by narcotics that their defenses were low. So low that she could please herself with whatever perverse sexual games turned her on . . . .

He could only guess at the degradation the set of six slaves had suffered, had had to live through and it had only strengthened his belief that Elizabeth had to die. Humans euthanized dangerous dogs, dogs that were a danger to the public . . . . Well, Elizabeth was exactly the same. She needed to be terminated.

He'd only managed to gain entry to her cabin because one of her drugged slaves had staggered to the door and opened it for him. He'd heard some of the others hiss at the obliging slave, a blond man, for being stupid enough to open up Elizabeth's suite without her permission. Why the blond had allowed him entry, Vincent didn't know. Maybe he'd recognized that he was, in a roundabout way, there to help. They all wanted the same thing after all, to be free of Elizabeth's presence in their lives.

Until he'd stepped into her suite, he'd never realized how one could be money rich but emotionally poor. Elizabeth obviously felt sufficiently dutiful to house her slaves in the very best of accommodation, to dress them in designer togs and feed them in the best restaurants money could buy. But at the same time, he could see with one glance that she treated them like toys. Dressing them up and playing with them when the moment suited her. Otherwise, they were left to themselves and he could see that they were dying a slow death. It was in their eyes and despite the untold horror he'd played witness to over the many years of his existence, there was something entirely horrific about the way the shining light of life in their eyes was continuously growing duller, second by second.

It was almost frightening to behold. Their eyes were dying and almost dead. In a quick look around the room, and, more importantly, its occupants, he'd seen bruises on two of the men's faces and one of them had whip marks on his arms. A woman lay laxly on the bed, her back bloodied from the same whip. She winced and hissed as one of the other ladies attempted to ease her pain by cleaning the marks with some kind of antiseptic lotion. The final woman had chains around her feet and her hands were cuffed together behind her back. A ball gag was stuffed into her mouth and she was naked, apart from a bustier that covered her from breast to hipbone.

They'd all been in varying stages of desperation and each had touched him to the soul. That Elizabeth could treat them so shabbily really sickened him. It was easy to see that their souls had been locked up tight to protect themselves from the degradation that that bitch put them through and it merely justified his belief that Elizabeth deserved to die.

What he'd learned thereafter had only compounded that desire. When they'd first decided to go after her, it had been because of her bragging. At first they'd heard tales of her need to embellish the story behind her kills and while they'd believed it to all be bullshit, words of a vampiress whose sole intent was to brag to her heart's content, they'd slowly learned that the kills had actually occurred. It had disgusted all of them, her relish in the loss of human life. They'd deemed it necessary to exterminate her, like the insect she was. But seeing how she treated her blood slaves, because they were still human, was poisonous.

The blond man had stood before him almost defiantly. His body spoiled the show of defiance as it had wavered weakly, almost as though a weak breeze would topple him and push him to the ground. "Why are you here?" he asked roughly, his voice gruff with distress.

"For your mistress," Vincent had replied bluntly. One quick glance around the room told him that these people were allies, not enemies. Weak ones, drained ones perhaps, but the abuse they'd suffered at Elizabeth's hands would work against her and aid him. And it had. They had been an unexpected source of information and had given him a deeper insight into Elizabeth's plans.

"What do you want with her?" This muffled question had come from the woman lying face-down on the bed, her wounds being tended to by another slave.

"Her blood," he'd replied simply. Gently pushing past the blond man, he'd walked over to the wounded woman. "Why hasn't she healed you?" he'd asked, but a cynical laugh had exploded from one of the men, but the woman had only shook her head tiredly. "Because it pleases her to see us suffer," she replied wearily.

Vincent shook his head. "If I could heal you, I would. But I can't. It would harm both of us to exchange blood when you bear her blood imprint."

"I know," was all she said.

"Why do you want our mistress' blood?" the blond man had queried curiously.

"Well, because she's a danger to you, to the public, and to my mate and brotherhood."

"Well, that's true. Are you the slayers she's been seething about these last few days?"

Vincent nodded carefully.

"Then it's your fault Melody is laying on the bed then. Elizabeth doesn't like to feel threatened."

"Don't be ridiculous David. It's no one's fault apart from the bitch's. It doesn't take much for her to bring her whips out. Hell, she's brought them out over less than three slayers baying for her blood," the woman, Melody, had hissed.

"I can only apologize, Melody," Vincent had said quietly.

"No need to apologize. Just kill the bitch. That's all I need. Freedom from her fucking stronghold. Two hundred years I've been with her. And it's two centuries too long."

"I don't understand how she's been allowed to get away with this. Every vampire knows that to treat a blood slave so, so poorly goes against every honor in our arsenal."

"Elizabeth has no honor." As she'd spoken, Melody had slowly turned around so that she could face him and not the bed. Wincing as she'd moved, when she'd finally sat before him, sweat had beaded on her forehead and her skin had turned a pasty white. It had been a long time since he'd been whipped as a punishment, but the memories of the pain hadn't entirely faded. He could easily imagine how sore she was, how each move was excruciatingly painful.

For him, it had been the first and last time to experience a punishment of that nature. It had happened just after he'd been turned. He'd been seeking nourishment on a farm he'd stumbled across on his journey back to town and a farmer with some farmhands had come out to investigate the noises he'd been making. They'd managed to catch him, weak as he was from poor nutrition and had punished him with the whip. Perhaps it had been a well-deserved beating, trespassing as he was on the farmer's land, but the loss of the small amount of blood his new body contained hadn't helped him any!

It always amazed him how cruel other members of his race could actually be. There was always a small measure of cruelty in everyone, but there seemed to be more than most in vampires. What his brothers and himself had suffered, what these slaves had suffered-all at the hands of evil vampires.

It was true that there was always a fine line between humanity and inhumanity. As years, decades, centuries and millennia passed; a time where there was little true contact with humans, contact that would remind a vampire of a human's limits, would remind them of how weak they themselves had initially been. Without this constant reminder how could a vampire keep on the side of humanity?

Lazarus had found himself in a similar situation and Lazarus had had Nico and himself by his side to keep him grounded! No vampire was free from the evil in his nature, but it still shocked him to see what one of his kind could put humans through. It was a complete anathema to him. Especially now he had Scarlet.

"She doesn't care about anyone. All she cares about is herself," Melody had continued, her eyes were clenched shut, her mouth taut in a grimace of pain as she tried to adjust herself on the mattress. David had stepped up to face him."If you want her blood, then she equally craves yours. You've made a powerful enemy, my friend."

"No, she's made a powerful enemy. I may not even be classed as middle aged in vampiric terms, but one of my brethren has seen more sunrises than your mistress has seen sunsets. He is more than a match for her," he'd stated confidently. "Aye, he may be," David had replied scornfully. "But she's not after him. The red head woman, that's who she's after. I've seen her with a blond guy around the ship. It's not often she takes me with her on deck, but she took me to one of the restaurants one evening and I saw them together."

"That's another of my brethren. A werewolf."

David's eyebrow had cocked in disbelief. "Two vampires and a werewolf? I may look like a fool, but I've been on this Earth for ninety years. I've been with that bitch for sixty-eight of them. All of that time in the paranormal community I've never heard of two vampires and a werewolf setting up together. You're bullshitting us. Werewolves and vampires are natural enemies, for fuck's sake! What is this? A test? Has she asked you to come here and see how loyal we are? Is that what you're after?" he asked sarcastically.

"I want to know what Elizabeth is doing. What she's plotting. I want to stop her from causing any more pain amongst the human community. We know she brags about how many kills she's made, and we will put an end to that! I can promise you that!

"So are you going to help me? Because if I look like the kind of guy that would even lift a finger to help a mother

fucking whore like your mistress, then you are a fool.
Perhaps you've never heard of my brotherhood, never
heard of the unusual mixture of members, but that's no
matter. All you need to know is that we never fail.

"My mate, blood mate, not slave is lying practically
defenseless in our suite. Her other two mates are there, but
we're so fucked up over her that when we should have
killed Elizabeth on day one, instead, we're almost heading
into the second week of this damned cruise and she's still
alive, still a threat to my mate. I need your help, dammit,
and you need mine. We both want the same thing.

"Like any megalomaniac, she must talk. Pillow talk,
angry talk. Whatever. You must know something about
what the hell she's plotting. I need something that will give
me the advantage. Because no one is more powerful than
the men in my brotherhood but our senses are dulled by our
mate . . . I need to protect them all. Surely you can
understand that!" His words had powered out until they'd
near as dammit rang through the room! With a grimace at
how self-righteous he had sounded, Vincent had just shook
his head and looked at each of the three men and three
women.

He'd assessed from the start that Melody was
Elizabeth's weak spot. Maybe on an ordinary occasion she
wouldn't have spoken. But you couldn't whip someone
until their skin was raw, until blood poured in rivulets over
the fleshy expanse of their torso and until there would
always be evidence of the whipping in thick scars. You
couldn't then not heal them when it was perfectly within
your power to do so and not cause any resentment!

He'd walked over to her and just looked at her
imploringly. "Melody, this can all end today with your
help. I just need to know when and what she intends to do,"
he'd beseeched.

"Well, you already know what. She's after your mate.
The redhead?"

Vincent had closed his eyes despairingly and shook his
head in reply. "Right, that's understood. She wants
Scarlet."

One of the men in the background had snickered.
"Original," was muttered into the background.

Vincent had spun around to glare at the offender, but

Melody had spoken before he could do more than step forward aggressively.

"Stefan! Don't be childish," she said, pausing to look at Vincent critically. "You're really here to get rid of Elizabeth?" she'd asked earnestly.

"I'm really here to get rid of her," he'd answered with a reassuring smile.

"She's gloating because she knows how your mate, this Scarlet, is affecting you. She's confident because she got to her once and supped from her. She knows that if she kills your mate then you and the rest of your brotherhood won't be long behind in dying. Elizabeth likes to cause the most pain and the most humiliation. All of us have experienced that at one point or another."

"Right, so she has no plans for Lazarus? Just his suffering?"

He'd wanted to laugh. Just his suffering? Like that wouldn't hurt both Nico and himself to see Lazarus just suffering!

Melody had shrugged, but David had butt in before she could speak. "Lazarus, you say? Isn't he over two thousand years old? I've heard of him before!"

"Maybe you can understand why I'm so confident then!"

"Maybe I can. While she's never mentioned his name to me before, I know that he will be the major target. I'd expect more than just your mate's death."

Melody had held up a hand. "She's gone after you today. The bitch likes the taste of your mate's blood and wants more."

Just thinking about those words made his blood heat in his chest. He'd left soon after, swearing to hold to the promises he'd made.

Somehow he'd managed to retain his shield of invisibility throughout the hellishly long journey to their suite and it was with a sigh of relief that he slipped through the cracks in the door. Transforming back into his human form, he ran into the suite of rooms "Laz! Where are you?" he called out urgently.

Getting no reply, he quickly entered the three bedrooms and checked the bathrooms for the three missing members of his family. Seeing no one, he gritted his teeth as he

realized that they must have returned to Scarlet's suite and
he didn't have a fucking clue where that was. He'd have to
waste valuable time in returning to the damned purser he'd
entranced this morning and pull out Scarlet's suite number
this time.

His face like thunder as he stormed out of the room, he
damned himself for not having asked Lazarus or Nico
where the fuck Scarlet was staying. He'd never needed to
know, she'd always been in his suite of rooms, or Nico or
Lazarus had brought her to them. Now he wished to hell
that he'd just asked! It would have saved him precious
minutes and they weren't minutes that he could spare.

The thought of what could be happening to his blood
mate made his skin drain of color. He couldn't lose her, he
couldn't. His life would be an abyss of endless pain if he
did.

"Do you smell that?" Lazarus asked gruffly. Lifting his
head from the pillow of Scarlet's tits, he curled his nose at
the sudden stench that entered his haven and quickly leaped
from the bed. It was the only clue he would sense before
coils of ropes seemed to spring out of nowhere. They
gripped his wrists and ankles, holding them tautly before
carrying him to the wall and keeping him stuck to it.

"What the fuck?" Nico and Scarlet screamed
simultaneously. Both of them jumping off the bed and
running to him as they yelled out. Fear and panic etched on
their faces as they attempted to break him free of the rope's
hold but to no avail.

"It's no use. They're enchanted," he told them calmly.
"Only Elizabeth can release me." He knew full well who
was behind this ploy.

"That's right, Lazarus. Who's a clever boy?" Elizabeth
asked sweetly as she walked, bold as brass, into Scarlet's
bedroom.

Nico, teeth bared and claws now extended, rushed at
her, his body twisting and morphing into his half-shifted
form as he neared the vampiress.

She didn't even flinch. Her sole reaction was to fling
some of the ropes that kept him tied to the wall at the now-
turned werewolf and they seemed to spread out in mid air
of their own accord. As soon as they touched Nico, they
curled about him tightly, keeping him clasped in their

grasp.

Lazarus winced as Nico landed with dull thud on to the ground. His legs and arms had been roped together so that he could hardly move. Hell, he could hardly lay flat. His limbs were curled into odd positions and Lazarus knew that it was sheer luck that Nico hadn't caused himself further damage. A bruised hide was nothing in comparison to some of the other injuries that could have befallen him.

Lazarus' eyes tracked Nico's fall then Elizabeth's movements as she neared the wolf and prodded him in the belly with the pointed toe of her high heel.

Nico, still in beast form, growled menacingly but couldn't react any further. The rope held him in a headlock.

Lazarus' gaze then flashed to Scarlet, who, looking petrified, had managed to cover herself in the bed sheet.

"Why bother hiding what I've already seen?" Elizabeth asked scornfully, sneering at her stupidity.

"Because it was never for your eyes," Scarlet retorted angrily and wrapped the sheet more tightly about herself.

"You shouldn't be so insolent, human. You should show me some respect."

"You'd be surprised what I can be, slut. And why should I respect you when you've done nothing but disrespect me so far?"

"So, your mate likes to talk nasty, does she, Lazarus?" Elizabeth questioned him politely, walking towards him as she spoke, ignoring Scarlet as she moved closer to him.

Lazarus correctly assessed that Elizabeth didn't deem Scarlet to be any danger to her. Knowing what he did about Scarlet's new gifts, he doubted that Elizabeth was right to just dismiss his mate from her mind.

"I'm rarely on first name terms with people I've never met," he replied stonily.

Elizabeth's eyes narrowed dangerously. "Don't play with me, Lazarus. You know who I am. Just as I know who you are. It seems rather comical that you, as the elder, are being held against the wall when I, a mere child in comparison, am the instigator of your imprisonment. It's never a good idea to take your eye off the ball, Lazarus."

"Maybe if you had, then we wouldn't be here, determined to end your existence," he told her conversationally.

Elizabeth's hand came up to touch his pec and slowly slid down over his belly. "You're a handsome bastard, I'll give you that," she told him, ignoring his last comment.

"You're too kind!" he said sarcastically.

"I know. I am, aren't I?" she murmured in agreement, her hand trailing lower over his groin until she held his cock in her hand.

It was like being doused in cold water. If she was trying to turn him on then she was going to make a fool of herself! Hell, he felt his cock almost curl inwards. Superficially, Elizabeth was an attractive woman. But that was such a small part of the look she portrayed that he would have preferred to fuck a hag rather than touch this bitch's little finger!

He heard Scarlet hiss at Elizabeth's intimate touch and quickly, he cast his gaze over to her. His eyes were filled with a warning that brooked no argument.

Scarlet ignored him. "Get your hand off him, whore," she spat angrily.

"Who's going to stop me?" Elizabeth asked, her words redolent with taunting spite.

"If you're not careful, then I will," Scarlet said threateningly. As she spoke, she stepped closer to the wall where Lazarus was hanging, his wrists and ankles somehow magically clinging to the surface.

He watched her step sideways slightly and frowned as she pocketed something from atop a chest of drawers to her left in her hand.

"You? A human?" Elizabeth scoffed coldly. "How the hell do you even think you'll do me any harm?"

"You're arrogant."

"Is that supposed to hurt?"

"No. It's a statement of truth. You'll make a mistake somewhere along the line, and I intend to make the most out of it!"

"Ha!" Elizabeth laughed scornfully, her hand still cupping Lazarus' flaccid cock, her eyes looking deeply into his.

What she was looking for, he didn't know.

"You won't even be alive long enough to cause me any harm!" Elizabeth informed her in a voice dripping with disdain.

It was then that he understood what she was doing. She was trying to make him feel fear.

"See, there's your arrogance again," Scarlet murmured softly.

In a move that surprised even Lazarus, suddenly, rather than being ten steps away from the wall that he was glued upon, she was one step away.

That was one step too close for Elizabeth's comfort.

As the vampiress swung around at Scarlet's proximity to her, Scarlet raised her arm and brought the glass ashtray she'd picked up seconds before down upon the vampiress' head. The heavy glass glanced off Elizabeth's temple. Scarlet couldn't help but think that the dull thud was most satisfying.

Elizabeth staggered backwards. The high heels she was sporting were an aid to Scarlet's attack, causing her to stumble, one ankle turning over in the dangerously high shoes. She fell to the ground, her eyes shooting daggers at Scarlet as she sprawled back against the floor.

Now winded by the surprise of the sudden attack, she tried to catch her breath. "Bitch, what the fuck do you think you're doing?" she spat a little breathlessly.

"That's a rather dumb question. I was capitalizing on your arrogance, just like I told you I would."

Quickly rushing forward, she grabbed one of Elizabeth's shoes that had fallen from her feet during the fall and swiftly dropped to her knees and hammered the heel, which was as sharp as a stiletto, downwards.

Until the blood squirted out, Lazarus didn't see where it had come from. Elizabeth's hand came up to cup her now ruptured eye, and she wiggled on her ass as far away from Scarlet as she possibly could. When her back hit a wall, she stayed put and began sobbing loudly.

Scarlet ignored her and looked almost blankly down at the bloodied stiletto heel. It took two tries for Lazarus to gain her attention. "Mellita. Mellita."

"Lazarus," she replied woodenly. Her body tense and stiff, frozen in a block of ice as the repercussions of her actions dented her conscience. "What have I done?"

"You've defended yourself and your mates, delicia. That's all. Come, the ropes are enchanted but if you wipe some of her blood on them then they should release me."

Scarlet stayed where she was, her eyes on the blood that had stained her hands and the sheet that was covering her.

It killed him to see her so uncertain and so afraid of her own behavior and not be able to help her. "Scarlet, come here," he said loudly. He tried to add a commanding note to his voice, but she was so distressed that he couldn't stand to do it.

She ignored him, totally focused inwardly.

His ears perked up at some sounds that were coming from the outer room. He hoped to God that it was Vincent coming in. If it was, then he wasn't calling out or making any untoward sign that it was.

Wondering who the hell it was, he could only breathe a sigh of relief as Vincent's groomed head popped around the door and took in what was happening. "Get the shoe from Scarlet's hand. Elizabeth's blood will release the ropes," he hissed quietly and glared impatiently at Vincent's frown.

"Scarlet attacked Elizabeth?"

Lazarus nodded. "Get the shoe and I will explain," he said and almost sang hosannas as Vincent finally complied and walked over to Scarlet, placing an arm around her shoulder, he hugged her to him as he walked them both towards Lazarus. He could see from his position that her hand was holding the shoe in a tight grip and he hated that she'd been placed into this situation, especially when it was down to their ineptitude.

"What the hell happened?"

"I'll tell you that later, but Scarlet's obviously inherited rather more of our gifts than we'd first expected. Although I doubt that she'd look upon that in the same light as I do. I can only thank God that she managed to attack Elizabeth, because fuck knows what the bitch would have done otherwise. Now quickly, lift Scarlet's arm and place the bloodied heel against the ropes. That should free me."

He watched impatiently as Vincent gently took their dazed mate's arm in his hand and lifted it slightly. A slight movement in the background jolted into his awareness. "She's going to get another rope, Vincent," he yelled out.

Scarlet's bewildered eyes suddenly focused and she spun around, the hand that still clutched the ashtray, raised and her gaze accurately pinpointed on the hand that was yielding the rope and quickly moved upwards, to the arm that would throw it and the shoulder that would enable that toss. Her eyes narrowed and in a show of perfect marksmanship, she flung the ashtray in a direct hit at Elizabeth's shoulder. The other woman slumped against the wall and the dull thud of the hit seemed to reverberate sickly around the room.

Lazarus watched as the arm went limp and had he been able to, he would have applauded his mate's skills! He highly doubted that before this cruise she would have been able to accomplish something of that nature. It could only be the addition of her mates' talents to her own genetics that enabled her to do something so swiftly, accurately and successfully. He could only be grateful that she'd somehow taken on more than just a fluency in French and Latin!

Scarlet spun around and began rubbing the heel of the shoe against his bindings, her lowered head gave him the perfect opportunity to watch Elizabeth and almost in slow motion, he watched as her left arm came up and lobbed the ropes at Scarlet. Before he could even mutter a word, or even cry out, the rope snapped around Scarlet's neck, tightened and tautened until it began to choke her. Her hands clambered at the rope, trying to pull it away from her throat in an attempt to breathe.

"Quickly," he spat. "Leave me, there should be enough blood on the rope to work through it. Rub it on Scarlet's bindings. Do it! Now!"

In the two heart-stopping minutes it took for Vincent to release the ropes, Lazarus feared they'd almost lost her. Something which had caused untold problems earlier, the fact that the claiming had partially been undertaken, had probably just been Scarlet's savior. Had that happened to an ordinary human, they would more than likely died without prompt medical after care. And that wasn't exactly on location at that exact moment. Her skin was tinged with a hideous shade of blue and he knew that even though she was still alive, that it had been too touch and go for his liking.

Finally free from the stasis that had overtaken him, he began pulling at his bindings. The blood had worked like an acid against the fibrous material of the ropes and even though it was damned difficult, he managed to free himself from the restrictive fetters.

There was nothing more that he wanted to do than go over and comfort Scarlet, but he couldn't. Elizabeth was slumped almost quietly against the floor, but he didn't trust her one inch. She was more than likely faking. And so, he walked up to her quietly and crouched down before her. He placed his hand underneath her chin and nudged her head upwards.

Her remaining eye was as befuddled as Scarlet's had been earlier, her skin was ashen and copious amounts of blood were weeping from the wound that Scarlet had caused with the unlikely weapon of a high heel! Even though she looked so pitiful, it stirred no pity in him. Perhaps it was because she deserved to die, or perhaps he felt nothing for the woman who knowing she was beat had still tried to take out the only woman that would ever matter to the three men in this room.

There was a streak of vindictive cruelty in Elizabeth's nature. Something that no amount of understanding and empathy would ever soften. She was rather like a wild animal in that regard. Where her so-called prey was concerned, she spared no pity for humans and treated them accordingly.

As he looked at the diminished figure slumped against the wall, he recognized what he'd come so close to becoming. He'd felt the coldness seeping into his veins. Year after year, he'd moved further and further away from the most basic of human contact, when he should have moved towards it. Having Nico and Vincent as constant companions had softened him, of that there was no doubt. But having Scarlet in his life was like a balm to his soul. Vincent and Nico could never replace that, would never even come close to that. He needed them in his life, but he would die without Scarlet. It was as simple as that.

He realized that the position Elizabeth found herself in, could so easily have been one he too could have found himself in. The thought was a shock to the system, but then the truth often was. He watched her lips pull back and saw that her fangs had dropped down in an instinctive search for blood to replace the amount she'd lost. Unfortunately for her, there would be no more blood taking. No more loss of innocent lives just for her blood sport.

Reaching down beside her, he took the chipped and

battered glass ashtray in his hand and deploying a great force, smashed it down against the ground. "Keep Scarlet's head turned away, Vincent," he yelled out and then gripped the now-jagged and lethal ashtray in his hand and sliced it down over the veins on Elizabeth's wrist. He grabbed the other one and did the same. Tilting her head back, he sliced the sharp glass along the curve of her throat and watched unemotionally as the small amount of blood housed in a vampire's body slowly seeped out of the cuts he made. Until he witnessed her death firsthand, he wouldn't believe she was truly exterminated.

"How does it feel to die, Elizabeth? Do you regret murdering all those innocent humans now?"

"You are the unnatural one, Lazarus," she muttered huskily. Her mouth was dry and the words escaped sibilantly. "Humans are our prey, not our equals. I feel nothing for those I killed."

"My blood mate is human." Or was. "Just think the kind you hate and despise utterly, could have been your salvation."

She glared at him but said nothing,

He stepped away from her, not wanting to breathe the same venomous and poisonous air as she did. He'd coated his hands in her blood before he'd moved from his crouching position before her and walked over to Nico. Sliding his wet hands along his bindings, he quickly freed the wolf who taking advantage of his liberty, hurried forwards and stood growling before the dying vampiress. His teeth bared at the enemy; Lazarus felt safe in leaving Elizabeth in Nico's paws.

He strode over to Scarlet, who was enfolded in Vincent's embrace and above her head, directed for Vincent to release her. It was begrudgingly done, but Vincent moved out of Scarlet's embrace and Lazarus quickly unwound the bed sheet that Scarlet was using to cover her nakedness and before she could complain, tucked her into his embrace. In his experience, there was nothing better than skin to skin contact to make someone feel more secure.

He was correct as she soon snuggled into his embrace and began to sob silently against his chest. He only knew that she was crying because the wetness of her tears touched him. Apart from that she made no other reaction. It frightened him because he knew how badly shock could affect someone and that was the last thing he wanted for his mate.

Without needing to speak to the other two, he recognized their shame at Scarlet having to handle Elizabeth's mistreatment, at her having to do their job. She should never have been included in this entire damned situation and that she was now in shock and crying just hurt him even more. He couldn't believe that she'd practically fought the vampiress all by herself. He was proud of her, yet concerned and he could only hope that this was the final flaw in a beginning that had been redolent with the damned things!

"Grab two bathroom robes, Vincent," he directed at the other man and quickly shrugged Scarlet into one as Vincent handed them to him. Covering himself up, he quickly picked her up and lifted her into his arms. That she didn't grumble about his cave man tactics caused more concern than he thought possible.

He spun around and walked to the bedroom door. "Is she dead?" he called out.

"Yes," Vincent replied triumphantly.

Nico's response was a satisfied growl.

Heading out of the suite, he quickly walked into the corridor and moved towards the elevator. He wanted to get her showered and into his bed as quickly as physically possible. The sooner he washed away the memories both figuratively and literally, the more normal she would feel.

* * * *

"Ma'am, you know the rules. No dogs allowed on board the cruise liner. That is unless you're registered blind and have the documentation to prove that or have paid for your pet pooch to stay with you."

Scarlet jolted into sudden awareness. Having been sat slumped in a deckchair for the past hour, watching the scenery, the glistening and ever turbulent ocean ahead of her, as she tried to contemplate what she'd taken part in the night before.

"I beg your pardon?" she asked the steward in a voice husky with disuse.

Honestly, it was difficult to take the man seriously when

he looked at her as a teacher reprimanding a five year old would, but dressed like a rebellious teenager!

The obligatory ripped jeans that exposed more than they covered. A groupie T-shirt that looked like it needed a wash. Safety pins through the ears. The whole ensemble was enough to make a granny shudder with distaste.

The man harrumphed at her polite query and repeated his earlier statement.

"Dog? I have no dog on board," she stated, her confusion evident. "I don't even have one at home!"

"Ma'am, there's no use in lying. The couple in the suite next door to you complained about animal noises in your cabin last night. I've come to ask you to declare the presence of an unaccounted dog on board the ship!"

"Steward, I will not tell you again, I have no dog!" She was extremely grateful for the sunglasses that covered her eyes as they would hide the guilty look in them. She had no dog, but there had been a wolf in her cabin last night, hadn't there?

"You're not in any trouble, Miss Reves. Please be aware of that. I just need to know, that's all. Your dog cannot leave the ship when we're in port, and I need to know where it is when you leave for a visit on dry land. You shouldn't really have brought one on the ship without a pet passport. You do know that, don't you? But as you're a competition winner, we'll go lightly on you."

"For God's sake! I have no damned dog. Why won't you believe me?"

"Because there's no need to disbelieve your neighbors, ma'am."

"Is there a problem here?"

Lazarus' voice was a soothing balm in her annoyed state. Five minutes ago, she wouldn't have welcomed the intrusion, but now, she was most grateful for his presence. He'd deal with this stupid steward where she couldn't.

"No, sir. There's no problem. Last night, a couple in the cabin next door to Miss Reves heard the sounds of an animal, more specifically, a dog barking. I'm only asking that Miss Reves declare that the dog is on board and then pays the fee for its accommodation."

"I heard her tell you that she has no dog."

"Well, she would say that, wouldn't she, sir?" the

steward asked in an obnoxious man to man tone of voice.

"Yes, she would, seeing as it's the truth! She has no dog on board. As far as I'm aware, she doesn't even own one off board!"

"Exactly, Lazarus. I told him that, but he won't believe me!"

"You won't believe her?" he asked, his voice a tad lower and slightly more threatening because of that.

"Well, she's bound to deny it, sir. The couple heard distinct sounds. There is no reason for them to lie!" he repeated firmly.

"There is no reason for Miss Reves to lie either!"

The steward glared at them both. "I'll be keeping your group under observation for the duration of this cruise. If there is one more complaint about animal sounds then I will expect you to pay the full fees for accommodating this creature. Good day to you both," he finished politely and stalked off with one last angry glare at them.

Watching the man walk off, Lazarus shrugged and settled down in the vacant deckchair beside Scarlet's.

"We'll have to inform Nico that no animal sounds are to be heard for the next two weeks. He'll be the one that has to pay the damned fees, after all," he joked slightly. When she said nothing, he just sighed and settled back into his chair. Minutes, hours passed and he allowed silence to reign, even though it was damned hard not to ask her to talk to him about what had happened the night before.

Ultimately however, his patience was rewarded. "I didn't know I had that kind of violence in me," she murmured softly.

"Everyone has that kind of violence in them, Scarlet. It comes from the days of fight or flight. Don't be ashamed of fighting. Of protecting two men from someone who would gladly have killed them. Especially two men who I hope you're coming to love."

She didn't reply for a moment or two. "It doesn't make it right. I blinded her, Lazarus. It wasn't just a jackpot hit. I knew that if I aimed there, it would cause the most damage in the quickest time. I just knew what I had to do. It was instinctive. It makes me feel sick to think that I'm capable of such bloodthirstiness," she finally said.

"Scarlet, you're not bloodthirsty. You were smart. Do

you realize that what you did to Elizabeth was nothing in comparison to what she would have been willing to do to you? Vincent probably hasn't mentioned this, but to discover more about her plans, he went to her cabin. Do you remember we discussed blood slaves? Well, her blood slaves were abused. Whipped and beaten. She did that for pleasure, Scarlet. Imagine what she would do for pain?"

"It doesn't matter that she was a sick, perverted bitch, Lazarus. I'm not like that! I'm not sick or dangerous, yet I behaved as though I were!"

"For God's sake, mellita, you defended yourself and protected Nico and myself from harm. How can that be shameful? How can that be sickening or wrong? The answer is that it can't be. It's neither. Perhaps it isn't modern to be seen as the protector, perhaps we no longer need to fear dinosaurs or wild beasts haring after us, but there are very real predators out there, ones with two legs. They're not always of the animal variety, Scarlet. Bitches like Elizabeth will kill you if you show any sign of weakness. They don't have to be vampires. You know from your human press the sick side of humanity. You are not a part of that kind. You are everything that is human, you're a beautiful person, mellita. You protect and defend where necessary, not attack or maim for the sheer hell or pleasure of it! Surely you can see the difference?"

"Maybe I do," she replied huskily on a deep sigh.

"Well, there should be no 'maybe' about it," he said stoutly. "You don't know what that woman was capable of, Scarlet. Last night, when he ensured that she was really dead, Vincent discovered who she was. Or to be more precise, who he'd known her to be in the past."

"Who was she?" Scarlet asked curiously.

"She was the woman that plotted the demise of his fiancée because he hadn't wanted to dally with her. The woman that attacked Vincent and tried to kill him and instead turned him into a vampire and all because of a jealous rage. Elizabeth was capable of such evil that neither of us can comprehend. She is no loss to the world, mellita." She smiled softly and turned her head to look at him more closely. As the words escaped her mouth, the smile disappeared and a stark light seemed to enter her eyes. "I couldn't have allowed her to hurt you, Lazarus. Not on her own merit or through me."

"I know delicia. Do you think I would have allowed her to hurt you if I was in the same situation? Of course, I wouldn't. We protect our own, Scarlet. It's only natural."

She hummed a little and sat herself more comfortably in her seat. "Do you love me, Lazarus?"

"I don't think you even need to question that, mellita."

"Don't I?"

"No. You know I love you. You know that you are the center of my, Nico's, and Vincent's existence. And if you don't, then you're a bit slow, amor meus."

She rolled her lips over her teeth to hide her smile but then gave up and chuckled. "I'm not slow, but I guess that every woman in love is a little insecure. I can't guess at your feelings, Lazarus. I need to know."

"As do I, Scarlet. Don't discount that just because I'm not female. And I'm pretty positive that Nico and Vincent feel exactly the same way as I do."

"No, I guess you're right."

"The trouble with blood mates is that because they're imprinted on our souls we sometimes have a tendency to take the other for granted. Because our genes say it is so, the need to tell each other we love one another is diminished somehow.

"But I think we should act differently, mellita. I've waited for you for over two thousand years and even when I thought I didn't need a mate, my soul was crying out for yours. I guess the only thing I can say to you is . . . where have you been all my life?"

Epilogue

What a difference twelve months made. It was incredible to even contemplate how different a person she was, how her life had changed, and it had all happened in the space of a year. The only thing that had turned out as Scarlet had planned, pre-life-changing-cruise, was her graduation from law school. An unexpected bonus of that was that she'd somehow managed to graduate magna cum laude.

How the hell she'd managed to do that, she didn't know. When she'd expressed her shock at how well she'd done, Lazarus had just quirked his eyebrow at her, quickly tugged her into his arms and then kissed her to keep her quiet. The thought still made her chuckle, because the celebratory petit mort she'd received afterwards had been far more satisfying than the culmination of almost a decade's worth of hard study and toil.

She dreaded to think what that said about her as a person! There was something special about how they always thought the best of her, even when she didn't. In their eyes, there was no question of her receiving honors at her graduation. To them, it was just as read. It was wonderful to be supported so entirely, and, in a way, it was something she'd never really had in her life. Although her mother believed in her, Scarlet had always felt as if she had the most responsibility in their household. As soon as she'd become a teenager, she'd taken up balancing the check book, ensured that the majority of the bills had been paid, and shopped at the store for food. She'd had the responsibilities of an adult as a child and, subsequently, had grown independent.

Now, she didn't have to be. She had a support system by her side made up of three wonderful men who thought the sun shined out of her ass! It was truly marvelous to feel so secure in their love. In a strange way, she had realized how her life had all been geared towards the discovery of these three men. That the role she'd played as ice princess with her hard-to-get facade had merely been tactics used by fate to ensure that her heart remained untouched for her mates. Her childhood had made her immune to the bullshit men spouted to get women into the sack and thus she was prime pickings for the three men that held her soul in their hands.

She often contemplated how bizarre it was to realize that the Fates existed. Having always been so down to earth, she'd never believed in anything like that. But now, she realized that her whole life had been organized and planned by those same Fates. In reality, she'd had it easy. She'd never longed for the love between a man and a woman, so had never missed it. But Lazarus, Nico, and Vincent had all been raised in loving homes, with parents that adored each other. Vincent had actually experienced love with another woman. Yet they'd waited so long for their mate to actually appear.

When Lazarus had said to her, 'Where have you been all my life?' it was hauntingly true. For countless centuries they'd been waiting for her and seeing how Elizabeth had turned out and all because she hadn't met her blood mate in time was a reminder of what could have happened to Lazarus, what had come so close to happening.

While she'd been given a relatively good hand in life, Lazarus and Vincent and Nico had all had to wait so inordinately long to meet her. When she'd told Vincent how cruel she thought it had been, especially on Lazarus' part, he'd just said that she'd been worth the wait. The words had been simple, the truth of them had been in his eyes, and it had made her love him all the more.

It had been a tough and rocky road, but the brotherhood had made it. Perhaps it had been a close call. Elizabeth's specter was still in their memories. The monstrosity and evil in her nature wasn't an easy thing to forget, and she could only thank God that while they'd had a long wait on their hands for her, she'd come at the right time.

The thought of that night had never really left her. She doubted it ever really would. But maybe that was right. Maybe that was the way it was supposed to be. She couldn't regret protecting those she loved, but the violence in her nature still frightened her. She still thought it was going to leap out at any moment. Nico had told her to stop fretting about it, that unless anyone in her close family was under attack, it would likely never occur again.

She could only hope to God that he was correct. Their first year together had been hectic- to say the least. Underlying everything had been a basic contentedness, a rightness to the whole situation. The medley of four people's wants and desires, goals and dreams, had been a difficult thing to handle, but compromise had sorted all that out. They'd settled in her hometown, had lived a relatively quiet life while she'd completed her studies, and everything had been going according to plan until she'd fallen pregnant.

As MJ had termed it, Nico had gone completely 'whacko'.

Wrapping her up in cotton wool wasn't enough. He'd seen threats everywhere, saw danger in the safest of situations. His hyper-protectiveness and need to ensure her safety at all times had been rather cute at first, then at the end of the first trimester, her morning sickness had started to worsen and she'd quickly felt worn down and tired. Unable to handle this cosseting on such a massive scale, she'd broken down to Lazarus who had explained that her mate wasn't insane-thank God!

According to Laz, Nico's wolf had taken control. In an unsecured area, in a town he didn't know surrounded by people he couldn't trust, Nico's beast was going mental. Laz had also explained that if she didn't want a twenty four hour bodyguard, in the shape of Nico for the following six months, then maybe it was wise to return to Nico's homeland, a place where Nico could relax and where he knew that she and their children would be safe.

And that was how she found herself in the depths of Russia, surrounded by werewolves in a rural pack land that beggared belief. She'd expected snowy desolation, what she found was an ancestral home that would have put Rockefeller to shame! She'd heard of Russian oligarchs but this was positively indecent.

On the private flight over from Domodedovo, Moscow's busiest airport, to Nico's pack lands, he'd pointed out the areas that belonged to him, and it was larger than the state of Colorado. Hell, probably even larger than that! She'd never suspected that Nico came from such stock, hell, he'd always been so unassuming! She'd known they were wealthy, their suits and cabin had indicated that, but so much land in oil-rich Russia? It had definitely been an eye opener.

Then when they'd driven up to the pack lands in cars-bulletproof and fireproof, of course-that probably cost twenty times the amount she'd likely earn in a lifetime, Nico had turned almost bashful at the exorbitant wealth his family home exuded.

It had equally shocked her to learn that Vincent was considered a multimillionaire in his own right and Lazarus, well, he was richer than Vincent and Nico combined. The number of zeroes of his estimated wealth was enough to make her eyes cross.

It was the strangest thing. From having to work three jobs just to make ends meet to having so much money that there were no concerns about anything-a true rags to riches story. If the car broke down, then it didn't matter. Hey, there was always the helicopter to get her where she needed to be. If the boiler broke down, there were the four back up boilers to keep the place warm. She could only liken it to living in a world clad with down. Everything was cushioned. There were no nasties waiting to spring out at you because, if they did, they'd be handled, and not by her, but by one of her mates.

Over the last few months, being cosseted had been most welcome. But she doubted that that would continue for too long. She was far too independent for her own good! Although it was difficult becoming accustomed to Russia, it was eased by her newly-discovered talent with languages. Unlike French and Latin, she hadn't immediately been fluent in Russian, but Lazarus said that was due to the differences between a were and a vampire claiming. But with Nico and some of the women in the pack's help, she was now fluent in another language!

Lazarus had been right once more when he'd said that as soon as she was on his turf Nico would make a complete about face, and he had. He'd stopped growling when men walked near her and he'd actually let her leave the house without one of them present.

Only the night before, he'd come to her with a working solution. It seemed that her mates knew her far too well and Nico had come to her asking for her opinion on something he'd been considering for a long time. He'd asked what she thought about him taking up the mantel of Alpha with his pack. And then, if she was okay with that, he'd asked her to reign by his side as his Alpha female, a role that made her responsible for all the women in the pack.

Even though she'd realized it would mean a huge life change for her, a constant stay in Russia, she'd seen how Nico had blossomed here on his own land, amongst those of his kind, and she'd easily accepted. It had also eased any qualms she'd had about being over-cosseted!

There was only one problem, and it stemmed from the distinct lack of welcome from the pack. Some women had been kind and had befriended her, but there were some that were jealous and resented her presence here in the pack, as they were used to being allowed to run free. The presence of a possible Alpha female definitely curbed that freedom! They'd also thought her mating with three men bizarre in the extreme.

It was definitely a role that was filled with pitfalls and strife, but she relished the challenge and looked forward to the reactions she'd receive when her new position was announced that very night. It was also a ceremony that would welcome and officially recognize the babies as pack members.

Her thoughts disintegrated into nothing at the sound of Nico's gruff voice.

"Where have you gone?" he asked, burying his noise in her throat before hooking his leg and arm over her hips possessively.

She grinned as she felt the prod of his cock at her side. "Again?"

"Of course. The day my cock doesn't harden in your presence, milaya is the day you need to worry!"

Scarlet laughed and, nuzzling her nose into his own throat, breathed in the pure essence of him into her lungs. "Like I'd ever let that happen, dorogoy."

She smiled to herself when she felt his body react to her speaking Russian. She'd swiftly learned that each of her mates found her talking in their mother tongue unbearably sexy. It was an unexpected avenue but one she was keen to exploit to the maximum! It was incredible how just one word could have them hard in less than five seconds!

"Mne tak kharasho stoboy," she murmured huskily.

"And I feel so good with you next to me, angel moy. Even better when you speak in Russian."

"I know, and I should hope you do feel good!" Scarlet teased and arched her back a little so that her breasts rubbed, hopefully enticingly, against his chest.

A small moue of pleasure escaped her throat as his hand came up to cup one of them and began to slowly tease the nipple.

His fingers pinched gently and twisted until they'd formed into erect little peaks.

She sighed impatiently as they began to leak milk on to his fingers and over the curve of her breasts. Having long lost any sense of embarrassment around her mates, she felt only annoyance at being interrupted. You couldn't be embarrassed around any of them, but especially not Nico. Earthiness wasn't the word! It came part and parcel of being a werewolf, or so he said . . . .

Almost on cue, she heard a soft tapping on the bedroom door followed by her mother's soft voice calling. "Scarlet? Scarlet, honey? The babies need feeding."

Groaning in frustration, she relaxed against the mattress and watched Nico slide off the bed, watched the muscles in his ass flex and release. It was very sexy. "Nico! Put some pants on!" she hissed as he reached the door and made no move to cover any of the good stuff up. She loved her mother, but there was no way she was going to give her a glimpse of what belonged to her!

That was another thing she'd noticed, she was unbelievably possessive now. She couldn't stand to have anyone touch her mates. Lazarus had explained that it was part and parcel of having three mates, but it was still alien to her nature.

The other day, one of the pack's women had brushed against Nico's arm and she'd had to literally stop herself from clawing the poor woman's eyes out!

"He doesn't have anything I haven't seen, Scarlet," her mother muttered wryly through the door.

"See, your mother doesn't mind!" Nico pointed out, chuckling in amusement.

"Tough! I mind! Here," she said as she flung the top bed sheet at him. The sight that was hers only! Well, Vincent's and Lazarus' as well as her own. But that she wouldn't change for the world!

He grumbled as he wound it around his hips and covered up.

Even though he grumbled, she could tell he liked this crazy possessiveness that was driving her around the bend. Maybe he was sick! Who the hell would enjoy being at the epicenter of something so covetous!

The thought made her laugh.

Laz, Vincent, and Nico, that's who!

"Here we are," Patricia cooed as she walked in with a gurgling baby in her arms.

Charles walked in behind her and carried the other two

of the demon triplets.

"Thanks, mom."

"It's my pleasure, honey. You know I love looking after them."

"Just put Seasar and Nadzia on the bed, that way they can play with Nico while I feed Alexis."

Patricia handed her Alexis and pressed a kiss to both her daughter and grandson's temple before she grabbed Charles' hand and led him out of the bedroom.

"I'll never get over my mother looking almost as young as I do!"

"Is she getting too many interested glances? Not getting enough attention, angel moy?" Nico teased.

She stuck her tongue out and settled Alexis against her chest. He immediately began to feed and until he did, she didn't realize how much of a relief it was! How she managed to forget that she was a milk machine, she didn't know.

But then she supposed that she had her mates to thank for that.

Even when she'd been looking like a female hippo, with three babies stuck to her hips in a bump that was a sight to behold, they'd made her feel like the most sexiest woman on the planet.

Just thinking about the positions they'd been in, the things they'd tried, made a twinkle light her eyes.

"Uh oh, Seasar, I know what that look in your mamulya's eyes means. Your father is about to be ravished!"

"You're not supposed to talk like that to them, Nico, you'll teach them bad habits. With you three as dads, Alexis and Seasar are bound to have hormones aplenty!"

"Bah, they're babies they don't know what ravished means."

"Lazarus said that we can't know how advanced they are until they start to speak! Which could be any day?"

Nico rolled his eyes and turned his attention to Alexis who was hungrily feeding, almost as though he hadn't been fed for the last week.

She still found it amazing that she'd had triplets and each one of them had a different dad. Lazarus had explained to her how it happened, but the science was beyond her. What truly amazed her was that they treated each of them equally. She'd thought that each father would be most fond of his own child, but it hadn't worked out that way at all.

They all doted on Nadzia- Nico's daughter, but the little boys were equally the center of attention. Even though they were only six months old, they were rambunctious little devils and her mates took great pleasure in seeing how much mischief they could get into. Nadzia on the other hand seemed to take after her. Quieter, laid back, happy; she snorted, not one of her mates would class her as quiet or laid back.

Happy was another matter. Scarlet couldn't remember ever being so happy.

"What are you snorting about?"

"Oh nothing," she murmured with a soft laugh. "Here, burp Alexis." Reaching for Nadzia, she said in a sing-song voice, "Zi-a, ya tebya lyublyu."

Watching his little girl gurgle happily before settling down for dinner, Nico grinned proudly then muttered, "You should not speak Russian when the babies are here, dorogaya! It is not good for my blood pressure."

She smiled triumphantly and whispered, "I know." She winked as he grimaced and began to pat Alexis' back to burp him. "But I like Nadzia to hear that I love her in her mother tongue. Just like I tell Alexis in French and Seasar in Latin."

"You do it to tease us," Nico said glumly. "You like to make us as hard as nails and always in situations where we can't take advantage of you, malyshka."

She said nothing just smiled naughtily. Then a little more soberly, "Do you think mom is alright?"

Nico snorted. "She's with her blood mate, Scarlet, of course she's alright. Are you alright?" he asked pointedly.

She wrinkled her nose at him and said, "I still can't believe that Charles is a vampire. And there was me thinking that he was a gigolo."

"Yes, I remember that conversation," Nico said with a chuckle.

"Well, at least she's safe and well looked after though. I'm glad she's been here for the last eight months; I think I would have freaked out if she hadn't been. I know I had you three but at first you were as useless as I!"

Nico grinned and shrugged his shoulders guilelessly. "We had no reason to be around babies, Scarlet."

"Neither did I!"

"You're a woman, it's instinctive."

"Not with me it wasn't. I think you should thank mom for having any babies left!"

Nico chuckled. "You're too hard on yourself. Patricia was indeed a great help but you would have managed. It's not in your nature to do anything else!"

"True," she admitted with a wry smile. "I'll miss her when she flies off next week." Then, a little shocked, "I'll even miss Charles."

"He's a good man and will take care of your rather hare-brained mama! Because she certainly needs looking after. One of the men came to me yesterday and told me that she picked up a wolf cub the other day. Patricia is lucky to still have her hands! You know how the mothers stay as wolves until the pups are old enough to shift - well, let's just say there was a small skirmish."

"If I've told her once, I've told her a thousand times! Dammit, I'm glad she's Charles' responsibility. My heart can't take the shocks anymore, not with the demon twins over there as well. Her excuse is that they're cute," she said sheepishly. "And they are, I know that. I said to her, 'Yes, mom, they are cute, but the mothers aren't!' So what does she go and do?" she rolled her eyes and then transferred Nadzia to Nico's arms and reached for Seasar.

"I think it's a good job that Charles loves her, let's just put it that way. If I'm honest, dorogaya, I don't know how she managed to reach her age! Such an innocent and so rare in these times," Nico said and shook his head amazedly.

"I know. I think it's good luck, and she's managed to make a lot of loyal friends."

"Thank God for that and thank God she's now immortal! Hell, Charles needs everything in his arsenal to keep her safe!"

"Do they really have to leave?" she asked with a pout. "I like having her here."

Nico shot her a wry look. "You know as well as I do that she'll be here every few weeks just to check up on her grand babies. They're only going on safari, Scarlet. Hardly going to the ends of the Earth!"

"I know. But can you imagine her amidst lions and elephants and God knows what? Makes me shudder just to think about it!"

"What makes you shudder, mellita? Me?" Lazarus asked cockily as he walked towards them from his office.

Their bedroom was at the very center of a suite of rooms. In a semi-circle around it were four offices, one for each of them. Although she hadn't had much chance to play with hers. Their bedroom had originally been a hallway for the offices, but she'd asked to renovate it into a living space. Not only was it huge, enormous, but it meant that they were always close at hand. There had originally been five offices, but one of them had been turned into a bathroom. Just beyond their bedroom, a gigantic five steps away, was the nursery.

"Of course, ocellus. But I was talking about Mom in the depths of Africa."

"Hell, more like a heart-attack. How she's made it this long, I'll never know," Lazarus commented blithely. His eyes focused on his son suckling at his mate's breast.

"Nico just said that. Maybe one of you should persuade Charles into not letting her go."

"She's immortal, Scarlet. What's the worst that could happen?"

"Elizabeth was immortal too and she died," she said soberly.

"That was different."

"Different how?" she jeered.

"It just is!"

Scarlet pointedly looked away.

"Dammit, Scarlet, the only reason she died is because we didn't let her heal herself. If we hadn't been there, then she would have just licked the wound and carried on as normal. To kill an immortal you have to drain them of blood and not let them heal themselves. That's the only difference. And unless both Charles and Patricia are attacked by a couple of cheetahs, then they'll be alright! I'm sure they'll both enjoy licking each other," he finished, winking at Nico as Scarlet glared at him.

She sniffed but changed the subject. "Is everything ready for tonight?"

"Of course."

"There's no of course about it where you three are concerned! I bet everything is half finished and won't be completed until ten minutes before the start of the ceremony!"

Nico had the grace to look sheepish.

Scarlet laughed despite her annoyance. "I knew it. And dammit, it'll be me that gets the blame!"

She shook her head wryly and lifted Seasar over her shoulder to burp him.

"You know the women don't like me and this kind of thing is classed as woman's work. Vincent promised he'd get it all sorted for me!"

"And I have. With just a few minor glitches," Vincent conceded as he walked into the room.

"I'll bet. How long until it starts?"

"About an hour."

"Damn. That means I have to get ready," she said glumly.

Laz's lips quirked as he said, "Not looking forward to it, delicia?"

"Not particularly. They hate me. It's like being back at school again!"

"No, it's not, Scarlet. You're their leader. Remember that. You hold their lives in your hands- the Alphas have the right to condemn other weres to death. Naturally it doesn't happen often, but you're their judge and jury, leader and friend. They will grow to respect you. Never fear."

Depositing a cooing Seasar on to the bed, she watched as he instantly disappeared. A slight pop was the only sound he made. When Alexis did the same and almost instantaneously Nadzia began to cry, she glared at Lazarus and Vincent. "Tell them to stop! You know I hate it when they do that."

Lazarus just smiled softly and shook his head. "I don't have to say a word."

They all watched as Nadzia's hand shot out and grabbed an invisible limb, she tightened her little grip until an invisible Seasar- she'd recognize that cry anywhere- popped back into sight. Nadzia kept hold of the foot until Nico helped her let go of it.

"She has her mother's guts," he said proudly and lifted his baby against his chest.

Scarlet watched as Vincent and Lazarus grabbed a newly reappeared Alexis and a sobbing Seasar and began to comfort them all. She left them to care for her mischievous little devils and headed to the bathroom to prepare herself for the upcoming ceremony.

It was a big night, one that would reinstate Nico's Alpha status; would declare her as his Alpha female and would introduce their babies into the pack. Nadzia would also be announced as heiress to the Alpha role. She would govern the pack in conjunction with her mate. Whoever that was.

It was a night that she hadn't really been looking forward to. A night that would more than likely be full of boring speeches and equally tedious people. But as she looked back at the three men who made her life worth living and the children that had taken over all of their lives and all their hearts, she felt at peace.

She felt happy and healthy and so very lucky to have the best babies in the world- little devils or not, and the best mates that ever graced the planet.

Life was unbelievably good and despite the tedium of the night ahead, there was always the thought of what would happen in that huge bed afterwards . . . .

The End

Mandy Monroe loves to hear from readers. You can email her at themandymonroe@yahoo.com

Check out some of Mandy Monroe's other titles available at New Concepts Publishing:

In the Shadow of the Wolf
The Wolf Within
Dances with Wolves
Savage Heat
The Mating

Hungry like the Wolf

The following is an excerpt from an upcoming book by
Mandy Monroe:

An Ambush of Tigers

Prologue

"Here's Calendar News, bringing you all the latest news
on this, the fifteenth of March two-thousand and twelve.
"Today's top story! Harris County deputies were sent out
into the 'wilds 'of the Lone Star state armed with
tranquilizer guns in search of two missing Siberian tigers
that escaped from their cages just outside of Houston last
night.

"This recent escape comes weeks after an Indonesian
tiger mauled a young child in Victoria and another pet
Maltese tiger managed to break out of an inadequate cage
in a suburb in Dallas.

"The search for the two Siberians continues but this
incident has prompted legislators to consider the laws
surrounding the possession of wild animals and treating
them as pets.

"Estimates show that there are in fact more tigers in
Texas than roam wild in India. Tigers are indigenous
animals in Asia and Russia and vary in size depending
upon the country in which they're found, with the
Indonesian tiger being the smallest and the Siberian the
largest.

"Kept as backyard pets, tigers are not considered to be
exotic animals in our state and with their pricing structure
at a miserly one thousand dollars, for many they are an
impulse item. Federal law doesn't touch the owners and, as
our next guest can further explain, this can be a shame for
many of the Texan pet tigers aren't kept in the best of care.

"With us now is Abby Reynolds, a vet and owner of a

local animal rescue center, the largest in Harris County, who handles many of these mistreated tigers on a daily basis." Jane McGannis, the reporter, turned to Abby and smiled. "Welcome, Ms. Reynolds."

"Thanks, Jane. It's great to be here, to clarify the situation a little," Abby said with a nervous smile as she tightened one clenched hand about the other. She felt sure her body language was more than likely as awkward as she felt and transmitted her terror at being in front of so many cameras, but even if it frightened the life out of her, publicity was vital where this cause was concerned. She knew in her heart that she just had to grow some metaphorical balls and do it.

The most horrifying aspect of this entire interview process was the studio lights, which were shockingly bright. If she'd been in this kind of light outside she would have slipped on her sunglasses. How people worked with them on a daily basis she had no idea.

Dragging herself back to the matter at hand with a mental shake, Abby forced herself to focus on the blonde woman's rather blank face. She was fully aware that the host of the local news was not interested in this story. That was clearly evident by the look on her face. Despite that, she did her job and asked the questions they had rehearsed earlier, which had Abby almost sighing with relief. She was nervous enough as it was without being asked questions she wasn't prepared for.

"Perhaps you would like to tell us why you handle tigers on such a frequent basis?"

"Well, as I'm sure the majority of the people watching have already figured out, I care for tigers that are abused by their owners or are simply discarded like unwanted toys at Christmas. Naturally, some of the pets are cared for and treated well, but, unfortunately, not a week passes by without an animal entering my shelter for some reason or another. I can truly say that it breaks my heart to see the state that they're in."

"Perhaps you can describe their mistreatment for our viewers? If it's not too . . . sensitive?" she countered.

"Tigers aren't meant to be held in captivity. They're supposed to roam wild and free in their natural environment. Unlike the dogs and cats you can buy at your local pet shop, they're not meant for a domestic lifestyle. Mostly through my experience I have found that the mistreatment stems from a simple lack of knowledge. I don't normally deal with cases of physical abuse, because even the weakest tiger can defend themselves. No, what I handle on a regular basis are tigers whose needs aren't being met."

"What needs are those, Ms. Reynolds?"

"Anything and everything from the sheer amount of food they need to survive, to the amount of exercise they need. The environment they're in can truly affect their quality of life. It's not natural for them to be restrained to a small area and so to cage them in the back yard is truly abhorrent to their way of life, Jane."

"Legislators are trying to impose new laws whereby tigers are properly housed and are insured with indemnity insurance to protect the public if they're attacked. In your opinion, are these adequate measures?"

"No. They're not adequate, Jane. That pair of Siberians you were talking about earlier . . . well, fully grown, they can be as large as a station wagon and can weigh up to six hundred and fifty pounds. I cannot honestly believe that animals of this size should be roaming around people's back yards. I think the majority of your viewers will, in truth, be shocked to hear that there are over three thousand tigers captive within this state, which, as you said earlier, is actually more than the number that roam wild in India. I work with that statistic on a daily basis, and it's implausible even to me."

"I'm afraid that's all we have time for at the moment, but, thank you, Ms. Reynolds," Jane said before turning back to give her full attention to the camera. "If any of our viewers would like more information about Ms. Reynolds' animal shelter, the details are currently being displayed on the bottom of your screen. And now, over to Paul and the weather."

A beep sounded from out of nowhere and a station hand counted down from three on his fingers. By the time he'd reached one, Jane, the newscaster, had started to fluff her hair and fiddle with her papers.

Abby was rushed off the red sofa she'd been sitting on across from Jane and out into the area behind the cameras.

Within the span of what felt like five minutes, she was being guided out of the studio.

It wasn't long before Abby was jumping into her car and starting the long drive home. As she sat behind the wheel of her old battered four by four, her shoulders slumped at the thought of the four hour drive ahead of her. While all the effort she had put forth had been worth it to publicize her shelter, she'd been up since six waiting on the station to call. They'd finally gotten around to contacting her at eight. She'd had the four hour drive after that, then all the camera nerves, and, now, she was going back home.

Lifting her right hand from the wheel, Abby began to rub her left shoulder. The relief wasn't all that great, but it was what she needed at that minute. Hell, she needed a damn sight more than the meager comfort her own hand could give her. What she wouldn't give to be rubbed down by some huge masseur with biceps the size of footballs. Unfortunately, massages cost money and that was what she didn't have at the moment.

That was why this opportunity had come at such a great time. The publicity that would come from this could fund the shelter for the next couple of months. At least, she hoped it would, that way she wouldn't have to dip into her own funds to pay for everything, as was usually the case.

Dealing with the aftermath of a tiger being handled poorly by its owners was one thing, but to be able to act in a proactive manner, to perhaps have stopped someone from buying a tiger . . . well, that was magnificent, and the feeling boosted her overall well-being immensely.

It seemed incredible that in those five minutes she could possibly have done more good than in all her years of working in this particular field. That comparison was mildly depressing, but, at the same time, nothing could stop her from feeling flushed with pleasure at all the good she might have done.

For the last ten years, she had been working with animals in general, the latter five of those included working with tigers. While all that hard work had been for something, that tonight she could have tripled her efforts was deliriously exciting. Not even the knowledge that when she returned home she would be thoroughly picked on about her appearance on the local news could dispel her good mood.

Abby contemplated the possible donations the news program might reap. After this broadcast, and with the advertisement of her shelter at the end of the segment, she hoped that there would be an influx of funds that would pay for her next purchase. Tigers needed lots of space, and, with her services in high demand from the local government, she needed all the land she could possibly get her hands on.

Beside her property was a lot of land that she wanted to purchase so that she could spread the shelter over that area. She crossed her fingers in the hope that there would be donations that would cover the cost of that land and perhaps even a portion of the building costs, too. Okay, so perhaps thinking like that was a tad bit greedy, but it was all for a good cause.

The problem was that no matter how many cages she had, she never really had enough. It was an easy enough calculation to think that one animal could go in one cage or two in a double-cage. But sometimes, especially with Siberians, a double cage could be taken up by just one of the big cats. And so, there was never enough room, hence the need for more land.

The government helped. She received handouts for the animals that came her way via the welfare field agents, as would the two tigers, which, if they were caught alive, would be winging their way to her shelter, but it wasn't enough. It was never enough.

When she'd first bought the shelter, it had taken up one plot of land. Over the last five years, she'd purchased a further two plots and this next one was the last free lot of space. After that, and if demand for her services continued to be so high, she would have to contemplate moving. That was not a thought she relished.

Shaking off her troublesome thoughts, along with the fatigue that came from the first three hours of driving, Abby pulled into a drive-in restaurant that was just a few minutes out of her way. The sky had become a lot darker, and she knew that it would be fully night by the time she reached home. Her stomach rumbled with hunger almost the moment she drove into the ordering lane.

Today had been an odd day. Ever since she'd received

the call that morning to appear on the news, she'd been in a state of . . . well, not exactly panic, but nervousness. She hadn't eaten a damned thing all day because of her nerves and felt almost as hungry as one of her tigers.

"Welcome to Awesome Burger. May I take your order?"

She perused the menu and with a wry, self-deprecatory grin, damned the calories. "Yes, can I have a double bacon cheeseburger, an order of extra-large fries, and a large coke," she said as clearly as she could as she pulled up beside the speaker.

"That will be six dollars and ninety-five cents. Please pull forward to the first window."

Pulling forward and paying at the first window, she moved on to the second window and collected her food and then pulled into the parking lot to park and devour her meal with the ferocity of a beast. Feeling marginally better when every morsel was gone, she drove out on to the road again for the remainder of the drive.

As Abby guided her car home, she contemplated what to do with the two Siberians when they were eventually found and ended up at her shelter. It was a negative train of thought, perhaps, but, such was life. It should have felt wrong to be thinking so precipitously, but, after all her years of experience, she knew that when they were eventually found, they would be heading her way, just as the Maltese and Indonesian tigers that were mentioned in the news broadcast had.

People didn't seem to understand how often tigers needed to eat or how much, which was why the majority of the tigers brought to her were undernourished. It wouldn't have surprised her if the two escapees had in fact escaped their cages simply to find food. Stranger things had happened. In fact, in her line of work, that wasn't really very strange at all.

The feeling of excitement from her earlier on air appearance had dissipated almost entirely to be replaced by melancholy. Of late, she had been feeling as though no matter what she did, no matter how hard she worked, it wasn't enough, and, while tonight had helped to cast an illusion over herself that she was in truth doing a lot of good, that buzz had not lasted nearly long enough.

Just around the next bend she spied the sign for her

home town of Fullonton and was filled with thanks. She
wanted to be home and now.

A few minutes later, as she pulled into her driveway, her
thoughts were still on the two tigers that had managed to
escape from their cages.

Where were they? Would they survive the night without
being shot

Chapter One

Three months earlier

With a leering grin, Brad Locke slammed the handle of
the brush he was holding against the steel bars of the cage
before him and then ran it along the length of the six foot
by nine foot metal box. The clatter it made stung his own
ears.

The already agitated tiger within the confines of the cage
jumped up, startled, and then roared his fury.

Rather than jump back, Brad just laughed mockingly
and rattled the bars again.

This had become their little joke.

Every time he was in the yard, he always greeted them
this way.

Not that the cat found it funny, just him. But then, who
was the owner and who was the pet, huh? There had to be
some advantages to owning a big cat, and, if having the
power to scare the shit out of one of them wasn't one of
those added bonuses, then what was? Lions might be the
king of the jungle, but tigers were pretty high up there on
the scale, too, in terms of being really fucking scary and
intimidating. Yet, he, Brad Locke, could scare a tiger. It
was a fact of which he was proud.

"You shouldn't piss them off, Brad," the voice to Brad's
left warned.

The lecturing tone fired up Brad's temper. "You pussy,"
he taunted, sneering. "What's to be frightened of? They're
behind fucking cages!"

"I ain't no pussy," John, Brad's friend, spat. "But you
shouldn't mess with these fuckers. They'll rip you limb

from limb."

"I know! I'm the one that feeds the bastards. You should see all that blood spurt out! A real fucking sight that is."

John winced at the visual the comment created. His reaction made Brad laugh. "Look, do we have to talk about this?"

"You're the one that brought it up, not me." Brad glared down at the growling tiger and then turned around to nudge the female that was lying supine on the scorched grass.

There was no reaction.

He nodded with satisfaction. "The drugs have worked."

"Drugs? You didn't give them human medication, did you?" John shrieked and jumped backwards.

He was almost out of the postage stamp sized yard before Brad waved a hand. "Come back here! Don't be stupid!" he hollered after him. "I gave her tranquilizers that I got from the vet. She won't wake up."

"She better fucking not!" John retorted as he grudgingly returned to the center of the yard before stopping to look around. "This place is way too fucking small for cages this size," he muttered.

Brad shrugged. "You have to use what space you have."

John hummed disbelievingly under his breath. "This place must stink in the summer."

"Yeah. Fucking dirty beasts."

With a grimace, John absorbed Brad's comment and took in the still growling and obviously furious tiger in the cage and then the sleeping female on the grass and then the last creature in the second smaller cage at the opposite side of the small yard, which had also been drugged.

"This better be fucking worth it," he muttered and then walked over to the female and nudged her gently with his foot. When she didn't move, he inhaled deeply with relief. "The only reason I'm doing this is because I want one of the cubs and you know it. I had better get one, Brad."

Brad grunted. "We'll see. We don't even know if it's going to fucking work."

John shot his friend an irritated look. "Of course it will work. A girl tiger and a boy tiger . . . and you said that the vet said she was in . . . I dunno . . . heat?"

"Nah. They don't go into heat," Brad replied with a sniff. "I looked online and in the wild this is the time they're usually mad for it, from November to April. The vet also said that she's 'receptive'. So, I don't know, maybe they do go into heat."

"Why have you got two males and just the one female? Surely it would make sense to have the opposite?"

"The damn breeder I bought the first two off of didn't tell me until I'd already parted with the cash that they were brother and sister. Bastard."

John snorted then burst out laughing. "You twat! You bought fucking siblings? I love it!"

"Fuck you," Brad hissed and shot him the bird. "Come on! Are you going to help me or what?"

"Yeah, I'll help, but only if you swear that you'll give me one of the cubs when she gets pregnant."

Disgruntled, Brad nodded. "Yeah. Alright. Do you want me to swear on my life or is my word enough?"

"Your word will do, Brad," John replied wryly.

"Let's get on with it then."

Brad stalked to the smallest cage in the garden and, through the bars, prodded the big cat again to ensure he was asleep. Konar, thankfully, was slack and supine on the concrete floor of the cage and didn't even budge an inch.

Konar was the largest cat he owned, and, while the vet had reiterated the dosages of the tranquilizers he was supposed to give the tigers, he didn't fancy losing a hand because some jerk-off vet just out of school had messed up.

Taking the lack of movement as a positive sign, he unlocked the cage and pulled out the door as wide as was physically possible. Once that was done, he retreated to the side of his female tiger, Tiana, and then bent down and awkwardly pushed his arms under her torso. "Go on then, John. Get your arms under her, otherwise we'll never get her fucking moved."

His order was swiftly obeyed. John maneuvered his arms under Tiana's torso opposite Brad.

"One, two, three-lift!" he spat with a grunt.

Heaving pants escaped both men as they attempted to lift Tiana and immediately failed. Instantly, their shoulders began to protest at carrying such a leaden weight. "How much does she weigh?" John asked, huffing for breath.

"The vet said she's underweight for a Siberian. She's only a couple hundred pounds-ish."

"A couple hundred pounds? You moron, why the hell didn't you ask Jim to come and help, too?"

Brad snorted. "Because I thought we'd be able to handle her, that's why! She's small!"

"Fuck you. You didn't want to promise him a cub either! Tight bastard. I'm not wrecking my back because you don't want to give Jim a cub!"

He shrugged. "Maybe. Maybe not. I thought we could handle it," Brad reiterated with a scowl.

"Yeah, well, we can't, jackass! I can't even bench press one hundred and twenty pounds, so I sure as fuck can't lift two hundred plus!"

"Course we can, pussy. Come on, let's try again. We just weren't prepared, that's all."

"No. I told you, I'm not fucking up my back just to help you. We need, I don't know, a sheet or something. Do you have a tarpaulin?"

"Yeah, in the house somewhere."

"Go and get it then. It would be a lot easier and less cumbersome to carry her like that. How the fuck did you get her to the vet?"

"I didn't. He made a house call."

John looked around with disgust at the pigsty of a backyard. "I hope you cleaned the place up or the SPCA will be flooding the yard any minute!"

Brad flipped him the bird.

John simply rolled his eyes.

Brad straightened up and walked the twenty steps to the back door that led into the ramshackle house. Within minutes, he came back with the large plastic sheet in his hands.

John strode forward and grabbed it from him, spreading it out on the ground. "Let's try and lift her the same way but spread her on to the sheet. That way, we should be able to manage it," he muttered.

Brad nodded in agreement.

They both returned to their earlier position. In moments, they managed to heave Tiana a few feet off the ground and on to the plastic sheet. They took a moment to get their breaths back and straightened out their backs with mirror-image groans and grimaces then grabbed the two corners of each side and began to stagger their way to Konar's cage.

As they moved her, Damian, Tiana's brother, growled. Of course, he'd been growling throughout the entire process. Brad had to admit, if only to himself, that some of the sounds Damian emitted freaked him the fuck out.

With a grimace and sighs of relief, they managed to deposit Tiana inside the cage. When they dropped her, the sound echoed around the small, walled yard as her body slumped against the concrete floor of her enclosure.

Damian's growls grew even more furious.

As Brad shut the door and locked the cage up, he slumped on the yellowed and dead grass next to John, who was sitting hunched forward trying to regain his breath. He'd noticed John's head was turned towards the pissed off tiger that was stalking the length and breadth of its own cage.

John issued a pained sigh. "You would think by the way he's acting that he actually knew what was going on, wouldn't you?" John muttered a little breathlessly.

Brad shrugged. "They've always been like that."

"Like what?"

"Aware, I guess is the word."

John snorted. "Aware? Of course, they're fucking aware."

Brad punched John on the arm. "You know what I mean. More . . . intelligent than I'd ever reckoned, that's all."

John raised his arm and then wiped his brow on the sleeve of his shirt. He grimaced at the moisture the act retrieved from his forehead. "Cats are clever, so I imagine that a big cat would just be doubly so."

"Maybe." Brad shrugged again. With a groan, he climbed to his feet. "I think we deserve a beer after that," he grumbled.

John followed with a heaving sigh. "I think we deserve two!"

Brad slapped John on the back. "Come on then, two beers here we come."

Having said that, they returned to the back door and headed into the kitchen to enjoy two long, cool beers.

* * * *

As a rage that seemingly encompassed all the anger he'd ever felt in his relatively short life began to overtake him,

Damian felt almost like exploding from the emotions that were rocketing through him.

Not for the first time since his parents' deaths, he wished that they hadn't died before they'd passed on knowledge of the shift. By all the Gods he wished that he could turn into his other form and release both himself and his sister from the clutches of the bastard who called himself Brad and who held the keys to their damnable cages.

Now it was too late.

Knowing what he did about what would soon be happening in this yard had nausea flooding his stomach. Damian cringed at the thought of his sister being mated to a . . . a wild beast and just that thought alone had him rattling to escape all the more. Frustration swamped him, and he began to roar out his aggression. He had learned from the very beginning that his captor didn't give a shit about him or his sister. When the extra male had been brought in, he had known what that meant, as had Tiana.

While Damian had been angry, Tiana had been more accepting. But then, she always had been more accepting of their fate, more accepting of the fact that they were completely unaware of their heritage, of the fact that they were completely in the dark as to how to access the other half of their nature. She had learned to accept the things she had no control over while he had rejected all of it and now this was her fate.

It wasn't right. It simply wasn't. The entire situation was so wrong, but there was nothing he could do to change it.

Damian felt so fiercely enraged by it all and even more so because this morning, when that tranquilizer dart had penetrated his hide, only then had he realized that Brad's intentions were to join his sister with that . . . beast in the other cage. By then, there had been nothing he could have done. And now, well, now he felt both incensed by their treatment and the prospect of his sister's rape and very disheartened. He felt disheartened because a part of him had always believed that when he was as furious as this, as maddened and as raging as he was now, that that ever-mercurial shift would come upon him and so, too, would freedom.

And yet . . . here he was, still a tiger.

The truth behind his heritage was still hidden, still

secret. When that was combined with his anger and frustration at his situation, it had a further dampening effect on his mood.

The already small cage seemed to have halved in size overnight, which Damian knew was a physical impossibility. Tiana been taken from his cage, which meant he had more space in which to move around, but that did little to stop the feeling that the bars seemed to be closing in on him, seemed to be ever circling him until that desire to escape strengthened tenfold.

He could feel the beat of his heart pound through his body and thunder like a flood in his ears.

It wouldn't be long before Tiana and that male they'd put her with would wake up and the natural conclusion would occur. It wasn't the other tiger's fault. It was their captor's, but, knowing what was about to happen and in such a small space as this yard, Damian felt like ripping apart both the other beast and the man who'd put him in a cage with his sister.

To turn away from what would happen in the cage opposite wouldn't be enough. He wouldn't be able to escape the sounds . . . the scents . . . hell, merely the thought was adequate enough to torture him, never mind being faced with the reality of his sister being mated.

There were times when he damned his human half and others where he longed for it and prayed for it with a fierceness that surprised him. At this moment, however, it was the former that haunted him rather than the latter.

The human half of him brought sensibilities into this situation, and, in circumstances that were already emotive, it was just the last nail in the coffin of his sanity.

He began to dread the moment that both tigers would wake up, and, the more he dreaded it, the more he began to pace, and the more furious and angry he became.

The heat of the day had already dissipated but the cages were dappled with the still-bright sunlight that shone through the trees that shadowed the yard. As he stalked around, the scents of the trampled and scorched grass assailed his nostrils and when that was combined with the scents of his captor and his aid and then that of his sister's heat . . . . They roiled about his senses sickeningly. He wished by all the Gods that he could hide from what was happening here, but he couldn't. He couldn't, and, already, Konar and Tiana were starting to wake up and soon . . . very soon . . . it would happen and then every part of him and his sister would be violated. Perhaps he should have grown accustomed to that, but he hadn't. He never would. And even though he was part human, and it was a part of him that he had yet to really tap in to, Damian knew that he would forever despise humans, forever hate them for what they had done to him and his sister.

Made in the USA
Charleston, SC
02 August 2013